By Emily McCosh

SHORT STORIES & POETRY
All the Woods She Watches Over

NOVELS & NOVELLAS
Under the Earth, Over the Sky
The Sea at the End of Everything

SERIES
In Dying Starlight

THE WIND AND THE WILD

— a KEEPERS OF FAERIE novel —

EMILY McCOSH

OCEANS IN
·THE SKY·

Cover design, illustrations, and formatting by Emily McCosh

Edited by Natalia Leigh (Enchanted Ink Publishing)
Proofread by Crystal Blanton

Published by Oceans In The Sky Press
OceansInTheSky.com

OCEANS IN
·THE SKY·

For the house I grew up in.

*It was not built in a meadow on the edge
of Faerie, but at one time it was close.*

Chapters

Names

Niamh: *Nee-ve*

Aidyn: *Aid-yn*

Niall: *Ni-all*

Una: *Oo-nah*

Tynan: *Tie-nan*

Dauna: *Dawn-ah*

Emma: *Em-ah*

Blain: *Bl-ain*

Olivia: *Oh-livia*

Andrew: *An-droo*

Cara: *Car-ah*

Cillian: *Kill-ee-an*

Athol: *A-thl*

Fiona: *Fee-oh-nah*

Niamh's Cottage
Where the Lost Enter Faerie
The Old Hawthorn
A Library on the Edge of Faerie

A Village on the
Edge of Faerie
The Wider World
The Vast
Human Woods

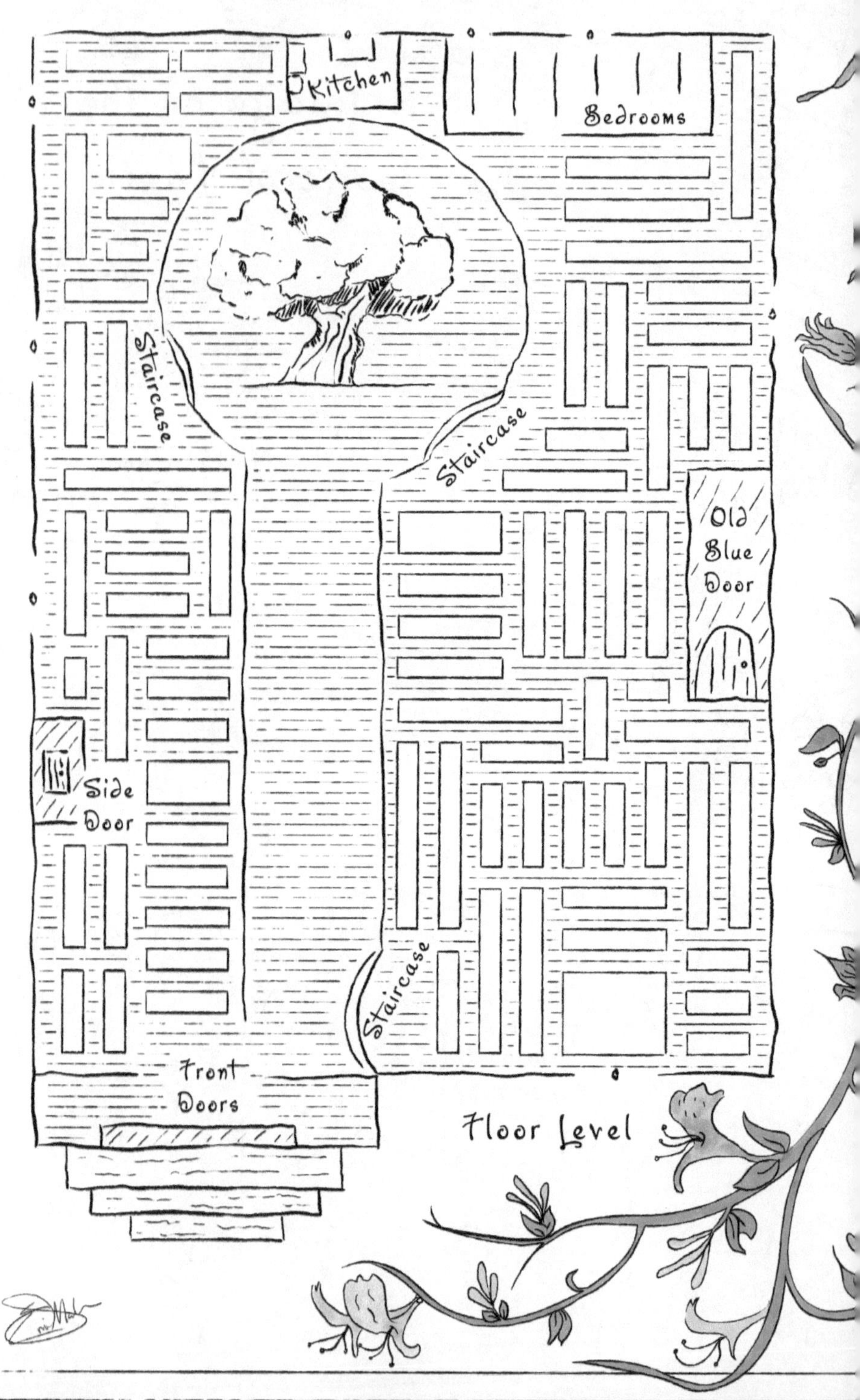

Kitchen
Bedrooms
Staircase
Staircase
Old Blue Door
Side Door
Staircase
Front Doors
Floor Level

A Library on the
Edge of Faerie
Upper Level
Aidyn's Room
Back Door
Staircase
Staircase
Staircase

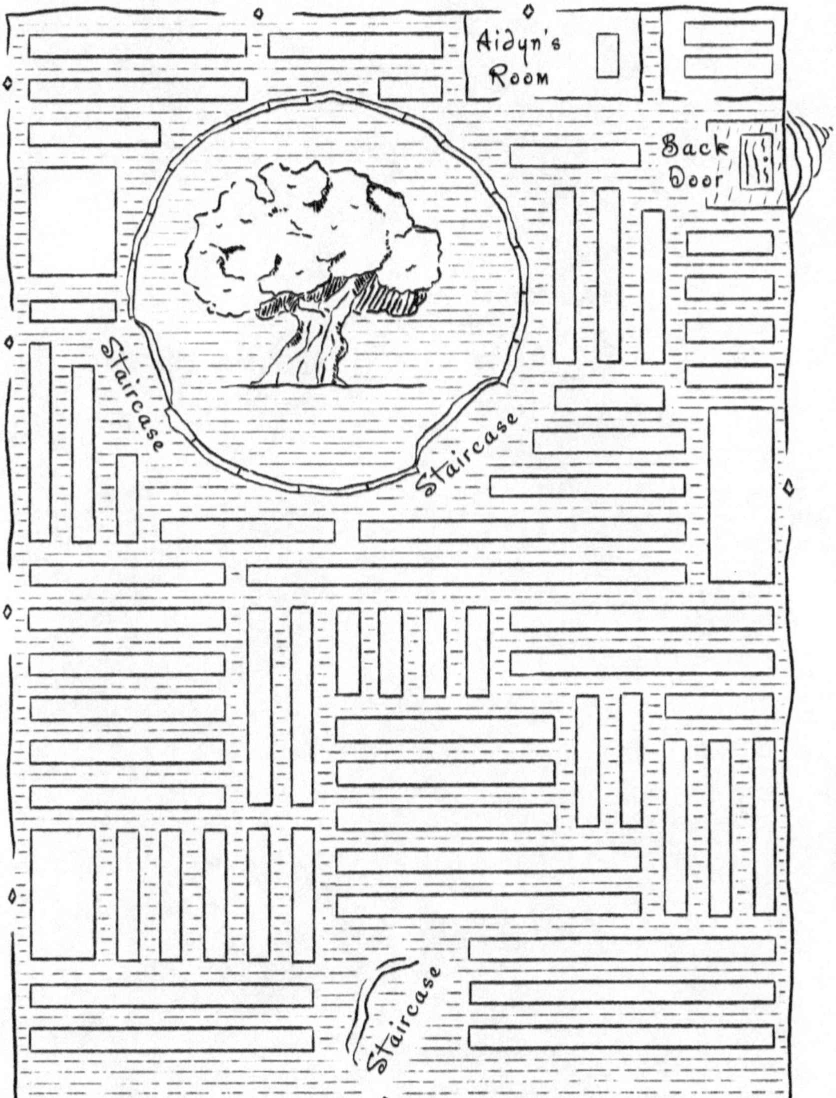

Part 1
Honeysuckle & Silver

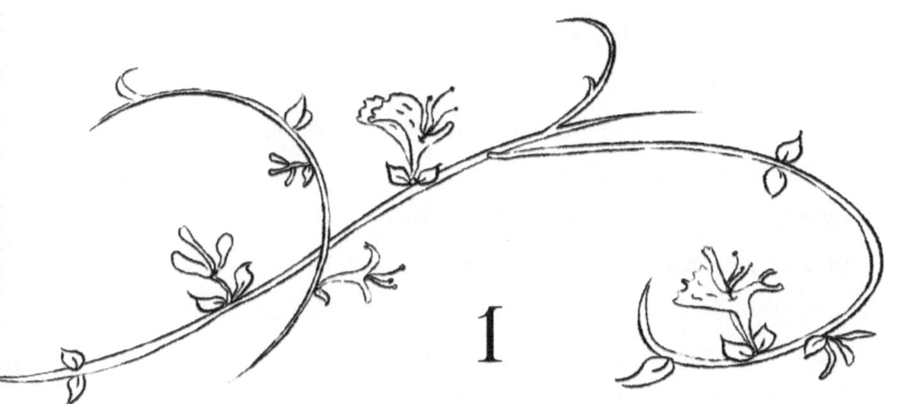

1

On the Edge of the Woods

No one finds Faerie unless they are lost. Or, more often than not, Faerie lures in those it desires.

In Faerie, names are not known. Water tastes like sunlight, food like sugar with the barest dash of needed salt. Music is spun for dancing until toes fall off and the cobbler comes to rebind shoes in the dead of night. Songs are sung until no one can speak their own name in the morning, if they remember it at all.

In Faerie, everything is strange, incorrect and too beautiful, which is why I know the little things wriggling in the leaves just outside the thickest portion of the trees have come from those lands.

I almost fell across them, almost trampled them beneath my boots, eyes half closed as I picked a tree to get lost beside. One let off a squeak, and I nearly leapt from my skin. I've met faerie monsters on the edges of Faerie before, but they did not make such harmless noises.

But I am not lost between the trees, so these little beasts should not be here. Carefully, I turn the nearest plump body over with my pinkie, worried of getting bitten. I cannot say precisely what they resemble—barn cats, perhaps, or newborn mountain cats, or something else entirely. Blue in fur like the night sky, mainly black and speckled with white, they bear long flat faces and tiny needle teeth. I've never seen the like.

"Hello, little things," I whisper, for it is always too quiet when nearly lost on the edge of Faerie.

If I bring them to the village, they will simply be tossed back into these trees or set in one of the little shrines along the edges of the woods in hopes one of their own kind will discover and retrieve them. There are a few who may simply dispose of them in the river and pray that puts an end to it, but most know better. We do not tempt faerie curses.

I glance through the thinning trunks, considering. No path weaves this way. I was on my way to becoming lost, but not quite. Wind clips a springtime breeze through the new buds and the winter-cold needles of year-round trees. Briars poke my ankles.

Something smells of blood.

I step over the kittens, taking a few paces into the trees, which are perfectly normal now that I've paused to gather my surroundings. Red taints the leaves of a nearby bush. It is too dark, and I keep my fingers to myself. More tufts of the strange blue-black fur are scattered here and there, caught in a bloody bramble, brushed against the rough bark of the nearest tree.

Hunt hounds on the border. They will eat anything they pass; strange faerie kittens doubtlessly receive the same treatment. I chew the insides of my cheeks until I taste iron.

Returning to the kittens, I scoop them into my satchel one by one, counting nine in total. They nip sleepily, their eyes barely open, but can't break my skin. I ventured here meaning to gather berries—Mam and Da are leaving tomorrow, and I mean to send them away with a few tarts—but it isn't a wise idea, not now. I'll make do with what I have in the house.

I can keep the little things in the barn. My parents won't mind. I won't be telling anyone else about the blood and traces of whatever larger beasts there were so close to our trees, but they'll need to know. Da holds weight in this village, even if he and Mam are leaving for a few weeks. I can decide what to do with the kittens when they're not clinging to life.

Where the trees thin, spring grasses rise, whispering in the breeze not blocked by trunks. A half dozen old shrines, piles of stones no taller than my knee, dot the edges of the woods, but we do not often leave offerings to the fae—not until mid-summer arrives. The village is between me and home, so I skirt the edges of it, sprinting in my light rough skirts meant for traipsing about the woods. Hiking them up to my thighs so I can run uninhibited, I hold my satchel to my chest and bolt past the outermost houses. In the spring, they are half hidden by high golden-green grasses, dandelion tufts catching on thatching newly replaced with the ending of the rains.

Una waves as she pauses beside her cottage, eyebrows bunched. I wasn't supposed to be back so soon—and certainly not fleeing full speed with grasses scraping my legs.

I drop my skirts to wave back.

A fence runs up one side of the road from the village to our cottage. Da has earned a fine living organizing the trading of our excess crops and the skins the trappers bring in with the closest cities in exchange for items we cannot so easily produce in a tiny village. After a few decades, he and my mam gathered enough to build a tidy little cottage at the edge of the trees.

You're practically the noble daughter of our little hamlet, Una once told me with a laugh when we were not much higher than the grasses ourselves. Our house is perhaps a third larger than hers, but it matters not. We have enough money to worry less, and this is a boon.

"That's a bit of running," Da says as I bolt past him through the entrance to the barn just tall enough for our draft horse. Sweet hay and horse dust hangs in the air, familiar and warm, baking in the oven of the barn's rafters. Our cow, Primrose, lows at me from the fence outside.

Da's in one of the stalls, brushing out the mare with her blue-gray coat and dark nose. I shuffle to a stop and open the gate to her stall, closing the wailing thing with a grimace.

Mam learned long ago not to dissuade me from sprinting wherever I'm going, and now that I've reached two decades, there's no stopping me. But I did nearly spook the horse this time.

"Sorry. Da, look—"

He takes an eyeful of my dress, not my satchel, with the knowing eyebrow of *my daughter has been in the woods again*.

I open the loose top and lift out one of the wriggling creatures, ignoring when it gnaws on my thumb. Its teeth are sharp, but there isn't strength behind its jaw yet. Da pauses, setting aside the horse brush and taking the little monster with more than some hesitation. It fits neatly within his palm with fingers to spare. He is a large man, broad in the shoulders, and probably should have sired a larger daughter, but I was born under the moonlight, and children born under the moon are always smaller and wilder than they ought to be. With his height, I manage to be a hair above the other women in my village.

"In the woods?" he asks, turning the creature over.

"Just on the edge. I hadn't stumbled in yet."

I used to give both him and Mam a fit, purposefully dropping myself into Faerie, but I don't go far, never enough to become fuzzy-headed or lose my way back. It's strangely easier leaving than it is finding my way in. Besides, plenty of beautiful and delicious things grow just inside the spot where the air shimmers—I needn't go farther. There are rumors of more dangerous places near the edges, of course, hag huts and old abandoned libraries, though I've never seen such things in the few places I've found safe to enter.

Then again, I've never searched them out.

"I think there was . . . something else," I hedge, picking leaves off my skirt. "I saw blood on a bush. I don't think it was from a person."

We're both thinking of hunt hounds, which haven't touched the border in years. I rub my arm and wait for him to speak.

"Don't show these to anyone," he says, handing back the squirming creature. "I'll tell Cillian I saw the blood when I was walking through the woods. Where was it?"

"Beside a small pine near the large hawthorn. I think you should find it if you walk straight out from Emma's cottage. I can show you."

He shakes his head. "I'll look. And show these to your mam so you don't give her a fright if she stumbles across them. I'm going to put off our trip for a day"—he eyes me from over his bushy red beard—"and I want you to stay out of Faerie for a few days until we figure out what's happened."

I nod, not particularly happy but more than willing to do as he suggests if there are hunt hounds near the border. It's easy to still feel their claws in my hand, to remember the certainty I would die.

Da must know I'm thinking of it and takes my face in his rough hands to kiss my forehead. His beard tickles my nose.

"Go tell your mam," he repeats, and I take the little creatures with me, still catching my breath. They are small and barely moving. I can keep them in my room. In the barn, something may discover them.

Mam is still folding away some of her things; I hear her upstairs. The cottage isn't large by the standards of the city Da took me to once, but it's comfortable. A nice little second story fits both my room and my parents', the walls whitewashed and soft. I thump up the steps, careful not to frighten the babies in their satchel, and bump the door to my parents' bedroom open with my shoulder. It's a quaint room, large enough for their wide bed and two dresser tables with their little matching carved washing basins. They're entirely too cute with each other, which drove me mad in my younger years. The white linen curtains are thrown back, letting in the sun, but they'll be closed when they leave for the few weeks. Open windows at night is an invitation for the fae, after all.

"Mam?"

She pauses in her folding of extra socks into the thick embroidered bag. "I thought the market was setting up early?"

And I thought you'd be off in the woods, is the other question behind the words. My parents don't mind my little adventures so long as I come back with suitable ingredients and promise to run with everything in my legs if I see anything resembling a faerie—humanlike or otherwise.

"Never made it past the trees," I say, ignoring the market comment, and settle the open satchel onto the edge of the quilt. She pauses, hands me the socks, and leans over the bag.

"Did one bite you?"

"Not very successfully. They're too tiny." I repeat the tale I told Da and watch crinkles form around her eyes as she thinks. Absently, she takes my hand and rubs the old place where the skin was once torn apart. It's still tender after years, but her touch is gentle. I let her and Da inspect it whenever they're concerned, as if sometimes they believe it'll reopen. Even faerie scars do not do such things.

"Da's going to handle it," I say with ease when the crinkles don't even out. "I won't go around the trees for a few days, until we make sure no one's seen anything."

Finally, she quirks a smile, scooping up one of the kittens and giving its head a scratch. "We have milk you can try."

I don't know much about faerie creatures, but everyone knows to leave out milk as a gift. Honey or sweets of any sort also work, but these are baby animals. Kittens themselves need milk, after all.

For the rest of the day, I comfort myself by baking with ingredients found in any old mortal market—apples and dough and spices—and several pies later, I have flour in my hair. I move on to roasting a quail that Niall snared on the edge of the thinner trees, where getting lost is less likely to end in an accidental trip to Faerie. He's sitting at the table with Una—the two of them pretending they *aren't* making eyes at each other and very likely poking one another under the table—both inspecting the little kittens. The creatures refused their milk, as well as the honey, bread, sugar, berries, *mashed* berries, *softened* bread, and scraps of yesterday's pork I tried.

Perhaps they are frightened, though they seem perfectly happy in the old quilt I found them, and they take water well. Perhaps they are homesick or miss their mother. Perhaps they do not care for human food, which will be quite the problem. I consider leaving them back at the border and slam a few potatoes down harder than necessary. Una and Niall exchange looks.

"Don't look at each other like that," I say, brandishing a squash.

"You're stressing and cooking," Una says, and Niall tries to hide a laugh in the too-short beard he's so proud of. Though rather nice, it's not nearly enough to hide his amusement.

"I need to find something to feed them." I wave the squash

at the wriggling kittens. "Unless you have anyone in Faerie I can drop them off with."

Una wrinkles her nose. She's a long-haired beauty with skin like Mam's smooth porcelain plates and eyes as spring grasses. A braid keeps her golden locks together. She and Niall are adorable together, even if most of the village has no idea anything is happening between the two. Even Da has hinted once or twice that organizing my dowry with Niall's parents would be a wise match. He is strong and broad shouldered, as a blacksmith's son would tend to be, with a kind face and kinder heart. If he hadn't been in my life for as long as I can remember, the three of us growing taller with grass scratching our legs and soaking ourselves in frog-croaking ponds, perhaps it would be a lovely match.

In private, the three of us had a fine laugh about my da's hints. Besides, everyone will eventually figure out the two are spending too much time with each other past childhood friends. Even *I* don't spend every waking moment with either of them.

"Niamh, tell me you wouldn't," Una says, and I watch her delicate shoulders shudder. She glances across the kitchen and through the house as if she can see past the walls and the woods beyond them. She has always been more nervous of Faerie than I am.

More so in the past few years.

Niall says, "She would."

I throw a peel of the squash at him. It gives a wet smack against the middle of his temple. Una giggles, though it holds some tight nerves.

I truly would not. We do not meet the fae. We do not make eye contact if we stumble into their path. We do not disturb their mushroom circles, and if we hear their music, we stuff our fingers into our ears and run with a prayer. In such ways, we maintain peace with our otherworldly neighbors in the woods. Old tales say they protect us from monsters leaving their borders, and I tend to believe so.

Hundreds of tales were passed down through warnings and songs until they became less individual events and more a blanket draped over the village, a constant murmur in the backs of our minds: changeling children who eat their siblings and run wild back to Faerie, girls who go tumbling in the grasses with faerie men and lose their minds forever, young men who chase after the calls of what should be a woman's voice in the trees only to never see the sky again . . .

Of all these tales, we keep in mind one thing: if we are being protected from monsters by other monsters, we do not irritate Faerie's more benevolent inhabitants.

We leave milk or honey or sweets whenever we stumble across a place they frequent.

Only on midsummer do we listen to their music.

Getting a little lost to enter the edges of Faerie to pick berries does not precisely equate to disturbing their peace. I've never, not in all my years of stumbling in and out, seen more than a few flashes of a bird's wing or other small creature in the undergrowth. A few times, music passed over my ears but was gone the moment I raised my head in preparation to flee. Likely it was my own fear playing on my mind.

On the edges, Faerie is much like our kingdom of Nevyan,

if the air were not so strangely heavy that I can taste the sweetness of it upon my tongue.

"I truly would not," I repeat aloud, in case my face betrays me.

2

The Other Side of a Hawthorn

Da puts off their leaving for a time, as he promised, though it makes little difference. He speaks to the other men in the village, who take up their wood-chopping axes and hunting bows and give the trees a cursory check. They find the remnants of blood I discovered, but without other signs of any creature, there's not much to be done but keep the animals penned at night and the children inside early in the evening. Even we adults will not venture so close to the trees in the evening.

It is just as well, for there are houses to be rethatched, fields to be plowed, and pies to be baked in preparation for midsummer eve, where I shall certainly take the ribbon. I did not last year, beaten by an admittedly delectable boysenberry pie made by a sweet girl named Maeve from the next village over, but with a bit of experimenting and more sneaking through the trees once they're clear of monsters, I shall make one quite better. Una and Niall will be happy to taste test.

Mam and Da leave three days later than intended, just to be safe. The roads in this part of the kingdom are never dangerous—they've only stayed out of worry for me. But I will be spending most days in the village and likely most nights with Una, helping with her dress for the dance, which shall last all midsummer evening and night.

Mam smooths some hair slipping from my short braids and kisses me, walking about with me under her arm while Da takes her bags into the buggy. Blackberry, our big draft horse, snorts and paws at the ground, happy for something to do.

Da squeezes me too tight. I hook my arms under his and breathe in the fresh smell of his coat. It's not that I need them here, but I'm missing them before they've left the barn. They'll return in several weeks, which will be taken quickly by a warm spring sun and the village out and about after a long winter, but I'm anticipating their return.

"Stay in the mortal trees," he says with a squeeze. "And think about what I said. We want you to be loved."

"I know, Da," I say, giving his beard a gentle tug.

He doesn't mean Niall specifically—it could be anyone from the village who catches my eye, or from just around the bend, a few hours' walk. They aren't pressuring me, but some gentle pestering is practically in their duties as parents. No one's caught my eye, but I'll think on it, as they say. As I often do.

Eventually, I'm sure I'll be ready once more.

With another hug and much waving, I watch them bounce off down the path in a puff of dust. Una trots up the path to wave goodbye, then drags me off by the side of my skirts.

"I haven't had breakfast!" I protest.

"Emma has too many eggs—you can make yourself at home!"

In the back of my mind, I know she's distracting me, maneuvering me out of the house so I don't while away the hours in my kitchen with no one to talk to. But the little kitten creatures did take some milk this morning, if only a few licks, and they're sleeping happily in a blanket in a crate in my bedroom, so I can leave them a while.

"Fine. Race you."

"Wait, no!"

I'm already sprinting down the path while she scrambles after, yelling about cheating before she has to save her breath for catching up. We're both in skirts short enough to hike up and take off as fast as our legs will go, but I'm taller and spend an awful lot more time running pell-mell back across the border of Faerie.

Una is correct—Emma does have too many eggs—and I trade an hour of making omelets for taking another half dozen home with me. She has onions in her garden, and Una was harvesting mushrooms in the bright section of the forest yesterday, so I'm content to overtake someone else's counter space for a time.

Emma is a gentle, round sort of woman, not quite the oldest in the village but close. For her years, she appears remarkably young. Her chickens are her grandchildren—when her own grandchildren aren't uprooting her yard, that is. She is, perhaps, one of the only people here to have seen a faerie and walked away unscathed—not that she's told me anything of the incident. Even with years of poking and prodding when I was shorter than her knee—including bringing her cakes when I was old enough to be let near the stove—I never received much more than a hint about not getting lost in the trees and that old library the fae built and abandoned long ago. It's been on my mind these past three days. Apparently, it is much closer than any other structure built by the noble folk, which makes it worthy of her memory, but she's said nothing more.

I never did find it the few times I looked, and I gave up some years back. There are some things not to be trifled with without good reason.

Thinking of the kittens and their cute dotted fur and needle teeth, I glance over my shoulder from chopping onion stalks. Una is at the table helping Emma unwind some of her yarn, which has become tangled by a few too many curious grandchildren. She might need to keep her colorful wools on a higher shelf.

"Emma," I say, "remember when I was a little thing? You told me about a library on the Faerie side of the woods?"

Una gives me a disparaging look, and I shrug. Emma ignores me—until she, too, glances up. "Why, girl?"

Another shrug. "I've been thinking about all the things you've told me. Hounds and such."

She looks at me and my hand. I have dresses with long sleeves, but the air is warming, and the boy who left me to monsters never lived in these cottages, and everyone here cared for me as I recovered those years ago. I receive a glance of pity every so often, compassion usually, but mostly, everyone is accustomed to the girl with a scar on her hand who wanders into Faerie.

Besides, if I were faerie cursed, we would all know by now.

If I've somehow become cursed with cooking faerie food, no one seems to mind much. In fact, there are always children and many of the adults lining up at our cottage windows when I get to baking large batches of bread and pies.

"Do you remember?" I ask again, lighter.

"Of course. How old do you think I am?"

I manage to keep my laugh silent. "How do you know about it?"

"The library? I saw it. It's not too far in. Have you never seen it? I know you go in there."

She gives a squint that mostly impacts one eye, but I only shrug again. It is not an unknown thing. Besides, if I'm the one risking my mind and sanity, who wouldn't want tarts and pies and jams made from Faerie fruit?

"No, never quite stumbled upon that one. Never stumbled across any building, actually. I can barely tell Faerie is Faerie, if I'm being honest."

Una shakes her head. I offered to take her in with me a handful of times. She, much like the rest of the village, thinks I'm mad to do so—not in a harmful way, just born-in-the-moonlight mad.

"Good," Emma says with a wave of her hand. "Best you never stumble across it. Berries are one thing. You should not touch anything built by their hands. Even things abandoned."

I shiver despite the warmth the kitchen is gaining. I believe her, and there's a far cry between a little exploration on the edges of the fair folk's lands and entering a space touched by their hands. Still, it nags at my thoughts—those little kittens abandoned at the edge of the border, something taken from them. I know little of faerie creatures other than what I've been told. Something in me insists they are not mere animals.

How can they be? From Faerie, they cannot be mindless creatures. Even the hunt hounds I met so long ago . . . Their most frightening aspect was not the claws or even the teeth; it was the second between thinking them monsters and realizing there was deep intelligence within their pure white eyes. They knew what they were doing and continued on anyhow, which makes it all the worse.

If these little kittens grow, will they grow into something wise as us? Otherworldly, certainly, but perhaps wise nonetheless.

An old faerie library.

On the border somewhere.

With knowledge of their creatures, perhaps. Knowledge we certainly don't have.

It has been several days, and there are no traces of monsters, no blood or strange paw prints or markings. If I hadn't stumbled across the kittens and the ensuing scene, no one, me included, would've realized something was amiss. It's been ages since anything dangerous crept from Faerie, anyhow. What are the chances something would happen with a little more exploring?

Besides, if I go into the woods alone, *there's nothing to fear.*

If I told Niall my thoughts, he would probably put aside his desire to never step foot inside the border of the noble folk's trees and join me.

I would feel safe with him at my back, wouldn't I? Most likely. With his stable hands and broad grin, he is one of the few I trust, besides Mam and Da. Una too, but she would rather drag me out by my ankles than venture in. I cannot blame her for such determination.

I have never needed a shield mate when venturing into Faerie. I shall not need one for a little adventuring on the border. I do it often. I simply need to be more purposeful with my getting lost.

"You," Una says after we have eaten omelets and untangled a great deal of wool and I am carrying a handful of eggs home in the pockets of my skirts, "are scheming."

"Scheming?"

"Scheming," she sings, looping her arm through mine.

"How is Cara?" I ask, hoping she has something to say about her little sister.

"Ha! In love with a boy she met from the next village when Da took them both to market day. Have you ever seen a ten-year-old give another ten-year-old a daisy? Adorable. I'm not that easily distracted."

I *have* known her to be that distracted, but I might as well explain. She and Niall are already sworn to secrecy about the kittens, which means they'll gossip to each other and no one else. She has never shared a secret of mine, and I never one of hers, and I doubt she will be the one to break the safe walls of trust the three of us have built around one another. I lean my head against the top of hers as we walk, careful not to crush the eggs by bumping my pockets into her legs.

"I'm going to try to find that library Emma told me about—"

"I *knew it.*"

"—*just* on the border, where I normally go. I've sort of half figured out how to pick landmarks. Find a tree you can remember, close your eyes, and run a dozen steps ahead. It will pretty much put you out at the same place every time."

"Pretty much?"

I shrug. "Every time I've ever tried. Within a few steps."

"Be honest. Have you ever plowed into a tree doing that?"

"Well, I pick a clear path."

"That is *not* what I asked."

I sigh as I open my cottage door, holding it open for her. "Perhaps . . . once."

With a giggle, she skips in, heading to my room. I deposit the eggs on the counter save for one and take a tea saucer, scrambling after her.

"When are you going?" she asks, already with the kittens spread out on my bedquilt and attempting to pet all nine of them at once. For all her fear of Faerie, she certainly overcame any hesitation with these little ones rather quickly. Not too difficult when they're helpless as the kittens my mind insists upon calling them.

I move aside the curtains and the dried bee balm and fox-gloves hanging in strings from the window, shedding more light onto the little creatures.

"This afternoon, I think. I don't want to frighten anyone

about going in. I don't go in the dark, so don't fret."

"I don't fret," she says, which is another lie, and watches me crack the egg into the saucer and try it on the kittens. Their rough little tongues scratch a little bit of yolk off my finger, but not nearly enough. "Niamh?"

"Hmm?"

"Please don't go in when it's dark. They come out in the dark."

Hounds. I force myself not to shiver. "I know, silly. I never do."

Late afternoon? Sometimes. Night? *Never.*

When she's quiet, I take her hand. I cannot tell her not to fuss. She has been worried over my uninvited trips to Faerie for years, and my reassurances are not going to wipe such things aside.

Finally, she smiles and tells me, "You can take Niall."

I give her a look portraying how we both know he wants to go in as little as she does. "This is nothing different than usual."

"Niamh . . ."

"*Una.*"

She shoves her shoulder to mine, which sends us both onto the smooth wooden floor. I grab the pillow from the top of the bed to enact my vengeance.

In the end, it isn't nearly so difficult to find the library as I anticipated.

In a thinner dress against the afternoon spring heat and sturdier boots so I don't twist an ankle on all the fallen branches, I stand at the edge of the trees. I haven't ventured here since three days back, and my skin itches beneath the weight of the trees' watchful eyes. Briars attempt once more to poke at my now-protected ankles.

I pass by the place where I found the kittens and discover the bloody leaves washed clean by morning mist. I run my fingers across the hawthorn and pick a different spot. A few dozen steps down, I find a tree I haven't marked. Every time I find a good berry patch on the other side, I scrape a little line into the bark of the tree I used to jump in. It looks like nothing, just a scratch from an animal or a natural flaw in the tree's flesh. It is a mark I recognize and needs be nothing else.

I pick an unmarked tree, face myself down a path where I *won't* smack into the rough bark of another oak, close my eyes, and run a half dozen steps.

Before I open my eyes, the air warms. A thick, hot summer day after a thunderstorm, moss and berries fat with juice and growing honeysuckle. I crack an eye and find myself in a section of the Faerie wood.

Otherwise empty.

I wander a half dozen yards in, but it is easy to see in all directions, even in the afternoon light. Nothing.

Turning on the spot, I close my eyes and run back until the air chills slightly, catching myself on the familiar oak tree on the mortal side of the border.

Another handful of spots turn up fruitless—besides the new blackberry bushes I discover. Constantly, I find myself glancing at the hawthorn. Late-day sun is beginning to cast long shadows against the leaves. A few beetles take to the sky. A gentle breeze swirls against the heat of afternoon.

I stop my search for another unmarked tree and return to the hawthorn.

Its trunk is wide and old, soft in the bark. It has grown short and gnarled, and such is the way of faerie trees cursed to live in the mortal lands. I put my fingers to it, avoiding the nearby bush once splattered with blood. Carefully, stepping over briars, I turn and face the very human wood.

Pick up your feet, Niamh, I tell myself, then close my eyes and run until the air turns soupy and sweet.

My shoulders tense, and I take a breath before daring to crack open my eyes, prepared to turn and run if anything resembling a monster or other creature I have never seen makes itself known.

No monsters.

Instead, there is an overgrown hedge of honeysuckle. It would not be blooming this early on our side of the world, and I find a smile tugging at my lips. Taking one of the flowers, I lick the sugar off the stem, mouth momentarily hurting with how overwhelmingly sweet it is. But a beautiful hedge of honeysuckle does not make for much of a clear view, so I pick up my steps, now on slightly evener ground of moss and fallen maple leaves. Moths flutter dusty-blue wings, tongues finding the insides of flowers. My boots crunch crispy leaves, a subtle disturbance of the ever-present stillness. My breath comes in a misty puff as if it is not a hot summer afternoon this side of the trees. Only three dozen steps in, the honeysuckle spreads, giving way to a straight line, and I realize it is growing along walls to either side of me that deteriorate into nothing a ways down, where the vines cling instead to bushes and trees.

Tall maple trees hang in the ensuing woods, leaves fluttering in the stillness, pale trunks like watching figures. A chill of sweat drips down the back of my dress, tickling my spine.

Sitting among the pale bodies of trees is a building strangely gentle for its massive appearance. It is not as otherworldly as I expected a building of Faerie to be—at least not in the individual parts. Largely wooden, it hangs with shingles of the same material, a base of stone supporting it. Pillars of marble—no, pale ash wood—ring the entrance. A small set of steps leads up, but the front door has been blocked by such an overgrowth of honeysuckle that I don't believe I'd be able to break through even had I brought Da's sheep shears or a kitchen knife.

Yes, it is mostly stone and old wood standing the test of time, with a sharply sloped set of roofs and several chimneys, but something about it makes me off-balance. I step sideways as if I'm about to tip over onto the flat forest carpet.

No trees have fallen in the area, none at all, and the uncanniness of the fact nearly has me turning on my heel.

But there are no other signs of life, just the trees and the honeysuckle and the moths. No monsters, and certainly no fae in this fallen building. If a single thing about the stories of the fair folk is true, it is that they are vain beasts, pretty monsters, and I cannot imagine one would dwell in a half-fallen library.

It should not be much to one of them, but it is the largest building I've ever seen outside the few visits to the city. In the mist and silent watchmen of trees, it seems to stretch forever, though I can see all its edges.

The border is very near still, and there is plenty of light. Farther in I have traveled merely to gather berries. This is not much of anything at all. There is nothing I need fear. When I glance back, the honeysuckle is the same. Everything is the same. There is nothing different here.

I can always turn and run, put my fingers into my ears and shout over the music. I have found Faerie, so Faerie cannot find me.

For now, I can walk forward.

3

An Inside Too Large

Perhaps I expected much worse—music or mocking creatures or ancient faerie traps or something discernibly *other* about the place—but it is only a library, after all.

Empty, abandoned, and strangely solitary, but a library nonetheless.

I do not make my way in through the front door, running my fingers across the thick briars and honeysuckle vines before deciding against a single attempt. The second-story windows are greatly unblocked, and many possess balconies and high, tall windows of pure glass, all unbroken. But it is a ways up, and I am not happy to fall and twist an ankle or knee on this side of Faerie. Instead, wandering around the porch, I find a small secondary door beneath a set of windows. Its burnished silver knob turns with only some struggle, and a gentle shove of the shoulder has it brushing open with a hush of sound in the eerie still of the wood.

Niamh, perhaps this is not worth it. There is nothing promising I will find any information about the kittens, but chances are, I might discover *something* they will eat.

Otherwise, I am truly a fool for stepping foot here.

I push the door fully open and find myself between two large bookshelves. I was momentarily entertaining the idea that this was not a library at all—though what other massive building could be just on this side of the woods?—but even our little village has something resembling a place people can read books they cannot buy. Dry paper and dust are familiar scents, mortal and comforting, and I creep between the bookshelves into even more eternally long hallways of books upon books.

Carefully, I touch the nearest spine, surprised there are volumes still here. *Why didn't they take them?*

As if in answer, a few bound spines crumble beneath my fingers, no more than dust themselves. I wince.

They could've been taken when they were still readable, couldn't they? Perhaps something here will tell me what happened.

Feeling strange but knowing any living and intelligent creature dwelling here would already know I'm in its domain, I whisper, "Hello?"

No answer. I allow myself a slow relieved breath and leave the door cracked open as I find the nearest break in the bookshelf leading deeper within.

Walkways of books weave inward like worm tracks in bark.

They stretch too high into a dark ceiling, the tops disappearing into shadow. It is late afternoon outside, and inside it is quite closed off and dark, at least in this section. Picking the most straightforward line through the shelves, I wander, hoping for a wider area where I can gain my bearings. Perhaps none of these tomes will be in my language—I have never heard a faerie speak, after all—but I've gone far enough there's no use in turning back without more investigation.

It truly is dilapidated.

No fae would dwell here, would they? Perhaps something small, like a brownie or another of the harmless creatures that tend to visit our side of the border.

After a few minutes, the maze of shelves breaks into a wide circle of a room.

It is too large in here.

As broad as the building seemed on the outside, this cannot all fit into it.

It is all in your mind, I tell myself, then glance over my shoulder, finding the front door mostly intact from the inside, with a sturdy-enough bolt that I wouldn't have made it in were vines not crawling through the cracks. It is shaped like a wolf's head, and I'm surprised to see something so normal, so *mortal,* on the decorations of a faerie door.

Perhaps the wolves here are not so benign as our own. They don't look enough like the hunt hounds to make me shiver.

"Hello?" I ask again, perhaps not wisely, and watch a smattering of leaves drift from the second level railing of the main room. Creeping out farther, I find nothing of note save for more books.

And trees.

Maples have somehow invaded the interior, large and many branched, having dwelled here since long before I was born. They drop a few spare leaves here and there in a strange breeze from nowhere. In one spot, the roof has crumbled, giving a glimpse of a bruise-blue evening sky. But the leaves atop do not shiver in the wind, only the bottom ones in the library itself.

What spell is upon this place? I shudder and shake away the thought. For all I know, this is a usual occurrence in Faerie. I have never been in one of their buildings, after all.

Hesitantly, I brush my fingers across the nearest spine as if touch will bring out creatures of this world. Again, nothing stirs, and I allow myself to relax a bit more. This book does not crumble, and I slide it from its space, letting it fall open in my hands with a well-aged crinkle. It is straight lines upon lines of text, and I squint. The words are familiar, and so are the letters, but they make little sense. I start over the paragraph at the top, mumbling to myself, but still they are lost to me. Carefully, I creak the spine shut and return it to its place. Three more books on this shelf match the odd language, and I try the next one over with a huff.

Whatever magic lives in these lands, it evidently doesn't allow mere mortals to read through even long-abandoned books.

A few shelves I try in this manner, but when I dare to pull out the ones not crumbling to dust, the words are the same.

"Upper level," I whisper, rounding the closest smooth pale beam lining the interior of the space. I am here—and do not know if I will have the courage to return—so I should try as many shelves as possible.

It is still a few hours from twilight.

The second story is much like the first, and no markers of any sort line the shelves, so I pick at random, finding book after book thick with lines of unreadable text. One, bound in heavy blue leather and smelling of it still after all these years, appears to be nothing more than charts upon charts of constellations. In the brief minutes I allow myself to flip through, I do not recognize any of our own. I set it on the closest dust-coated table in case I return and can inspect it further.

A platform crosses over the hallway of books below, and I touch the railings lightly, treading carefully lest the wood crack beneath my feet—or something hear my boots. Even inside, it is warm, though slightly chiller, as if the building only holds the night's cold and never catches the day's warmth. Outside, it smells of summer, heavy and damp. In here, it is fall, still hot but edging into winter.

I file through more unreadable books. I don't need much, just a catalogue of creatures, perhaps, or an ink sketch with information listed.

If I bring back paper and a quill, can I copy the letters one by one until they form something coherent on a piece of mortal paper? Pleased with the idea, I search more diligently. Books, books, and more books. All shapes and sizes, all seeming to have been written by hand, with different tilts and swoops and personalities.

All this work. Abandoned.

Shaking my head in the failing light, I step over one of the shivering maple branches reaching through the railing and into the middle of the upper shelves.

Something snaps.

I go still as a deer caught in the aim of Da's crossbow. Glancing down, I find my boots on the solid old floorboard below, no twig I've stepped on. I scan the area and discover nothing I haven't noticed before.

The tree leaves shiver.

A soft moan like an old door blowing shut has me backing away from the turn I was about to take, shoulder blades pressing to the shelves, heart thumping against the inside of my chest bone. Chills dribble down my skin, and my fingers tremble.

There can't be a faerie here. This place is abandoned. They are vain and selfish and too beautiful for abandoned libraries.

Besides, they don't come to the border and have not in many years.

I let out a long breath, rubbing the comforting coarse wool of my skirts between my fingertips. No other noise permeates this place save for the silent skitter of leaves across the bottom floor.

The breeze.

The breeze blew one of the old unhinged doors open.

I let my head thunk quietly against the rough wood of the bookcase, rolling my eyes up at the beamed ceiling.

"Frightened of the wind. Very well done," I whisper.

Besides, what did I think? That hunt hounds can open the latches on doors?

Shaking my head at myself, I lean off the bookshelf, still too nervous to return to my path. Stalling, I check the books

I'm beside, ears strained for any sounds, for a predator stalking when it thinks I'm distracted.

I flip open the crispy pages and find sketches of monsters. My heart jumps in a much happier way. In my haste, I partially rip a corner of the ancient paper trying to turn it.

"Sorry," I whisper, as if it can hear me, and turn the leaflets with more care. Perhaps I can take this one back with me, though I'm not sure bringing faerie things besides *berries* into the mortal lands is wise—

"Are you apologizing to a book?"

I gasp. The book slips from my hands, striking the floor with an uncannily loud noise in the silent library. My heart picks back up a too-quick rhythm, spots clearing from my vision. Turning in a circle, I can't find the source of the voice, but the unmistakable sensation of being watched crawls across my skin. The words sounded strangely far away, as if carried over a breeze, but it saw me with the book—

The same creak of a door crackles across the silent space, definitely on the same upper floor this time, and I run.

The stairs are close by. I edge around the railing, glancing back and catching the outline of a shadow in the dark aisles. It is darker suddenly than it should be, not nearing night but too dark for the afternoon, and there is nothing but a sleek shadow of a tall figure among the dust-catching moonlight. Bright eyes narrow, and its head cocks as it steps forward. Moonlight cuts across the open space before the bookshelf. A face—pale as milk, long and strange but mostly human— peers at me. He looks as confused about my appearance as I am about his. A wave of ink falls across his shoulders. His clothes are mostly unnoticeable, pale and embroidered, a long lithe blade in his hand, brushing the floor.

I back down, catching my arm on the railing when I nearly lose my footing and go tumbling.

He makes a strange jerk of a motion, as if meaning to step closer to me, push me the rest of the way down. His lips part. A thousand wary tales about fae and their music, their songs and ensnaring words, rush through my mind.

Daring to turn my back on the creature, I flee. Fingers shoved into my ears, I stumble through the bookshelves, ankles unsteady on the dusty cold floorboards.

For a moment, I'm certain I'll take the incorrect turn through the maze of bookshelves and never find the door, but I nearly knock into it in my haste, stumbling to the leaf-strewn ground outside. *No music.*

The sun has fully gone down. I wasn't here nearly long enough for such a thing.

Scrambling to my feet, I drag the door shut with shaking fingers and turn for the honeysuckle, feet pounding on the quiet forest floor, legs burning, breath refusing to come quickly enough.

I shouldn't have dropped the book, I think, casting a last glance over my shoulder to check if it's following me. In the dark, the library is nothing but a shape in the moonlight. It may be my imagination, but I'm certain I catch a flicker of movement in one of the broad glass windows of the second story.

Honeysuckle cuts out my vision, and I sprint a half dozen full strides through its corridor before closing my eyes and losing my way back into the mortal realm.

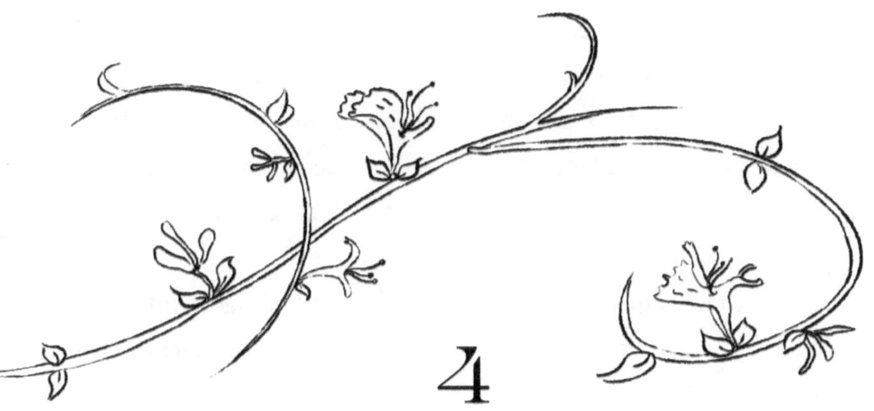

4

Honeysuckle and Silver

As Una teased me for, I nearly smash into the haw-thorn tree, tripping over a root and tumbling to the leafy ground. Rolling over so quickly I make myself dizzy, I stare at the path and all around where I first found the kittens . . .

And find myself alone.

Huffing out a breath, I drop my forehead to the scratchy leaves, groaning.

"Never again," I whisper. "Niamh, you're a moonlight-born fool. Never again."

Crawling to my feet, I wobble toward the edge of the woods before steadying, glancing back too many times in the dark. I will *not* be telling Emma about this, not even a hint—

"Niamh—"

An undignified scream rips from my chest before I recognize Niall's gentle voice. He starts, gazing around as if we're being attacked. He's coming up through the trees, from the direction of the village. As soon as my heartbeat returns to normal, I'm fairly certain I frightened him as much as he frightened me.

"Oh, fae help me." I wave a hand at him, fingers on my throat. Then I punch him in his big shoulder. "You scared me half to death!"

"*Me?*" he yells, then lowers his voice and chuckles. "I don't think I've ever heard you scream like that. Are you cursed?"

I roll my eyes, then hug him. With another laugh, he rocks me back and forth. I'm three months older than him and take after Da's stature, but he's still bigger than me. If anything, he's much broader, which makes for safer embraces.

"No," I answer, "just terrible at judgment."

"So I see. Una said you went wandering around in Faerie again, but you usually come back before dark."

I lean my head back to look at him. He doesn't go into Faerie, but he'll come wander the border for me. "I'm all right. It wasn't dark when I went in."

As I say it, releasing him, I can't help another glance over my shoulder.

It wasn't dark when I went in. When I turn back, I get the distinct impression Niall's trying his best to inspect me in the low light.

Lowly, he asks, "What did you see?"

I hurry him back toward the flickering lights of the village on the edge of sleep. "What makes you think I saw anything?"

"Other than the banshee screech?"

I wrinkle my nose, shoving into him as we walk. "Don't say their name."

"Sorry." Likewise, he glances over his shoulder.

I sigh, dropping my face back to stare at the sliver of a moon, not nearly so bright as that in Faerie. Ours is losing the fight against the dark of the evening sky.

Dust in the moonbeams.

Bright eyes, a tall shadow, a long blade.

Suddenly too cold in the spring night, I drag Niall back to the cottage, intent on hot tea and the hearth.

"Did Una go home?"

"She wouldn't until you came back."

For no good reason, my throat gets tight, and I swallow lungfuls of night air.

Well, I suppose I won't have to explain twice.

Una clutches two of the kittens, one in either hand, while Niall tries cold milk instead of warm with another one, his scruffy face scrunched in unhappy concentration at the animal's lack of cooperation.

Or perhaps it's the description of the faerie I encountered that's haunting his expression. Perhaps I made it sound worse than it was, but once I opened my mouth, I began rambling, voice rising. Now Una is cuddling the kittens—who seem happy with the attention, purring as if they are indeed cats—while giving me uncomfortable and often rather severe looks.

She's probably wondering if I gathered a faerie curse along the way. I don't blame her.

I wonder too. I suppose by morning we'll know.

At least she's distracted from the idea of hounds on the border shredding me to pieces. I'm uncertain which I'd prefer she fret over—since she certainly must fret.

"You are never going back in," she says with a tone that is not to be defied, stroking the kittens' soft heads with her thumbs. "You're lucky you're even back with us. What is your mam going to say?"

I give her an even look. That threat hasn't worked in ages. I'm not young enough.

Though I hope she doesn't tell her.

"Don't worry, I have no plans to," I say, curled on the pillows beside the hearth, tea in hand and an empty plate beside me where pie once sat. With my friends on either side of me, the cottage warm, and my mind clear, I feel foolish for my overreaction. After all, whatever type of faerie it was, all it did was stare at me.

And ask me why I apologized to a book—not even for my name so it could drag me away into Faerie forever.

Now that I consider it, picture the scene more clearly in my mind, I'm not certain it was a long blade in its hand. Warriors do not lean on their blades, gripping the top as if they are an old man gripping a walking stick.

Silly as it seems to consider, I know little of fae and the ways they dress, the ways they decorate themselves. Perhaps walking sticks are a common practice, such as gentlemen have in the larger cities. It's a funny thing to imagine, but barely less threatening.

A faerie does not need a weapon to wound and drive us mad, after all.

"I don't know what I'm supposed to do about them," I say, picking up the nearest kitten. Its bony body seems to settle between my fingers. I let it sniff my cooling tea, but it turns its nose up, wrinkled eyelids scrunched shut. Sighing, I set it on my chest, where it settles with a flap of its tiny tail.

Una waves me off. "We'll find something they'll eat. Don't worry about it, Niamh."

"And if you go back in, I'll tell Emma too," Niall adds, giving up on the cold milk.

I drop my head back against the pillows and groan.

They don't need to, but Niall and Una stay the night, sleeping on the pillows with me beside the dying fire. Restless, I dream vividly of waking with my teeth falling out, my skin dripping off my bones, and dancing until my toes break away. Each time, I wake and tell myself to stop being so ridiculous. But I find little sleep by the time the morning is graying.

Frustrated, I throw back the quilt, check on the sleeping kittens in their crate, and head to the kitchen. After dragging in logs for the stove, I get it started and roll out dough for fresh bread, then for a new piecrust.

If I hadn't dropped that book, maybe I'd have more than a few licks of egg yolk for the kittens.

I know exactly where I dropped it. All I needed to do was

retrieve it before I ran.

Why didn't I just think enough to pick it up?

Whoever that faerie was, it certainly took him a while to find me. I must have been there at least an hour. He likely didn't hear me come in until I was tromping around the top level in my heavy boots.

I pause, staring at the flour on my palms, at Una and Niall sleeping by the fire. Their hands are close in the space I left, and my chest gives a squeeze—not with jealousy of *them*, but of the feeling, the sensation. I remember it, but remember it more clearly turning bitter. They fell in love, and deep down in my chest, I love it for them.

The strange faerie didn't hear me come in, and I know exactly where I dropped the book.

By the time the sun has risen in full, the gnats swarming in the tall grasses in the cool morning dawn, Niall is up, stretching and gathering the eggs from our three chickens. I still have the extras from Emma, but they'll be put to use quickly enough.

Yesterday's bread gets sliced and toasted, and I stir porridge and sizzle salted ham over the stove. Niall yawns and steals one, nearly burning his fingers. I smack his arm with the nearest wooden spoon.

"Sleep all right?"

I wrinkle my nose, leaning back onto my heels. "No."

"Bad dreams, or something else?"

"Something else" being a faerie curse. "Bad dreams. Plenty of them."

He nods. "Try again after you eat. Daylight can chase things away."

Una comes stumbling in, hair unkempt. Someone in the village will have a good laugh about the three of us sleeping over together as if we are still children.

I eat, and food grounds me, makes my stomach stop churning. While Una pokes about in the garden, I milk Primrose, feeling happier with my forehead leaning against her warm belly. Frothing milk collects in the bucket, and I watch it, thinking of fae bribed by humans.

We have honey in the cupboard. I shake myself. Sitting in the garden with Una, I dig my toes into the soil and feel the heat of the morning sun on my face and neck and shoulders and bare arms. I lie back and doze. Una hums. Niall takes the pail of milk inside and calls goodbye before he runs down the path to his duties with his own family.

"I'm all right," I murmur. "I'll come down later and help with your dress."

"You're sure?" Una asks, trailing her fingers through my hair where I still lie in the hot soil.

"I feel perfectly fine, just tired, I promise."

"If you go back in, don't let it be to the library."

I glance at her.

"The woods with these hounds are bad enough. Do not add another monster to the mix."

"I'm not sure about 'monster,' " I mumble, squinting at a ladybug crawling over her toe. "I keep remembering things differently . . . in the daylight."

"How?"

It feels strange and silly saying the words aloud, but Una is accustomed to me by now. "All he did was stand there and ask me a question."

She huffs out a sigh, but the consideration is there in her eyes. "Perhaps. That is all they need, isn't it? A question answered."

What is your name?

He didn't ask.

"I suppose so, yes."

"Still, if you go back in, it better be when the sun is high, or so help me, I will find out."

I manage not to laugh, squinting at the heat of the day on my face. "I am only sporadically that foolish. And now is not one of those times. I'll pay more attention to the light, now I know it changes in such a way."

"Please keep your head about you, Ve."

She sounds so uncharacteristically sober that I tell her in the same tone, "I will."

She gives my forehead a kiss. I watch her disappear down the path and stare after her for a while, the sun beginning to burn my face, a beetle crawling across my foot, my finger tracing the tender scar wrapping around my forearm and across my fingers and palm. It doesn't bother me when I cook. It bothers me it exists. It bothers me that the boy who left me to it is happy in the next village over.

I sit up.

Digging the jar of honey out of the cupboard, I tuck it into a basket with half the fresh loaf of bread and the newly baked pie. I'm not planning on being caught, no faerie eyes pinning me in place, but it never hurts to be prepared.

Besides, something about the creature's existence doesn't

sit easily in my mind after considering it for more than a few minutes. I have never seen one, so how should I know, but he didn't quite appear to move correctly, and if that was indeed a walking stick in his hand, I almost begin to wonder if there is something wrong.

Either way, fae are swayed by sweet things, are they not?

Trying again to feed the kittens and having less success than last time, I tuck them back into their crate in my bedroom, pull on my lighter shoes, and sneak out the back door with the basket. Una is not above spying on me with the state I was in last night—it is broad daylight, and I do not wish to be caught.

The long way through the woods is warm and shady, leaves fluttering green with spring, happy and normal and of the mortal world. The heat is of springtime: thinner and not so oppressive, nothing like the swampy night air of Faerie. *Will it be even hotter before noon?*

I find the hawthorn tree sitting still and proud and touch the soft bark. I did not mark it, of course, but it is quite easy to find. In the daylight, there is nothing frightening about the little clearing around it in the thinner trees. I have passed it a dozen times before, and besides the kittens and the blood, it is nothing to fear. It is not even the place where I gained my scar.

Voices call from the village, but they are the greetings to neighbors I know so well. From here, I can just see the tops of thatched houses. Later, I should help with the newest rethatching. No use in anyone worrying I've locked myself away after a little blood was found on some leaves.

Facing the clear of the deep forest, endless and eternal until one becomes lost and enters Faerie—I do not know what exists on the other side of it, nothing perhaps, perhaps eternity—I wring the handle of my basket.

"It's an old library," I tell myself, though that is not the part making my skin cold in the warm morning. "And he's probably gone. Why would he stay? It's an old library."

I close my eyes and run half a dozen steps.

Honeysuckle drifts over me, and I skid to a stop. When I open my eyes, it is so benign it almost seems strange. In the slightly brighter daylight—the trees still obscure much of the sun—it all appears much less threatening, even when I creep through the walkway and peer around the corner at the library itself. With the leaves falling around it, it is more a painting, a picture from a children's tale.

The window where last I saw his flickering shadow is empty.

You can turn around, I remind myself, then crunch across the leaves to the little side door, almost expecting it to be locked. It is not. The handle is chill beneath my fingers, but inside, the library is warmer than expected after last night's cold. Perhaps magic warms and cools it. Little is known of how magic exists or works—many say it is a myth, like the fae themselves, but they do not live in a village on the edge of Faerie.

Picking my way through the maze of tight bookshelves, I come to the same hallway. My heartbeat thumps behind my ears. My fingers grip the basket so tight they ache. My soft footstep feels too loud on the wooden floor.

I step out once. Twice. I hear nothing besides the leaves still coming to rest along the floor. There seems to be an unlimited number of them. If they fall this way constantly, they would be long gone from the broad branches by now.

Leaning forward, I catch sight of the bookshelf at the edge of the upper railing, where the corner of the book rests. All I need to do is creep up the stairs, snatch it, leave the honey and bread and pie, and sneak back out.

Simple.

Perhaps the moonlight blessed me instead of cursed me, for the steps do not groan on the way up. On the tips of my toes, I make my way back to the correct shelf.

The book is gone.

I freeze. *Did he take it? Why would he take it? Only because I was interested?*

Perhaps he put it on a different shelf; the spot I pulled it from remains empty—

It's atop the shelf.

I squint at it. *Why would he put it up there?*

Perhaps he is attempting to trap me. If I must climb to get it, it will take more time. But I've been standing here for minutes. If he were trying to catch me, he would not need to lure me to the top of the shelf to do it. I glance around, then into the nearest rows of shelves. Empty. I don't feel eyes on me. I think I would know the feeling of them, after everything.

Setting the basket on the floor, I step just under the bookshelf, looking up at the familiar spine. The shelf itself is not terribly tall. I can nearly reach it if I stand on my toes. The tall figure last night could certainly set it there with ease. I test my weight on the bottom step, and it gives a faint squeak but holds me. I boost myself up and slide the tome to me. Dust comes scooting off the edge, catching on the waist of my dress.

Past the shelves, something creaks.

I was starting to believe he wasn't still here.

Chills catch along my skin. Against better judgement, I step one more rung up, nudging a few spines with the toe of my boot, and look over the rows leading back into the room. I don't *see* anything, and the moon knows anything in here could be making the noise.

A footstep. A breath. My own catches in my lungs.

I turn my face ever so slightly.

He is not a shadow anymore.

And he is so *close.* I flinch. Somehow, he stepped around the bookshelf and right up under me with not even a sound— not a sound until he wanted me to turn and find him. And he is *tall.* I didn't realize how much so in the dark. Now, when he stands just under me with his pale flat face and slightly too-long neck, leaning right up under my shoulder, eyes seeming too close, I realize just how frighteningly large he is. His limbs are all long ropes of thin muscle. He's too thin and tall and ungainly but moved with such grace the night before.

Now he is still.

Incredibly still.

He does not so much as blink, head caught in a perma-nent slant of curiosity. I am staring into the face of an owl, or a hawk, or a night monster the thoughts of which make my scarred hand gripping the bookshelf ache. He is not *moving,* and I realize how uncannily strange it is to watch something living that doesn't even appear to shift with breath. My fingers are shaking, my heart hurting with panic.

I should've left Una and Niall a note so they'd at least know why I never returned.

Somewhere in the corner of my panicking thoughts, I recognize that it is indeed a walking stick in his hand, not a long blade as I first feared. Quite heavily, he leans on it, and I think perhaps it is more a cane.

Can fae be wounded?

I must say something, must speak. I am in Faerie, and I should not be, and he has not killed me in the first few seconds of panic. Perhaps I can say something, *anything* . . .

Words flee my thoughts, and I find myself whispering, "I . . . brought you honey."

Finally, *finally*, a muscle twitches in his face. *Amusement?* I grasp on to it. Amusement is good. You don't kill something you think is funny and pathetic—not when you're human, at least.

I dare to shift my foot a bit, and the ancient wood snaps. My fingers slip off the top shelf, and I drop to the ground. An arm catches me, and the side of my head smacks against a rather distinct cheekbone. He lets off a small grunt, stumbling, leaning more heavily on his cane.

I freeze, one foot on the floor, awkwardly caught against him. His hand is iron around my elbow, and I feel each and every joint of his fingers. I don't know why, but I expected fae to be cold as the moon they're born under, cold as the claws of the hunt hounds in my arm. When I glance up, the line of his jaw is closer to my face than expected, and the strange silver eyes gaze down at me in open curiosity. A branch of the tree shifts, a shaft of sunlight cutting farther in, and his pupils dilate. Honeysuckle has spread its scent to his clothes.

Gently, he sets me down.

Every muscle in my body tells me to get *away* from him, put as much space between us as possible, but I'm much more frightened of running and angering him. Right now, he looks curious, and that can't be worse than angry.

His hand moves, and I flinch despite my best efforts. He pauses, slim eyebrows quirking together, before moving slower. Up to the top of the shelf, where he eases down the book and offers it. I'm more than a little suspicious it's a trap to take it, but it could be a trap if I *don't*. Slowly, being as submissive as possible, I put my hands around the edges. His fingers are longer than I realized, and I accidentally brush them with mine under the bottom cover.

"Thank you," I say, and my voice comes out weaker than intended.

"You can read it?"

Such a normal question. His voice is gentler than his tall form, quiet—a stream over river stones.

I open and close my mouth a few times, throat tight, and say, "No, I . . . There are pictures . . . I . . ."

He is a faerie . . . He is a faerie, and he seems friendly enough. Perhaps I don't need to find the little kittens in the book and try to guess at the words written around them.

They should be on this side of Faerie anyway, should they not?

"I . . . found some kittens by the edge of the woods. They

are not from our side, and I don't know what to feed them—
they aren't eating anything I give them—so I thought I'd try
to figure out what they'll eat. I didn't know anyone was in
here. I didn't think fae came to the border—" The words all
come out in a huff of breath.

His eyebrows go a little higher the more I ramble on.

Definitely amused.

"Kittens?"

"Well, I don't know what they are, but they're . . . a little
like kittens."

He waves a long hand toward the book. "Point them out
for me. I will be able to tell you."

Still friendly enough. I hold the book awkwardly, worried
about opening it and tearing a page again. "I . . . didn't actually find them in here . . . yet. I was looking when you startled
me . . . last night."

"I didn't mean to."

I find myself nodding, for he says it so genuinely. I remain
expecting a trap, but fae cannot lie, and he seems . . . uninterested in hurting me, at the very least. If nothing else, I seem a
vague curiosity, a strange beetle he's come across.

He nods to the book, and I realize he expects me to look
through the ancient pages. Right now. Right here. With his
sharp inhuman eyes staring at me. I shift the book a little into
one arm. It is rather large, and he watches me hold it in the
crook of my elbow before shifting aside and gesturing along
the railing. A table sits farther down. It would be easier, but
I don't want to walk past him, don't want to turn my back to
him.

He gestures again, and I don't dare refuse despite the pin-pricks of chills rolling between my shoulders as I make my way toward the table, very aware of each thump of my boots on the floorboards. Behind me, his feet make barely a noise save for the gentle click of his cane. There's a lilt to his soft gait—he's certainly injured himself, or it's an old wound. But from all the stories, I'm not sure fae retain old wounds.

There's some relief when I set the tome on the dusty table and he comes to stand within my vision, gaze on the movement of my hands as I turn the pages with care. Hopefully he isn't irritated by my slowness.

"Why didn't you leave them where you found them?"

I start, not having expected him to speak again. *Get ahold of yourself, Niamh.*

"They were just there by themselves. And there was . . . blood on the nearby bush. I thought perhaps something had killed their mother. Someone had to help them."

He nods, which is a strangely disarming gesture when expecting a violent creature.

I'm more than halfway through the book and beginning to wonder if they are not even here at all when a passing sketch catches my eye. The adult versions of the creatures, I don't know, but the kittens with their flat little faces and needle teeth—those are unmistakable.

"Here," I say, touching the leaf-dry paper and edging the book toward him. He leans closer, and I am very aware of his tall presence over my shoulder.

He turns the book a bit more toward him, and his expression darkens.

5

An Echo in the Dark

Heart leaping, I step away. He blinks and catches what must be my frightened expression, and his own relaxes, though tension remains.

"You found these by themselves? There was blood?"

"Yes . . . Are they dangerous?

He turns back to the page. "Yes. But not to you."

I'm not sure if his words are meant to comfort me.

Fae cannot lie, can they? So, they must not be dangerous to me. Unless he is mistaken and only *believes* he is telling the truth—I do not know if such a thing is possible. He leans against the table, other hand on the grip of his walking cane, looking over the book once more. Ink-black hair spills over his shoulders, longer than my own. Mine was hacked off a few years back, so it isn't as full as it could've been. Otherwise, he is utterly still once more, just the occasional muscle shifting as he appears to bite the inside of his cheek in thought. He looks . . . human enough, though when taken in all at once, it is rather obvious he is not. A set of individual mortal features does not a mortal make.

Finally, he shifts the page, turning it to check the other side before closing the heavy cover. All at once, I have his full attention, and this is not where I wanted to be.

"Bring them here," he says.

I blink. "What?"

"You can bring them here tomorrow. They won't eat of mortal foods. I can care for them."

"Oh." It's an easier solution than I expected.

When I don't know what else to say, he clarifies, "If I frighten you, you may leave them at the bottom of the stairs so you do not have to see me."

His lip quirks, and I wish I weren't so *obvious*. Perhaps if I were braver I would be able to better trade words with a faerie. On the other hand, perhaps it is well enough he think me fragile and too stupid to hold a conversation—there is less opportunity to anger him.

"All right," I whisper, because I am still staring and don't want him to think me rude.

Rather suddenly, he cracks a smile. "You think I am trying to trick you."

"Occurred to me, yes," I say, then put my palm over my mouth.

"I am not," he says slowly, as if I'm not bright enough to catch it. "You are free to leave."

Fae must tell the truth, but they can also change their minds. I nod, unable to stop a glance at the cane he leans against. His clothes, now visible in the daylight, are lovely if simple, a drapery of fine fabric, embroidered in places, but mostly an unassuming pale tunic and dark pants. The shirt is open around the neck, and I can see the uninterrupted line of his throat. He is prettier than any man has the right to be, and I feel my face heat despite what I know of fae—they are vain, they are gorgeous, and they will ensnare humans if given half the chance.

He has been given more than half a chance.

When I realize he's still staring, he looks me up and down pointedly, blinking as if to say, *Would you like to look me over further?* A faint curl remains on his lips.

"Do you need help?" I blurt before I can stop myself, not realizing the words are out until the amusement falls from his face.

"If you were capable of such a thing," he says, looking to the tree, "I would be quite impressed."

The dismissal is there in his tone, his body language, rippling off him. I can practically taste his discomfort in the air.

Is Faerie having an impact on me? I shouldn't remain here.

Glancing at the book, I think of asking if I can take it with me, but it's no use. I'll bring the kittens to him tomorrow, and then there won't be any reason for it. I have not dismissed the idea he will grow angry with me for some unforeseen slight.

"Thank you," I whisper, and think about curtsying, but it would look awfully ridiculous in my old dress meant for traipsing around the woods. Instead, I scurry to the stairs, glancing back to see him running a finger over the spine of the book and not paying me any mind.

As quietly as I can, I take the honey and bread and pie from the basket and set them on the nearest empty shelf, where he will see if he turns, and flee with the empty basket back out the library and through the honeysuckle.

On the mortal side of the woods, I stop at the edge of the village and stare as close to the sun as I can until my eyes ache. I walk straight past the houses without bothering to hide in the trees or speak to anyone. Depositing the basket back in the kitchen, I pace before checking on the sleeping kittens. Nothing is to be done for them—in fact, I shall take them back this afternoon, for they have gone much too long without proper food as it is—so I stare out the window over the kitchen counter, out at the path leading to the cluster of cottages. From here, I can just see the house they're rethatching, the shirtless backs of the men in the sun, the flashes of women's hair or their airy scarves covering their necks from the burn of the spring heat.

My heartbeat is slow under my palm, though it feels strained in my chest. My breath hitches, though I don't know why. Humans are not meant for Faerie, certainly not for long. But that was not long. That was not even an hour. There is nothing wrong with what I did. Eating their food is nothing, interacting with them without giving your name is nothing. Terrifying, but nothing. He did not curse me or ensnare me or even play a trick on me—cut my hair or tear my dress or any other such cruel and nonpermanent ways of frightening.

I rub my hands together and watch the village work.

"Back in the bright sun," I mumble, then head out the door. "I have been in and out of Faerie a hundred and more times. It is nothing."

It is Athol's house they are rethatching, and I join the other women cutting and binding the thatch.

Una waves at me from the well, where she's collecting water for the men up on the roof.

Niall is taking a break with two of the other men his age, shirt off, flexing his muscles. He catches my expression and laughs, head thrown back. I roll my eyes.

Emma passes by, and I keep my eyes on the straw, focusing on the sweet dried smell of it, the roughness of the twine beneath my fingers. The world no longer smells of dust and honeysuckle, but my dress does, as does the lock of hair that falls from its braid and over my eyes. By the afternoon, sweat is trickling down the back of my dress and through my hair, and I feel better, more grounded.

While I'm busy splashing ice-cold well water over my hair, I consider telling Una and Niall what I snuck off to do when I claimed I was going to nap. Only a few hours ago I was looking into those silver hawk's eyes and thinking I should have left my friends a note so they would know where I disappeared to.

Now I am only going back to drop the kittens off. It is nothing particularly threatening. He found me a little pathetic and stupid perhaps, and certainly not hostile. I won't even see him, as he suggested. I'll leave the helpless creatures on the top of the dusty staircase and leave.

And I shall not go into Faerie again unless I am collecting berries and flowers, and never again shall I lose my way near the great hawthorn.

I find a pair of arms weaving around me from behind, and Una rocks us a little. "You're sweaty."

"Mmm."

"Have a nap?"

I sigh. "No, but I'm feeling better."

I will deliver the kittens, then *I shall tell them, when there's no more upcoming danger for them to fret over.*

Remembering Niall searching for me in the evening, I breathe around the tight feeling of knowing the two of them love me, that they would wander up to the edge of Faerie for me. I give Una's hands a squeeze and return to washing as much of the sweat from my arms and neck as I can get without drenching my poor dress.

"Want to help me with my midsummer dress?" Una asks, voice far away.

Glancing sidelong at her, I find her holding an empty water bucket in her hands, looking back at the house. I follow her gaze and find Niall still shirtless and returning to bouncing around with his friends. The man can thatch a house and still be full of energy.

"Boys," I mumble.

"Mm-hmm," Una hums, still running her eyes across every inch of him.

I try my best not to laugh. "I *cannot* believe I'm the only one who notices."

"*Shh!*" She swats at me and misses with her eyes still on him. "He's going to be my dance partner at midsummer. He'll put flowers in my hair, and everyone will know."

I smile at the tradition, weaving my arm back through hers. "A hopeless romantic, as always."

"Who's going to dance with you?"

"Oh, I don't know. Perhaps I'll steal you."

She giggles but doesn't press the subject. Running back to my cottage, I change into something less dirty and sweat soaked while she waits in the garden. The kittens are still asleep, one yawning widely when I pet its ear.

"A few more hours," I mumble. *When I can get away from Una without being suspicious.*

After I have returned the kittens, I shall tell her. *After.*

A few more hours, and my fingers are sore from helping Una with her dress—which is admittedly gorgeous, and I'll be proud to see her wear it and know I helped—but it's a while before late afternoon yet, and I can confidently declare I want to fix dinner before evening.

With several hours to think it over, and more time while I'm cooking, I tell myself this isn't such a foolish idea. *No one can be angered by being offered food.* I think of his eyes and his strange clothing, but more so whatever he was hiding under them. *What can wound a faerie?* His hand, leaning too much on the cane when he was lost looking at the book instead of me. And he is there alone.

Are they vulnerable to their own monsters?

Into the basket go more bread and honey and another slice

of pie, this time alongside roasted potatoes with herbs from the garden and a few slices of cold ham. I have no idea what fae like other than sweets, so it should be enough. Upon further thought, I find a jar and add in milk.

Digging a second basket out of Mam's cupboard, I unearth another old quilt and make the kittens a new nest. It'll be easier to carry than the crate. They mewl and nip at my fingers, and I murmur soothing things as I reach the bottom of the stairs. The whimpering keeps up, and I am more assured of my decision to take them back this afternoon. They have eaten some, but after all this time, they must be bordering on starving.

Someone knocks.

I pause. Una or Niall would be shouting by now, and I'm not eager to speak to anyone else. Carefully, I set the basket in the kitchen, in with the broom and kitchen rags, where no one can see or hear them, and open the front door.

"Mister Haskel," I say, too surprised to sound properly dead.

"Ah, oh, Niamh, are your folks home?" The man is a nice-enough fellow, a tall, skinny reed not much older than my own father.

Still, he knows what his son did and nevertheless comes by every so often. It's been so long I've nearly forgotten the discomfort of it. Last time he was here, Niall stood in the background and glowered, which was perhaps unfair but made me feel better nonetheless. I like to think I am not bitter, but I know I have not rid myself of that certain fault. Heat is already rising behind my chest, and my hand is aching as if it is possible for the scars to split back open and pour blood.

"They won't be home for a few weeks." I hear my heartbeat behind my ears. "Are you here for any particular business I should pass on?"

"Ah, no." He gives a little wave of his hand and backs up to his horse, who's currently eating the tops off Mam's carrots, sticking his thumbs into the pockets of his bright red vest. The fabric is finer than any we have here; Una would be jealous. "Just arrived back from the city and had a few things to do in the next village. I was merely heading through. I have some things to discuss with your father, but I'll call on him in a few weeks."

I manage not to let my eyes narrow. "I'll pass it on. Have a fair day."

Watching to ensure he heads down the path, I shut the door too hard and stomp back to the kitchen, the nerves of returning to Faerie replaced by a familiar pit in my stomach. The gall of that man to still interact with our family after his son's actions. Perhaps he has never believed it—I am merely a girl from the next village over, after all. Everyone probably thinks I had a lie in the hay with him, which I would have. I am very aware that I would have, with very little prompting, if I had not been left to the trees and the monsters.

And Mister Haskel has business to attend to with my father, *evidently*. Da is the wealthiest man in our little cluster of cottages, so I am not surprised. Raging, but not surprised.

It has been ages since I've visited the city, but that hardly has me interested in what he's doing there. I wish to be *unin-*

terested in them for the rest of my days.

Feeling the anger all the way to the tips of my fingers, I watch out the kitchen window until he disappears before retrieving both baskets and taking the back way out once more.

I half expect something to have changed with the hawthorn tree, but it remains as it was, pale and soft and stable. I close my eyes, and honeysuckle envelops me. Much as the afternoon before, it is deathly still, leaves swirling to the forest carpet with nay a breeze to knock them down.

As I maneuver through the walls of books, I push aside the unwelcome visitor in the mortal world and consider what I'm going to do. This morning I had quite decided to leave the kittens and make a run for it, sacrificing the basket along with them. It remains an option. I could leave the basket, then the honey and milk and wrapped food on the floor beside them. They will not get dusty. Una would certainly prefer I never lay eyes upon the faerie ever again and will likely take my own basket to my head when she discovers I have.

Another part of me considers.

I could call out to him. Or, at the very least, call out so he will know I'm leaving them here. He only suggested I leave them on the steps because it was obvious I was fearful. I could call out to him, yes.

And ask again if there is something I can do to offer help.

It would be a foolish thing to do, Niamh. I know it, and I still creep to the top of the steps, set the baskets down, then pick them up again. For a few minutes, I simply continue to stand there, wondering if he'll notice me a third time and come looking. Perhaps he will not, for he promised to stay away so I would not have to be frightened of him.

It seems a deceptively kind thing to offer.

Perhaps not. *What use would a faerie have for an uninteresting village girl?*

"Hello?" I whisper, then curse myself for doing so. He *did* mention to bring them tomorrow, so perhaps he is not paying attention, and I should leave them—take the safer route and leave while I can.

On the empty section of the bookshelf, the honey and bread and pie are gone. He took them. A smile curls at my lips. Perhaps it should not, but someone from Faerie was pleased with my cooking.

I creep a little along the bookshelf, glancing down the aisle leading to the back of the room where he must be staying. He came from this direction both times. The late-afternoon light makes it all slightly more unsettling than this morning, but what can it hurt to deliver the baskets?

"Hello?" I try again, and receive no answer.

Perhaps he is not staying here after all and is only intending to return for them. But he was here this morning and the evening before. Frowning, I consider again leaving the baskets before creeping down the hallway. Reconsidering, I stop making my footsteps silent. I'm not trying to sneak up on the man . . . creature . . . *faerie.*

At the back of the room, around the edge of yet another dusty bookshelf, is a room with a door ajar. Faint warm light filters out. I watch it for a moment but see nothing else of note—not from this angle.

"Hello? I brought the kittens." I look down at my white knuckles, fingers clenched around the basket handles. "And more honey."

Silence.

As carefully as possible, I step up. Knock gently on the jam of the open door.

It slams shut, a blast of air sending my hair and skirts back. I yelp, nearly tripping over the edge of the nearest shelf. My heart leaps into my throat, and I lean against the wood, smelling the dust disturbed into the air.

A moment later, what I've just witnessed catches up to me. *Magic.*

I shouldn't have come up here. I don't belong in Faerie. He may have looked friendly enough, passive enough, but he was not *human*. And I was fully ready to walk into his lair.

Idiot girl, I tell myself, then push off the shelf.

The door cracks open. I freeze, instinctively clutching the basket of kittens closer. A familiar shape of fine clothes and long dark hair stands silhouetted against the warm light in the room.

"What are you doing?" he asks, and his voice is rougher than before.

Why did I come a day early?

"Kittens," I squeak, trying to clear my throat without making too much noise.

Even in the dark, I can see he's staring as if I've lost my mind, which I've just decided I have. Before I can think through the words, I find myself saying, "I'm sorry, but I wanted to bring them back tonight since they're not eating and are probably terribly hungry. I thought I could just bring them now—"

"You were to leave them on the step."

He's quite correct. "I know, I'm sorry. I, um . . . brought more food?"

He's quiet for so long that I don't know what to do. In the dark, I can't make out enough of his expression to truly read it, which might be preferable. He doesn't have his walking cane and leans heavily against the doorframe, and I see the same long hands gripping the edge of the frame too tight. When he shifts, he looks shaky, as if I've caught him in a worse state than before. Many men—human or otherwise— would not appreciate such a thing. Behind him, I can't make out the room, but there's a crackle of a small fire, likely from one of the chimney hearths I saw outside.

Perhaps I merely startled him. I remember his expressions in the light of day—frightening and nonhuman but not unkind.

Gathering my courage, I take a step forward. "Here, I can bring these in for you—"

"Get out."

I falter, pausing to set the basket of kittens down on the floor instead. "I—"

"*Get out!*"

His voice shocks me to my bones, an unnaturally high sound of pure rage. *Not human.* Despite my attempted bravery, I flinch against the bookshelf, knocking my shoulder blades hard against the edge of a book spine. He shifts against the doorframe, and whatever fear held me moments ago returns with force.

Not for the first time, I flee as quickly as I can in the dark, tripping over the bottom step and past honeysuckle until I am safe on our side of the woods and his voice is just an echo in my thoughts.

6

Uprooted Earth

Alone in the cottage, the kittens gone, I chew the ham I didn't manage to take to the strange monster and consider the cruelty of the people who have passed through my life.

What a morose topic, Niamh.

I've finally managed to rid myself of the fear of the place, the strange chill of the library at night. A hot bath helped, as does the smell of soap still lingering instead of honeysuckle and book dust.

I have the best people here—Mam and Da, Una and Niall, and others less close but loving nonetheless. The singular things stick out. The sensation of being abandoned, a cold shaft of ice that never melts in the warm summer heat of the people who are near to me. Any little thing reminds me, even a strange and terrifying faerie I have no attachment to screaming at me in the dark.

I curl up on the cushions beside the hearth, pulling the blankets nearly over my head, feeling the heat of the flames and the comforting scent of crackling wood.

I may as well tell Una and Niall tomorrow since it is all over.

It is all over.

A little thing as it was, it is all over.

I wake late in the morning. The cow is lowing, and I go stumbling out of the house barefoot with hair askew, bucket in hand. There are no kittens to check on, so I'm returning to my usual chores at their usual hour—if I'd *awoken* at a reasonable time. The air is hot. My breath is clean in my lungs. Someone waves to me from the edge of the village, and I wave in return.

Once in a dress not slept in and my hair reasonable, Primrose happy and the chickens fed, I start down the path, intent on finding Una.

She is not in her cottage, and neither are her mother and father and little sister. I wrinkle my nose, looking around their garden. It is not a large village, so many out of their cottages at once is unusual—

Someone is running down the path, and people are gathering at the far side of the edge of the whitewashed cottages, near the faerie side of the trees. Ice floods my veins, but it is more for the memory of the creature and his scream than any tangible threat. They are not even near the path that would lead to the hawthorn.

Still, I trot down, glad for the gentle overnight rain so the path does not kick up dust. A few too many people offer me sympathetic gazes when I pass, and that sets more of a chill into my bones. Two dozen people are clustered, and half as many children. Niall is closest to whatever they're looking at, and so is Una, seeming to perch behind him as if he'll protect her from the gashes in the upturned soil. When I push my way through, her hand grabs mine and drags me closer. There are indeed breaks in the soft earth, doubly as long as me and distinctly animal in pattern but much too large to be from wild pigs or anything else in this area.

No wonder everyone is clustered and quiet. The fragile skin on my hand suddenly feels raw. Una's slim fingers wrapped around it is comforting. I give her a slight squeeze in return and feel the lack of Mam and Da in the village. It is not as if they can protect anyone from faerie monsters—but I'd feel safer than I suddenly do in our cottage, alone.

"No one saw anything," Athol says, scratching the back of his hair. "We'll just keep a better eye out. If they came too close, the animals would have been braying. Maybe they aren't here for us."

"Perhaps the fae will do their duty and protect us on their side of the border," someone else mumbles, and I think of the wounded creature in the library, his hand gripping the cane too tight, the high pitch of his voice in the night.

It is said hunt hounds only emerge to enact revenge. Ages ago, when they attacked me and the boy I'd been foolish enough to kiss in the forest, it hadn't been about *us*. Some small child—it must have been a child, for everyone knows to walk with care where mushrooms grow—had kicked down a faerie circle with no one the wiser.

If the little girl or boy had been out at night instead of me, they would've been killed. Eventually, the mushrooms regrew and the slight passed, the hunt hounds along with it. No one's heard their haunting barks since.

Apparently, something else has offended the fae. A little blood at the border is nothing; claw marks in the field outside of the village is *too much*.

"They got through before," another says as the crowd begins to disperse, and a comforting hand touches my shoulder. I look up into one of the familiar faces I've grown up with and smile, hoping it says, *I am well.* I receive a few more pats on the shoulder and squeezes of my hand not currently being crushed in a death grip by Una. Once, it irritated me, but the protective sympathy is now rather comforting. I dig my toe into the unoffensive upturned earth. In the village, a few are already sprinkling salt along the edges of the paths, away from their gardens, a ward against malevolent creatures of Faerie.

For hounds, I doubt it will be of much use.

Cara runs past, casting troubled gazes at the gouges in the earth. She skids to a stop, glances at her sister, and then tucks herself under my other arm.

"All right, Ve?" she asks. I can hardly stand the sight of her near the marks in the soil, imagining those claws in her instead.

"Yes," I say, combing back her hair, hoping my voice isn't shaking.

"Will you spend the night with us?" Una asks, her hand still wrapped around mine.

It's more a relief than I'd like to admit. "Yes."

"I took the kittens back to the library," I admit to Una.

They have enough space that I could've taken a spot on the floor by the hearth with its thick woolen rug and some extra blankets and pillows, but Una insisted I share her bed. Perhaps she is as frightened as I am. It was only a few years ago now, and we have been friends since we were little things. She sat by my bedside then and followed me around when I was up and about, constantly worried.

A few times, Niall told her with a laugh and a smile not to smother me, but he did nearly the same thing.

It is dark, and the moon is outside, and Una's bed is not quite large enough for the two of us to fit comfortably, so we're squished back-to-back.

"I knew it," she mutters, then reaches back to slap me in the thigh as hard as possible. Only the blankets keep the noise from sounding sharply through the house.

"*Ow*," I hiss, then smack her back.

"Why are you such a fool all the time?"

"He said he would take care of them, and what was I supposed to do, let them starve?"

She sighs and rolls over, her shoulder jabbing into my back.

When I squirm onto my back, she's facing me, hands under her cheek, giving me a dirty look in the dark room.

"*What?*"

"Don't *ever* do that again without telling me."

I grimace. "I admit that occurred to me."

"Oh, *you admit that occurred to you*, wild woman. *Don't* do it again without telling me."

"*All right*, heavens."

She pinches me hard on the arm, then hugs me. I roll my eyes, but her concern is heartening, and I'd be just as—if not more—worried for her under the same circumstances. Next time I venture into Faerie, even if just to pick berries on the edges, I'll only go in the daylight, when nothing threatens the edge of the trees. It is frightening at night anyhow.

Hounds are awake at night.

We lie there for a time, warm, staring at the dark ceiling, until she finally says what I assume she's been considering for a while.

"Do you think he has something to do with it?"

It passed through my mind a dozen times today, along with something else. "Actually, I was wondering if it's the opposite."

She rolls back onto her side, watching me. "How?"

"He doesn't seem well. I wonder if he's hiding out from those hounds. One faerie wouldn't be much of a deterrent if they decided to attack him."

"You think fae attack one another?"

Well, they are certainly different types *of fae.* "Faerie is violent, isn't it?"

"Hmm," she agrees, propping her head up on her hand. "Well, I'd ask if he needs help, but I don't want you to go back there. You brought him honey, and he wasn't too thankful, was he?"

"I . . ." I pause, unsure how much detail I should give of the last encounter. "I tried to bring him more yesterday. I don't think he expected me to come. He screamed at me."

In the dark, Una's eyes widen. "*Please* tell me you didn't tell him off for it."

I scoff, then clap a hand over my mouth so no one else in the cottage is woken. Una has her own small bedroom, but it isn't a large house. Cara is in the other room just over—or more likely, she is tucked in between her mam and da, needing the safety.

If Una met the strange creature, she'd have no illusions of me reacting how I would if one of the village men tried to yell at me.

"I ran for my life," I admit. "He's not . . . human, Una. I know how that sounds—of *course* he isn't—but you have no idea what it's like to stare one of them in the eyes."

"How?" she whispers again.

On this side of the border, safe in her bed, having no memories of Faerie and having never stepped foot past its borders, such creatures are only pretty stories. Mysterious and a little romantic, she may be frightened of it in theory, but it's equally as fascinating. Even *she* knows this is not the same as the hounds. I understand. Even having been there, even having been frightened out of my wits, just speaking of the place brings a dull ache behind my ribs, a speeding up in my heartbeat. We are lying in a cottage not a mile away from a few lost steps into Faerie, and I've *been there.*

"He's probably the most beautiful man I've ever met," I

admit, and Una giggles. "But I think I might even stare into the eyes of those monsters and be less frightened."

"You went back."

"He wasn't so awful . . . when he was trying to be kind." I bite the inside of my cheek, frustrated with myself. Only now does it occur to me that he may have been putting on the air of being more human, if only to not frighten me. Of course, that in and of itself is not awful. Kind of him, in fact. But I believed in it, fell for it with a little bit of reading a book with him standing near me, and every faerie tale and cautionary word I've heard about Faerie and those that dwell in it left my thoughts the moment I met one.

"You're going to go back in."

"What?" I ask. "No?"

She stares at me with her pale eyes.

"No!"

"*Shh!*"

I wave her off, rolling my eyes.

"Look, I can't stop you, but if you do it, would you at least tell me first?"

"Why would I go back in right now?"

She gives me such a look that I know she's probably right.

"Swear it."

"Fine, I *swear*—"

"And *only* in the daytime."

"I've agreed to that already."

She glowers.

"Una, I *swear* I will not go at night. I don't even go in the evening. Happy?"

"Hmph." She pulls the blankets up to her chin and rolls back over. "I'll believe you when you tell me. Oh, and when you are back well before evening."

I roll my eyes again and turn over onto her, using her back as my pillow.

Perhaps I should not, but I find myself watching the trees the next morning. There are more monster tracks along the edge of the village and others in the fields this time, not close to the houses but causing even greater concern nonetheless.

Someone's chicken was found in pieces near the trees, feathers scattered in the morning wind, caught on blades of grass, a few splatters of blood and meat left. It must have gotten free of its coop, but if they are eating our livestock, it was not purely a passing incident.

It will worsen.

I think of Una and her soft hands and pretty eyes, her unblemished skin. Of Niall and his easy strength. Of Cara, who likes to wander out in the fields, gathering mushrooms. We're all so vulnerable and always have been, rooted as close as we are to Faerie.

But these monsters shouldn't be coming out of the trees, and everyone realizes it.

Likewise, other fae do not venture near the edges of the border. Those more human in appearance have not been seen in decades, long enough that they have mostly fallen into stories, though we all are aware of their existence. It's more likely to get a brownie in one's sock drawer than it is to come across one of the tall beautiful fair folk I found in the library. In truth, I'm shocked he's even there, let alone for long enough to take up residence.

Would he know why the hunt hounds are here?

"Una," I say while she's stitching a pattern of lace out in the sunlight. "I'm going back in."

"Any particular reason?" Her voice is calmer than I expected. When I look over my shoulder, she shrugs as if I'm dense. "I knew you were always going to go back in—I'm not an idiot. I just want you to let me know so I can decide if I'm supposed to go in after you. And if you make me do that"— she brandishes her needle at me—"I will cry the whole time and punish you for life."

"I wouldn't want you to do that," I say, then go and kiss her forehead. "I'll be back long before nightfall."

"You still haven't told me why."

I sigh, putting my hands on my lower back. My dress is nicer than the one I usually wear into Faerie, but I'm not planning on traipsing through berry brambles, and I don't wish to return to my cottage. "To ask if he knows why the hounds are coming out of the trees."

And to ask if he can make them stop.

"And if it's him?"

With more bravery than we both know I have, I tell her, "I'll ask him why."

She looks up at me for a long time, then glances at her mam where she's hanging sheets on a line. "Don't do that."

I shake my head and flap my hand at her. "I'll be back

when the sun is still up, I promise."

"I'm warning you, I *will* throw a fit if you don't—"

I wave over my shoulder as I leave their garden, likewise waving at her mam so she knows I'm only going for a walk. I take the sunny path out of the village before easing into the tree line and doubling back, telling myself I am as much a fool as Una claims. Pausing at the hawthorn, I look up into its calm branches, considering that perhaps I should turn around. Going back might end with my body strewn across the honeysuckle outside the library or me dancing for his pleasure until my feet break bone by bone and fall off.

Why am I going back in?

Because he may have answers.

Because he may be the protection we all pray for at night.

These monsters cannot keep slinking into our lands. Eventually, the claw marks will cease being in the soil and will instead be in our skin. Perhaps they don't know the beasts of Faerie are sneaking out of their borders and informing him will put an end to it. He can tell the others of their kind who keep the dangerous beasts away from the fragile humans, and that shall be the end of it.

A strange part of me, I can admit to myself, wants to return to see his strange features and intelligent eyes again, even if they are frightening.

I close my eyes and walk forward until I smell honeysuckle.

Of course, the library is as I left it. Fingers trembling, I edge around the wall until I find the side door and let myself in.

There is no reason to sneak in or creep about. If I am in here, he will know.

Instead, I stand under the massive tree sprouting from the floor and call, "Hello?"

7

An Unanswered Question

Dust motes descend through the sunlight, and I feel suddenly watched. With the knowledge of monsters on the border, I rub my arms, knowing I'm defenseless. I could've brought a knife or a pitchfork or an axe, but what would be the use? Perhaps I could score a few small cuts into the impenetrable hide before it shreds me.

"Are you still here?" I ask to whatever pair of eyes is watching from behind one of the bookshelves. "I . . . wanted to ask a question."

A brush of a footstep, and I am looking up the steps at his silhouette in the gentle sunlight. Momentarily, I don't believe he'll speak, not after his quiet and screaming the other night, but he gestures. Surprised, I force my feet up the stairs, carefully, as quiet as possible, still considering that perhaps he is tricking me now I've had the stupidity to return.

"A question?" he asks, and his voice has returned to gentle music. "You returned to this place for a *question*?"

I force my hands to be still. I'm standing far enough I'm not forced to tip my head to look at him, but in the daylight, I am more aware than before that he should make my skin crawl. Though my fingers tremble, he is quite the most fascinating thing I've ever encountered. Perhaps I should not, but I glance away from his face, down his clothing again—the same as last time, though they seem clean—and to his hands. One still grips the cane, his thumb digging absently into the wood, a strangely human fussing. The other rests carefully against the nearest bookshelf, fingers decorated with rings I didn't see the last time.

When I look up, he is doing the same for me. Though I am considerably less impressive, and need not be, I smooth my hands across my skirts absently, embarrassed. I wonder how many humans he has met, considering how reclusive they are as a species, and if I am as strange to him as he is to me.

Unlikely. He must be hundreds of years old. Plenty of time to see more interesting things than a village girl.

Finally, I remember he asked me a question. My voice comes out as a whisper but doesn't break. "It's important."

"Oh?"

I can't tell if he's mocking me, but I won't be giving in before I even broach the topic. "There are . . . monsters . . . coming out of Faerie and into our village. They've come out before, years ago, and all we know is that other fae put a stop to it, and the times before that when it happened. I wanted to know . . . if you know anything about it? If you can help?"

"Monsters," he repeats.

"Yes?"

"Like me?"

My mouth pops open, and the first words that spring to mind are "not as beautiful as you," but that wouldn't be wise. "No. Real monsters. Monsters who will rip us apart and shred us to our bones and eat us."

If I expected another quip, I am sorely disappointed. He gives a visible twitch, which sets him a little off-balance, and the tip of his cane taps softly against the wooden boards. His head cocks as he regards me, and I stare back with wide eyes, blinking, feeling better now I've asked but concerned by his reaction.

Finally, he asks, "*Not* like those . . . *kittens* you brought me?"

I shake my head, feeling the sting of my hand. "Definitely not. Hunt hounds."

He drops his hand from the bookshelf, thumb rolling the rings around his fingers. "I know of no such name, nor of monsters who would go into the human realm. Such things do not happen."

Disappointment floods me. If he knows nothing about it, he cannot be expected to help. Quietly, I say, "They do."

"How can you know?"

I glance at him. It is not accusatory, but neither is he giving me much faith. I suppose he shouldn't, not if he believes it not to be true and humans to be fanciful creatures tending to panic over little things they think to be fae playing tricks.

Rubbing my hand, I work on stepping toward him. It is not as if I am ashamed of the scar, but it is also not as if I appreciate bringing it under people's noses.

He does not back away or make any indication I should not approach. His eyes follow down to my feet, then up again, and I ignore the flutter in my chest those silver eyes present.

Stopping more than an arm's length away, I hold out my hand. "I remember. I cannot forget it."

I expect him to merely observe from a distance—certainly, his sharp eyes are quite enough for that—but he steps forward. Before I can snag my hand back, his ringed fingers catch mine. I would yank away, for no one has touched my hand besides Mam and Da, Una and Niall, but I am frozen in sudden shock under the unexpected and sudden fear of a faerie touching me. He leans his shoulder against the bookshelf so he can use his other hand as well, still holding his walking stick. Cool fingers turn my palm over, brushing along the tender scar, the littlest finger, which took the most damage and didn't heal well, barely recognizable as what it used to be. It isn't too noticeable—when one isn't expecting it.

"This did not heal well," he murmurs. "Who tended to you?"

"My parents and the village apothecary. It is not as if we have tools to deal with faerie wounds," I say more than a little awkwardly. "They did as much as they could. It healed."

"Not well," he says again, still not releasing my hand.

Finally, I give a gentle tug, aware of the tingle along my skin where his fingers dance against the back of my hand. He releases me, and I press my palm against my leg.

He rubs the rips of his fingers together, still leaning against the bookshelf, and gestures. "When did that occur?"

"Years ago. Nearly five, I believe."

He gives a nod, eyes on the floor, unfocused, as if remembering.

"Do you . . . remember?"

Blinking, he returns his gaze to me. "Hmm? No, no. I was not fighting at that time."

Fighting. My lips part, and I don't know how to continue. Without meaning to, I glance at his walking cane, at the leg he seems to favor, wondering what is hidden under all the clothing.

Clearing his throat, he inspects the nearest branch of the tree growing into the second story of the library as if realizing what he revealed.

"I apologize," he says suddenly, turning back. "For my treatment the other night. You startled me."

My cheeks warm. I remember that only mere hours ago I was considering how foolish I was for being taken in by his pretense at human charms. *I am not being taken in*, I tell myself. *I am simply listening.*

"You frightened me," I tell him, and his lips quirk down in rather genuine unhappiness. "It's all right; I know I wasn't invited at night. How are they?"

"Hmm?"

"The kittens, or whatever they're really called. How are they?"

"Oh." He looks me up and down as if considering, then hesitantly gestures to the back of the library, toward the room

I found him in the night before. "You may come see them."

I open my mouth to insist that I am only here to ask about the hounds, but he is looking at me gently, he has not harmed me past a few good startles, and I *am* curious to see them again. I was becoming attached and was sadder than I'd like to admit that I had to give them up.

What would be the harm?

Emma could likely think of a great deal of harm, as could Una and Niall, and Mam and Da for that matter, but I find myself nodding. When I don't immediately move, he nods in return and leads me back. I wonder if he doesn't want to turn his back to me as well. Much more dangerous for my back to be to *him*, and he must realize. Carefully, I follow with as quiet of steps as possible, twisting the front of my dress in my hands. His hair is always smoothly brushed, falling between his shoulder blades, and if I weren't walking so far back, I'd almost be tempted to reach out and touch it. It must be soft, like running a hand through summer grasses still fuzzy with new sprouts.

Perhaps I should leave. I am too easily drawn in by this creature, and he is a god compared to humans—I could fall prey to anything he says, any movement he makes. It is up to him whether or not I am trapped here forever.

For this reason alone, I pause in the doorway of the room where he's taken up residence.

Peeking in, I find what must have once been more shelves and bookcases, for there are a few along the opposite wall. Half of the room is open. A hearth burns low coals, though it's plenty warm, muggy even. I cannot know the depths of the illness or injury that afflicts him, so I do not comment. A window along the opposite wall lets in dim Faerie sunlight, catching dust motes in the air like spinning stars. He seems to have cleaned up, but there is only so much to be done in an ages-abandoned library, and injured atop it all.

He has found what were once old cushions as well as blankets and furs and has made a rather luxurious bed near the fire, enough space to recline comfortably any way he likes, with room as well to sit propped against an old couch with its wooden legs crumbled off. Rather comfortable—and rather human. A few baskets are strewn about, though from here, I cannot see what's in them, and I spot my own basket in the corner, which must still hold the kittens.

What else could I bring him to help? I shake off the thought—returning once was foolish, returning thrice and perhaps Una should have me seeing a doctor.

He bends and plucks at the blanket holding the kittens with careful fingers.

Though I don't want to offer it in return, I find myself asking, "What is your name?"

Unexpectedly, he lets out a gentle mock of a laugh, straightening. "Would you tell me yours?"

An expected answer. Disappointment floods me nonetheless, tightening my chest. "No, but I cannot do anything to you with yours."

Cocking his head at me, he nearly looks . . . *charmed.* "You are correct, aren't you? Aidyn."

I blink. I didn't expect such an easy offer. It feels important, and I open my mouth before closing it, lost for a way to respond. Finally, I manage, "Aidyn."

His eyes drag down across me, settling on my nervous hand wringing. "Are you frightened?"

Fae cannot lie. Likewise, they know we *can* and must know when we are, considering how old and wise he likely is. Lying to his face is quite too much for my nerves. "Yes."

Perhaps I expect him to mock me, knowing the tales of the noble folk. Instead, his eyes might soften for how gentle they are—strange and frightening, but gentle. "I will not harm you. But what am I to call you?"

"I wouldn't mind 'human,' " I say, because from his mouth it might sound like a compliment.

He wrinkles his nose, unexpectedly crinkling his eyes warmly. "No, no. You do not have a pet name your friends call you?"

I shake my head, which is a lie, but it feels less so with no words spoken.

"Hmm," he says again. He gestures to me, then to the kittens. "I will have to come up with my own."

It does not sound threatening—not in his gentle voice. He is merely considering, and I creep up to his side and peek at the little animals squeaking and crawling across one another, eyes mostly closed. Without meaning to, I smile. Picking one up, I let it nibble on my finger.

"They are very picky creatures," he muses, cocking his head at the ones still in the basket. "They will not eat human food, and the food they eat from Faerie must be fresh. It must be soft things, but not more than a day or two old. Sweet things, more than meat until they are grown." He shakes his head.

"You were fighting an uphill battle taking them into your home. It is well you returned them to me. They would have died."

I nod, unable to keep from glancing up at him. He is unfairly tall, and I can see the wires of muscle in his neck. Everything about him is graceful and delicate and ethereal . . . and powerful.

How would he appear at full strength? I am seeing him weakened, injured, possibly kinder than he normally is. My fingers tremble a little, and I distract myself with the kitten's silky fur.

He lets off another sudden chuckle. "Shall I call you Bluebell, since you will not give me a name?"

My cheeks warm, and I say, "Bluebell?"

He gestures to my dress. "This is the third blue dress. Different hues each time, but this one looks like the bluebells that grew outside the walls . . ."

I look down at my skirts, considering his trailing words. He almost spoke of his home, which is not here, and stopped himself. *What is haunting his steps?* Hopefully not monsters.

"I don't mind," I whisper, cheeks still hot.

He looks quite pleased with himself but leans against the wall again.

Is he only standing so long because I am here? I don't want to leave, not when he has not answered my question, but I am also hesitant to mention anything of his obvious weakness. He did not appreciate it last time, and I can hardly blame him. *How do I find a way to help without saying so?* Perhaps he was only angry because I startled him—

"What is it?" he asks.

I start. "What?"

"You look to be trying very hard to think of a way to say something."

"Oh." *Am I that obvious?*

"Ask. I will not yell again." He seems so genuinely regretful that I feel bad for even being frightened. It may be an act, but if he's lying by dancing around the direct truth, he is doing a fine job of it.

Still, he said bluntly that he will not yell, so that must be true. "I was just going to ask . . . if you want to sit down?"

He looks at himself, then smiles without humor. "It is good for me to take a little walking about."

Not truly an answer. But the suggestion was made, so I don't push further.

"What are you feeding them?" I ask. When he blinks at me, I clarify, "You said they're picky eaters."

"Ah, yes. There is a beehive out into the woods a ways. They seem quite happy with the honey."

Something about the image of this pretty man accosting a beehive has me biting the inside of my cheek so I don't laugh.

"Though I should find them something else," he muses. "It is a rather small hive, and I don't want to upset the bees."

"What other kinds of things?"

He shrugs. "I don't know. I'm not enthusiastic for long hikes at the moment." He gives me a wry twist of the mouth that has me smiling in the same way.

"I could help" almost leaves my lips, but snooping around an old library on the edge of Faerie with a single mostly friendly faerie is far different from venturing deeper. And I *don't* want him coming with me. No one shall accompany me into the woods again, particularly not whatever rabid creature lurks beneath the beautiful face across from me.

But I want him to tell me what he knows about the monsters. Something about his silver eyes when he cradled my scarred hand told me he knows more, that he is as haunted as me, perhaps more. I glance at the walking cane he leans heavily upon, at his clothing likely hiding some injury.

"I could help you get the honey," I offer. "Where is it?"

He cracks a smile, which seems genuine enough. "I believe I can manage that quite well on my own . . . unless you're looking to see more of Faerie?"

I'd like to say no, but I'm still not comfortable lying to his face. "I am, but I also don't want to get eaten by anything. Or . . . ensnared."

His smile is soft. "I wouldn't let that happen."

It doesn't feel like a threat, but neither is it comforting. On the other hand, it is not a lie. Perhaps he would not let it because he would only do it himself.

If he wished it, I would have long lost my own mind.

He gives another little smile, carefully replacing the kitten and taking my hand, leading me out with sudden quickness. Startled at the cool contact, I follow him. His two fingers curl gently into my palm, soft but with obvious rough patches. *From a sword?* I cannot much imagine him chopping wood or washing clothes enough his palms became rough. And he mentioned *fighting*. I don't ask—not yet—and instead trot after his long stride. He leads me not down the main hall but off to the left, deeper into the upper story. A door sits at the back, and he leans against its handle, opening onto a metal swirl of a staircase returning us to the forest floor.

"Come, come," he says, pulling me carefully along.

Chewing my lip, I cast a look back into the safety of the library, then follow him down. This staircase empties onto the opposite side, so I cannot see the honeysuckle from here, just smell its presence in the air.

Open trees loom, otherworldly in their silence. Ancient. My steps slow to a halt as he wanders ahead.

"How far is it?" I ask.

He flashes a smile, and I am very aware of the way the sunlight catches his eyes. "Frightened of the woods?"

8

Into the Trees

"**N**o," I tell him, bracing myself for a challenge I must rise to.

He merely cocks his head. "What is it like?"

"What?"

"Being able to lie. What is it like?"

I try to give him a disparaging look, but it's difficult under his gentle sharp gaze. "I'm not afraid of the woods. I'm afraid of Faerie." A half lie. "And it doesn't feel like anything; you can just do it. Some people lie badly, and you can feel your heart react to it, or your face gets hot, or your hands sweat, but that's worrying you'll get caught."

"Do you get those things?"

"Depends on the lie. And who I'm lying to." *To a faerie in a hidden library? All of the above symptoms.*

He leans over me, enough I must force myself not to step back, but he is only curious. I stop myself from wiping my face to ensure it is clean.

"You don't look red in the face," he says.

"I'm not lying."

His brow furrows. I press my lips together, trying not to laugh. He brushes a light finger to my chin, as if testing if my skin is hot, then twists his lips in confusion and turns, gesturing for me to follow again. My face burns *now* at his brief touch, but he isn't looking. Or perhaps he saw it and realized.

Can they hear our heartbeat? I hope not.

"Not far," he calls back, and I'm relieved he didn't ignore the question. Pointing, he says, "There, you can see."

Following his finger, I do indeed spot a swarm of bees a few dozen steps into the open trees. There is no reason to fear such a thing. These are bright open woods with a gentle-enough faerie.

No reason to be frightened.

It's as if my feet have sprouted roots.

No reason to be frightened, Niamh.

Trotting after him, I slow just behind his long gait. My heart is pounding.

Turn around, turn around, turn around.

I'm uncertain why I don't. I already hate my own fear. *What if he sees it as well?*

Despite the cane, he walks quickly. When he glances back, my hesitation seems to amuse him, and he catches my hand again.

"It is all right, this section is not the Faerie you hear about in your little human tales. These trees are not empty, but most of what dwells here would not harm you and certainly would not come out in the sun."

Truly, I believe he means to comfort me, but such words only have chills crawling across my skin. After the sun set early that first afternoon in the library, I keep an eye on the morning light.

Releasing me a few steps from the hive, he approaches with caution. A few dozen bees buzz leisurely, and I wonder if they collect from the honeysuckle. They look just as our mortal human-side-of-the-border bees, and I watch one buzz past my face on lazy wings.

Aidyn hums something. The words are recognizable, but my mind grasps at them uselessly, and I'm unable to keep them in my thoughts for more than a moment. He continues the strange humming, soft under his breath, a sleepy lullaby tugging at the memories of my childhood: gentle high grasses on a hot summer day, lying atop the covers with the windows flung open on the sticky dark nights, moths flying in heady stumbling paths about the outline of the moon—

Gasping, I stumble back, my feet ready to flee.

He's going to sing me into this world forever.

This is why I venture into the forest alone, only alone.

Even without my name, he can—

With a start, Aidyn goes quiet, and he stares at me with likewise wide eyes. Turning his head, he glances into the trees as if searching for a predator.

Finally, he whispers, "What is it?"

As the panic fades, something between confusion and

humiliation replaces it. "Why . . . were you singing?"

He blinks a few times, then points to the hive with an uncertain hand. "The bees? So they won't sting you? Their sting is quite bad for humans. Very painful."

Oh. Full embarrassment takes hold, and I glance at the waves of golden combs sitting within the bark, dripping honey. His hand is rather close, and bees drift through his fingers without harm. They're more aggressive in their flying patterns around me, though I'm not standing close enough to be a threat.

"Sorry," I say, still feeling more than a little silly for such an immediate and aggressive overreaction.

His own confusion still sits in his eyes. "What was wrong?"

Now that I'm forced to explain, I wave my hand a little, rubbing my neck, feeling too silly to admit it. "You hear sto-ries . . . about fae who . . . sing humans to sleep forever. Or make them dance themselves to death."

His eyes flicker away, and he drops his hand with a thought-ful expression. "This is true, it has been done. But we sing for many reasons. Again, it seems I must apologize."

"It's all right . . ." I whisper.

"It will not affect you . . . That is, it *will*, but there will be no permanent spellwork."

I nod, expecting him to once again pick up the tune, but he only gives me a concerned look and pulls a small comb of honey from the bark before returning and handing it over. Slowly, I take it, uncertain what he wants me to do. He puts the rest in his mouth and smiles, gesturing.

He wants me to try it. I don't know why this startles me—I have been stealing berries from this side of the border for years, after all. The comb crunches against the roof of my mouth, and my gums hurt with how sweet it is.

"The cakes I could make with this," I say, thinking about glazes and possible icings, let alone the cake itself. When we were younger, Una and I would dip figs into honey, though that seems too sweet now.

Aidyn quirks an eyebrow. "Cakes?"

He sounds so much like a child being offered a pie that I snort, licking the remaining honey off my fingers. "If you hadn't scared me half to death the other night, you would've ended up with another pie."

Heaven knows why I'm suddenly feeling so brave, but the look of deep offense lighting his face has me laughing again.

"If you're nice to me, I can bring you another one." *Niamh, why are you offering to return?*

Regarding me with low-lidded eyes, he hums and passes me on his return to the library. For some reason, the offense doesn't seem nearly so dangerous. I wonder if he has brothers or sisters and if he is practiced at fake anger.

Taking a final glance at the bees, I trot after him.

"You enjoy cooking?" he calls back.

Surprised by his interest, I say, "Yes . . ."

"There are many books here. They will have recipes you can try."

My heart expands, and I can't keep the grin off my face. *What kind of midsummer pie could I make?* "I can't read them."

"I can pick some and tell them to you; you can write them with your own hand. You will be able to read them then."

He pauses at the base of the curling metal stairway, letting me pass by first. Brass flowers decorate the undersides of the hand railings with many unfamiliar petals. Three steps up and I am looking him eye to eye, perhaps even a little down at him. Amusement quirks at the corners of his lips, his eyes inspecting my hair. He takes a strand that has unwoven from its braid and tugs it carefully before letting it bounce back.

"Red is a lovely color," he says. "Autumn leaves."

You have such nice hair. Women with such hair have fire, don't they? I wince a little at the memory, but the way he says it is so nostalgic and faraway I can't compare the two—not truly.

"What is wrong?" he asks at the same volume.

"Nothing. It doesn't matter."

"Now that is a lie, correct?"

I try to smile, and it comes out funny. "Correct."

He nods but doesn't pry. Eventually, I move out from his gaze and climb the stairs, hearing his soft steps behind me. I want to ask him a dozen things, including *why are you here?* But the question I came here with still presses against my thoughts, and I look back at him as the safety of the dim library envelops us. He catches up to my stride, though we're in no hurry.

Quietly, I ask, "Do you know about the monsters coming out of Faerie?"

His already faraway expression twists into something slightly more pained, if only for a moment. "Yes."

I wait, and finally, he continues without prompting.

"I will get word to someone who can fight them back. It may be a few days, but I will."

"Are you leaving?"

He shakes his head. "I have my ways."

I leave it at that—if he wished to explain, he would have.

"Why do they come out? For the most part, they don't hurt anyone. They'll eat our animals, but we don't even see them. Until we do. We figure they attack if we've done something to offend one of your kind, but it is only a theory—and a way for parents to keep their children from treading on faerie circles—so I'm not sure it's the truth."

"Why?"

I blink at him, pulled from my thoughts.

"Why did you encounter one? You are correct: they rarely interact with humans. I don't know what exactly you're witnessing, but there are a few things humans could mistake as *hounds*. Any one of them would eat just about anything, but generally, all fae are attracted to those with magic in their soul. Humans do not have enough."

"I was . . ." I pause, not knowing how to answer easily. "Near the border . . . and not paying attention."

Perhaps I can find their picture in the book, and he will know precisely what I am referring to.

"I do believe humans generally have enough fear not to do such a thing." He doesn't sound amused but is nearing it in a wry sort of way. "You were certainly frightened enough by a few words of song."

He seats himself at the same dusty table where I set the book. I hover near the railing, touching the soft leaves of the tree growing over the second story.

"A friend asked me to bring him to Faerie. We got to

talking. I was a bit enamored with him, so I wasn't paying very good attention. Trust me, it's not a mistake I repeated."

Another half lie, and something about his sharp eyes lets me know he is aware of it. Kind of him to not say so. Perhaps he is dancing around topics as much as I am. I know him very little, though it seems we share a certain understanding. Or perhaps that is simply whatever faerie magic clings to his skin.

His fingers tap at his leg as if he's thinking of rubbing it but doesn't want to draw attention. Feeling suddenly brave, I crouch near him and touch the back of his hand.

What is possessing you, stupid girl?

His skin smells fresh and sweet, his clothes like clean cotton, and his eyes crinkle with amusement at my sudden closeness. He is entirely the opposite of everything I imagined a faerie to be and yet precisely as *other*.

"Can I help you at all?" I whisper, a gentle nudge of a suggestion this time rather than a shove of it as the night before.

As he promised, he does not yell again. In fact, his expression barely darkens, just becomes tired. "How would you accomplish such a task?"

It is not mocking, but I am at a loss for words anyhow. "I . . . don't know. But I'd like to if I can."

He shakes his head. "I do not believe you can."

It is such a straightforward answer I must believe he is telling the truth. I nod, suddenly self-conscious of my hand on his, the cool metal of the rings beneath my fingers. "If you think of something, I would be happy to try. We don't have much in our village, but we have people who can aid with healing."

His eyes flicker to my damaged finger, but he mentions nothing of it and gives another polite nod. I drop my hand, the awkwardness overwhelming.

"No one should know I am here," he says evenly. "It is not a time for our kin to be near the human border. Your village should not know."

Of this I was already well aware—not specifically for his sake, but certainly for mine. I am well loved but already born under the moonlight and strange. I am not afraid of my village, but neither am I a fool.

"I know," I tell him. "If you think *I* was frightened, you ought to meet the village."

His cheek twitches as if he wishes to smile but does not manage it.

Playing with a wrinkle in my skirt, I regard him as equally as he regards me. According to his own words, he will send help for the hounds—and whoever arrives can figure out which kind of monster they are—which is more than I ever expected.

I stepped into the trees with him, and nothing terrible happened.

I have done all I need to do in this place, and the sun is heading toward the horizon.

I would not like to be all alone in a crumbling library if I were wounded.

Una must be worried, and I promised her I'd be back soon.

Did someone he loves abandon him among the trees?

There is no reason to tarry here and less reason to return.

"Might I return?" I ask.

He blinks, long and slow, and a few seconds of silence pass between us. "Yes."

Una is glowering from the edge of the cottages when I wander back, my feet heavy, my head spinning, shocked with the interaction now I'm no longer in his presence.

There is still plenty of hot bright afternoon sun.

"What happened?" she asks, scurrying up and taking me by the shoulders. "You look upset. Did he hurt you?"

I shake my head. "No, not at all."

"Did he yell again?"

"No, he was lovely."

She pauses, staring at me. Puckering her lips up, she asks, "*Lovely?*"

Her tone takes me out of my daydreaming. "Yes?"

She sits me in the long grasses as if I am a child in need of chastising. Plopping down before me, she holds up her hands. "Explain."

Giving her a long tired look, I glance over her shoulder at Niall chopping wood at his cottage. He squints but leaves us alone.

"How's the dress coming?"

"*Niamh.*"

Sighing, I repeat every bit of the conversation I can recall. It is twilight by the time I finish, but the air is still warm and the light enough that the fear of monsters does not yet drive us back to her cottage where there would be listening ears.

"He says he can stop the monsters . . . ?" Una whispers when I have finished.

"*Someone* will. He will tell them . . . I'm not sure. He wasn't giving many details. It may take a few days. He doesn't seem to know what they are . . . or he doesn't want to say."

"Do you think we will see them?"

Them. Other fae.

Will they come out of the trees to drive them back? Or will they perform their magic in the dead of night, as the hounds lurk in the dead of night, and we will never know hide or hair of them?

"I don't know."

Glancing at the trees, Una is suddenly more skittish of the falling dark. She grasps my hand, hauling me up and back to her cottage.

"My animals—" I begin.

"I fed them for you. I don't want to be out after dark."

Hugging her around the shoulders as we walk, I let the door of her cottage close behind me. Warm light from their hearth and lanterns brightens the room. Suddenly starved and still tasting the sweetness of the honey on my tongue, I let Olivia, Una's mam, shove supper my way—recently caught rabbit stewed with early-spring carrots and various garden greens—and am drawn into Cara's game of making dolls out of old scraps of cloth not used on her sister's new dress. It is all very human and gentle and warm. I sigh, relaxing into the cushions of their couch, comforted. My muscles unclench. I hadn't realized how nervous I was until getting home—or close enough to it.

Una and Olivia talk about Fiona's new baby due in a few

weeks, and I find my mind drifting to a lonely faerie sleeping in a library with no one to tend to whatever wounds he's concealing. A thousand reasons could be behind his hiding. He could have performed some horrible deed, and for a faerie that would have to be a truly wicked thing—murder of someone innocent, or worse? Does such a thing even occur to them? Perhaps he abandoned those with him during the fight he mentioned. Perhaps others of his kind are hunting him as we speak, ready to stumble upon his hideout in an old abandoned library, and will find me with him.

Would a human in such a situation be put to death?

Try as I might, I cannot imagine him performing a heinous deed worthy of such secrecy. Perhaps that is what I shall do tomorrow—bring food, cook him something from one of their own books, and ask him why he is there.

He must understand why I would ask, if only for my own security. He was concerned for my safety in other situations. He must be capable of understanding. Even the wild noble folk of Faerie understand the act of protecting oneself from harm.

"You are going back, aren't you?" Una asks that night when we are once again lying safely in her bed.

"Yes," I whisper, a hum of a noise befitting the quiet night and the singing insects.

"I know he is enchanting, but you know better." There is no accusation to her voice.

"Yes."

"Do you think you can actually help him?"

It takes me longer to consider this, and I settle on, "I don't know. I hope so."

"Has he asked for help?"

I don't wish to answer, because it makes me feel entirely more foolish. "No."

The question hangs in the dark of the air between us. *Why go back, then?*

"I don't know, Una." I sigh, though she didn't voice the words. "Wouldn't you want someone to help you if you couldn't ask?"

"Yes," she admits. "But I should hope I would be capable of asking."

"Me too. Maybe it is much more difficult when you are a strange old creature."

The night is dark and the moon is slim, and crickets and water bugs sing. I put my hand to my cheek where he touched an experimental finger to discover if I was lying. My heart is strange in my chest, and I see his eyes when I close my own.

Long after Una, I do eventually find sleep.

9

An Uncanny Thing

In the early morning, when the light is gray and the sun still struggles to warm the air, I slip out of bed, restless and uncomfortable. After writing Una a note, *I will be back before night*, and easing out the front door, I return home and gather food into a basket. The cow needs her milking, and I toss hay in for her to eat while I fill the pail, leaning my forehead against her warm side. She gives off a low, and the world feels normal and like any other springtime. I stand in the open barn doors as the sun finally creeps over the edge of the trees.

After scattering feed in for the chickens, I set their warm eggs into the basket and take the long way around the edge of the woods, avoiding anyone up and about at this hour.

At the hawthorn, I close my eyes and step across, and a chill crawls over my skin.

To my eyes, there is nothing different in the air—the same distinct stillness with the barest rustle of the leaves in strange places, the honeysuckle nearby, and nothing in the trees. Something about the smell is different—a thick uncomfortable musk like mud or animal fur beneath the strength of the honeysuckle. Stepping out from its maze, I gaze into the empty trunks.

Perhaps Aidyn has a visitor. I did not tell him when I was coming.

The thought is both concerning and heartening. Perhaps he is not alone after all and someone much more capable than a human from a tiny village is offering him aid.

Hunt hound.

A distinct memory of their smell pricks at the back of my mind, and I freeze halfway to the library. I glance toward the treetops only to realize the dim light is not that of the normal Faerie morning. The sun is not quite up.

It is only a few steps from the honeysuckle, not even ten seconds of a walk, but I almost turn and run. *But crossing the human border will not help me, will it?* They can cross the human border—they *have been* crossing the human border. If I turn and run—

A subtle growl echoes through the trees.

One bark. Then two.

Three is my death.

My feet carry me a step back before I tell myself, *No, do not run. Think.* It isn't much use. My heart is beating too fast. *A fleeing human will certainly attract them.* They will hunt me down. Perhaps this time they will be more interested in killing me, not just wounding me in a moment of startled panic. If I move, they will certainly kill me. If I do not—

The library door creaks open. My breath comes out in a huff. A familiar pale hand on the door handle and a fall of dark hair as he leans out. Gesturing wildly, his eyes too wide even from here, he waves me toward him more aggressively when I do not immediately move.

Glancing around, I am still frozen, frightened my movement will attract them.

"*Run*," he hisses.

My muscles unlock as if the voice of an ally is all I need. I bolt across the empty dozen steps between us.

Aidyn does not move out of the doorway quickly enough, and I nearly stumble into him in my haste. His arm catches me as he drags us both inside, shutting the door in a fluid movement and leaning against it.

As the safety of the library wraps around me, my breathing catching up, I wonder all at once if I was overreacting.

Were they even the same monsters?

Of course they were; I heard their barking.

Putting a finger to his lips, Aidyn keeps his weight on the door and whispers, "Shh . . ."

I catch my breath and hear footfalls—giant paws on the other side of the door, claws on leaves. My body goes still. I'm aware of each and every noise I might make. In this section of the library, we are in the dim little cramped corner where the books are nothing but dust. For one of the noble folk, it is not as much room as I would have expected for a library of Faerie. Aidyn is close enough I can feel the heat of his skin, the subtle brush of his uneven breaths. Too frightened to move into the more spacious hall, I stare at the embroidery on the neckline of his shirt, unable to be properly embarrassed past my terror. Softly, his hand drifts up to touch my elbow as if he wishes to steady me.

Like a breath of wind through the leaves, he whispers, "They will leave."

I wish his certainty comforted me. "Did you send word for help—"

My voice is not as controlled as his, and his finger touches my lips. He nods, and his silver eyes are steady on the crack between the door and floor. I do not have the courage to look down. Despite the fear—*can he hear my pounding heart?*—his touch is comforting. His skin smells sweet and clean, and I wonder if he's found a river nearby to bathe in or if this is what all fae are like. Honeysuckle clings to his clothes. Perhaps he has been walking through it. His eyes drift back to mine, then fall across my cheeks and lips before returning to my eyes. He's slightly bowed in the cramped hallway, putting most of his weight as a brace against the door, and his face is as near to mine as when he first stood under me beside the bookshelf. His breath tickles my cheek. The gentle touch of his hand through my long sleeve feels heavy, stable.

Long after the footfalls and snuffling have disappeared, he finally shifts. I look away, blinking, cheeks suddenly hot, still startled and glancing at the pitiful barrier of the door.

Running a hand down the side of his loose shirt, he says quietly, "Come upstairs with me."

"Are they gone?"

"From the door. They may roam for a time more. They like the dark but should not be here so late in the morning."

I nod, feeling even more foolish. As he glances my way sheepishly and heads through the shelves, I feel the sudden lack of his safety by my side and stumble after. Following the click of his walking cane to the middle of the library, I watch him sit on the bottom step as if his body weighs on him. Resting his elbows on his knees, he regards me strangely, as if the little interaction was as odd to him as it was to me.

"I'm . . . sorry I made you come down," I say, regretting the pain he's evidently in. "I thought there was enough light. The sun was higher at home."

"They behave differently here than there, and so does the light. It is not your fault. The sun does not rise at the same time every day. It will be dealt with shortly. You won't have to worry."

Belatedly, I realize, "You know what they are."

Letting out a long breath, he whispers, "*Cù-sìth.*"

The word sounds strange upon my ears and slips from my mind in a moment, same as the faerie words in the books. This one I can just barely cling to, perhaps because he said it directly to me. The impression of his tone has my heart squeezing.

Still, I realize I have no idea what he's saying. "Pardon?"

Blinking, he looks up. "They are . . . not hounds, though I realize they resemble your human dogs. They are not dangerous in and of themselves. In the past, they simply lured humans into the realms of Faerie."

"That is dangerous," I whisper when he does not continue.

"You're correct," he admits, leaning his shoulder into the railing. "In the past, that is what they were. In the generations leading up to these . . . they have become more dangerous to all, even our kin."

Without meaning to, I glance at the cane still held loosely in his fingers. But he is not looking into my eyes enough to catch the question, and I have no heart to ask.

"You may be correct," he mumbles. "They may be coming across your borders if you disturbed something they do not appreciate. I did not realize they still venture to the human realm. What disturbed them when they injured you?"

So, we're just speaking of these things now? Now he has asked me, I don't wish to bare it all to him when I still can't grasp why he is here or what crime he may have committed. It is ridiculous—he's attempting to help—but I cannot calm my nerves. "We're not certain. But later we found a crushed faerie circle. We think perhaps a child trod on it."

He nods, then shrugs a shoulder tenderly. "It was too long ago for us to know now. If they have just begun to come out once more, you may still have a chance to figure out why. If you see anything of note, please tell me."

My brow furrows without me meaning for it to. "I thought there are others coming . . ."

"There are." He looks away. "Soon. But it would be helpful to know why they have crossed the borders."

It makes fine-enough sense, and there *must* be others on the way if he says so plainly. Still, something nags at me. "Will you go with them? The . . . others?"

A wince in his expression has his jaw twitching, but it

doesn't appear to be anger. Discomfort, perhaps. "No. They will not know I am here."

There is something in his tone that is not to be argued with. Of course, I could insist upon those particular details, but who am I to ask? He does not know me, and it is not as if I would tell him all the details of my life.

I will not even tell him my name.

There is, though, another matter. "Are you hiding here?"

No confusion enters his features. Perhaps he expected the question—if the stories are true, fae are wise. "Yes."

Such a blunt answer was unexpected, and it has my heart jumping. "Have you done something awful?"

The moment the words leave my lips, I know I should not have asked—not in such a way. It is not only too personal but may ignite his anger. I have not forgotten the sound of his screaming, and I never shall.

Opening my mouth to bury the question, to say anything else, I'm stopped by his soft, "Nothing that would bring harm to you."

At the very least, he understood the concern behind my question. I'm not certain I believe him—not because he could be lying, but because he may believe something untrue. But he knows the ways of Faerie and his own kind far better than a village girl who does not even know the proper name of the monsters who attacked her.

Of course, this point would be moot if I never returned to these lands.

"Thank you," I say kindly.

With a nod, he mumbles, "Your *hounds* will be dispatched

of shortly. You will be safe."

His eyes flicker to my hand as mine fall to his cane resting against the steps.

Will you be safe? Not the question to ask—not when he is avoiding the rest. Gripping the basket handle, I edge toward him, sitting on the same step but leaving space between us. I do not know if my presence irritates him once he is not panicking over monsters.

"Do you need to return to your village?" he asks.

Numbly, I shake my head, still feeling foolish and wishing I could look into his eyes again—not from across the room, but from under his chin as I did minutes ago.

"Stay until the sun is high, if you can. I would walk you back to the border but . . . not today."

Tightness lodges in my chest at how miserable he seems from just his venture down the stairs. It's a far cry from yesterday and our little trek to the honey hive. I don't wish to be incredibly blunt, not with this gentle creature, but my hints have gotten me nowhere.

"Are you dying?"

His eyes find mine again. "I hope not."

Not the answer I was searching for, and not even a little comforting. However, I already asked him if I could help and was denied. I fear asking too many times might have him chasing me away.

What would be so wrong with that? Perhaps it is what I should be hoping for.

"What do you have there?" He nods to the basket I cling to like a toddler's blanket.

I look at the cloth covering the items. *I cannot go back to our world—not for the next few hours.*

"Food. Can I borrow your hearth?"

His eyebrows twitch, and he glances away in thought. "I believe there is something you'll like better."

Frowning, I follow as he finds his way through the bookshelves on the ground floor. Directly above us should be the room where he's taken up residence. Pushing open another door blocked by a few fallen books and old hinges, he tosses a knowing smile over his shoulder and disappears inside. Though I've long since determined I am safe enough within these walls, I follow as if the room will swallow me up.

When I find my way inside, my feet fall still.

"Why does a library have a kitchen?" I ask, too thrilled to be properly confused.

"Our kind often taken up residence where we make our work. The sprites and nymphs who resided in these halls would care for them, so it would have all the comforts of home. There are bedrooms close by. They were too dusty for my liking. The hearth upstairs was friendlier, anyhow."

It is a small thing; no more than a dozen paces long and wide, the little kitchen is fitted with a large hearth of its own and has a sturdy dust-laden table in the center. Any remnants of food are long gone, but pots and pans and utensils of all sorts hang along the walls. Cupboards sit carefully closed, perhaps stocked full of plates and cups and bowls. Wood is still stacked by the hearth, so ancient it has turned full of holes and old soot. Spiderwebs hang in silky threads in the corners, their dust capturing the bright morning light from a high window.

Aidyn leans against the table, his back to me, observing the window or whatever lies beyond that his faerie eyes can better see. The sun catches on the edges of his pale shirt and along the few stray hairs that aren't combed. He isn't even looking at me, and I can't imagine what must be going through the mind of such a creature.

"What happened to this place?" I ask as soft as possible, unwilling to disturb the strange spell that's fallen across the kitchen with the sunlight and Aidyn in its midst.

"I do not know," he mumbles in a matching tone. "It must be an ancient place indeed for us to have abandoned it."

His free hand gives a small movement, and the red-orange maple leaves strewn across the dusty stone floor go skittering around my feet before settling. Not for the first time, my heart jumps into my throat. I gaze up at him. My hand twitches to reach out and touch him again. Ridiculous. He's taken my hand once already. There was nothing strange about it, nothing magical, truly, but suddenly, I wonder what it must be like to inspect the fingers that can send magic out into the world.

Finally, he checks back over his shoulder—hopefully I don't look as if I've been gaping at his back.

What is your magic? I want to ask, but instead, worried of irritating him, I ask, "What is your favorite food?"

Quirking an amused eyebrow, he seats himself carefully on the edge of the table, eyeballing my basket. "Nothing you have heard of. What do you have in there?"

Forcing my feet forward, I set the basket down and begin taking out my store: eggs, milk (no more honey, considering he has eaten it all), smoked bream we had in the storehouse, potatoes, and an assortment of vegetables from the garden as well as what berries I've been gathering on the human side of the border this early in the spring. They're a tad pathetic compared to those that grow year-round just within Faerie, but I've been too nervous to go to my usual places.

Perhaps I should be more nervous to be here with this creature.

Without meaning to, I glance up, finding his eyes on my movements with that same predator-bird intensity of when he first startled me on the bookshelf. This time, he smiles. It does something human to his eyes.

"What are you going to make?"

He looks so purely happy to have someone to make him something to eat—or perhaps only to have some company—that I can't help a nervous giggle. "I don't know. I don't suppose you have any of that honey in here? I could make the cake I mentioned."

"I actually did bring more in just for myself," he says, eyes flickering to the door, and I realize he plans on hiking back up and down the stairs. "I can—"

"You"—I point at him, backing toward the door—"stay there. I'll get it. Don't . . . rot the eggs or anything."

"That is a *myth*," he calls, offended, as I trot back for the stairs.

Another giggle bursts out. It's the uncanniest thing, joking with this creature. I have to wonder what Una will say about this development.

I take the stairs carefully, creeping into the room he's taken up with more nerves now that I'm here. This is his private place, and though he didn't object to my presence, I don't want to touch anything. It is much as it was the day before, with his blankets and pillows by the dimly flickering hearth. A few clean shirts and other things are folded neatly beside the bed as well. Beside them is the crate of sleeping kittens. When I lift the blanket, they don't wake. He has a few items stacked on the shelf near what books he's taken for his own store—knick-knacks and such, acorns and winter honeysuckle flowers and a small box of something I itch to look into but don't dare snoop.

And several faded glass jars of honey. Taking one and sending a last inspection across his few private things he's brought with him, I turn for the stairs.

Something glimmers under the blankets of his makeshift bed. With a furtive glance at the open door, I nudge the edge of the blanket up with the toe of my boot. A sword hilt sits comfortably among the pillows and blankets.

I've never seen a sword, unless I count the ink illustrations in our little excuse of a library. We have no need for them in this little side of the kingdom. Certainly, I know there are places where warriors and knights are common and that faerie weapons are considered the height of craftsmanship, but I didn't expect to ever see one myself.

The closest thing we have are kitchen knives, and what pitiful comparisons.

My fingers twitch to pick it up, to take it from its scabbard and stare at the work of violent art, but again, these are his items, and it was covered up.

Did I not think his hand was rough from a sword and nothing else? I nudge the blanket back into place, then hurry down before he becomes suspicious.

I was not fighting at that time. Yes, that is what he said. Thinking of his walking cane, I wince.

Clutching the jar of honey to my chest, I trot back into the kitchen. He is brushing a thick layer of dust off the stovetop with the bottom of his cane, wrinkling his nose. The glance he sends my way has me thinking that perhaps he knows I was snooping, but he mentions nothing of it.

"There are some cloths and such in the next room over, where the bedrooms once were. They're old, but they're probably fair enough for cleaning this place up a little. Would you rather me help with that or find a cookbook to translate?"

Whatever propensity fae have for liking to be cooked for, he evidently wants to involve himself. Considering his unsteady stance, I tell him, "I'm going to make a cake, but you can find a book for next time."

If he's reading, he'll have to sit down.

Another knowing glance, but it could be for anything. He taps his dusty cane on the edge of his boot.

With a tiny bow of the head and a flourish of the hand to match, he says, "As instructed."

I watch him disappear into the bookshelves and consider how I'm going to tell Una about the frightening faerie in the library who wants to help me bake a cake.

10

Honeyed Cake

"Why didn't I see them in the trees?" I ask when the constant fixation of his eyes has me feeling anxious and more than a little embarrassed.

"Hmm?" he hums while I crack an egg into one of the large and rather ancient wooden bowls we found under the cabinets. There is a water pump in the corner. Though likewise as decrepit as the rest of building, we got it to work, and I washed the dust off everything I needed.

"I could hear the hounds," I say, shivering at the thought of them but determined to learn all I can. "But the forest is so open, and I couldn't see anything for ages. But you knew they were there. Did you hear the barking?"

Absently, he nods, then adds, "We have keener senses than

humans. I could smell them long before I could hear them."

I blink, unsettled by the idea he may *smell* when I enter the library. "Is that how you knew I was here?"

He nods, flipping through an ancient leather tome and looking at me as if it is nothing unusual. I was successful in my scheme to get him to sit on one of the stools still stable enough to hold his weight, and with him leaning over the table where I'm working, he seems more comfortable.

Distracted, I ask, "What do I smell like?"

"Human."

I give him a look portraying how unspecific that is.

"Well, you see how animals all have their own scents that don't necessarily smell like anything else? It is its own description. You could say something smells as a horse smells, and that would make sense to anyone who's ever been near one. Humans just smell . . . human. If you don't know what I mean, I can't describe it to you. I had never been close enough to a human to smell one before, but I have been in contact with things they have touched. Now that I've been close to you, I know."

It makes sense. In an odd way, but enough sense.

"Though you also smell like hay," he says conversationally, returning to his book.

His hair falls over his shoulder, exposing his ear, and I catch not only that it is pointed but is also slit at the top like twin knives. With the other still covered, I can't tell if it's natural or an old injury. It doesn't look like a scar, but perhaps fae do not scar.

"I milked our cow," I mumble.

"Our?"

It feels dangerous to expand, but he could easily step across the border and know every single person I hold dear in our village. "My mam and da. We have a cow and some chickens and a draft horse. I used to ride her when I was a girl."

A smile dances across his lips. "Do your parents know you are consorting with a faerie?"

"No," I say primly, unwinding the sack of flour. "They are away for a few weeks. But they know I go into Faerie to collect berries. They'd probably be surprised you're the first faerie I've encountered."

He blinks. "The first?"

"Well, I'm not counting brownies and such. Everyone has seen a brownie at some point. We had a whole summer when I was twelve when a brownie made her home in the eaves and cleaned our kitchen in the night. Then she left. They always leave in the fall—" I realize I'm rambling. "No, I mean I've never met a faerie like you." I wave my wooden spoon at him. "The kind that sing you into Faerie forever."

"The Keepers," he says. "And we're not the only ones. Beware anything you see in these trees."

I nod, suddenly colder.

"Don't ever do anything in the woods of Faerie."

His tone has me pausing to meet his eyes.

"You said the trees were empty when you came here, but they weren't. They're never empty, no matter what they look like. Something is always watching you; it's just a toss of a coin whether or not what's watching you is interested in harming you or not. Don't ever speak of private things in the woods.

Everything will hear you."

It takes me a moment to resume my stirring, my stomach churning.

Silence stretches, but finally, he adds, "You're safe in here." I give a doubtful eyebrow, and his serious expression falls away to a chuckle. "I mean it. The places we build for ourselves are sanctuaries, even if they're long abandoned."

"I hope so," I manage, praying he doesn't notice the tremor in my voice. "Otherwise I don't think those hounds would be deterred by a few old doors."

"They shouldn't have much interest in us," he says a little curtly. "Certainly not with me, and so not with you whenever you are near me. But do not test fate."

I try to match his earlier laugh. "No intentions to."

"And you're the first I've met as well."

Blinking, I pause with a spoonful of sugar. "What?"

"A human. You're the first human I've met."

"*Ever?*"

His eyebrows quirk. "Yes. I said as such. Is that a shock?"

"Well . . . I don't know," I say, comforted by the change in topic, finally realizing the implication of his words. "I figured when you're hundreds of years old you'd have plenty of time to go bring yourself down a few levels and interact with the little humans—"

"*How old?*" he asks, his calm musical voice rising so much it reminds me of Una when Niall brought her wildflowers.

I freeze, unable to stop a nervous laugh at the shock on his face. "Fae are . . . old?"

He pauses, staring, then gives off a laugh I'd describe much more like a giggle than any of the ones he's given before. "Well, not *all of us*! We have to be young at some point, you realize?"

My face heats, but I put my hands on my hips. "Is that so? How old are you, then?"

Snickering again and putting a hand on his middle in a way he probably hopes I don't notice, he says, "Twenty-three."

Squinting, I look at his beautiful ageless face and realize I wouldn't know if he was lying—but no, he cannot, can he? "Truly?"

"Yes, *truly*. How old are you?"

"Twenty. But . . . how do you age?"

Dragging my bag of sugar toward him as if I will not realize if he does so slowly, he says, "It varies by species. For us, we tend to age until sometime in our twenties, then it will slow down to nothing for many hundreds of years. Some stop aging by sixteen or seventeen, I've heard. Some stop at thirty. Usually it's more around where I am. I may have stopped, though such a thing is too incremental to tell."

"What dictates how long you live?"

He shrugs. "Nothing, really. Or fate, if you will have it. It's easier to tell by how long those in your family lived before you. We creatures you humans all group into *fae* either grow long and slow lives or grow quickly but usually just as long. We are all called the Keepers, sometimes, whatever form we take. We Gentry, specifically, are adults in our second to third decade of life. The Unblessed take hundreds of years to mature; a twenty-year-old human may be the equivalent of a several-hundred-year-old Unblessed—"

"Unblessed?"

He blinks up at me. "What you usually refer to when you think of fae who trick or kill with no provocation."

"There's a difference?"

His eyebrow quirks as if in mild offense. "We all can . . . *enchant* humans, but the Gentry, in general, are not malevolent. Unblessed tend to live solitary lives and are often unkind."

I sift the flour absently while he licks sugar off his finger. I very much doubt Aidyn's view of malevolent and mine are similar. Likewise, I wonder how terrible Unblessed fae must be that the others of their kind consider them so.

He is alone.

"My point," he says. "The Gentry do not have many children. I am one of two offspring—we do not bear young well. The only thing that truly affects our lifespan is too long dwelling in the human world. Eventually, we can become mortal if we don't stay in the magic of Faerie. We'll still live long compared to humans but nothing close to what we should."

My mouth opens. I've never heard Faerie itself having any effect on their age. Though I also didn't expect this creature sitting before me to only be a few years my elder.

"Wait, does that mean that any humans who live in Faerie . . . ?"

"Stop aging? Yes, after a few years of complete exposure to the magic here. If they ever return to the human kingdoms after spending centuries in ours though, well . . ." He makes a face and a waving gesture that says enough: immediate death, or something worse.

"So, me being here doesn't have any effects?"

He shrugs. "Not particularly, though anyone who lives on

the edge of Faerie will feel the pull of it. It is not so strange that you've been drawn to coming in here over the years."

His eyes skim over me, and I wipe at the flour on my skirts, only succeeding in making the blue lighter as I spread the powder. Something admiring sits in his gaze, and it makes me shrivel. I am still very aware of the animal-predator nature of his eyes, though they seem to hold mostly kindness . . . if not a little flirting when he thinks he's been clever.

Eyeballing the honey and how his shoulders droop even as he sits with his elbows leaning against the table, I ask, "What are you going to feed the kittens today?"

He spins the honey jar absently, digging pieces of the comb out and putting his finger into his mouth. "There is enough for today if you don't use too much of it, and I have more. At this size, they barely eat anything. They'll mostly sleep for weeks, then become heavier eaters. As soon as that happens, they'll be competent at hunting on their own. It's a born trait."

"So, you need more food for them?"

He eyes me. "Eventually, yes."

"Would you like me to go get more from the hive?"

He regards me momentarily, something strange and knowing in his gaze, before his eyes rest on my hands around the bowl of batter. "Tomorrow I will go with you. I have enough for today."

If he is feeling poorly enough that he does not want to make that small walk, he certainly should not be down here with me, but I say nothing of it. I know little of how fae and their bodies are built, and I know Aidyn less. I shouldn't tell him off to bed like some small child . . . but I'm not above it.

Anyway, I'd prefer to go without him . . . once the hounds are gone. Once with him standing beside me among the trees was enough.

"It isn't far. You may watch me from the window if you like. I can light some pine needles for the smoke—"

"*No,*" he says with such sudden harshness that my hand stills at my mixing and I'm suddenly reminded of what he is. It is not a bad thing in and of itself, the fact his kind are so dangerous—many a human hand could injure me (and one has)—but his sudden intensity is startling.

"No," he says again, much softer, spinning the honey absently. "The farther in you go, particularly alone, the more danger is present for a human. And those creatures are not the bees buzzing around your gentle trees. These are excruciating—to a human much more so. No. Tomorrow I will go with you. Or I will go alone." He eyes me suddenly. "Do not think to go deeper by yourself."

I hadn't been considering it—Faerie frightens me enough—but if these woods can unnerve a creature born to them, I am in no mood to set foot on the other side of the library.

"Well," I murmur, "you've suitably frightened me off."

This doesn't appear to please him. Perhaps he is as unhappy about frightening me off as I am. It is no matter. I don't believe he will let anything happen to the kittens, and if he says he has enough for today, I shall take his word for it.

He must believe it true, after all.

"Three days," he says suddenly.

"What?"

"Don't return to Faerie for three days. The . . . *hounds* should be long gone by tomorrow, but take two extra for safety."

A part of me wonders if he doesn't wish me here so I do not attract the attention of whoever will be coming to drive the beasts away. Perhaps he is hiding so desperately that he does not even wish to be noticed in passing.

I open my mouth to ask but instead say, "I suppose I can manage three days."

"Manage" is dramatic. With the knowledge of the hunt hounds nearby, staying out for three days will be as easy for me as it is for every other human who has no wish to step foot within the bounds of Faerie.

Easy as breathing.

Una has her arms folded at me when I return. I pause, feeling strangely heady after returning to the human lands and having forgotten she would certainly be waiting to pounce. I left before she awoke, after all.

"Hi," I say, then head for the well in the center of the village, suddenly thirsty in the overbearing sun.

"You're going to be the death of me," she says, following and giving me a splash from the bucket when I haul it up.

"Knock it off." I splash her in return. "Besides, I left a note."

She rolls her eyes so dramatically they twitch. Across the small square, Niall watches us from his father's workshop. It is mostly his own now. His shirt is off, and he's working at some sort of tool I can't make out from here.

"Niall's shirtless," I say casually.

Una glances back only to do a double take at me. "That is *not* a distraction."

I raise my eyebrows.

"Not *enough* of a distraction," she mutters, then swats me on the shoulder again. "What happened?"

"Um," I hedge, watching Niall abandon his project in favor of heading our way with long strides. His expression holds less of his usual calm cheer, and something sits uncomfortably in my chest for it.

"What are you two discussing so vigorously?" he asks, then pinches Una on the leg. She swats at him and glances about to see if anyone noticed. Most everyone is in their gardens or the fields, out of the stuffy heat of their houses, not paying us much mind. The three of us talking by the well isn't precisely an unheard-of event.

"Niamh went back to visit the pretty faerie," Una whispers conspiratorially. No one is close enough to hear.

I ignore her. "What's wrong?"

"Well," he says, casting a glance over his shoulder to the field where midsummer festivals are thrown. The closest two villages gather here on the day, considering our own cluster of houses is closest to the woods and therefore closest to honoring Faerie. Our little village will more than triple in size, and preparations are slowly being put together weeks early. It's difficult not to smile at the thought.

"Well?" I prompt, and Una has given up her glowering to look up at him.

"Some folks from Brym came to deliver poles for the May dances."

My stomach twists before he finishes the thought.

"Blain is here. So are his father and sister. And a few others. I thought you'd want a warning."

Without meaning to, I glance at the field. Several figures and wagons dot the landscape, but I'd never be able to tell who they are from this distance. It's only their silhouettes in the hot spring air.

"Oh," I say, and nothing else. *What else is there to say?*

When neither of us speaks, Niall grunts, grabs each of us by the hand, and drags us in the opposite direction of the meadow. I trot along gratefully, a weight in my chest, Niall's warm rough hand around mine. Una casts a disgusted glance at the meadow and makes a face in my direction. I force a smile.

I knew something like this would happen—and will continue to. Blain lives in Brym, the next village over, after all, and it makes sense that he would help with the preparations and that he will eventually show up the day and night of midsummer. I've been planning on ignoring him. In fact, he hasn't shown in years—not since that night—so I figured he and his family wouldn't have the guts.

Evidently, they have decided enough time has passed.

"I can't believe they have the gall," Niall mutters when we settle into the long grasses on the brighter side of the woods—the side less likely to get one lost into Faerie. I set my basket between them, along with the third of the honeyed cake Aidyn insisted I take with me. I tried to gift him the whole thing since he was alone and not in great supply of food.

I suppose you'll have to return and make me something from the recipe book, then. There was a gleam in his eye.

My face heats.

"What's this?" Una asks, taking some of the cake. Her eyes widen at the honey. "Oh, sprites."

I snort without meaning to. Niall eyes it before taking some as well, looking me up and down. "Why are you blushing?"

"I'm not!"

"You are. Those things will enchant you, you know. Don't blush at the pretty faerie, Niamh."

I swat him gently on the leg. "You're not my brother *and* I'm older than you. Don't tell me what to do."

He grasps his heart in mock hurt.

"Fine. I'm older than you, at least. Don't tell me what to do."

He sends Una a conspiratorial smirk, but she's too busy making eyes at the cake. I bury my face in my hands, suddenly overwhelmed and feeling silly for being so.

"Is this about the pretty faerie or the stuck-up son of a mongrel over there—"

"Niall."

"I won't apologize."

Snorting again, I say through my hands, "He's very nice."

"Well, I know you're not talking about the stuck-up son of a—"

I shove him, though it doesn't do much to move him. He snickers. Either one of them can make me laugh, and he knows it.

"He's definitely hurt himself somehow," I say, rubbing my hands together. "And I think he's scared of something, but he's not insisted upon my name, and he's warning me where not to go in Faerie in concern for my safety."

I carefully *don't* mention the hounds or how I went in *much* too early this morning, even if by accident.

Niall raises an eyebrow, not convinced. "Moonlight born," he mutters, edging into amusement.

I take some of the cake and make a face as I eat. He's correct, after all.

"You're going to go back, aren't you?" Una asks, trying to take more of the cake slowly, as if less of it will disappear if she does. "And can you give me a good reason why?"

I can, actually. It occurred to me as I was walking out. Aidyn insisted upon leading me down, his hand on the inside of my elbow as he checked the few dozen steps from the library to the honeysuckle for monsters. The wind had picked up about him, and I've learned enough to realize it was his own magic.

I can still feel the touch of his hand on my skin.

"He needs help getting food for the kittens until he feels well. And besides, who would want to be alone while they are hurt?"

"Him, evidently," Una says, though not unkindly. "Since he's hiding there."

She is correct, of course, and I nod, unable to bring that to change my mind.

"Because I wish to," I say gently, and the two exchange looks but do nothing more than smile.

Niall whispers, "If he threatens you once, you'll—"

"I am no longer that type of fool," I say in a matching tone. "I'm not going to give myself or either of you a reason to worry. If I think he's dangerous, I won't return."

"I think they're all dangerous," Niall mumbles.

"And I've seen you throw an axe," I point out. "*You're* dangerous."

Despite the point he's trying to make, his ears turn pink, and he's clearly pleased with himself.

I squeeze his knee. "I know. And I'm being careful."

"Promise?"

I think of Aidyn and his gentle movements, the way even the slight bite to his words was in panic over wishing me to understand I could be terribly hurt in Faerie. "I promise."

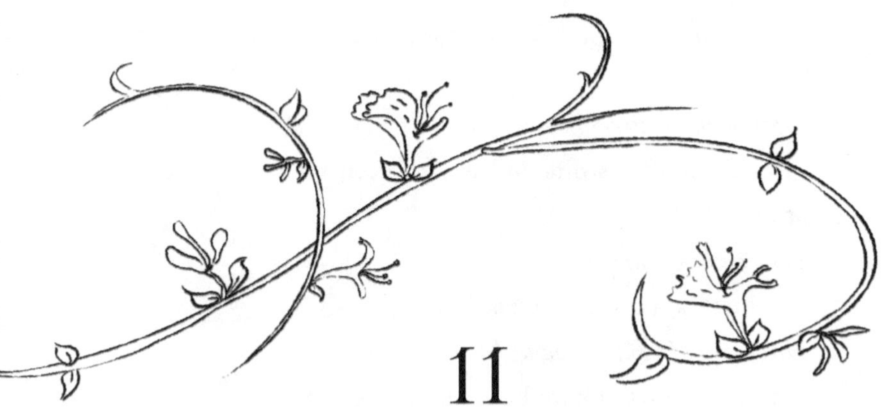

11

An Old Blue Door

For my own sanity and Niall's and Una's, I promise myself I will not go into Faerie until the three days have passed, and for good measure, I will wait until late morning.

That evening, Blain doesn't enter the village itself. Perhaps he realizes my two friends and I are not the only ones dwelling here who would not be pleased to see his face. When I watch his and the two other wagons bounce down the path into the setting sun, the remaining heaviness eases from my chest.

With the animals tended to and dinner eaten at Una's, I am back sharing her bed. She wants to know details, and I cannot blame her.

What does his voice sound like?

Like a soft sigh in a quiet morning. A creek running peacefully over river stones.

Does he more resemble a human or a faerie monster?

Human in all his bits and pieces, monster when taken in all at once.

Does he have magic?

Yes, but I am unsure precisely what it is.

Have you discovered what has hurt him?

No, and I don't believe he shall ever tell me.

Will the others arrive soon to save us from the hounds?

Tomorrow, hopefully. If we can, we must try to discover if anything is causing their anger.

Thinking of them has me shivering. Still, I haven't mentioned the hounds' closeness to either Una or Niall—I don't want them throwing a fit next time I go to the library. And I will. I was trying to tell myself I would not, but I cannot deny it any longer. Better to embrace what I know to be true.

I am going to visit the strange faerie again, and I will continue to until he does not need help and I no longer feel the need. Running my tongue over my teeth, I imagine the folktales of all the ways a faerie curse can twist one's soul and body. I dreamt of my teeth falling out that first night after meeting him—the image has stuck in my mind, but they are healthy and smooth as ever.

Stop being paranoid, Niamh.

We must try to discover if anything is causing their anger.

I try to run through all the things that have happened in the village in the past few months. Fields are being grown and harvested. Houses are being rethatched. Cows and sheep are being moved from pasture to pasture. The river is being fished. Midsummer is being prepared for. The same has been done every year.

Perhaps it is truly a circle of faerie mushrooms that has been trampled by the careless foot of a child.

Rolling over, I twine a strand of Una's hair between my fingers while she sleeps.

In the morning, Una and I trek around the fields. Cara is in tow, stomping down the lanes and picking flowers. We don't generally beware faerie things on this side of the woods, as those that exist are rather obvious, but I watch my steps.

There are mushrooms, of course, but no faerie circles. Instead, I pick the edible ones and think of making Aidyn something heartier, like a soup. Or perhaps something simpler—butter and garlic. Neither of those things are sweet, but so far as I know, fae do not eat *exclusively* sweet things. Either way, I suppose I shall find out.

"You're smiling to yourself," Una says dryly, picking an early fruit from a huckleberry bush and wrinkling her nose at the unripe sourness.

"No, I'm not." Her severe expression has me admitting, "I'm just thinking of what I can make with the mushrooms."

"Something for your new friend?"

"Perhaps," I say primly, pretending to be very interested in the fact that Cara has caught a frog.

"Are you *certain* he hasn't done anything threatening?"

"I am *certain* you have both asked me that eight times now. Do I seem cursed to you?"

"Well, no—"

"And I don't feel it." I loop my arm through hers.

"You're being careful of faerie mushrooms, aren't you?"

I manage not to roll my eyes. "I'm always careful of that. Sometimes I wonder if it was my own foot that stepped on one those years back."

She is momentarily quiet. "It could've been anyone."

"Hmm," I agree. "But yes, I've always been careful since. And besides, I don't think he has any intentions of cursing me. I think he merely likes having some company."

Una wrinkles her nose again for an entirely different reason, but eventually there are other duties to attend to than looking for disturbed mushrooms.

Three days is not so much when I am glancing sidelong at the woods, wondering if hounds will appear in the twilight shadows, or jumping at anything rustling in the undergrowth, which always turns out to be a rabbit or a deer or anything else safe and of the human world. It is not so much when I spend the time assisting Una with her dress, helping Cara make dolls for the other children at midsummer, and helping the men in any way possible with the preparations. Blain and his kin even stay away for the remaining days, which leaves me in a considerably finer mood.

It is much longer when I am still or quiet for any length of time. Or in the hot afternoons when the spring heat shimmers over the grasses and a chill finally descends into the air, the world not yet full of summer. When I think about how, if

Faerie were not only accessible through becoming lost or getting taken, the top of the library would likely be visible from the top of the village, if from a distance.

For all three nights, I expect to hear the hounds' shrill barking or to find signs of the Keepers, as Aidyn called them, dispatching of the creatures. All three nights are suspiciously quiet. Perhaps this is a good thing; perhaps it means the fae have done their duty and driven the creatures from our lands and we are none the wiser.

After all, we are not to see the fair creatures outside of midsummer—at least not the kind like Aidyn, tall and strangely human yet as far from it as a creature could possibly be.

I consider what he must do when not being entertained by my lack of knowledge and human talent at cooking. To consider he thinks of me at all is arrogant, but it fills my mind nonetheless. He is bewitching as any of his kin, but it does not mean I am *bewitched myself.* If I know it and can consider it with such logic, it cannot be true.

Still, it is barely midmorning on the third day by the time I'm hiking up my skirts and bolting for the trees through the hot grasses.

Emma glances my way, but she's the last person to stop such behavior. She'll judge me, certainly, and I'm worried for the next time I bump into her, but I don't mind being caught. If anything, she's likely shocked this is the first time in days I've done such a thing.

This time around, I am much more careful when I first step into the honeysuckle, and I waste no time in sprinting into the library. No more lazy wandering for me, even in the safety of the sunlight.

I'm not catching him at a strange hour of the day, but I make my footsteps heavy on the stairs and call out, "Hello?"

There's a creak of a door farther down, and I follow it to find Aidyn has pushed open the back door of the upper balcony where he's seated himself. I see the silver of his eye through the crack.

"Hello, Bluebell."

Ignoring the heat in my cheeks, I nudge my way out. "I'm not wearing blue this time."

"I'm scandalized."

He's stretched himself out parallel to the door, seated on the top step, back against the wall. The basket of kittens is out, and he has three of them circled between his two long hands. Still with the rings. I'll need to ask about them.

"You waited three days," he says with a note of amusement.

"Is that so shocking?"

"Well." He shrugs a shoulder. "There's a reason we can sing humans into Faerie. Once you step foot in, you don't appreciate going back out."

I match his shrug. "I'm accustomed to it."

He grins.

"Feeling better?" I ask, sheepish to bring it up but likewise wondering.

He doesn't appear remotely offended. "Yes, very fine."

It must be true enough. I glance around the Faerie woods. No signs of a struggle or action of any sort; it all remains perfectly calm and pristine, leaves drifting gently in the lack of wind. I attempt to imagine others like Aidyn nearby and the hounds themselves, though I did not see them truly the first time in the dark. Picturing it is difficult—I can barely imagine Aidyn perfectly when I am not before him, as if such a strange creature is not meant to be remembered by the mind of a simple human girl.

"They are gone?"

Something flickers in his expression, but something does in mine as well each time someone brings up the beasts.

"I . . . do not know."

My eyebrows bundle together.

There is a distinct downturn to his mouth. "I do not believe the . . . others came. Neither did I hear hide or hair of the beasts, but I cannot say for certain they have been dispatched of."

"Could they have come without you knowing?"

The twist in his expression is barely readable. "That is a decidedly small possibility."

Folding my hands, I wander nearer, uncertain where to go from here. Finally, I settle on admitting such. "What happens now?"

He takes a long, deep breath, eyes on the kittens. "Hopefully they have gone on their own. I shall keep listening at night, and you shall keep telling me if there are signs of them in your trees. Do *not* go into the woods at night and nothing shall harm you."

I'd smirk at how everyone keeps warning me away from the night woods if the reasons weren't so dire. Truly, it isn't needed. I haven't had ideas about Faerie in the dark since the hounds first stepped into our little village.

"You and my best friend keep telling me that same thing," I say in an attempt to lighten his expression once more.

It works . . . barely. "Your best friend is obviously the wisest of the group."

I snort. "Careful saying such things. She's not so certain I should be visiting you." His lip quirks, and I change the topic before he can decide to agree. "How are the kittens?"

"Quite well enough. They like the honey, though I'll need to begin finding them fruit soon—I am well and truly irritating the bees with my theft."

I manage not to smirk. The jar of honey we used most of the other day is now much fuller, and the kittens are licking his fingers. Sitting, I take one and pet its soft fur, feeling the bones beneath the fragile skin. They are no larger, but he mentioned they will not be for a time. As long as they are awake and eating, I am satisfied.

When a moment of silence passes, Aidyn sits up taller. "Come with me."

Before I can ask, he rises, returns the kittens back to his room, and is maneuvering out before I can even catch up. Even with a walking cane, he is faster and more graceful than I am.

It's a little endearing.

"What are we doing?" I ask, ignoring the jump in my heart when he hooks his fingers against my palm once again and leads me into the center of the library.

"I would like to show you something."

"That's a little unspecific, *Aidyn.*"

He gives an odd laugh, like a bird's warble. "I was exploring the library further. I found something I believe you'll like."

Down through the rows and rows of bookshelves we go, until we are far beneath the level where I first stepped onto a shelf and was caught by this strange faerie. From the small building, I still cannot imagine how so many shelves fit in such a small space, but it seems to go on and on forever. Running a finger across the nearest row of spines, I find many more falling to dust, only a spare few that jostle when I touch them, still in one piece.

"There are so many of them," I mumble.

"Yes. I still have not gathered the purpose of this place. Some things are unknown even to us. I don't suppose anything or anyone would remember the reasons behind this place—not anymore. It has too many oddities to be a simple library."

"I wonder if humans did not even exist then, when it was made."

From behind, I watch him cock his head. "Perhaps not. We are an ancient race. If this place has fallen into such disrepair, you may be correct. Ah, here."

Finally, he seems to have found the nearest wall. Gazing back over my shoulder and above my head, I am met with a dizzying combination of shadows and bookshelves; it is possible I would never find my way back to the main hall on my own. Without meaning to, I squeeze Aidyn's hand a little and am startled when he squeezes back.

The door is small and perhaps was once blue, though it's difficult to tell beyond the age and the dim light of this cobweb-strewn section of the library. The handle appears silver.

Twisted into a rope of fine intricate flowers and vines, it looks to fit perfectly in the hand. Without thinking through the gesture, I touch my fingertips to it. Nothing other than a chill smooth surface greets me, but I don't quite wish to step away.

"Fascinating, isn't it?" Aidyn's eyes sparkle when he glances down at me. "I went through three times. Let me show you."

His hand replaces mine over the handle, and he twists it and leans in to jog it properly loose from the ancient wall. Dust shimmers down in the scant light, and I step out of the way of a small sprite that goes leaping to the floor and dancing into the bookshelves.

"What do they eat in here?" I ask, watching its pale body disappear.

"Likely it has found a passageway outside. Those specific ones dine on the bark of trees."

I turn to ask how he knows so much about every little creature of these lands, but he has cracked open the old blue door, and the underside of a tree greets us.

No, not quite. A long, thin passageway of a tunnel goes downward only to slope up again. Daylight filters in. The tunnel is of no handmade creation but of countless roots wrapped round and round and bound together until a passageway has formed. A few more small creatures hanging from the ceiling like dusty cobwebs go scattering out into the light. Leaves rustle down onto the root-bound floor.

"Another back door?" I ask softly, though as I say it, I know it does not seem correct. "There wasn't one before."

"Yes and no," he says, stepping down in. "Each time I go

through, it puts me in a different place, each where I needed to be."

I blink at him.

He waves his hand in a loose circle down the passageway. "I tested it. The passageway remains open so you can return. The first time, it put me right back beside the honey hive, as I was looking for something to feed the kittens. The second time, I thought it was simply a passageway just outside beside the hive, but I was thinking of finding another water source, and it put me out beside one. I'm not precisely sure how it functions, but it put me there again when I wanted to return."

Blinking a few more times, I crouch and look deeper into the tunnel, nervous of venturing in, even if it is only daylight a few paces away.

"Come along," he says with a chuckle. "I shan't let you get lost."

I know not why it makes me any more nervous than the rest of this place—I am already in Faerie, already in close quarters with a creature who could sing me away forever should he wish it. A dozen steps through a tunnel of roots and out into the daylight is no different.

Taking his offered hand, I drop into the tunnel, noting no difference in temperature, just a stronger scent of earth and roots. He is forced to duck his head to make his way through, but I can stand straight and only need to avoid one lower-hanging root. Bright daylight shimmers in through a smaller hole with enough space for us to fit one at a time, and Aidyn boosts himself out carefully, sitting just on the edge.

"Come along," he says again, and I hear something else

over the sound of his voice: a few bees and running water. Poking my head out into the strange sunlight this side of the border, I squint at a thicket of berry hedges among the familiar trees. My heart squeezes a little.

"You can see the library just there." He points behind me into the trees. "It's a ways and mostly hidden, but it's there."

Getting to his feet, he brushes off his trousers and gazes down at me happily, offering his hand. I don't think he should be pulling me out when he already leans on his walking stick, but I'm more concerned with truly stepping into the trees, even if the library is just there. Another sprite bumbles past, knocking into Aidyn's leg before climbing up the nearest tree. My lips pull up at the corners.

At my stillness, Aidyn points the other way, into the deeper forest. "There is what I believe you'll like. Come along."

The smile falls from my face. "How far in?"

"Not a few dozen steps into those trees there." He gestures again through the hedge of berry bushes. "We are perfectly safe in the daylight."

I glance up as he gazes down expectantly. His eyes are earnest, curious. He appears no more than a child who wants to show something they've made.

It's not particularly the daylight I'm worried about.

I would like to go with him, I realize.

"I . . . don't want to go into the woods."

"The monsters are not here. Anything else in Faerie will not bother you with my presence."

I wonder just how frightening he is that others dwelling here will not harm me so long as he stands by my side.

And how much more frightening the *hunt hounds* are that even he grows paler when they are mentioned.

I shiver. "I know. I still do not wish to."

He squints, gazing at me as if he is trying to decide if a lie is sitting on my human features. With a slight smile, he asks, "Why not?"

Most people wouldn't have a reason to ask—not when living in a village on the edge of Faerie means *going into the woods* could leave you forever lost within its depths. This is no danger to Aidyn, and of course no danger to me, and so *of course* he is going to ask.

"I just don't wish to."

Glancing at the library, then into the woods, he says once more, "There are no monsters at this time."

He's trying to reassure me. "I know—"

"And if I wanted to enchant you, I wouldn't need to lure you into the trees." He says this with a gentle laugh, and I believe him for more reasons than simply because fae do not lie.

I try to match his smile. "I just . . . don't wish to."

He squints again. After regarding me for a long moment with that confused smirk, he shrugs a shoulder and turns on his heel, heading into the trees by himself. "Very well. I shall go."

I open my mouth at his retreating figure but don't know what to say.

Was that supposed to convince me? Or has he simply given up on my company and is going to whatever place he's found on his own? Am I meant to wait here until he returns? Frowning, I fold my arms and watch him disappear into the brambles with a friendly wave.

I snort.

And I am left alone. Squinting after him and leaning my arms against the top of the tunnel, I consider that I am no longer going into the woods with anyone at my back, and suddenly I feel silly.

I could sneak after him.

But no, that is likely *exactly* what he was trying to get me to do.

I do, however, wish to know what he's excited about.

Simply climbing out will do me no harm.

Glancing at where the library should be but unable to find it from my height, then into the surrounding woods, I pick up my skirts and scramble fully out into the sunlight.

12

Berries and Brambles

Spotting the path Aidyn's boots made through the leaves, I take a few steps into the brambles, half expecting him to be peeking back at me through the spring leaves.

"Aidyn?" I call.

"It's only a few dozen steps down!" comes his faint voice. I don't see anything through the thicket, but perhaps that means nothing. Rushing water beckons in the Faerie heat.

Of course he expected me to follow.

A little arrogant, but such is to be expected.

He was not incorrect, after all.

Glancing at the bees humming nearby and remembering his warning not to get too close, then at the little tunnel we crawled from, I creep between the path of gaps in the undergrowth. Water trickles nearby, small rivers gathering toward the falls. It's so oddly peaceful here, the stillness to the air indescribable and impossible in the human world.

If Una and Niall would ever dare come here, they would love it just as much. In a way, I am grateful they don't. I watch the way Una worries over me, and I'd hate to be fretting constantly if both my best friends took to traipsing off into Faerie whenever it suited them.

Hypocritical of me? Perhaps.

"What are you?"

I squeak, caught off guard for the countless time. Whipping around toward whoever spoke—it was certainly not Aidyn with his water-calm voice—I spot a pair of eyes gazing out at me from beneath a clutch of berries. Cocking my head, I crouch to get a better view of it under all the scrubby little leaves. I've seen brownies before, of course, cute things that nest in cottage eaves.

This is not a brownie.

In truth, I've no idea what it is. A squat little body and frogish legs crouch beneath the prickly leaves. Little pale hairs sprout from gray skin, and its face is squashed and flat, stuck into a permanent scowl.

It would be a little cute . . . if I weren't looking at a creature on the dangerous side of Faerie.

Aidyn is a creature on the dangerous side of Faerie.

Glancing around, uncertain if I'm more concerned if Aidyn *will* or *won't* reappear, I say, "Hello."

"What are you?" it asks again.

Not exactly a normal question, but this is the side of the

woods where humans are not the only things that speak. "Um . . . a human?"

It blinks at me and says nothing more. I peer into the brambles at the thin path Aidyn has taken, then back to the creature. It seems strange to turn my back on it but stranger still to linger.

"What happened to your finger, little human?"

I bite the inside of my lip. Coming from a tiny creature, the question is almost funny. I try to pick out memories of all the tales I've heard of Faerie and how to converse with one. It cannot be the same as conversing with Aidyn, and I never know if I am doing *that* well. The only thing of value I can pick out is not to be rude but not to be weak.

"I was attacked by a Faerie hound," I tell it, not remembering the term Aidyn used and less willing to speak it if I did. I don't wish to act as if I know too much.

Is Aidyn supposed to be interacting with me?

Glancing his way, I find the brambles empty as ever. I am almost certain this means nothing—Aidyn appeared right beneath me on the bookshelf with barely a brush of his feet. He may be about to appear from behind the nearest leaf.

"Why so?"

Honest again, I say, "Because I knew no better."

It cocks its head at me. Unfolding its legs with a series of pops and clicks, it unravels into a much longer creature than I imagined, all legs and arms and bony joints, crawling up through the brambles to look me in the eye. I manage not to step back. Though still no taller than my knee, it is distinctly unnerving nonetheless, and I press my hands into my skirts to hide my fists.

"You think we pretty things are less dangerous than the boy who left you to die?" it asks, head rolling so far against its neck it appears to have no joints.

I blink, stepping back. A sharp pinch behind my chest has me catching my breath.

"How did you—"

"Know?" it asks, drool seeping from the corner of its mouth. The strange pain grows sharper. "I—eeek!"

A long hand snatches it from its bush, and I jump at Aidyn's sudden presence. He drags it out of the thorns and holds it to eye level, displeasure twisting his mouth. The pain breaks like a string snapping, and I find my hand on my chest.

It shrieks and flails like a dragonfly caught by the tail. Aidyn's expression turns unimpressed.

"What do you think you're doing?" he asks as if someone has spilled his porridge, and I take a moment to realize he's asking the creature, not me. "I thought I chased you off."

It continues with its flailing and shrieking, and Aidyn sighs. Letting it go, he bends and hisses, "Stay away," as it flops into a ball and scatters away in a tangle of limbs.

Straightening, he smooths his pants and wrinkles his nose.

His eyes drift to mine, then float to my hand still cupped against my chest. I drop it, feeling strange. Now that the little creature is gone, I am suddenly very aware that I am alone in the woods with this strange faerie and that I was planning not to be. There isn't room to step back among the brambles— they're already poking gently through my dress—but my legs are ready to run. I remind myself there are no monsters here, but that is of less comfort than it should be.

Aidyn's eyes return to mine, and he offers something akin to a smile, though it doesn't touch his eyes. "I didn't realize it was still lurking here. I haven't seen it in days." He wrinkles his nose again. "Even when you are a creature of Faerie, you are often surprised by its inhabitants."

I stare up at him, unsure what to say.

He adds, "It drinks off your emotions. Painful memories are strong. It likes discomfort."

How did it know? I don't want to ask because then I may have to explain. "Why is it here?"

With a shrug of the shoulder, his eyes skid away, inspecting the berries. "Me."

"Oh." I don't want him to ask, so likewise I don't push. If he wanted to share, he would. Faerie knows I've nudged him enough already. Still, I glance at the cane beneath the palm of his hand and wonder about the specifics of his painful memories.

Suddenly, he straightens, offering a better smile. "If you come across it again, just walk away. They are not physically dangerous. They do not even have teeth."

He flashes a bit too much of his own, but it's a strangely gentle gesture, an unnerving but friendly wolf. I try to match it and don't care for the result.

"Come along, Bluebell," he says with the same great attempt at true cheer, making a gesture as if he's going to take my hand again, then catching my tension and heading back through the brambles without me.

Watching him go, I get the sudden impression he knows

what has upset me. At the very least, he's not pestering me, and he's giving me space. For a strange creature of Faerie, it's much more than expected. Still, he pauses at the edge of the thicket and gestures, just the tops of his fingers visible.

"Come along!" he calls again. "Just to right here. I don't want you getting lost."

Glancing at the top of the library peeking through the trees, the burrow we came through, and back to him, I tell myself, *A few more steps is no harm.* The way he says it is not patronizing. He seems genuinely concerned.

I have never walked in the woods since, not with anyone else. Not if I don't count Niall or Una wandering the edges of the trees with me. And those two I would never count as a danger.

His hand pops up again to usher me along, and I stare after it.

You think we pretty things are less dangerous than the boy who left you to die?

Suddenly hot with rage at the petty little creature, I force myself after him.

What is that thing to attempt to frighten me? It does not even have teeth or claws.

And I have met *things with teeth and claws.*

I wish to spend time with Aidyn, and so I shall.

I can still see the library, and these woods are open and bright. It is about time I rid myself of this ridiculous fear anyhow. At the very least, I can try.

Heart thumping, I maneuver through the sharp thorns and ripe handfuls of berries until I nearly bump into Aidyn where he has paused to wait for me. All at once, the ground falls away, and the gentle rush of water becomes louder. It pools in glistening swirls beneath a gentle set of falls, berry bushes circling the stony ground.

I didn't see this at all. The waterfall is tall enough to see. Glancing back, I still catch the top of the library through the trees and over the brambles and the tree from where we came. Frowning, I look back and forth.

"Distances are strange things here," Aidyn says, his soft voice startling me atop all my nerves of being alongside him. *Una would be mortified.* "So is time. As I mentioned, you should not be wandering farther without me."

Something about the quiet way he says it has my heart jumping. When I glance up, his eyes soften further.

"Do not worry," he says. "It would take a great deal for me to be lost in this place. I was born of these lands."

He can be as comforting as he likes—my heart is still pounding against my ribs. All the bravado disappeared the moment he came into my line of sight.

Trading the woods with one stranger for another, and this one dangerous more than cowardly, at that.

Hopefully I am a wiser choice in my friends than I once was.

Can he see my pulse in my throat?

Abruptly, his expression brightens. "Come, come," he says, maneuvering down the rocks toward the edge of the water. After another comforting glance at the library, I follow. My legs move as lead, but they move.

He is bringing me here because he thinks I'll like it, I remember, the thought previously lost over the strange creature and my nervousness. His excitement is a bit too infectious to resist. I follow him down, stepping carefully on the sun-hot rocks. At the edge, he sits himself down and begins unbuckling his boots, setting his cane aside.

My face heats. "What are you doing?"

He looks up as if I'm missing something quite obvious. "I'm not going to get my boots wet, am I?"

My face turns hotter, then hotter still with the realization he may be able to tell. At least he isn't inspecting my cheeks this time.

His knowing grin turns to a fake-scandalized hand over his heart. "Fear not, I would never disrobe before a maiden."

Whatever nerves have been tightening my chest abruptly turn into a laugh. It's strained, but it's real. My cheeks don't entirely lose their ridiculous blushing, but I'm suddenly much more comfortable. Down here, I cannot see the library, but the path we took is there, and I don't suppose Aidyn would be out here if he believed monsters would arrive. Certainly, he seemed as frightened as I was, if in a hidden way. He believes we are safe, and I do not take him for a fool.

Perhaps he'll regale me with what he knows about the other fae who should've *come . . .*

Watching him take off his boots and the heavier overshirt, I catch the way a swirl of a gentle breeze circles him in the otherwise calm woods and can resist no longer. "You have magic?"

He unbuckles his pants but is only taking out his belt. It is a pretty thing, carved with flowing organic patterns of no particular plant I can recognize. Niall would likely be impressed with the workmanship on the silver buckle. Once again, I wonder what is hidden beneath the clothes that causes him pain. Perhaps he *would* simply disrobe in front of me if those injuries did not exist. I don't know if I'd be particularly averse to the idea, embarrassed as I'd be.

"All fae have magic," he says conversationally, as if we're discussing the weather.

"Well, all humans do not, so I'm curious." I match his tone.

Something about that has him grinning. Leaving his cane, he rises and sticks a toe into the clear water. The undershirt is much looser and cuts down his chest. I believe I catch the edge of a bandage, though apparently this will not dissuade him from swimming.

"What would you like to know?" he asks, then simply drops off the edge of the rock into the water. When he surfaces, hair plastered over his forehead, he watches me expectantly.

"What . . . is yours, exactly?" I ask, edging up to the water and gazing into the clear depths. Nothing about it seems dangerous, and less so with Aidyn casually treading water. The day is hot, as if midsummer is already upon us, and the linen dress is tight and too warm for Faerie. He is watching me as if expecting me to *disrobe* as well.

Perhaps I shall.

Carefully, I undo the simple laces down the back. I have a thin shift beneath, and I don't mind him seeing a little more of me. It seems remarkably different than anyone else seeing my shoulders or my legs when I pull up my skirts and run.

His eyes trail along my fingers undoing the threads. "I can bring the breezes to my call. It is one of the less violent magics in existence, but it certainly has its uses."

He speaks of it so casually, as if its gentleness makes it less impressive. "So, it will just . . . do anything you want?"

He floats back a little, his dark hair stuck to the white fabric of his shirt. "Most anything."

"Is it difficult to do?"

"Not terribly so." Lifting a hand from the water, he gives a small flourish. A breeze swirls about my feet, dancing all the way up through my dress as if it is a cold winter storm. It's surprisingly warm. Fingers of air tickle my stomach and chest and out through my hair. I stop short of yelping in surprise, but it's close. It doesn't quite lift my skirts, but I get the distinct feeling he did it to make me blush again. Glowering but not managing to make it angry enough, I pull off the dress, air touching my bare shoulders. At least it's not *his* magic, just the forest sunlight.

Pretending I don't notice his staring, I kick the fabric away and pull off my shoes, the smooth rock hot on my bare feet.

Trying to think of a different question to follow up the staring, I ask, "What *are* the more violent magics?"

He wrinkles his nose. "There are too many to count. We all have various levels of abilities to *ensnare others*, as you like to put it, though that is more difficult outside of Faerie, and we need your name for such things. Then there are the separate things, like this"—he sends more leaves skittering across the ground—"and some are used mainly as an aid for fighting."

"Examples?" I ask.

He merely gazes at me.

Perhaps not, then. "Very well. What is the most impressive thing you can do?"

"That would be bragging," he says mildly, then dips below the surface of the water.

I didn't much expect him to answer, but those words have me shaking my head. If nothing else, he knows how beautiful he is, but either this is where he draws the line at impressing me, or he doesn't want to speak of it.

Either way, I may as well stop standing here like a fool. Creeping back to the edge of the water, I peer in, barely believing anything isn't dangerous in Faerie, let alone a body of water.

Do merfolk exist? Probably not in a tiny waterfall pool.

"Can you not swim?" Aidyn has resurfaced a little farther away, and I shoot him an offended glare.

"Of course I can swim. I'm trying to decide if anything in here's going to eat me."

I can't tell if he's amused or thinks I'm simple. "Why would I bring you here if something was going to eat you?"

"I don't know," I say, sticking my toe into the water the same as he did. Though it should be the spring snowmelt, the water is nearly warm and balmy. The air is thick and heavy, and the pool beckons, which could be anything from some spell cast upon me to the magic of Faerie. I wouldn't know the difference. But I haven't known the difference from the moment I stepped foot inside the woods. "Perhaps you have a pet out here."

A sudden laugh echoes off the rocks, and he dips beneath the water a bit, laughter cut off in bubbles. I fight to keep a smirk off my face. When he finally resurfaces, he's grinning.

"Nothing is in the water that will harm you," he says, swimming nearer and holding his hand up. "With me, you are safe in Faerie."

As long as I don't wander off and talk to strange bramble creatures, at least.

I still can't see the library and *still* don't like being alone in the woods with this faerie who is indeed a stranger, but I tend to believe him. At the very least, he believes his own words.

Enough of this silly fear, Niamh.

His hand isn't needed, but something in me doesn't wish to pass up the opportunity. Sliding the tips of my fingers into his palm, I step off the stones into the water.

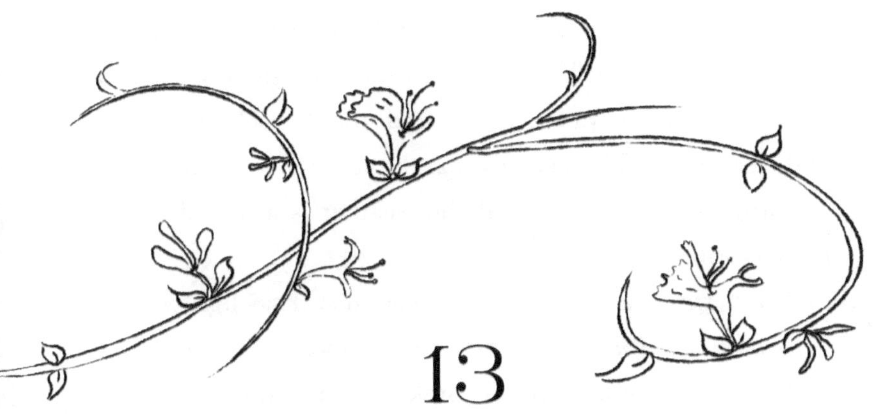

13

Beneath the Falls

It is deeper than I anticipated, though dark shadows of the bottom are visible.

Anything could lurk there. Resurfacing, I wipe the water from my eyes and find Aidyn closer than expected. He still has the same smile, his fingertips gently holding mine.

I realize what about it feels so strange. "We're finally the same height."

Grin widening, he relinquishes my hand to swim backward toward the waterfall. Again, I think perhaps I should not follow, but I am already in the water. A small bit of swimming won't do me any harm. I follow him under the gentle, slow stream of the falls, feeling strangely undressed in just my shift, even with the water to cover me. Dipping up on the other side, I find Aidyn propped on some of the partially submerged rocks, pleased with himself. It's dark here, the air frigid and crisp, smelling of cold stone and something sweet. Moss clings to the walls. My toes find smooth rock, and I look at the cavern roof. Ice crystals coat the stone. Even in the dead of spring, or summer here if the weather is any indication, there is still ice.

"Well, this is a fine place to ensnare me," I say lightly.

Niamh, you don't know what's good for you.

With a widening grin, he slinks into the water, pushing himself toward me. "Don't tempt me."

A nervous giggle bubbles up, and I swim backward, knowing that if he meant any harm, it would be a useless endeavor. Both Una and Niall would be appalled, but I don't mind.

"Are you really twenty-three?" I ask, for the oddity of it has stuck in my mind a long while.

He laughs. "That is very disconcerting for you, isn't it?"

"Well, of course."

"Yes, I am twenty-three. My father is several hundred years old. You can imagine how young I am to *him*."

The casual nature of the statement catches me off guard. I sit on the nearest stone, still in the water, aware of my shift clinging to my skin. Something about the situation has me thinking perhaps he is being a little childish—I imagine an ancient faerie whose very young son (relatively speaking) is hiding out in a library, evidently not wishing to be found.

He must read my funny expression. "What are you thinking?"

"Does your father know you're redecorating an old library?"

I say it with a tease in my voice, but some of the genuine

happiness falls from his expression. I wish I hadn't spoken. "No. He would be appalled."

Momentarily, I consider pushing the topic, but he has already looked away, toward the falling water, and I hate when the light falls from his eyes. It seems oddly incorrect, as if his pretty face should not bear the weight of unhappiness. I can ask later, little bits at a time.

It is not as if I am giving him all my troubles either.

I try a different approach, bobbing into the corner of the cavern and touching the ice crystals. "What is it you love to do?"

"How do you mean?"

It's difficult to tell, but it seems as if his hand may be under his shirt, against his middle. Swimming was his idea, but I wonder if I should try to coax him into the sun. "I could cook all day and never grow sick of it. It makes me happy. I have a friend who loves her sewing. What do you love?"

That gets some of the crinkles back around his eyes. He opens his mouth, then pauses. His eyes flicker to the wall of the cavern. I glance over my shoulder but see nothing save the cold damp stone. I can never tell if his expression should be judged on how humans act, and I don't know how to react to his sudden stillness.

"What is it?" I ask.

His expression turns cold, and he drifts toward me, eyes still on the wall. Putting a finger to his lips, he bobs close enough I feel the heat from him even in the water. I'm suddenly much more aware of my lack of clothing and dress clinging to my skin.

His intensity has my stomach twisting.

Conspiratorially, I whisper, "What do you see?"

He shakes his head, opens his mouth again—

A sharp yip of a bark breaks the gentle rumble of the water. My heart leaps into my throat, all joy turning to cold dread.

It's broad daylight, nothing can be out here.

He promised I was safe out here with him . . .

I turn to him, intent on saying as such, but his wide eyes match mine. He's considerably better at hiding the fear, but it's there. It cannot be an intentional trick, then. It *cannot* be.

Get ahold of yourself, Niamh.

We must be safe back here, mustn't we? Thinking of his sword buried beneath his blankets, I wish very suddenly that I had mentioned it to him so perhaps he would have brought it on our little excursion.

His hand returns to my elbow, and he puts a finger to his lips. *No more questions, then.*

Another bark.

I can't help but flinch. The water is unpleasantly cold. Aidyn's eyes follow the dips in the rocky cavern, and he shakes his head slightly.

Annoyed with the other fae who didn't come?

For a long time, I hear nothing else. Then he's releasing me and slipping toward the waterfall.

"Aidyn . . ." I hiss, snatching at his arm.

He shrugs me off, waving his hand as if to shush me, still about to swim out of the safety of the little cavern, leaving me here. Catching his sleeve, I attempt to drag him back. Why he wishes to go out there is beyond me, but he's *not* leaving me in here alone.

He's the one who brought me here—against all my better judgment, no less—and I'll be damned if one more person leaves me in these woods.

I may as well be fighting a statue. Attempting to drag him back only succeeds in plastering me against him as he refuses to budge even in the water.

Scowling, he unwinds my hand from his sleeve. "Let go, and *be quiet.*"

"What are you doing? Don't go out there!"

"Shh! I'm getting *rid of it,*" he hisses, his voice so suddenly and unnaturally low it has me frozen.

Weakly, I say, "You said they don't come out in the day-light—"

"They do not. And the others should have *arrived* by now. Apparently, *I'm* not the only incompetent one here."

There's more behind that statement, but he's pulling away again. Panic leaps into my throat, anger along with it, and I grab his shoulder for better purchase.

I give him as solid a pull as I can in the water. "Don't—"

An angry inhuman noise rips from him, his hand wrapping like iron around my wrist, yanking me off as if my fingers are made of paper. Only his shirt tears a bit under my grip. With a shove, he pushes me back through the water, away from him. When I surface, coughing, he is already disappearing onto the other side of the falls.

And I am alone.

Clinging to the nearest rock, I wait, attempting to catch my breath, my wrist stinging where he shoved me, though there isn't a mark to be seen. My breath hitches, and I bite down on my lip hard enough that the pain distracts me.

Seconds pass. *What would I do if something happened to him? Would Faerie not let me find my way back to the library? Would the hounds come through the water?*

Cursing myself, I swim to the edge of the falls, to the little sliver of light between the water and the cliffs of frigid rock, and attempt to peek through the mist spraying my eyes. A tendril of warmth from the outside air slithers across my cheek, but the light has gone, as if twilight fell all at once.

Darkness fell early again.

I dare to press myself out enough to see, praying not to glimpse a pair of bright rabid eyes meeting mine. Aidyn will have left, I'm aware. Much easier to return to the library without attempting to drag a human along behind him—

The first thing to meet my eye is a shadow. A shape sits among the brambles and bushes wrapping around the little woodland pool. Again, my breath hitches, my eyes burning. It is not clear even in the brighter twilight, a strange patchwork of blending into the undergrowth and standing as a stark contrast against the light. Even from here, I cannot quite make out its features. I do not *have to*. I remember vividly the scent of it, the cold of its claws, the rabid intelligence of its eyes. I do not need to see them to know it is looking directly at—

Aidyn.

It is looking directly at Aidyn, poised on a rock in the center of the pool, standing on a ledge I do not see, one hand on the sun-dried stone, barely his shoulders out of the water, watching it in return. He is utterly still, dripping black hair plastered against the bright white of his shirt, a frozen guardian in the middle of the water.

I've held my breath so long my entire chest burns. I cannot convince myself to release it.

The hound slinks through the brambles, circling above the edge of the pool. My eyes cannot discern each of its movements—only every few seconds can I catch up to where it is. Aidyn's head tilts to follow it. His voice sounds gently across the roar of the water, a series of words I know are not my language, but I cannot grasp at them, just as I cannot with his books or his songs.

A rippling growl slithers across the empty trees.

A third bark.

One of its massive paws touches the path down to the water.

All the trees rage at once, a twirl of wind stronger than any winter storm I've witnessed swirling down upon the slinking monster. Aidyn's hands rise from the water, and that is all I see before the force of the gales drives the waterfall into a frenzy and I am swimming back in a desperate hurry. Water hovers sideways, drawn by the air, and I glimpse the hound with its paws off the ground for a split moment before a deafening crash. All at once, the water returns to normal.

I take a gasping breath in the ensuing silence, merely the roar of the falls to break it.

"Flower," comes Aidyn's soft voice through the falls. "Bluebell, come, hurry now."

A full five seconds pass before I can convince my screaming muscles to unlock. Unsteadily, I paddle through the water and into hot twilight, peeking above the surface and ready to dive to safety the moment a slithering shadow enters my vision.

Nothing.

The Faerie woods are much the same as they were, save a coating of leaves in places they were not.

And a massive fallen tree with a splinter of its trunk still rising into the sky.

No sign of the hound, just of Aidyn still perched on his rock, leaves caught against his wet hair and clothes and skin. He dips once below the surface and washes most of them off, gesturing for me to hurry to him. I swim through the layer of golden-red leaves, following him to the edge where our clothes were blown against a nearby boulder.

My voice finally returns to me, though rough and unsteady. "Where—"

"I am not certain it is dead," he says, sounding similarly unraveled. "Let us hurry. Do not forget your things. Put your shoes on."

Yanking on my shoes and gathering my dress to my chest, I gaze into the woods as Aidyn takes his things, forgoing his own boots, and grasps me by the elbow. I start, remembering the harsh dig of his fingers as he dragged me off him and shoved me aside. No time to dwell, he is likewise dragging me up the path, albeit much gentler. Neither of us is particularly steady, and even in the panic I see how he leans heavier against his cane than previously. The wet soles of my shoes slip on the rocks, my underdress heavy with water, and my knee stings on a sharp edge. With my arm holding my dress, the only reason I do not fall harder is Aidyn's unmovable grip on my elbow.

At the top of the pool, past the brambles, deeper into the woods, I see precisely what felled the massive birch tree.

Twisted limbs lie in a pile of golden and green leaves and greener fur. Splintered logs and branches are strewn across the otherwise bizarrely calm and pristine woods.

He sent it flying through the trunk of the tree itself.

Aidyn pauses, his breath coming quicker than I believe it should. Inspecting his handiwork, he glances down at me, then back at the creature. I can't read the interaction, not with my heart still threatening to pound its way out of my chest.

He killed it.

A leg twitches.

Aidyn says something my mind can't grasp, but the tone is clear. He doesn't need to haul me off this time; we're both sprinting back through the brambles to the small tree where we first climbed from the strange tunnel. If anything, I'm faster than him with his hidden injuries, and I find myself grasping his hand as we run, his fingers twined tightly between mine.

As I drop into the root-bound space, a deeper chill settles across my soaking clothes. Up and through the little blue door, we push our way into the library. Shoving the rusted hinges into place, Aidyn leans against it, dust trickling from the rafters. Quiet falls. His gaze is on the bottom of the door, and my eyes cannot leave his face. All at once, I see the thread of crimson down his shoulder, where my desperate grasping tore his shirt. All my anger at him shoving me aside turns into cold mortification at the reason.

I tore off a bandage. And reopened a wound in the process. It looks no larger than the tip of my finger, but a rivulet of blood finds its way down his skin, staining the pure white of his shirt.

My eyes burn, throat closing up. No wonder he shoved me aside—

His eyes slide up to mine, then down to his shoulder as if he's only now remembering its existence.

" 'Tis small," he whispers, and then his eyes turn all cold, glancing at the door again.

Grabbing my hand once more, he hauls me down the dusty hallway, weaving through the impossible maze of ancient shelves without hesitation, releasing me beside the stairs. I scramble up after him.

"Go back to Nevyan at once. Do not return until—" He stops and gazes at me strangely, as if wondering if I *will* ever return. "Tomorrow."

My heart leaps at going back out of the library at all. "What—"

"Go," he says, then disappears into his room. My feet are frozen to the spot, and I'm working out just what to say when he steps out again. His cane is gone; instead, he holds the scabbard of the sword I saw. It is still sheathed, and I cannot glimpse the bright blade. The presence of it hangs in the room. Aidyn pauses, staring at me. Still drenched, his shirt moved back into place but stained crimson, feet bare, he doesn't appear half the creature I first stumbled upon. "Go out the front. It . . . won't follow you."

Again, I open my mouth, but he says, "It is only one. Just

go. *Please.* I don't wish to worry over you if you are here."

I find myself nodding, for I do not *wish* to be here any longer. No longer do I feel as if the walls of this old library will protect me. I should never have returned to begin with. I am aware only that I broke my own rule and nearly paid the same price.

Still, the only words that manage to come out are, "Are you certain?"

Unlatching the back door where we first visited the honey hive, Aidyn pauses, hand on the handle, eyes avoiding mine. "You do not . . ." His expression spasms as if the words are difficult. "You do not *have* to return."

His gaze flickers to mine before he gestures to the stairs and disappears out the back door.

For a moment, I consider staying.

I consider if I may help.

Even if he walks back from that creature and is hoping to see me, should I trust him again?

As I flee down the steps and out the front of the old building, I wonder if there are more lurking nearby, ready to tear me to pieces, and he shall wander around and find my body strewn along the leaves. A harsh yelp of inhuman pain, precisely as I remember the hounds to sound, echoes across the utter silence of Faerie.

The scent of honeysuckle and hot grasses deposits me home.

Two familiar horses stand by my cottage.

There is also Niall, hands on his hips, sweaty from whatever he's been working on, gesturing angrily at the owners of said horses. My feet are rooted to the middle of the dusty path. I managed, after I'd finished crouching in the human side of the woods and weeping, to put my dress back over my damp shift. My shoes I've taken back off; my feet were uncomfortably wet inside and threatened to cause blisters if I walked in them much longer. I hold them by the laces and feel the caked dirt between my toes. My hair is tangled, for it came undone of its braid some time ago—likely in the wind—and still damp atop it all. I look precisely as if I've been wandering the Faerie woods like the moonlight-born child I am.

As I wept, I told myself I would not go back, that my time in the Faerie library is over. Quite obviously, Aidyn has no need of me, and whatever amount I fooled myself into believing is not true. He needs no aid and probably not even the company—not from a little human.

Now, walking in the hot leftover rays of the human sun, I am less certain.

You do not . . . have *to return.*

My throat burns.

I do not believe I should have *left.*

But I cannot return in the dark.

I stare at the horses, at the men beside them, and at Niall's defensive stature and very much consider bolting into the undergrowth along the side of the path. My hand aches, and I rub it against the rough material of my skirts, soaking up the damp from the shift beneath.

Blain sees me standing in the middle of the path, and I cannot run now.

I pick up my steps before it looks as if I was frozen. There is nothing else in my hands save my shoes—I must have left my basket there, but new ones can always be made—and I force myself not to attempt to detangle my hair with my fingers. It is no use. A memory of the hunt hound's eyes sit just behind my vision, the slippery nature of its shape among the trees. There is also the ghost of Aidyn's fingers over mine when he ran with me to the library. A gentle spring breeze whispers across the ground, and I half expect him to be hidden in one of the bushes alongside the path, offhandedly sending his magic across the ground.

I let my shoes swing by their laces from my fingers, as if my heart is not pounding its way out of my chest.

Niall finally hears me and glances back. His expression is tight—I would imagine he is being polite, though his body language says the opposite. Eyes narrowing, he takes in my appearance. I had forgotten about my skinned knee until he looks at it, and I force myself not to follow his gaze. His arm goes around my shoulders immediately, and I lean into the embrace. Perhaps it is good that everyone thinks we should be engaged despite how he and Una and I have a good laugh at the idea. It appears more than just a friend standing by my side at the moment, and I need that before these two people.

Besides, his safe touch grounds me. I'm nearly surprised that Aidyn's grip on my arm felt more solid, more secure.

"Mister Haskel," I say. "I thought you were going to call in a few weeks."

Perhaps I should not be so terse, so blunt, but I have had quite enough of this and had a considerable scare as it is.

I decidedly *don't* look at Blain, though I feel his gaze on me. From the blurry shape of him in the corner of my eye, I see he is petting his horse's nose, nudging one of the plants in Mam's garden with the toe of his boot.

I should fling my shoes at him.

Mister Haskel hooks his fingers into the rings of his vest pockets. They are more richly embroidered than the last time. "Ah, I was planning on it. We came a bit early, so I figured I'd try again."

I nod, and when the silence stretches, I gesture to the obviously empty house. Niall's arm over my shoulder makes me braver. I imagine Aidyn looking down upon these two humans with the height he has on them and the sharp predator-bird intelligence of his eyes, and it *nearly* improves my mood.

The older man clears his throat, glancing at his son. Still, I ignore him. I did not invite him here. It cannot be helped that midsummer is a festival that gathers all the closest villages together, and so *of course* he would eventually return. But I do not have to speak with him, and I do not have to acknowledge his existence.

My hand is hidden behind Niall's back, against the warmth of his shirt, and that is likely the only reason I manage to keep my expression neutral.

"The preparations seem to be going well," Haskel says.

How much small talk will he attempt?

Bored, Niall says, "Yes."

"The weather is warming up much better this year," Blain

says, and I nearly start at the sound of his voice. It has been ages, and I do not appreciate the sound of it. Worse, I do not appreciate how it is understandable that I once found that voice so alluring.

Again, Niall says, "Yes."

I stare at a nearby tree in the ensuing silence, wondering if the ground might open up beneath my feet.

"You look lovely, Niamh," Blain says.

Niall's arm tightens ever so slightly about my shoulders. I hope it doesn't look too much as if I'm leaning against him.

Finally, I look at Blain. He's grown into himself well enough. With the broad shoulders and pretty sweep of hair, I'm certain there are many women who would chase after his hand. Just as well. Most women do not wander the edge of Faerie, so they should have no qualms with his . . . courage.

"I know," I say, ignoring the tight burn in my chest. I can't tell if it's embarrassment or something worse. I decidedly do *not* look lovely, not in this state, and it is just as likely he is mocking than genuine.

I can't read his expression, but the slight upturn to his lips has a decided tendril of disgust curling in my stomach. Why should I have to bear scars of those hounds only to encounter them again when this man stands perfectly well before me? Why should I have to gaze upon him at all, particularly when I've no clue why he is here, his father as some sort of shield from the very real possibility Niall would break his knuckles against that perfect nose?

Aidyn did not run into the woods without me. He did not leave me to those beasts.

I thought, for a moment, that of course he had, but the image of him standing between the waterfall and that creature is stuck in my mind.

No, Niamh, you will not return. My voice sounds weak in my own mind.

Perhaps it is not the same thing, not comparable between a human and a faerie. I am not a good-enough liar to tell myself so. The sudden calm certainty that I would not have left Aidyn by the waterfall either washes over me.

If he had asked me to stay, I would have.

I wished to, even as I didn't, even as I let him convince me to flee to my own kingdom.

As much as I am trying to convince myself I shall not go back, I find myself glancing across the village toward the trees that will become Faerie the moment I am lost.

Though he begged me to leave, I almost decide here and now to turn and go back, shrug off Niall's arm and run back through the trees. But it is twilight, some sort of strange time passing beneath the waterfall, and to return now would be a death sentence for me and possibly for Aidyn as well in his attempts to protect me.

Because he would, indeed, attempt to protect me.

In quite a terrifying manner, perhaps, but it is strangely comforting—the knowledge a stranger would stand between me and a monster he so obviously fears as I do.

Tomorrow, when the sun rises.

"Who are you dancing with?" Again, Blain's voice startles me.

I'd almost entirely forgotten he's standing before me.

Who would want you at the midsummer dance? is what he's asking. I stare at him, suddenly very aware of what he is attempting. I know I am pretty and that my mam and da are wealthy for our little side of Nevyan, but surely he can find a better match. Perhaps it is his father encouraging him, and I cannot so much as begin to comprehend the thoughts that would pass through his mind to come to such a conclusion.

His eyes flicker over my appearance, and I hate that I am still embarrassed by my disgruntled state.

"Not you," I say too bluntly, then grab Niall by the hand. "Niall, you said you were going to make a candlestick holder with the silver that finally arrived. Show me!"

Niall catches on without a single hesitation, and he's hauling me down the path in a moment, before either of us can get a proper look at Blain's expression. The moment we reach the village, he slows and scowls. For no particular reason, I'm glad I bolted the front door to our cottage before I last left it.

"What are they up to?" he asks, more anger in his voice than mine—I am simply relieved to no longer be under their scrutiny. "Wait until your da hears about this. I've seen him punch a man before, did you know? My da will help him too, if you need."

I pause, staring at him. A laugh bubbles out, too loud, and I clap my hand over my mouth. The image of Niall's father, the boxy little blacksmith who raises puppies and couldn't hurt a butterfly, taking a fist to Blain's face is a bit too much for my nerves. Niall's face breaks into a grin, and those nearest us look on in confusion with matching smiles.

"No, don't tell him," I manage, heading for Una's and hauling him along. "I don't know what he wants, and I don't care. May he get eaten by banshees on midsummer."

I catch a gasp from someone listening in but refuse to look up. Niall makes a noise somewhere between a gasp of shock and a laugh.

"Sprites," he mutters, glancing down at me as we walk. "Are you all right?"

What a terror I must look. My knee no longer stings, but still I feel the ghost of Aidyn's hand beneath my arm, keeping me from falling farther. His hair plastered down by the water and the smile on his lips before we swam beneath the waterfall.

The regret in his eyes when he gave me permission to stay away. I need feel no guilt, not even for hurting his shoulder, for it was an accident, and he told me it was small. And in truth, it even looked a small wound. Still, I hurt him and am infinitely sorry for it.

The rest of his injuries, I am certain, are not small. I felt such sadness for him when I spoke to Una. Called him a strange old creature. He is not nearly as ancient as I believed, barely older than me. Somehow, in all this, that stands out as so much worse. To be young and alone and abandoned. I knew it for a moment, but I have Niall and Una and Mam and Da and the rest of my village to gather about me.

You do not . . . have to return.

The twilight is already falling to darkness. I do not know where Blain and his father are spending the night, and I do not care.

In the morning, once the sun has risen enough that time has no chance to play tricks on me, I can return.

In the morning.

I nod. "Yes, I am all right. I . . . have something to tell you both. And I need your help. Let's find Una."

Part 2
Shrines & Notes

14

Dinner Conversation

Spring is already falling headlong into summer; even by the next morning, the day on this side of Faerie is hotter, the world warm by the time I rise and dress. Later, I'm positive it will be blistering. Una wanders after me all morning, both of us in the lightest skirts we have—with Niall utterly shirtless again—as she makes offhanded comments about the hounds and nearly getting myself killed. About how Aidyn himself could have easily gotten me killed in his attempt to impress me—not to mention that he *was* rather impressive, even in my retelling of the tale. About how he obviously wished me away from him, so perhaps I should stay on this side of the border. At least for a day. Perhaps a few.

"It's like being pecked to death by a chicken," I tell Niall as the three of us help Emma clear her garden of the weeds that have invaded with a vengeance now the air is hot and the night damp.

The muddy roots of a weed smack into my back.

"I am the only one of us here *thinking straight!*" Una jabs a finger at me.

Emma pauses in the midst of eating one of her early-ripe tomatoes to stare. Hopefully she hasn't a clue what Una's going on about. More likely she does but already knows I'm moonlight mad, so there's nothing to be said.

"What have you been doing in Faerie?"

Or perhaps there is.

Wincing, I say, "What I've always been doing in Faerie."

"Is that so?"

I glance up from the carrot I'm checking. "Yes?"

Aidyn would be appalled at the lying.

"Try to work on the blushing," Una hisses. I step my bare foot onto hers.

Emma takes a seat on her porch, still working on the tomato. "I haven't seen as much of your usual cooking. You're usually our full-time town baker by this time of the year."

Nosy old lady—faerie knows I would be too.

"Well, I'll bring something over next time this one here doesn't eat it all." I smack Niall on the back of the thigh.

"I need it—I'm a growing man," Niall says, fake affronted, and turns his muscled arms toward us.

I manage, just quite, not to roll my eyes. Emma is regarding me with such an intense gaze that I'm forced to return to my weeding lest my expression give me away. Surely she's realized I went searching for the library, but whether or not I found it . . . Well, hopefully she shouldn't know. She *definitely* shouldn't realize I've made tentative friends with one of the noble folk.

She very well may realize.

As long as I don't bring it up, there's nothing to say. For all I know, she befriended one herself when she was my age. We all know she's *met* a faerie, but whether or not the creature was friendly is for anyone to know.

I'd ask her myself, but then she'll ask after the details of my own escapades to Faerie.

I yank on a particularly crabby patch of invasive grasses trying to grow between her potatoes.

"Will you be dressing for midsummer?" Emma asks.

Why does everyone want to know *so badly?* "Yes. It'll be nice to dance."

"Have you made your dress?"

I feel very certain she's hinting at something but can't grasp on to *what.* "Partially. Una and I are working on hers first. It's a bit more . . . lacy."

Una twirls her work skirts happily.

"Will you make your own mask?"

I glance at her. Finishing off her tomato, she levels an interested stare at me. She's *never* interested in the silly little things the "children" do, and anyone under fifty years is a child to her.

"I'm not sure," I hedge. "I might just take one of the paper ones the children make."

The masks are a midsummer tradition—dance with the fae where they cannot see your face, and never give them your name. Though it has been ages since any true fae visited midsummer, the tradition persists. There will be an overabundance of paper ones—the children of the villages are set to making them—but many make their own by hand. I have in the past. Very likely I would this year as well were I not so otherwise occupied with . . . certain things.

Emma is still staring.

She knows.

Well, I'm not precisely sure that's true. Furthermore, I'm not precisely sure it *matters*. If she does, she will not tell anyone. A part of me wonders if I should sit her down and tell her the details. Perhaps I will—when I have all the details myself. Another part wonders if I could simply take her to Aidyn, or bring Aidyn to *her*, if she would be able to aid him in any manner, and if I could trust her to do so. But if Da and Mam were home, I'm uncertain I'd even be telling them. I can't imagine encouraging him to interact with any other humans from our little hamlet, and so I put the thought from my mind.

Emma's suspicion of me is the single reason I don't leave her garden until near midday. By now, it is entirely too hot to keep digging about under the sunlight, and I'm less suspicious in appearance when I trudge back to my cottage to find a less filthy dress.

Hopefully less suspicious.

I exchange my usual basket for a larger one reserved for harvesting fruit. Two thick grass-twined straps hang off it for slinging it over my shoulders if I wish, but it shouldn't be too heavy. In goes an assortment of food and items that Niall and Una helped me scrounge the day before. I'm unsure how

Aidyn will take to such treatment, so I fold a few extra quilts over the top of the bundle. I can begin with those and reassess.

Una would be appalled to know I'm going back in directly the next day . . . I'll tell her later.

I take the longer walk through the outskirts of the woods to the other side of the village where the hawthorn stands. My heart is doing its very best to throw itself against my ribs until I hear my pulse behind my ears. I pause by the wide trunk, staring into the unoffensive trees.

The moment I hear a monster, I'll run back. It isn't a foolproof plan, barely a plan at all, but it calms me. Besides, it is perfectly bright on the mortal side of the trees, so it shall be in Faerie.

No venturing under strange waterfalls, and pay attention out the window while I am in the library, and all shall be well.

Closing my eyes, I take a long calming breath and jog a few steps with my heavy floppy basket. Honeysuckle and buzzing bees. I crack an eye and find the welcoming flowers with their scent that clings to Aidyn's clothes. Peeking my head around the edge of the vines, I see nothing but the stillness of the library. Eyeballing it, I consider what gruesome sight might await me should I walk to the other side, where the monster was tossed through a tree and where Aidyn went with his sword.

I don't believe I'm brave enough for that.

Creeping into the broad trees, I nearly jump from my skin at a flash of movement on the library roof. Squinting up and ready to flee, I spot a familiar set of boots. Aidyn leans against one of the chimneys, half hidden by the wooden shingles, and gazes down at me. I cannot read his expression from here, and he gives no wave or welcome, but I hardly mind. Only the moon knows what he saw yesterday, and I'm not about to leave because he is staring with some amount of chill.

I have already decided he is not a danger to me, only to other dangerous beings. I have no desire to step into the woods with him again, but I'm uncertain he would even wish to—not after yesterday.

Depositing the basket inside the door, I back up to where I can see him leaning over and gazing at me and hold my hands up.

Where did you climb up?

He points to the corner of the building just around the main door—*not* the back where there may or may not be the body of a hunt hound lying in pieces. Carefully, my fingers still trembling with nerves, I creep around the side of the overgrown door. A metal staircase winds its way to the roof. Apparently, the fae wanted easy access. Testing my weight on the old steps, I find them mostly as solid as those we've taken out the back and step up and up, one foot after the other. Aidyn did not lean over and tell me to leave, so I shouldn't be concerned.

I feel very well as if my stomach may empty itself.

He looks perfectly calm, so there mustn't be any danger—not in the bright of day.

The roof of the library is *mostly* stable, so long as I avoid the gaping hole in the middle where I've so often stood in the sunlight beneath the maple trees. Their leaves are visible below, and I wonder about how the inside of the structure appears so much larger than the outside and how it compares when I can simply look down into it from above.

Aidyn is on the other side of the gap, still leaning against the chimney, cane held loosely in one hand, his other elbow rested on his drawn-up knee, expression partially covered by his hand. His sword lies beside him, sheathed. In the broad daylight, in the dappled heat of the sun, his silver eyes appear sharper, brighter. Perhaps midday sun should make a monster appear less a monster than when they are steeped in shadows.

No such rule in Faerie, it seems.

"Hello," I say, still standing across the ragged shingles and a little too nervous to approach now I'm in his direct line of sight.

For a long few moments, he simply continues to gaze at me, his mouth hidden by his hand, until I wish to walk over and give him a tiny shake.

Edging around until I can lean carefully against the chimney and seat myself beside him, I smooth my skirts over my knees. The cut doesn't hurt much, and what does sting is probably due to a bit too much kneeling in the garden. My arms burn from all the work, and my lower back is happy to be upright again. I glance at his shoulder where I tore the bandage, feeling worse and worse for my ridiculous reaction and the pain I must have caused. There's nothing to see, but I'm going to ask about it.

Once I get him to speak.

He continues to gaze down at me, just his eyes following, the rest of him unmoving.

I am, perhaps, growing accustomed to his odd movements.

Or lack thereof.

Still, the silence is driving me over the trees. "Well, you need to say something profound. I'm just a human, and we're terrible at this."

He raises an eyebrow, which I count as making him move.

"You're the ones with silver tongues, are you not?"

Finally, he drops his hand, and I'm relieved he wasn't hiding some new injury behind his palm. "I've never been too terribly fair at such things."

There. He spoke. Perhaps that shouldn't give me such a sense of victory. But *I* ran home to people who cared about me. He did not. I know little of the fae and how they are put together, but no creature must find that comforting.

"I don't mind. Neither have I. Even for a human, I'm remarkably terrible at it."

He continues to stare down at me. *Am I going to have to pull each sentence from him?*

"Well, I brought more food," I tell him. "Today seems like a lounge-inside-and-cook type of day. It's too hot, anyhow. Maybe while everything's in the oven, we can pick one of those recipes you read the other day to write down. I need to be able to bake the most spectacular pie this midsummer. Last year, a girl from the village over beat me out of it. That's what I got for trying to bake something with *human* ingredients. This time, we're going to find the perfect filling on *this* side of the border."

"Isn't that cheating?"

I shrug. "If anyone else had half a mind to come into the edges of Faerie, they'd do the exact same thing. Besides, half of baking a good pie is finding the best ingredients to use on the inside. All I'm doing is finding the best fruit. It just happens to be over here."

His expression is heading toward somewhere between amused and baffled, and I smile up at him until I can't bear his intense gaze and stare out at the trees instead. He is facing my side of the woods, or at least my side if I get lost just past the honeysuckle. From here, they appear to be Faerie woods forever and forever, disappearing into mist quite quickly. I consider what might happen if I were to walk that way without closing my eyes and consider with more alarm that perhaps that is how humans entranced into these lands fail to return— they simply do not know where the border lies.

But Aidyn has been overlooking the woods in the human direction. It occurs to me he may have been watching for my appearance to ensure I arrived safely should I be foolish enough to return.

Apparently, he picked up on my senseless tendencies rather quickly.

Finally, I decide I may as well ask, considering he's spoken very little to my more cheerful promptings. "Do I wish to know what happened after I left?"

Finally, he stops giving me those intense eyes and gazes out at the woods instead. I'm not sure I prefer it.

"It is dead."

I nod, relieved but nervous on his behalf.

"I think it must have been alone," he says, voice faraway. "If it were not, the others would have come to its aid. I do not know where they ran—the Gentry have not come. I don't suspect there is danger of more, particularly not in the daylight, but let us not test that theory."

"No arguments from me," I say, looping my arms around my knees.

"Have you any idea what brought them here?"

I shake my head. "I looked for faerie circles and didn't find any, and other than that, I'm not sure what would bother them. Perhaps . . . you can help me look?" The idea has me nearly smiling. "You probably know what you're searching for better than I do."

After some silence, he says, "Perhaps."

It is enough. Attempting to imagine him on the human side of the border is useless—I'll have to see for myself.

"You came back," he says with enough calm I believe he must be disguising the emotion behind his voice.

I wring my fingers in my skirts, already sweating even in the thin, loose material. I didn't expect him to be so blunt, so I don't have anything planned to say. Instead, I shrug. "I was worried."

Not a lie. My face heats anyhow, and I hope he doesn't notice.

"I—"

"If you apologize again for frightening me, I'll be very upset. The hound frightened me, you didn't. And I'm so very sorry about your shoulder. I . . . panicked."

He shakes his head, but the accompanying shrug is mostly with the other shoulder. I think of trying to lift away the fabric to see if he's bandaged it. I keep my hands to myself. At his continued silence, I glance at his sword, thinking of picking it up but not entirely certain he wishes me here to begin with, let alone to touch a weapon he went out of the way to hide.

"Does it have a name?" I ask, and he follows my gaze to the scabbard between us.

Taking in a long slow breath, he says, "Yes . . ." What follows is a breath of a word as foreign to me as every other he's ever spoken in his own language. I keep in my mind that it is a short soft sound with a sharp note to the end, but I do not have a prayer of repeating it.

I give him a wry smile. "I wish I could understand any of your words. They leave my mind immediately."

He does not match the smile but nods. "It is a word meaning something like the cold of starlight. There is no direct translation for most of our tongue."

I inspect the sheath about the bright silver blade matching his eyes and wonder if the sound of his name in his own tongue sounds like the wind over the leaves.

"Is it heavy?"

"No," he says, but he does not offer it to me, instead turning his face aside.

I let the topic fade. "So, are we staying up here on the roof all day, or would you like to join me in the kitchen?"

He returns to that funny little stare from the corner of his eye.

"I will be very cross if you make me cook by myself," I say primly, picking leaves off the cotton of my dress. If he's going to act strangely, I may as well say whatever I like. Still, my heart is pattering in much too irritating a fashion—he may still ask me to leave or may simply not join me in the library. I

very much wish him to stay within my sight. We were beginning to speak to each other as friends yesterday, before the
beast appeared between the trees.

I can coax him back. Besides, he could use a good meal
and a friendly face after whatever happened when he took his
blade out back and bade me leave.

Stubbornness is something I got from both parents—he
has been much too kind a faerie to dissuade me now with a
bit of uncanny staring.

He lets out a gentle sigh like the breeze over the leaves, a
near-startling soft noise after all the human voices surrounding me in my mortal life.

Finally, he turns his face fully, which is no longer as strange
as it once was. "Can you make custards?"

As it turns out, what Aidyn can speak about all day without
growing tired is the creatures of his Faerie.

For the first half hour, he's utterly silent while I heave the
basket of ingredients onto the kitchen counter and get to
work on a large batch of soup my mam used to make when
I was sick—before I overtook the kitchen from her. I want it
simmering while I make a custard. I already checked on the
kittens, asleep as usual, and made a point *not* to look out his
window at whatever may lie in the woods.

Aidyn eyes the quilts on top but says nothing, handing me
things or wordlessly peeling the carrots I give him. He barely
looks at the blade as he does so, his eyes focusing on a random

point on the table. I glance at the delicate precision of fingers performing such a simple task as peeling a vegetable and shake my head to myself, chopping herbs too fast.

When the silence has begun to nag at me, I say, "You never answered my question."

He blinks, halfway into the potato I sent his way to peel. "What?"

"I asked you what you could do all day the way I can cook all day and never grow tired of it. You never answered my question."

Because we were interrupted by a monster. No use saying it aloud. I can read in his expression that he's considering it as I am. Each creak in the old library, gust of a breeze from outside, or leaf fluttering silently past the window has me jumping. Certainly he's seen. Still, I haven't yet had the courage to ask him what happened after I left or to take a glance out one of the back windows or doors. At least the broad kitchen window makes it easy to keep track of the light.

Better to start slow.

Aidyn shrugs.

I consider him for a moment. He isn't looking at me. A strong urge to sit near him lodges in my chest. I am quite accustomed to offering physical comfort when Niall or Una or my parents are upset, and Aidyn has taken my hand once or twice and held me under the elbow so I would not fall. Perhaps it should not be as intimidating as it is, the concept of getting within his personal space. But the idea of anything other than touching his hand has the human side of my brain screaming not to. It's not a side I've been listening to much, but I'm uncertain Aidyn would appreciate a human being so bold.

Instead, all I do is what he's done to me: I brush the tips of my fingers over the back of his hand. He glances at it, then at me. I offer a smile and take my hand back before I can feel even more like a fool. My skin feels warmer where it brushed against his.

He puts a slice of peeled uncooked potato into his mouth, the blade of his knife uncomfortably close to his lips. "Your . . . *kittens*, when they grow, will only ever have one litter."

I blink, uncertain what provoked *that* tidbit of information. "Oh?"

"I told you of the Gentry and the Unblessed—of the differences in aging and how many children they bear. Your kittens are much the same as the Gentry. The parents would bear one litter in their lifetimes, so they are quite rare. You should be proud to have saved as many as you did."

My face heats at the genuine honesty in his tone. Pulling out another pot, I get to work on his custard, cracking a few eggs. His long fingers snatch the discarded shells, and he pops them into his mouth without a blink. I stare at him while he crunches. His eyebrows pull together, and he offers me one.

Another laugh bubbles up. "No, thank you."

His frown deepens. "You do not eat them?"

"No, not generally."

Casting me a glance as if *I* am the one missing out on a great delicacy, he tosses another daintily into his mouth.

I give him the rest. "What else can you tell me about the kittens?"

Squinting as if my plans are obvious, he takes the rest of the eggshells and launches into a quiet lengthy description of every little fact it seems he can conjure to mind: that their fur is warm enough they have been known to travel into the far places where nothing but snow exists; that despite the size they will grow to, they are incredibly able to fit through small places, as if they can bend their very bones into any spot they wish; that despite their shyness and elusive nature, they have been observed taking in other small creatures when lost; and many other such things.

Once this topic has been exhausted, he begins on a variety of other animals I've never heard of and have no prayer of keeping in my mind. I stir the custard carefully, avoiding making it foam, keeping the smile off my face at my successful distraction. He is speaking again and seeming to enjoy himself.

Evidently, the answer to my question is *animals*. He enjoys studying, if he knows all these facts, but he must love raising the little creatures themselves, if the lists of detailed stages of their development he rattles off are any indication.

His eyes light up when he speaks about a certain strange creature he claims is no larger than my finger but flies about with a dozen tiny wings like dragonflies. I attempt to commit it to memory, though I do not understand the name he speaks. His long fingers turn the rings on his hand, and he's staring offhandedly at the hot custard I'm stirring over the stove, a slight smile on his face as he speaks. His eyes remain tired, but the enjoyment appears genuine. I may as well be listening to poetry—certainly, I would not sound so elegant if I were trying to describe to him how to perfect a soufflé.

More like a prattling child in comparison. The thought doesn't bother me in the slightest.

"Where are you going?" he asks once I've slid a bowl of soup his way and he's wandering after me with it clutched between his hands like an offering, ignoring the spoon I brought and sipping at the rim.

"Don't touch the custard until it cools."

" 'Tis not what I asked. *Where are you going?*"

"None of your business."

"You're in Faerie—it *is* my business."

"Nope."

"*Flower!*" he calls. At some point, we moved from Bluebell to Flower, which is more amusing than perhaps it should be. He can call me anything he likes. All words sound sweet from his voice.

"I'll be right back. Eat your soup."

Before I disappear into the shelves of books, I glance back and catch him staring, baffled offense in his eyes. Pleased with myself, I head to his room with the quilts. I'll leave most of the other items hidden in the basket, uncertain if too many things at once will leave Aidyn's pride wounded—he seems the type to never take aid until tricked into it . . . or introduced in small doses.

With a few blankets under my arm, I trot up the steps before he can snag my arm.

"What are those?" He is hustling after me the moment I glance back down the railing at him.

Stubborn creature.

Ignoring him, I take the extra quilts into his makeshift

bedroom. I have never been in Faerie in the dead of night—and have less intentions of ever doing so now, with the things I have learned from Aidyn—but for all I know, it may grow bitterly cold. And from the way he keeps the fire lit and his room too hot even in the muggy heat of the day, I'd say he struggles to keep warm in whatever state of recovery he finds himself.

"Quilts," I say in an obvious tone, though I'm certain his question is hinting at *why*.

Let him ask.

Depositing them, I stop myself from straightening out the old ones he found here. Well aware of the long blade that was once hidden beneath them but now sits by his side, I don't want to bring it out into the light, to make him feel as if he must answer questions about it. I do not wish him to become someone else with the reveal of a weapon of war—but perhaps he already has.

Turning, I find him in the doorway, squinting at me, expression unreadable. His eyes dart to the bowl of soup cradled against his chest as if he's just realized I'm making him soup and bringing him blankets, and both those things together are like I'm attempting to care for him.

Which, of course, I *am*, but who's to know how a creature of Faerie will react to such a situation.

His eyes do much more flickering about, such a stony expression in place while the kittens wake and squeak at us in their basket that I have a hard time keeping a straight face.

Finally, he nods his chin to the topmost blanket on the pile and says, "That is beautifully made."

Better reaction than I expected. "Thank you. Well, my mam made it, so I'll tell her you said so."

His shoulder twitches. "Does she know you took them?"

"They're away on business," I say, wandering up to him, enjoying the stark difference between what my heart does when I stand three steps from him and when I stand three steps from Blain. "But she wouldn't mind."

His lips press into a thin line. It's a human expression on an otherworldly face, and that, as well, has me wanting to giggle.

Get ahold of yourself, Niamh.

Finally, he says, "Hmm," and turns on his heel, returning to the kitchen. "Come along, I'll find a book to translate for you. Tomorrow we shall go out onto your side of the trees, yes? We might attempt to find what attracted the beasts."

Grinning, I prance after him, skirts in hand as I take the steps two at a time, trying not to slip on fallen leaves.

Again, trying to imagine him in the human sunlight is impossible. I suppose I shall know tomorrow, when we brave the mortal side of the trees together.

Tomorrow I'll sneak the medicines and salves in when he isn't paying attention.

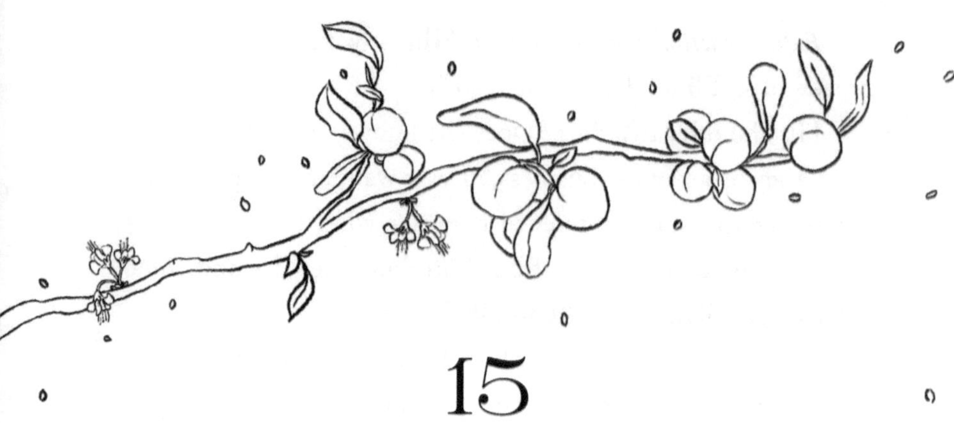

15

Faerie Mushrooms

As I'm tripping over a bramble into Faerie, it occurs to me that I could have brought Una and Niall.

Aidyn will be coming to the human side of the border, and I doubt he means anyone here a stitch of harm—in fact, he seems to be concerned for our well-being. But I'm uncertain that introducing him to the two people I care about more than life is a wise idea. I do not *know* him, after all, and though he seems a gentle creature, the moon knows he isn't. At the very least, he has the ability to be violent.

Perhaps soon. Soon, I will ask the two if they wish to meet this strange creature. Niall might. Una might not.

If I'm the first human Aidyn has met, how would he see the villagers?

I shake my head as I creep in the side door, casting about

glances for anything even resembling a hunt hound. I shouldn't be thinking along those lines. I shouldn't even be *speaking* to one of the *Keepers*, as Aidyn calls himself, even if he proclaims the Gentry to be gentler. I should be leaving an offering and sending a prayer and hoping his silver eyes never fall on me again.

"Aidyn?" I call cheerily, heading for his room.

"Yes?"

I yelp. His voice came from behind, and I turn halfway up the steps, putting my hands on my hips and giving him a glower across the library. He's found himself a nice spot across the upper level, half hidden by the maples, a book in hand. From here, it's impossible to tell the topic.

"What great amusement you must take in startling me," I say.

There's a flash of his teeth, and I'm pleased to see he's returned to smiling at small things.

"You're so easily startled, Flower."

Ignoring both him and the heat rising into my cheeks, I stomp to his room, uncovering the kittens and kneeling to scratch their cheeks and chins. Sleepy as ever, they are gaining weight and opening their eyes. A full jar of honey sits on the shelf where Aidyn keeps his little collection. He must have returned to the hive. Still, I don't glance out the window to see the back of the library.

A soft tap of his cane on the dusty wooden floor alerts me to his approach. "Shall we?"

"Yes," I say, covering the kittens and joining him in the doorway of his room. "Are they all right sleeping so much?"

"Oh, yes. They would be sleeping between their mother's

shoulders for weeks. 'Tis their nature."

I glance at him, thinking of the blood on the leaves near the hawthorn, and decide not to linger on the topic. "Very well, off on our little adventure, then. I'm not certain what you think you're going to find. Un—um, I've been looking for anything faerie that has been disturbed. I haven't so much as found a faerie circle."

If he notices I almost said Una's name, he gives no indication. Instead, there's a sly little upturn of his lips. "You think I cannot find my own kin?"

I open my mouth.

"Come along!"

Snatching my hand, he leads me back for the stairs. I'm forced to trot to keep up with his long strides.

"Do you know I am not a short woman?" I grumble as he takes the same side door out into the woods.

"Hmm?"

"You make me feel short."

Glancing back, his eyes roam up and down every inch of me in much too intense a fashion, eyebrows puckering together as they did when I turned down his eggshells.

"You *are* small."

"I am most certainly not."

"No?"

"You need to meet more humans. I can wrestle a good number of men."

He blinks, aghast, looking me over once more. The flummoxed expression grows wickedly amused. "Could you *wrestle* me?"

Well, someone's in a fine mood this morning. Or pretending to be—pretending is not lying, strictly speaking. "No, I prefer to live."

He leans against the edge of the honeysuckle. I imagine the heavy scent of it seeping into his clothes, clinging to him wherever it goes. I wonder if the others in my village smell honeysuckle when I return to the mortal realm.

"I could let you win."

"That wouldn't be too terrible."

His grin grows.

"But you would have to be very careful. If anything happened to me, I have a best friend who would come in here and enact her revenge."

"Ah, I see. Is she much larger than you, then?"

"No, not at all. It's much worse. She would cry at you."

His shoulders shake with a silent laugh. It's a shame, for I wanted to hear the sound. "I shall be very gentle, then."

The way he speaks has me wondering if he's not teasing as much as I am. Only the knowledge he's still nursing injuries has me thinking there isn't a *large* chance he'll spring upon me.

"Go on," he says, jutting his chin into the maze of flowers. "I do not need to lose myself to leave Faerie. You go ahead. I'll follow once you're safely through."

I blink. Never has it occurred to me how fae come and go from their own realm into Nevyan. Giving him a careful eye, I slip into the vines, glance over my shoulder to see him peering at me, and close my eyes, feeling silly now I'm watched. A few steps has me back in my own world, stumbling against the hawthorn in my hurry to turn and catch him. For whatever reason, I expect him to merely appear from thin air. Instead, he steps from behind a lone pine tree as if he were always hiding there, looking mighty pleased with himself.

"How did you do that?" I ask, keeping on the lookout now we're in the human realm. Most of the villagers don't wander on the edge of Faerie unless there is a specific reason—and there rarely is—but I'm still jumpy. If the kittens were worth swearing Una and Niall to secrecy, Aidyn is every superstition and fear we've ever had brought down upon our heads.

He shrugs. "I wanted to."

"That's all?"

"That's all. Why do you have to close your eyes?"

"We pretty much only make our way into Faerie if we become lost. If you close your eyes and run into the woods, you're pretty much lost immediately. Or I suppose the magic thinks so, at least."

I've no concept if magic indeed works that way, but Aidyn shrugs as if it's a reasonable answer.

He wanders past me. I squint after, wanting to warn him not to venture into sight of the village, and am caught strangely off guard by how he appears on our side of the trees. Remarkably normal if I look at all the little individual parts of him—his stable shoulders, the straight arrow of his back, the gentle fall of hair across his shoulders with the one strand newly braided in a fashion I've never seen, a ring of moss looped into it.

Remarkably like a wolf lurking along the borders of a village if I take him in all at once.

He is getting dangerously near where sunlight makes it

through the thinning trees.

"What are you doing?" I ask, voice rising, hurrying after him.

"Merely looking. You live here?"

He has stopped just inside the shadowy section of the woods, mostly behind a tree, taking a peek at the tips of the newly thatched cottages.

"Yes," I say, pausing just behind his elbow. *What does this place look like to him?*

"It's so small," he murmurs, as if he is not truly speaking to me.

With no concept of what he must be comparing it to, I nod, remembering how I imagined him walking by our cottages in the moonlight, gazing up at my window.

"You should not be seen," I whisper, trying to quell the anxiety within my chest.

"I shall not be," he whispers in return, then gives me a wink. With a frown, he glances back into the open trees as if looking for hounds or his own folk.

They still have not come.

Catching my eye, he offers a smile too tense to be properly happy and turns on his heel at once, tromping off into the woods with his hand back to being wrapped around mine.

Perhaps I did not believe him when he implied he could find a faerie circle, but within fifteen minutes, we've trekked around and through the edges of the human woods, taking very specific twists and turns, Aidyn humming under his breath, until spread before us in a particular little spot of sunlight is a circle of white death's breath mushrooms.

"Huh," I huff, and Aidyn releases my hand, leaning both palms on his cane, looking pleased with himself.

I am going to keep quite a good eye on whether he appears to be ailing, but for now, he appears full of energy. Besides, I'm not sure if yesterday's quiet was his body ailing him or his dark thoughts. If it was the first, I tell myself it was my soup that did the trick.

"Very impressive," I say, watching him step around the edges of the circle, inspecting.

He has kept us very close to the tree line the entire time. Certainly, more circles would be deeper in the woods, in places where humans are less likely to tread on them.

Is he doing so because of my hesitation to venture into the woods with him? It's oddly touching—the idea he would not only notice but care for whatever unsaid fear I maintain. Likewise, he did not suggest using the tree-lined tunnel at the bottom of the library. I stuff my hands into my pockets and watch him step gracefully about the long grasses, the stark human sunlight catching in shimmering dapples across his hair and his cheek whenever he turns his face up to me.

When he steps directly into the space of the circle, I squeak without meaning to, clapping a hand across my mouth.

He blinks at me.

"You know, monsters tend to come out of the woods when those things are disturbed," I remind him.

The grin returns. "I am not human, Flower."

I know that, but hearing him admit it so freely is unsettling.

Kneeling carefully in the center—I do not miss the way his hand touches his leg as he's careful to bend it—he spreads his hand across the moss growing in the center. "This is as much a creation of my own as it is of the little creatures who built it. Nothing I do will cause harm."

Crouching on the outside, arms folded over my knees, chin inside them, I watch him simply gaze about. None of the mushrooms seem disturbed, save one that's been eaten by ants. Not quite an actionable offense. I don't touch the pale white caps—death's breath, as its name suggests, could kill me within a few breaths if eaten. Touching can make one very sick. Not all faerie circles are poisonous, but all are never to be disturbed.

"This one looks fine," I say when Aidyn has not spoken for a long batch of time.

"It is quite fine," he agrees, then suddenly plucks one of the fungi from the circle, twirling it between his fingers. I grimace, wishing he wouldn't touch it. Perhaps his skin is tougher than ours, but the sight of it still has me squirming.

"They say no . . . hounds have passed by," he says, the same hint of amusement in his voice that I have named his strange creatures *hunt hounds* and *kittens*.

"*They?*"

He looks at me evenly, a little as if he wishes something. "You humans see very little."

Nothing is insulting about his tone, but I wrinkle my nose. "I see you just fine."

The wicked grin returns. From between the moss and mushrooms, he withdraws something I cannot make out—not until the form of a tiny creature clinging to his finger catches in my eye. It flickers in and out of sight, nearly invisible, before Aidyn offers it to me. Instinctively, I hold out my hands, and he deposits the creature into my palms. It more resembles a dragonfly but flickers into a little humanoid creature with arms and legs depending on how the sunlight catches it. Sticky limbs cling to me like a lizard climbing a wall.

"They're quite shy," Aidyn muses while the tiny thing peers up at me with two large eyes occupying most of its face. I want to ask if I can keep it but already know the answer. Carefully, he retrieves it from my hands and deposits it within the mushrooms.

"Shall we look for more?" he asks, rising smoothly, the picked mushroom still in his hand.

"Are you feeling well?"

He looks only mildly irritated by the question. "I am perfectly fine to continue walking."

I squint. Taking notice, he squints in return, leaning over the mushrooms until his face is barely a hand from mine. My cheeks turn hot, and I momentarily forget my suspicions. I scramble my thoughts back together enough to put my hands on my hips and maintain my stance.

"I shall continue asking," I declare, then attempt to leave with grace, though I'm nervous of stepping on mushrooms.

"Evidently," he says dryly. I glance back to ensure he is indeed following me away from the deadly circle of fungus.

He's stepping over them with ease, the picked mushroom still clasped between his fingers—

Which he promptly shoves into his mouth.

"*Aidyn!*" I smack it away before he gets it fully past his lips—his hand doesn't move, though the mushroom flies. "What in the stars are you *doing?* Spit it out, even if it just touched your tongue! Hurry!"

The mushroom goes tumbling to the grasses in two pieces. Startled, he nearly drops his cane and stares at me, eyes wide. A moment later, it catches up to me that I made a rather violent gesture at a rather violent creature, and my face grows hot all over again.

Blinking, he glances at the fallen mushroom, then back at me.

His lips twitch, and he giggles.

"*What's funny?*" I don't care how ridiculous I sound, and I consider if I should grab his face and try to wipe at his mouth. "Those are death's breath, you oaf—"

The giggling grows into a full laugh, and he bends and scoops the mushroom back from the grasses. "Are they poison to you?"

I pause, the panic momentarily halted. "Yes?"

Another chuckle has him shaking. It's a rather beautiful noise.

"We can eat them," he says, still grinning. "They're perfectly fine for us."

Somewhere in the back of my mind, I make a note never to eat anything he cooks unless the ingredient list is divulged.

He bites a bit off the top of the cap, and I restrain myself from smacking at him again. My heartbeat is still pounding too fast against my ribs, and I watch suspiciously as he twirls the remaining piece in his hand. After a full fifteen seconds where he hasn't keeled over, I admit that perhaps he is correct: they have no harmful effect on his kind.

Finally, I manage to say, "Oh."

If possible, his grin grows, showing too much teeth. "Though your concern is touching."

Every bit of me is hot, embarrassed. Glowering, I head off into the thinner section of the trees, still giving him a warning glare back. "You almost made my heart give out. Stop shoving things into your mouth. You're like a child."

He pops the rest of the death's breath into his mouth.

Moon help me.

" 'Tis fascinating," he says. "I didn't know humans were susceptible to mushrooms."

I suppose he wouldn't know much about how we work outside of Faerie. I shudder. "Only some of them. We eat plenty different kinds."

"Hmm."

I try to change the subject, still embarrassed I smacked his hand so hard. My fingers sting where I hit the rings decorating his fingers. "How many faerie circles are here?"

He catches up to me with ease but only shrugs a shoulder. "I can figure when they are close. I cannot count them all out without seeing each."

"Well, let's stick to the ones near the meadows and fields, shall we?"

"Yes, yes, no deep woods today."

Once again, I get the distinct sensation he understands what my fears must be, for it is broad daylight and he cannot be worrying about possible hounds—I can't decide if it's irritating or comforting he says nothing of it. Glancing up, I find him still smirking. He wipes a bit of mushroom stuck to the corner of his mouth and grins down at me.

Huffing, I stomp into the trees while his quiet laugh follows.

We make it all the way around the edges of the woods surrounding my little village without spotting a soul. We don't uncover another faerie circle either, but that only means it's less likely that one has been crushed by a careless foot. Aidyn and I exchange a steady stream of unimportant tidbits around whatever we pass in the woods—from me, which mushrooms we humans *can* eat (and are now collected into my pockets), and from Aidyn, which birdcalls belong to which set of feathers and other such things. He glances into the woods often and asks once if we have seen signs of the fae. I assume he means the other Gentry he called for. When he hears my answer, his lips pinch at the corners.

Only once do I find my steps hesitating, when I glance into the trees and see the long-overgrown footpath where I once walked with Blain toward Faerie. Aidyn's presence along and just behind my shoulder presses against my back as if a physical weight. There is nothing to fear in those particular bright trees, not when hounds could appear anywhere, but it slows my hiking nonetheless. Aidyn's finger brushes my shoulder, and I look up to realize I have paused on a patch of mushrooms covered in fallen pine needles, but no ring of them is to be seen.

I move my steps along and find relief in the way he does not push his concern into asking questions.

In the back of my mind, I plan on how to ask after more-sensitive topics surrounding his own presence here but am loath to sadden him when he is so cheerful.

Likewise, every time I ask after his walking so much and if he feels well, he gives no complaints. Eventually, we've wandered so far we're nearing the main road heading through the fields and the woods beyond. A part of me wonders if he warps time about himself as Faerie does, for we cannot have been walking so long.

"Where does this road lead?" he asks, leaning against a tree and pointing down the path. It's mostly unused but worn down now with a constant parade of wagons and feet back and forth putting together the preparations for midsummer.

"To the next few villages, then the larger city. We are the closest to Faerie on this section of the woods."

"Hmm." He squints at the birds above chattering at him, and in the way the sunlight is dappled against the ground and across his hair and shoulders, he hardly seems real. "I don't believe anything far away would've attracted them. We've passed something by." He looks at me thoughtfully, then cocks his head. "Or something is hiding from us."

I shiver and give up on hoping he doesn't notice. "You keep saying ominous things, and I think they're much more disconcerting for me than they are for you."

He shrugs, leaning farther over the tree. "Where Faerie and Nevyan meet are disconcerting places, and your little village is right upon it."

"It is an old village." Leaning forward, I attempt to bend over the tree and glimpse what has caused his fixation but am not tall enough. "Who knows the thoughts of those who first settled here."

He shrugs. "We are drawn to our own lands. It is only natural humans would be as well. They are less capable of resisting."

"Why would a faerie wish to resist?"

He blinks, then glances down. "I don't know. Stranger things have happened."

Perhaps he's seen the stranger things.

"Oh?"

A snap of a horse hoof upon dirt draws my attention. I still can't see over the twisted branch, so I find a foothold and boost myself up while he chuckles.

"Again, I will have you know I'm quite tall for a woman," I hiss, which only has him more amused.

"A human woman, perhaps."

I pause in my struggling, glaring over at him—we're finally face-to-face in height. "Are you tall or short for a faerie?"

He rolls his eyes to the treetops, considering. "Slightly below average . . . for the Gentry, at least."

I stare at him, the horse hooves forgotten.

His eyes flicker around some more. "What is it?"

"You are the tallest man I've ever met."

His lips twitch. I'm uncertain if this pleases him or he thinks me silly. Either way, I like what it does to his eyes.

"What are you looking at over here?" I ask, boosting myself farther up against the rough bark. Leaning over the nearest branch, I realize what's caught his attention: two people with a wagon, and their horse has apparently thrown a shoe. Whatever they are hauling is covered with cloth blankets, but it's likely something for midsummer. I consider leaving Aidyn here and going to offer help when I recognize the voice bouncing off the forest trunks.

". . . to the village . . ."

"What is it?" Aidyn asks, plucking a leaf.

My smile must have dropped. "Nothing. Let's avoid them."

His eyebrow rises.

"You said we must have missed something. Should we circle back?"

"Why?"

"Why what?"

"Why are we avoiding them?"

"Why shouldn't we?"

A smirk joins the eyebrow.

"You're not supposed to be seen here, you know. And I *very* much shouldn't be seen with *you*."

He readjusts against the tree, getting comfortable, one foot resting over the other. "Your pretty smile fell."

Stars is he blunt. My cheeks grow hot anyway. "What?"

"You no longer look happy."

I sigh, closing my eyes and resting my cheek against the rough bark I'm clinging to, acutely aware of his closeness. If I open my eyes, he will be so very near. "I do not like those people. Must we linger?"

"We mustn't," he supplies. "I wonder why you don't like them."

Of course he does. And I wonder why he's dwelling alone in a library. "Sometimes people are not so terribly honorable."

He cocks his head. Hooves on dirt, snorting horses, and the faint voices of the two men still drift through the trees. Aidyn leans over to look again, glances at me, and hoists himself off the tree, heading along the side of the road in their direction.

"Aidyn!" I hiss, dropping down and scrambling after him. "What are you doing?"

He turns momentarily to give me his finger over his lips. Taking one of the mushroom stems from my pocket, I throw it at him. It bounces off his lower back, and he only smirks at me.

Emma would be appalled by my behavior.

Then again, so would Mam and Da.

So would Una and Niall.

Well, a little late for that consideration.

"Aidyn," I hiss again, worried to make my voice more than a whisper. We're quite close now, and I slow so my footsteps aren't heard among the normal noises of the woods. Aidyn keeps his pace without making a sound. *How unfair.*

Eventually, I catch up to where he's peeking through the trees. I'm torn between wanting to give his arm a smack and being too nervous of touching him so casually. Instead, I stand by his shoulder and glower at the side of his face, ignoring the path he's observing so intensely. His eyes catch mine from the side, and he appears to be withholding a smile as he ignores me, returning to the men along the path. He can be as endearing as he likes—I'm not smiling in return.

When I'm ignored for more than a minute, I sigh and chance a glance to the side. A small mossy embankment stretches down to the dirt path, thick trees on all sides hiding us. Still, I'm worried about my dress—a pale red, but a different-enough hue from the trees they'll probably see me if they look this direction.

Mister Haskel and Blain are bent near the horse, discussing, not giving us any notice. When I turn back, Aidyn is watching me. I glower as best I can, which isn't much.

What? I mouth.

Leaning over, he whispers against my ear, "Which one makes you unhappy?"

Startled by the sudden closeness, I lose most of the glare. His face is a finger's breadth from mine, so close that when I attempt to glare his way, I see the filaments of silver in his large eyes, the little flecks of green I never noticed.

"None of your business," I whisper in return, though I don't think it carries much weight. If I lean forward a little, I would brush against his cheek—

You can show me Faerie? I didn't think any girls weren't frightened of Faerie. I wince, but the voice those words belong to is down on the path, not near me.

I glance down, stepping away from him. This is the human side of the woods, but I am not entirely comforted. Aidyn cocks his head again, like a cat, curious. Peering back over the nearest branch at the path, he gets a little glimmer of something in his gaze I don't particularly think is a good thing. My throat is tight, but I open my mouth to tell him off, considering just walking away to see if he'll follow—

He flicks his fingers in a little circular gesture, and I've no idea what he's trying to tell me until a yelp sounds from the path. I start, pushing a branch away so I can better see.

Blain spits out a leaf, swearing and coughing while his father looks on in confusion.

Aidyn's magic.

Aidyn, who is currently smirking in my direction.

Stop it, I mouth, but I don't believe I look angry.

It's . . . a *little* funny.

There's a sudden swoosh of wind through the leaves, and hundreds of fallen oak leaves smack into Blain. Mister Haskel yelps and takes cover behind the cart while Blain stumbles onto the ground, sitting up too fast when the leaves die a moment later, covering him. Scrambling to his feet, he keeps on swearing and glancing into the woods.

Aidyn giggles softly. I try to glare, but I'm forcing down both a smile and pure mortification.

"Are you satisfied? Can we leave now?" I whisper, gathering my courage and tugging on his sleeve.

Blain is looking our way. I go utterly still, gazing back, uncertain if he sees us or merely senses our presence.

Would I sense a faerie right beside me in the woods? I hope so, but I'm uncertain. His eyes narrow.

Aidyn huffs, and a twig smacks straight into the side of Blain's cheek. A little scream yelps out of him, and I clap my hand over my mouth, face burning but the built-up nerves bursting forth all at once. Aidyn's soft chuckle turns into a breathless belly laugh, and he shrinks down behind the tree before he can shake the branches.

"You idiot," I hiss, but he's successfully made me laugh, my face hot but a strange satisfaction sitting in my chest nonetheless.

Aidyn is *entirely* too pleased with himself.

Footsteps crunch our way, and all amusement dies in my chest. I open my mouth to say something about running, but Aidyn puts his finger back to his lips, suddenly weaving his arm about my shoulders, pressing me against the tree, half hiding me with his body. My cheek brushes his arm, and I don't have time to be properly embarrassed before Blain stops right before us. I put my hand over my mouth, hiding my breath. Aidyn is utterly still before me, head cocked, inspecting the other human.

The second human he's ever met, I suppose?

Frowning, Blain turns in a full circle, looking directly at us. Light dapples past the trees, and the grasses sway. Aidyn's fingers tug absently on the hem of my sleeve, fingertips brushing the underside of my arm, leaving tingling traces along my skin. His hair slips from his shoulder in a slight breeze, further covering me. Some part of me understands there is magic wrapped around him, and therefore around me pressed so close, but I find it strangely comforting. My heart is beating loud enough I'm sure both men must hear, but Blain only scowls in deeper confusion.

Turning, he says to his father, "Damn things shouldn't have so much magic with so few manners. I hardly pity them. Must've been something small. It ran from me."

I frown. I suppose he wouldn't like the fae either, having been scared out of his wits when I was. His reasoning doesn't seem as deserving. My hand aches—pressed against the warmth of Aidyn's back, it feels securely hidden.

Wiping remnants of leaves from his shirt, Blain stomps back down the incline.

Aidyn snorts.

Blain spins on the spot, but more leaves rush upon them, spooking the horses and sending them scattering down the path, both men chasing after and yelling. Once they're so far down the road there's no chance of hearing, the built-up laugh chokes out of me. Aidyn joins in, and with his back pressed against me, I feel him shake happily. My cheeks go back to red-hot; they're going to be fixed that way, it seems.

"You're a *fool*," I hiss again. "How did you *do that*?"

"Hmm?" He seats himself on the roots of the tree, chin in hand, twirling his cane.

"How did you make him not see us?"

He shrugs a shoulder. "It is an innate magic. Not difficult."

It hits me how there is a large chance of many fae being in these woods at any time—we would not know it. I've always known they are sneaky and able to hide from human eyes, but I did not realize it was quite so *strong*. Any faerie could be right across from me, and I would be none the wiser.

"Have I frightened you?" he asks, suddenly sober.

It's such a strangely sweet concern that my lips pull back up. "No, I'm just . . . I don't know what I am. Not frightened though."

He brightens once more, leaning against the roots. I expect him to ask me again why I did not like Blain and Mister Haskel, but he leaves it at that, warmth in his smile.

My own stretches in return.

"You're correct, 'tis turning late. I know a much easier way back—" He glances at the path, and his words die, expression freezing.

My stomach drops, though following his gaze, I see nothing among the trees. "What is it?"

My mind jumps at once to hunt hounds, but Aidyn rises with care, stepping from the trees and making his way down the mossy slope, crossing the path. I scramble after him, skirts in hands—casting glances down each side of the road lest someone be venturing toward us—and press through the thicket on the other side of the path, hoping not to lose him. He doesn't venture far and kneels among some grasses sprouting amid the thorns. I suspect he's found another faerie circle but see nothing.

"What is it?" I ask again, voice a mere whisper.

He glances back at me, expression twisted in such a way I halt my approach. Carefully, he takes my hand and draws me down beside him, guiding my fingers to touch something soft against the earth. I half attempt to pull back, but there is nothing to see, and he has not caused me harm a single time, even if my hand is still aching from my own memories. The woods have gone utterly quiet, not a birdsong or warble to be heard, not even my own breath.

My fingers brush something strangely like fur, and I see the monster lying among the grasses.

16

At Sunset

Crying out, I yank my hand away, tumbling against Aidyn's side. His arm is woven about my shoulders, so I do not fall far.

His whispered voice tells me, " 'Tis all right, you will not be harmed."

A moment later, I recognize that it is not the shadow of the hunt hounds and their dark green fur, their massive teeth.

It is, though, a great monster in its own right.

And appears not to be breathing.

Now my hand is gone from it, the body flickers in and out of sight, as if the grasses blowing gently about it could obscure it completely. Aidyn's free hand remains on the creature's massive paw—it is the size of a donkey from head to short tail, perhaps larger. I've heard of wildcats in other kingdoms but did not suspect them here on the edge of Faerie. Looking closer, I find it maintains that uncanny nature Aidyn is steeped in, as if the library and the feeling that washes over me each time I lose myself across the border has spread this far.

A wildcat.

Blue fur stretches across it, with very similar markings to—

"Is it . . . ?"

"Yes," he murmurs, and over my calming heart, I can now hear the weight to his voice. His arm remains across my shoulders, long hand wrapped gently about my arm. The rings rub through my thin sleeve. "I've seen only one grown before. They are much rarer than your hounds."

The kittens' mother, I think, then ask the question aloud.

"Very likely, yes. The markings match. Here, see?" His finger wavers above its blotchy fur. The pattern of the darker blue does indeed appear familiar. Aidyn's eyes likely see it better.

Even with the magic obscuring the body, I catch bloody marks along its torso. My stomach turns up, and suddenly my throat is tight, eyes burning. My hand flies to cover my mouth. *A dead faerie.* If the hounds and their wild, intelligent eyes are anything to go by, these are just as wise . . . and it is dead.

"Appalling, isn't it?" Aidyn murmurs, his tone much worse than his words. He sounds very well as if he may cry himself as his hold about me tightens. Again, he murmurs, "They are quite rare."

A moment later, my mind catches up to the implications. "Does that mean there are more hounds here since the other day?"

Uncertain, he shakes his head. "It may be from before. I . . . do not rightly know. I shall call for the others again—I do not know why they have not arrived. This may be beyond your little village if these two beasts have taken to fighting."

Finally, I tear my eyes away to glance up at him. "It is not because of one of us?"

Another head shake. "We are often at war with one another—we Gentry and Unblessed. If this is not an isolated incident, as I assumed, it may simply be our war spilling out the edges of Faerie."

At my stricken expression, he says, "It has been happening since before you humans walked your own kingdoms. Generally, it is not something for you to worry over."

I turn back to the wildcat, unable to keep my eyes off it. Aidyn's hand drifts over the bloody sections of fur, his brow furrowing further. Mumbling something I do not catch, he glances back at the path with a long sigh.

"Is someone coming?"

"No, I—" He draws in another breath, and I wonder if there is something he very much does not wish to tell me. "Some of these wounds are too small to be from a hound's teeth or claws."

Squinting at the body, I cannot discern what he is speaking of, not even when I touch the paw and find it a little clearer to my eyes.

"Are there other creatures that would fight them?"

"I—" Another long pause, as if he is picking out his words around a lie. "Possibly. But I am not positive what could have made all these wounds."

Not positive does not mean he doesn't have *theories*. He winces when he catches my eye, but this could be from anything, from simply the animal lying here.

"What is it, Aidyn?" I ask, voice so soft I barely hear myself.

Another small shake of the head. "I am not certain." Again, he says, "I will call for the others. This is more serious than the last incident—they should come."

I'm not sure I believe him—many things can be covered up with *I don't know* as the answer, but if I asked and he is still not telling me, I doubt that pushing will do me any good.

"Hopefully they'll come," I agree.

"No more hunting for faerie circles," Aidyn murmurs. "Not that you would, but again, do not come into Faerie too early or late. I do not believe they are here, but it would be better to be safe."

"What about the other day?" I finally ask. "It went from day to night so fast—"

"Some little pockets are like that, where time does not move the same. We will not go back under the waterfall. I had only been there once, for a few moments. Even we are susceptible to it all." He lets out a long sigh. "Let us return, I want you home early—"

"What do we do with it?" I ask, brushing my fingers against the same paw. Soft fur tickles my palm. "We must leave it here?"

It does not feel as if such a creature should be left for the earth to rot, though it may have been here weeks. The body is not decayed, but I know little of the workings of Faerie.

Aidyn's expression twists, and he avoids my eyes. "The others will take it away. You can cause it no change, and I cannot do anything in my . . . state. They are quite heavier than they appear."

Even now, kneeling beside me, some of his weight is pressed against me, taking the pressure from his injured side. I can imagine it took him a great deal to admit such a thing, so I do not push. Alone, I do not believe I could do anything to the creature, not even bury it. And as much as I wish to, I cannot bring Una and Niall here to aid us—I am doubly glad I did not bring them along or mention the last encounter with the creatures. I'm uncertain I should be witnessing this at all.

"Come, let us go," he says again, rising slowly, his hand on the nearest trunk. "Nothing else will find it."

His fingertips linger on my shoulder until I, too, climb unsteadily to my feet, eyes burning. "Who are the others you speak of?"

He opens his mouth and closes it, and for a moment I believe he will not answer, but haltingly, he tells me, "Others in my bloodline. Our kin are the closest settlement to your kingdom in this side of Faerie. We protect your borders."

"So, they are your family?"

His mouth twitches, but his expression remains stone, impassive. "To varying degrees."

And they did not come to his call? Perhaps I should let the topic drop, for he is still regarding the wildcat with grief in his eyes and I am still attempting not to cry, but this is the closest I've gotten to any true answers and can't allow the opportunity to slip through my fingers. "Why are you hiding from them?"

Finally, he blinks, eyes snapping to mine. Momentarily,

I think I've angered him, but all I can read is exhaustion. "Because I must."

He will not answer. I nod. Tempted as I am to step forward and hug him, I keep myself still. His arm was around my shoulders only moments ago, but it seems almost an accident—I fell back against him, and he steadied me. It seems so much different than looking directly up into the face of a creature much more frightening than I am and putting my arms about him as if he is Una or Niall or Mam or Da. Instead, I touch my fingertips to the backs of his knuckles where his fingers are gripped too tight around his walking stick. He does not attempt so much as a smile, and I wonder again if they cannot lie with their expressions as they cannot with their words.

"Come," he whispers finally, "I know an easier way back."

Taking my hand, he leads us carefully around the body already fading into the grasses the moment I step away.

"Close your eyes," he instructs, and I realize he means to take us into Faerie on this side of the woods. I did not realize such a thing was possible, but I do as instructed, tightening my hand around his, realizing how foolish I am being, heading into the woods with this man, my eyes closed. Threads of panic weave up my chest.

Perhaps I should not—

Honeysuckle wraps about us, the air turning to the familiar thick perfume I've come to associate with the library. Cracking my eyes, I find us alongside the wall of flowering vines, a ways down from the place where I usually step out, and my fear eases.

"How did you . . . ?" I trail off, still feeling strange to speak.

"I can go anywhere I wish here. Your rules do not apply."

Numbly, I nod, and without his prompting, I take up my skirts and trot back into the side door of the old building, up the stairs and into his room. Sitting beside the basket, I take the kittens out carefully, setting them in my lap and looking over each one. I expect to find nothing but wish to reassure myself that they are well and still growing. Crawling out onto my knees, they blink and mewl and gnaw a little painfully on my fingers. The faint blue markings are more pronounced, matching the body of the creature we found in the woods.

We found your parent, I think, throat burning, and kiss the nearest fuzzy head. Hopefully the Gentry will take it away. I hate the thought of it sitting there until the ground reclaims it. Tears are finally hot on my cheeks. Eventually, Aidyn's cane taps along the floor, and he appears in the doorway, watching sidelong, his shoulders not as straight as before.

"You walked too much," I tell him bluntly, voice rough.

Sighing, he seats himself on the pillows closest to the edge of his bed, his boots nearly touching my shoes. His sword he sets carefully along the floorboards beside the old mattress. I try not to look at it, more for concern of his discomfort than my own.

"Yes, ma'am," he says dryly.

His hand scoops up the nearest kitten, and he inspects it carefully, combing the short tufts of fur. I wonder how he tells the other fae they are needed here without revealing himself. I tuck the thought away as something to ask later, when I have better earned his trust. Besides, if he and these monsters are anything to go by, I'm not particularly comforted by the idea of running into another of his kin, Gentry or not. The more I spend my days here, learning the way Aidyn carries himself and the tidbits about his life he offers like crumbs, the more I come to understand that perhaps he is one of the kinder, gentler of the fair folk I could've happened across. If his kin are coming here to fight monsters he evidently fears, I should very much *not* like to meet them.

Glancing up, he reaches forward with a sudden movement and brushes at one leftover tear with his fingertip. No surprise is in his expression, but I cannot help but wonder if fae can cry at all.

"You are thinking," he whispers, and I hope he does not wish me away. The sadness has not left his posture, his expression.

I take a long breath, grasping for a different topic, something lighter. "How do you go anywhere you please in Faerie?"

He nods slightly. "Partially, it is our innate magic. We are born of these lands and have ways about it none can replicate. At least, we may go anywhere within our own realms."

"Realms?"

"Faerie is not all one place. The borderlands you think of are only part of them. I was born of these places, so I may go anywhere within them. But there are many realms and courts within Faerie—I cannot travel within them so easily. They are too far for you ever to become lost in."

I blink, slowly grasping at his words. Faerie is much larger than I ever imagined if these lands are no more than the edges. "So, you can go anywhere in your own realm simply because you are born to it?"

"Yes. But it is easier if we are given something of these lands by someone who dwells here."

Taking the honey off the shelf—it is getting low—I dig some out for the kittens and their tiny teeth. "How do you mean?"

"If we are gifted something, given with a full heart and not under any threat or duress—a pure gift, essentially—and that thing is of our lands, we may hold on to it, and wherever we wish to go, we are much more likely to find ourselves there, in much a shorter time than one would walk."

"Just . . . any gift?"

He nods. "Any gift. Usually it is something easy to carry with us." Working the smallest silver ring off his pinky, he hands it to me. "If I gave this to you and told you to keep it, or only told you to keep it for, say, a day or three, any time you held it or wore it, you'd very likely be able to walk anywhere you wish in Faerie and arrive there within a matter of minutes or hours. The purer the intentions of the gift, the better the magic works. It is not a thing easily given."

I cradle the tiny ring in my palm, feeling the cold weight of it, wondering at its value. "Is this the gift someone gave you?"

"Not that one, no," he says, retrieving it. "It was a gift, but not for that purpose." He twirls a ring on his forefinger, braided silver, with the smallest glimmer I think it perhaps may be a diamond or similar stone. "This was. It has not failed me."

"Who gave it to you?"

Expression twitching, he gazes at it for so long I believe he may not answer. "My father."

"It is very beautiful."

"Yes." Working it off, he hands it to me. I expect something strange when it touches my fingertips—some magic, like when Aidyn's hand brushes mine or when he sends the wind rising. But it seems no more than a ring, the glimmer of a stone I saw a strange blue-streaked gem no larger than a seed.

"Very beautiful," I mumble again. "Does he look like you?"

"Hmm?"

"Your father . . . Do you look like him?"

At his quiet, I glance up.

He is considering. "Perhaps a bit in the face. We have the same eyes. We are not alike—not truly." A moment passes. "I am told I have my mother's countenance, but I did not know her. Do you look like your parents?"

I wish to ask after the last comment, about his mam, but he is evidently changing the subject. "A little bit of each, yes. My da is a big man; he's the only reason I'm as tall as I am—"

His lip quirks.

"And I *am* tall, thank you very much. I would be taller, but moonlight."

"Moonlight?" he echoes.

"Children born in moonlight are said to be smaller. Didn't you know?"

His expression is impassive, thoughtful. "Hmm, no. No wonder you talk to fae. Moonlight."

I shrug. "You have better berries on your side of the border."

Another crack of a smile, but it hasn't touched his eyes

through the whole conversation. I am trying not to consider the wildcat but have the kittens clutched close to my chest, as many of them as I can gather into my arms, the rest in my lap, one still in Aidyn's palms. I wish to take them home with me, but I know they are safer here even if food were not an issue.

My eyes slip to the sword resting on the floorboards, harmless.

"Do I need to stay away again?" I ask, wondering if my voice sounds as sad to him as it does to me.

He shifts, no longer looking at me, just at the remnants of embers in the hearth. Between the muggy outside weather and the heat in here, I'm sweating. He appears unbothered.

"It would be wise. In fact, stay in your home after evening if you can. Or near it. The others may come into your human side of the woods, if they come at all. You should keep yourself scarce."

My heart leaps a bit as I consider the rest of the villagers. "Should I warn anyone—"

"No, that would be dangerous for you. I only mean that . . . you have spent much time with me, and if you were to come into direct contact with another of the Gentry, they may be able to tell. The rest of your humans are just . . . human."

"Tell how?"

He taps his nose, finally glancing my way.

Ah, yes, he can smell *me.* The concept that I may very well *smell* if I've been around Aidyn leaves me considerably unnerved, and I avoid his eyes, petting the kitten gnawing on my thumb.

"How long?"

He shrugs, but his expression does not match the casual gesture. "Another few days. A week if you're wise. Forever if you're wiser."

"Do you wish me to be wiser?" I ask, heart pushing against my ribs.

"Not at all."

I manage not to laugh. "Good. Do you still have plenty of that soup I made you?"

He rolls his eyes. "Yes. And I am perfectly capable of cooking for myself, yes."

I have no doubts, but I dislike the idea of leaving him here, alone and with the kittens to care for. I would hate if he were hurting, especially after all the walking. I glance at the salves I left in little jars on his window where he stores all his other knickknacks I've yet to gather the courage to snoop in. He hasn't appeared to notice their sudden appearance.

"Are you . . . going to ask them for help?" I mumble, uncertain I should be pushing the topic.

"Yes, 'tis why I will call for them."

"I meant for you."

He glances upward without raising his face, regarding me coolly, and I remember how dangerous he first appeared, standing below me on the bookshelf.

Bluntly, he says, "No."

I nod, face burning, not knowing what to say or how to say it. I wish to offer him better help but cannot drag a creature of these other lands into being better cared for. "Are you angry I asked?"

He lets out a long breath through the nose, and his eyes

soften. "No. You are quite a pushy little human."

I press my lips together—he is not incorrect, after all.

" 'Tis rather nice."

Watching the kittens as I set them back into their basket, most already back asleep, I ignore my burning cheeks and ears. "You're certain you'll be all right?"

"Yes, quite," he murmurs, then straightens as if shaking himself, putting a dramatic hand to his forehead. "How didst I ever survive before you snooped about where you weren't supposed to?"

I snort, then laugh a little more, not feeling it truly. My nerves must be weakening. It was already late in the afternoon when we returned here—no doubt I am pushing my luck in remaining.

As if knowing my thoughts, Aidyn rises, more unsteadily this time around; I don't mention it, having already pushed the boundaries more than once today. "I shall walk you back."

Perhaps I should not allow him, perhaps I should suggest he stay here and ensure the kittens are fed, but I already feel jittery, unsafe on this side of Faerie. I am jealous of his presence already, knowing I will not see him for more than a few days.

What have you gotten yourself into, Niamh?

Besides, he already walked the entire woods about our little village—if he is well enough for such a thing, certainly he must be well enough for the tiny stroll to where I can lose myself back into the mortal trees.

Aidyn's hand stays on my elbow as he takes me to the edge of the honeysuckle, our bodies long shadows in the gray light.

Pausing at the heavy flowers, he smiles slightly.

"Go along," he says. "I'd like to watch you disappear. It is too late to be out. Run all the way home at once."

I open my mouth to make a suggestion I know is unwise—that he might, if he wishes, stay in my own cottage for a while, if he'd like to feel more at home. We could even bring the kittens. He does not wish to be found by the other fae, for whatever reason, so it would be quite unlucky they would check for him in my own cottage—this abandoned library is much more conspicuous a hiding place. I don't believe he'd say yes. More so, I don't believe it would be wise. Not a single person would be able to suspect he was there.

Not unless it were midsummer night.

It is not so far away now.

I keep such thoughts to myself. Instead, I tell him, "I may stay home the week, as you suggested; my friends will be quite cross with me for spending all my days here. Everyone is making preparations for midsummer, and I need to pull my weight." I shrug. "A little."

It is difficult to see his expression in the lack of light, but he nods. "I will manage to survive a short while without you bringing me blankets, I'm certain."

His tone has me grinning. I don't mention the little jars I left in his room with scraps of paper under them, scrawled with notes for which is good for what injury. He didn't even notice them when I put the honey jar back. After all this time, I've still no concept of how he injured himself. He is careful with his clothing and never mentions specifics, no matter how the conversation drifts toward it, skirting the edge of something too serious for him to broach. Today was close, but not by much. Therefore, I left a bit of everything I have, made from varieties of herbs and such gathered throughout the seasons, little things for infections, cuts, burns, and fevers. All work well enough for us humans, so perhaps one of them will do his a little bit of good.

Hopefully by the time I return he'll have had time not to be annoyed with my concern. Besides, I'm not sure he's actually irritated or just acting the part.

'Tis rather nice.

"Pet the kittens for me," I tell him, bouncing on my toes. His hand is still on my elbow and slides down almost to my palm. Warmth from his fingers sits against my wrist. I learned my lesson and have begun to wear cooler dresses on my trips into Faerie, so my arms are bare. His head cocks slowly, and he looks down at me with the same strange faraway expression he had when I brought those quilts—though I noticed the next day that they were laid out atop the other covers, no longer folded up where I'd left them.

His lips part as if he intends upon speaking . . . or something else. All at once, I am tense, aware of the trees around us and the falling darkness. Aidyn's eyes fall to my hand, which has twisted into an unintentional fist. He takes a soft step back, and I nearly follow him forward, immediately regretting the distance. Bringing my hand up, he kisses my knuckles, barely the softest touch against the still-not-quite-healed skin. I stare at him, wide-eyed, not breathing, before he nudges his chin toward the woods.

Softly, he says, "The sun is going down."

I nod, still not breathing, and turn to take off into the honeysuckle before I can think twice, closing my eyes until I know I am home.

Slowing to a stop in the mortal trees, I turn to inspect the hawthorn, the easy stillness and breeze of the human lands. Touching my fingers to my hand where his lips brushed, I force myself to breathe properly and start up walking again. Just because I am not in Faerie does not mean the hounds may not appear.

Run all the way home at once.

There will be fae swarming these trees soon, if his warnings are any indication. I cannot help but consider how close the wildcat is, less than an hour if I ran as quickly as I could down the path through the village and toward the human kingdoms, its body sitting in the moonlight to be collected by others of its kin.

I shake the thought away.

If Aidyn kissed me on the edge of the Faerie woods, I do not think I would mind so much.

With such a strange thought swirling in my mind, I run home to my empty cottage.

17

A Wail in the Dark

For two whole days, I do nothing much but watch the trees.

I assist Una with her dress and my own, attempt to assist with the last of the houses needing rethatching, and throw myself into the midsummer preparations as the heat of the day grows overbearing.

And throughout it all, I keep my eyes on the edge of the woods.

I do not dare travel the path where the wildcat was found—only the moon knows if I'd be able to find it on my own, its body hidden from my gaze as it was—though I consider often what other possible wounds the creature could've had. I trust Aidyn's judgment in thinking it was not just a battle with the hounds, but I cannot imagine many things could fell such a large and magical creature. Still, I dare not return. Aidyn's warning sits in my ears: not to go where other fae might find me. I have spent too long with him to be passed over as a regular human.

The thought is unsettling.

And strangely touching.

Aidyn has spoken to no other save for me, does not wish to be seen by the other humans here, and is hiding from his own kin—though I do not know why, it seems a strange solitary honor that he enjoys my company.

I enjoy his.

"You're blushing at a blade of grass," Una says, deadpan.

I blink, looking up from my staring where we're both seated under the shade of the edge of the woods, methodically bundling thatching. The trees are cooler here, and we're both in shorter light dresses, no shoes or stockings, our legs on the dirt to soak up the cold. Close by, the men keep up with the midsummer preparations, some of the other girls from the nearer villages helping as well. Some are giving Niall appreciative glances, but Una doesn't seem to notice, nor does Niall appear to care.

I manage not to smirk.

We are quite close to Faerie here, but it is broad daylight; besides, it isn't so obvious I'm staring into the trees if we're right inside them.

"No, I'm not."

Una's eyebrows go up.

"Well, it's not about the *grass*."

She smacks my shoulder with her bundle of thatching

before tossing it with the others. Nearby, a dozen children are working on their own bundles, albeit with more time wasted. They're not close enough to overhear our words.

"I'm worried about Aidyn," I say, pulling the rough twine too tight against my finger. "I wouldn't like being in that library all by myself for so many days."

She smirks, much too knowing, but glances at the woods herself, gnawing her lip. As before, I confided in both her and Niall the warning Aidyn gave to stay indoors. I don't wish them in even a bit of harm's way—most of the villagers are prone to staying inside all night as it is. One becomes used to such things, dwelling in a village on the edge of Faerie, with midsummer approaching upon it all.

I rub my hand. The twisted little finger doesn't appreciate the manual work, but it'll stop being sore after another day or two. Besides, it's good to keep that hand as strong as I can manage.

"I haven't heard anything at night," Una whispers, glancing at Niall as much as I'd be glancing at Aidyn. I should tease about *her* blushing as much as she teases me.

This doesn't feel the same.

"He didn't necessarily say we'd hear anything, just wanted us to be cautious."

I say it with a shrug, but my unconvinced expression matches hers. Something feels different from when Aidyn first asked the other Gentry for aid, either because I saw the wildcat or because I never could bring myself to check for the body of the hunt hound Aidyn dispatched of that wasn't supposed to still be haunting the borders of Faerie.

Or perhaps because the first time they did not come at all.

"Perhaps they've already come and gone," I add. "Aidyn only said a few days again, just told me if I was wiser I'd stay away a week."

"Ah, so he knows you're a moonlight-born fool as well," Una says dryly, still not appearing soothed.

"Yes, he's quite aware. I think he is too, he's just too elegant for it to be noticeable."

"Elegant," she says, as if I've been caught saying something embarrassing.

"Yes," I say primly. "*Elegant.*"

"I can't believe you brought him into Nevyan and didn't tell us. We were in the same lands."

"Do you *want* to see him?" I ask, knowing the answer but wishing to watch her squirm.

Squirm she does, readjusting on the grass. "I've never seen a true faerie, and you keep *speaking* about him."

She has me trapped in that respect. Smirking at the bundle of thatching, I toss it onto the pile. "I thought about it as I was going to get him, then couldn't decide if I should. We're not supposed to be doing this, anyhow."

"No, you're not," she agrees, unbothered. "Niall is becoming quite concerned."

"Oh, simply Niall?"

"Of course. You've said he isn't dangerous." She gazes at me intently.

I roll my eyes. "Very subtle. I didn't say he's not *dangerous.* I said I don't believe he's malicious."

These days I've remained home, I haven't rid myself of the

memory of his expression when he looked down upon the creature we found in the grass. Struggle as I may, I cannot imagine myself under any threat from a faerie who mourns over things most humans would not. Dangerous creature or not, he is all gentleness and concern, even the few times he's been angry and close to truly frightening.

"And the other fae might be," Una mumbles, and we both glance again into the trees.

"Might be, yes."

Half a dozen girls from the next village hustle our way—after baking for years of midsummer festivals, I'm rather well-known in the two other little hamlets. Three baskets I brought for lunch, and the girls are starting to get the hint.

Una and I exchange glances, the topic dropped.

"Help yourselves," I say, pushing the basket farther toward them with my foot while they settle and pull out breads and jams and help with the thatching. They all echo hellos and continue with whatever boy they're talking about and who he'll pick to dance with. Una looks to be trying not to laugh and stuffs half an oil-cooked cake into her mouth, sugar on her lips. Boys are always the main topic of conversation around midsummer, and this year is no exception. I'm positive that were I to eavesdrop on the cluster of men and boys where Niall is working, I'd hear nothing but talk of girls.

Glancing again at the sun-bright trees and picking up my own pastry, I squint into the depths where it finally grows dimmer. Aidyn could be out there watching over us. I'd be none the wiser, and it almost seems like something he would attempt, especially with the way I found him perched on the roof the other day, guarding the trees for me to appear. Hopefully he is resting well after our little adventure through the woods—

One of the girls pokes me in the leg.

"Hmm?" I ask, blinking at the group looking at me expectantly.

Una snorts. I restrain myself from pushing the cake into her face.

"Have you seen him lately?" the girl asks. She's no more than a few years my younger, with pretty brown hair. I remember her vaguely from the previous festivals.

"Who?"

"Blain. Everyone says you two courted?"

Una stops chewing. I'd be more irritated if I weren't concerned I'll have to wrestle her down. Gossip travels, but I suppose these girls haven't heard the specifics, or they wouldn't be asking.

"Oh," I say a little lamely. "No, I haven't."

She seems disappointed.

Another says, "He's handsome."

The group dissolves back into chatter as another says, "He and his father just returned from the city. I heard they're growing their business larger than they can account for here—"

I manage not to roll my eyes as I return to my thatching. They can have him; perhaps he's entirely less a coward when he's in the city. He and his family work in trading all sorts of items, and I've no idea what's earning them so much they need to expand. I couldn't care less. All the gold in the world wouldn't have me touching him even one more time.

Niall heads our way, eyeballing the basket of breads and pastries, and I relax. His presence, and Una's furious expression as she chews her cake with some amount of violence, are steady, comforting.

"Don't return yet," she whispers to me softly, and I don't need ask what topic she's switched to while the girls ignore us.

"I'm not, not for a while," I remind her . . . and myself. "The others have likely already come and gone. I'm merely staying extra days as a precaution, because *Aidyn* is worried."

"Yes, already come and gone," Una mumbles, picking at the tangled twine.

"Come and gone," I say again.

Come and gone.

Aidyn folds his hands across his chest, gazing at the bright midday tree canopy. I cannot directly picture his face. How we got here, on the human side of the woods, I'm uncertain, and I don't much care. Rolling onto my stomach, I prop my chin on my hands and gaze at him. His hair falls in gentle locks around his shoulders, and it is high time I put my fingers in it as I've been considering. As I imagined, it's soft as water.

"Are you enjoying yourself?" he murmurs, sounding half asleep, but his lips are tugging into a smile.

I braid the tiny section of hair at the end. "Whatever do you mean?"

"Hmm."

I toss the lock of hair over his face, and he blows it out of the way, cracking one eye to look at me. "Why do you like to come here, Niamh?"

He knows my name.

No, that's not right. I never told him.

"What?"

He rolls over, turning me onto my back, face inches from mine. His breath smells strange, not sweet as the few times he's leaned close. It smells human.

"You know what happens to silly girls who like to venture into Faerie. Their clothes are torn as their minds. Maybe I should protect you—"

His dark hair is replaced by a familiar shade, his shoulders different, no more cool rings where his fingers are too tight around the back of my neck.

"Maybe you should show me the way into Faerie," Blain tells me, and my scarred hand connects with his face in a sharp streak of pain.

A soft wolf wail has my eyes opening. My shoulder hurts from staying huddled on one side of Una's little bed, a piece of straw poking me through the cloth of the mattress. My hand is tucked under my leg, fallen asleep under the weight of my body and aching. I ease it out and wiggle my fingers.

If I would just return home and sleep in my own bed, there'd be much more room. Silly woman.

I'm glad I didn't.

Rolling onto my other side, I rest my cheek against Una's back, her warmth comforting. I haven't dreamt of such things in a long time. Feeling particularly miserable and wishing the remnants would leave my mind, I wiggle out from under the covers. Spring has fully turned to the beginnings of summer, and in nothing but a nightgown and bare feet, I'm not cold. In fact, I was too hot beneath the covers.

Creeping into the kitchen, I dig out yesterday's milk and warm some over the remnants of the stove. Another wolf howls, low and lonely. They are quite a different noise from the sounds of the hunt hounds, and I find them wonderfully comforting in comparison. Leaning over the sink, I glance out the window, at the moon well on its way to becoming full, listening to the crickets. I wonder if Aidyn is a restless sleeper or if, like Una, he lies dead as a log through the whole night without so much as a rolling over.

Do fae sleep the same as humans? All bundled up under blankets, curled into a ball when they're cold or stretched out when they're too warm. He certainly has enough blankets, and even more now that I've taken to bringing him supplies. It is a silly thing to picture. I imagine I shall never know, for Faerie is not a safe place at night—less safe than usual, at least. Still, I can daydream.

Another wolf howls, slightly closer this time. We have all our livestock up for the night, and the guard dogs are curled on their porches, so I'm not worried about our cow or chickens. It's been ages since a wolf or fox managed to do any damage here—

A scream rends the air, a low otherworldly wail of a sound. Jumping, I knock the steaming milk from the stove, sending the pot and its contents scattering across the floorboards. Cold crawls across my bones and under my skin, and I stay ducked behind the counter, unable to move myself into standing.

It lasts too long for any living creature, then warbles into silence before starting again. Closer. Much closer. I force myself to look out the window, over the edge of the counter, to grab the shutters and turn them closed before I can glimpse whatever cursed thing I may see.

"Niamh!" cries Olivia, flinging herself toward me, grasping my shoulders, trembling beneath her nightgown. I grab her hands where they dig into my muscles. "What is it?"

"I don't know—"

Another scream, and she's hugging me closer before fleeing to her children in their beds. Dogs bark outside, and Una's father, Andrew, joins me at the counter, rubbing sleep from his face. "Did you see anything?"

"No, I was too frightened to look."

His hand goes to my shoulder as everything falls quiet. Outside, a few panicked voices are yelling in confusion, then fall quiet as well, the whole village listening. Una scurries in beside us, her mother and sister just behind, the five of us huddling in the kitchen, not knowing what to do. Andrew's hand drifts carefully to the massive hunting bow always sitting by the door, but he doesn't pick it up.

I glance at Una, and her eyes meet mine.

Fae, she mouths. We've both been thinking it, and I wonder exactly what could've caused such a noise. It is not the hunt hounds—I'd know the sharp pierce of their bark anywhere. Perhaps it is the wildcat, another of its kind, but Aidyn spoke of how he'd only ever seen one other grown, they are so rare.

What else could it be?

"I've never heard anything of the like, Andrew," Olivia whispers.

"I know," he murmurs in return.

Una's hand slips into mine.

For a long few minutes, there is no other sound. Even the dogs have gone quiet.

The next wail is so close I imagine it beside the border of the village.

Swearing, Andrew runs to bolt the other windows—no, he's throwing them open to look outside. Una does the same with the one over the counter, and I cannot help but join her, crawling atop it to press my face to the glass over her head. I don't dare open the window itself, just gaze past the misted warped glass. Shadows flicker through the trees along the border of the woods. Squinting, I imagine seeing the top of the library over the hill and through the forest.

The Keepers?

I find my feet back on the cool planks of wood, flying to Una's room and the steps to the attic along the wall. Pressing up into the cold loft, hearing Una calling after me, I push through the slats of thatched roof and into the night air, crawling up the rough grass to crouch beside the warm bricks of the chimney.

More shadows flicker along the edges of the trees, *not* the shapes of the hounds . . . not yet.

The dogs have taken up their barking, voices growing in panic.

A fourth piercing wail begins, like a warble of an other-worldly bird, a trill fleeing across the landscape—three rapid barks that barely have time to send fear piercing my heart before they are cut sharp and dead. My breath hitches. Still, I do not see much more than shadows. A few houses down, someone else has gotten the same idea and crawled onto the roof, drawn by the sounds, unable to resist. Even more are opening their windows, throwing salt onto the sills and before their doors, wards against monsters. I search for Niall in the few people who've stepped outside and cannot find him, relieved he is inside and safer.

My fingers grow chill against the hot stones, my breath fogging before my lips. It is not so cold, not in the dead of summer.

A hound stands in the grass between the trees and the edge of the village.

It is not looking at me, it cannot be, but I am frozen, unmoving.

Aidyn was right.

They did not leave—they have been haunting these trees all this time.

What if . . .

He didn't realize there are more . . . *What if he stepped outside the library at night?*

He could be gone, and I wouldn't realize.

A sudden urge to flee through the trees to find him claws up my chest, and I wrap my arms about the heat of the chimney, clutching myself in place. Tears burn my eyes. The hunt hound stands rigid among the grasses.

Something shimmers, as if the air is a rippling heat wave in the hottest of midday sun. A figure is there beside it at once, a billow of long dark hair and thin limbs, graceful in the hips and shoulders. In the slivers of moonlight suddenly flooded by clouds, a female face is visible, long and large eyed and nothing resembling human. Her hand is raised, the other cradling a long blade. Her mouth is open. The word is the long hollow wail of sound.

The beast's vivid barks clash against it, its feet spread, the two glaring each other down. The air ripples. It pounces. A rough cry jumps from my throat, my hand clapping over my mouth a moment later. Its feet come to a skidding stop mere inches from the woman, a posturing dog against a much wilder wolf. Its shadow mingles with hers in closeness.

She does not step back, her hand unmoving, lips spread wide in sound. Another figure behind the hound, and it is ribbons of black shadow among the grass.

More hounds and more figures in the trees.

The male joins the woman, his hand passing against her shoulder. Her wail does not cease. Her face turns toward the village and slightly up. From here, I see her pale lips open in their strange song, her bright eyes directly on mine. Hand slipping from my mouth, I am unable to blink.

She cocks her head at me, and the ear-shattering song ceases.

A few rustles in the edges of the trees, and they are gone.

I rest my cheek against the hot bricks, smearing the tears on my cheeks, breath coming in gasps.

Gone.

18

Shrines and Notes

Gashes line the fields and grasses, great claw marks of upturned earth. Small shrines are being assembled around the borders of the trees. I move past them numbly, toeing at the loose soil. It took each and every one of us hours to venture into the sunlight, and I doubt anyone else received much sleep. The rest of my night was plagued with more dreams, Blain and Aidyn and different faces of everyone I've ever known morphing together. I rub my eyes.

Niall wanders near me, watching the closest shrine. We've never had much to offer Faerie. A small village hasn't much to give, not to such creatures, but we try. We saw the fae drag the monsters away with our own eyes, and suddenly the trees are lined with more offerings than I've seen in my lifetime—dozens of little piles of stones with scraps of food and pretty cloth. A piece of Una's lace sits beneath the stone of the nearest one.

Last night shall be added to the hundreds of stories that exist in our minds, yet another time a faerie monster came from the trees and was chased away by the other creatures of its kind. Of all our myths and tales that have become one being, one mist lying over this valley—last night will, for a time, be a full tale for parents to tell their children when warning not to tread too close to the woods of Faerie.

If I could force my legs to move correctly, I'd run straight into the trees.

It hardly seems right to stand here, let alone go farther. A few of the men are taking their farming hoes and shovels and filling in the gashes of claws. There's no reason to, not in the fields where we don't plant and rarely walk, but they wish for no reminders.

The woman's song still sits in my ears.

"Una says you saw something," Niall murmurs, leaning his arm against mine. "I looked out the window but only heard the screaming. Barking." He shivers.

"I climbed onto the roof," I mumble, voice faraway, as if words are incorrect in the quiet morning. "I shouldn't have. I couldn't help it. There was a hound. They cut it to pieces."

"Aidyn?" he asks, and the sound of his name spoken aloud startles me.

"No, most definitely not. A woman. There was a man with her . . . It didn't look like him at all."

"You could tell in the dark? From that distance?"

I consider Aidyn's shape, the slope of his shoulders, the

slight sideways tilt of him as he finds different ways to lean casually against his walking stick, the way he carries himself. "I could tell."

He nods, slumping, perhaps relieved the creature I have been spending so much time with is not one of the wild monsters who appeared among the trees to drag the hounds away.

"The woman," I say, aware of Emma glancing our way. I'm surprised she joined in on the efforts along the forest edge, but perhaps she is the most likely to do so, as I am. "I feel I have seen her before, but I could not have; Aidyn is the first I ever met."

Niall glances sidelong at me, a frown bunching his eyebrows. "Perhaps it is only the magic? Who knows how the fair folk affect us. Only Emma's ever met one. Well, other than . . ."

He shrugs, and I'm glad he doesn't mention it. Though my friendship with Aidyn is perhaps the only reason the Keepers appeared to chase the hounds away, I don't believe anyone should know.

I'm almost surprised they came from their borders to help—I wonder how Aidyn has taken this development. Given how irritated he appeared when they did not first arrive at his calling, I'd suspect him to be pleased. But I am not entirely certain how he should feel when calling to his kin for help while hiding away in an old library at the same time. Not that I suspect he'll explain it to me, but I'm more determined to ask.

Emma is looking at me still.

Even *her* interactions with fae are funny little things of myth in our village, more a gossip that started long before I was born than any fact or significant situation.

She does not appear terribly flustered by last night's circumstances.

When Niall returns to his parents, I wander Emma's way. She hasn't taken her eyes off me and raises her brows when I get close. I don't very much know what to do, but my own grandparents are no longer with us—I hug her about the shoulders. She is shorter than me by some means, so it's an easy task. She huffs a little, amused, patting my back.

"What did you see?" she asks.

Releasing her, I repeat in low tones what I told both Niall and Una. We are a ways from the group, but I wish for my words to be private. Una's eyes stay fixed on me across the grass, but I don't expect her to stop staring for a long while.

"Did you see anything?" I ask.

"No," she muses, pulling her shawl about her even though it's warm. "I know better than to be climbing onto roofs."

She gives me a dry gaze, and I look at my feet, toes bare and dirty.

"Are you going back in?"

For no good reason, the question startles me. "Probably. Not today."

I don't bother asking why she wishes to know—it's rather obvious I've been wandering the woods and will be more obvious to her I've been going into Faerie. I glance at the path through the village, toward the opposite end where, if I were to walk far enough, I would pass where the wildcat lay. Perhaps now it is gone. I hope they've done for it whatever fae do for one another in death.

"Hmm," she says in a way the reminds me all at once of Aidyn.

I follow her gaze through the village, where I was just looking, at a few wagons making their way down the path. Midsummer approaches. I'd forgotten. Blain may very well be with them, since he and his relatives appear to be nosing their way back into my life.

You know what happens to silly girls who like to venture into Faerie. Their clothes are torn as their minds. Maybe I should protect you—

My nose wrinkles before I can wipe the look off my face. Emma is staring at me deadpan.

I attempt a smile.

"Would you like me to cane him?"

I blink. "*Excuse me?*"

"Your old admirer," she says mildly, giving her walking stick a shake. "Would you like me to hit him? No one will mind. I'm old."

I imagine Aidyn giving the man a good smack with his own cane, and I don't know which scenario I'm laughing at as I giggle nervously into my palm.

"No . . . Well, I mean . . ." Covering my face with my hands, I tell her, "Don't suggest such things to me."

Emma shrugs, unbothered.

"I should check on my animals," I mumble, not daring to look at her scheming expression. "I'll be by later and cook you something?"

"If you'd like. Bring your other two ducklings. They're not subtle, you know."

Whipping my head around to glance at Una and Niall, then back at Emma, I manage to close my mouth. "They're trying."

"Not well. Lucky for them, everyone in this village is a little too innocent for their own good."

I snort too loudly, glancing at the shrines with their ribbon scraps and eggshells and little bits of honey combs in jars. It seems incorrect to laugh so close to the border with all that happened the night before and all that is being set up in honor this morning.

"Did it frighten you?" I ask softly, not knowing why. Perhaps because she is the only other who has seen the same side of the woods, and I both feel as if I should not be so afraid as I am and much more terrified as to never step foot within the trees again, neither alone nor with another.

I have been in the woods with another many times now.

Emma regards me for a long moment. "Yes."

I nod and give her another quick hug before heading for home, arms around myself, glancing at the woods and feeling chill in the hot summer day. Niall trots after me, apparently not intent on letting me leave his sight, hands in his pockets but bumping his arm into mine. I'm glad for it.

It's cooler than yesterday, but we are not fully into the warmest weeks of the year. Some spring chill still makes itself known every now and again. The air smells of rain.

Aidyn, what are you doing right now?

Perhaps he needs help.

Probably not from me, but I am the only one he appears to have.

Unless he left with his kin.

He would not, would he? Not without saying goodbye.

Niall heads to the chicken coop, casting me a glance as if he's worried I'll run off into the woods. I match his mild glare, then make a face, disappearing into the barn as dramatically as I can while he scoffs.

Our cow is lowing to be milked, and I trot in, mumbling, "Sorry, sorry," under my breath.

She's giving too much milk for me to drink—I'll bring some to Emma, or to Olivia, since I've been eating her food more than I should. She seems happy to let me in on their stores as long as I'm the one cooking for hours. We are both content with the arrangement. Still, I should bring her today's eggs as well, and whatever our garden spits up this early in the year.

It is not as if I will be bringing them to Aidyn today. My stomach twists.

I am doing as he instructed; there is no reason to feel guilty. It has not been a week yet, after all. If I hadn't had such a fright, I might've ignored him and been sprinting off into the trees by now, eyes closed, a basket of food in hand.

"Coward," I mutter, glaring at the frothing milk as it splashes into the pail. It isn't a very convincing argument, even to myself. "He told you to stay a week, and he knows better. There's no reason not to do as he says—"

"You still talk to yourself, I see."

I jump up, knocking the stool aside. Primrose moos and bumps her flank into me in complaint.

For some naive reason, I didn't expect him to ever come

into my barn, at least not when I was alone, and *he* is alone atop that. He can see my hand fully, and I consider what he would do if I simply punched him. The thought startles me—I am not the violent type. Perhaps if I return to Emma's, he'll follow. I don't believe for a moment she was kidding about taking her cane to him.

If Niall saw him come in, he'd be at him with a rake by now.

"What do you want?"

Blain leans against the door of the barn, looking into the stalls in mild curiosity. "Heard you all had a visit from the fair folk last night."

I stare, lips pressed together.

"Did you see any of them?"

Slowly, I right the stool and sit myself down, back to him, heart pounding, continuing with the milking as if he isn't here. I feel his presence still as I move the bucket aside and lead Primrose out the back for grazing. The chickens are clucking to one another, but Niall won't hear unless I raise my voice. I consider it, just to see him come flying in a rage.

Sunlight hits the back side of the barn, hot and stabilizing, but I feel Blain lingering, wandering behind. I tell myself to ignore him, *keep* ignoring him—after all, he isn't going to *do* anything to me. He did nothing to me the first time, just ran for his own life without a thought.

A speck of blue catches my eye, and I stare at the flower left on the fence railing against the back wall of the barn. Continuing with my ignoring, I step over and pick it up. A clump of bluebells, heavy with dew, likes of which I've never seen in this area, stem wedged between a crack in the wood so it won't blow off, a little piece of paper folded about.

Tomorrow. There's a tiny doodle of a flower beside the elegant handwriting.

Momentarily, I forget who's standing behind me and smile.

He is all right, and he says I am safe to return tomorrow? I cannot figure any other meaning. My lips curl at the edges. Again, I feel like crying, but there is no reason this time, so I bite my lip until the discomfort distracts me. Off into the trees, a soft breeze blows, and I squint into the shade of the leaves, wondering—

"I didn't think those grew around here."

I start at his closeness, finally turning to glare properly. Blain steps back, but his eyes are on the flower with its little note. Heat bubbles up my chest at how he dares step anywhere near, dares interrupt something precious left for me. My own internal violence surprises me, how protective of Aidyn I feel in the face of this man. I needn't be, I know. I have the distinct impression Aidyn could snap him like a twig beneath his boot. The realization is rather consoling. Drawing myself up, I walk past with all the calm I can muster, back through the barn. It's time to check on Niall with the chickens.

"You know you're going to have to speak to me sometime." I hear his boots on the hay as he trots after me. He is not as graceful as Aidyn. Neither am I, but I don't think nearly as high of myself as Blain does.

I continue *not* speaking.

His hand circles my arm. "Come along now, Ve—"

Yanking away without success, I give his boot the best

stomp I can, regretting my bare feet and no sharp heel with which to crack on his toes. He huffs but appears more flustered than in pain. If he touches me anywhere near my face, I shall bite his—

Wind crashes all the barn doors shut at once. Outside, Primrose lets off a startled groan, and the chickens in their attached pen squawk and flurry their feathers.

Blain drops me, something knowing flicking into his expression. "What—"

The doors burst back open, and I yelp more in surprise than fear, getting a sudden suspicion and sitting hard on the hay-strewn floor without bothering to run for it. Wind howls through the center of the barn, a vicious spring gale if not for the heat of it, leaves and twigs and small wild apples from the edges of the trees blowing straight through the tunnel of the barn. Debris pelts Blain, streaks of red appearing with sudden scratches from twigs and thorns. A few stray leaves find their way to me, but from the floor I am safe. Blain stumbles to the ground but doesn't seem to realize it's safe here before he's scrambling to his feet and running for it, cursing the fae and whatever brownie he thinks has taken a disliking to him.

No brownie could do such a thing.

But he does not live on the edge of Faerie, so how should he know?

As if a living thing, the wind follows him out, flattening a few of Mam's poor carrot tops—they'll be fine in a few hours.

The howling continues for a full ten seconds more, ridding the barn of any remnants of his presence, before drifting to a gentle breeze. Hands over my ears, hair disheveled, I glance into the trees.

Carefully, I call, "Aidyn?"

A gentle chuckle carries its way along the breeze to me, and for a moment I catch what might be a rustle in the undergrowth before it, along with the wind, disappears entirely.

I drop my hands between my knees, gazing at the mess he's made of the barn and garden and at our very flustered cow standing just outside, gazing my way. If she weren't half so lazy, she'd have run for it. If the chickens weren't still in their pens, I'd be hunting down hens for the rest of the day. A handful of leaves fall from my hair. Niall comes scrambling around the corner, scraps of hay flying, eyes wide. No one from the village seems to have noticed, but I see Una running up the path, skirts bouncing.

I put my face in my hands and laugh so hard I might cry.

19

Uncertain Paths

"Are you certain?" Una asks, following me only to the edge of the trees and no farther, pausing at the hem of shrines about the trees. "Because it hasn't been a week."

I hold up the scrap of paper once more, as if she hasn't seen it a dozen times by now.

"Yes, but . . ."

She trails off, and I wait for a further argument. It appears she cannot come up with one. Instead, she gnaws her lips, glancing into the trees.

"I keep wondering if it will happen again, Ve."

Her tone takes me off guard. "What will?"

She twines her pinkie into my weak one, holding up my hand.

"Oh," I say, not knowing what else to add. "I worry about it sometimes too."

She lets out a long breath, keeping my hand in hers. "I realize you would be going into Faerie even if he were not there. It's part of us all, I suppose, even if I would *never* step foot in there"—she sends me a look—"but it bothers me that any little thing could make them angry. We still don't know what caused it the first time. It could've been anyone walking in the woods that disturbed them—"

"Is this what you do all day while I'm not here? Worry through different ways I could die?" I ask, trying to tease.

"Oh, no, I do it when you're here too." She waves her hand. "You're a wild thing, and atop it, you're your parents' only daughter—it is my role to be the mindful one."

I press my lips together, trying not to laugh.

"It's not as if Niall's going to be," she adds. "He thinks you're mad too, he's just not going to threaten you about it like I will." She smiles, pleased with herself, though it's shaky.

I take her about the shoulders and hug her, comforted as I often am by the knowledge I have her to return to on the human side of the trees. Niall and Una, her parents and sister. I have one foot in each side of the world, but never both feet in Faerie.

"I'm being as careful as I can be," I assure her.

She rolls her eyes, grimacing, but appears to be hiding a laugh.

"And I don't know if you've told him about us, but if you have, tell Aidyn that your friends are properly appreciative of his antics."

I give her an even stare. Once she recovered from the idea that Aidyn can both use magic in a tangible way and that he's evidently used it on this side of the Faerie border, she joined Niall in the laugher he'd started up as soon as the wind died. It seems a silly thing for them to think better of the strange creature with such an act, but Una only argued a *little* when I told her I'll be returning this morning. From her, after all the drama of the other night, it's practically an endorsement.

Niall simply did not stop grinning.

I wonder if these strange dreams of mine will cease as soon as I see Aidyn again.

"I'll tell him," I say, heading into the trees.

"Wait, you haven't told him our names, have you?" Her voice rises a few octaves.

"Una, I haven't told him *my* name," I toss over my shoulder dryly, hoping suddenly that he isn't lurking behind one of the trees. Foolishly, I feel as if I'd be able to tell.

"Niamh?"

I glance back.

"Careful."

I nod. One day, I'll get Aidyn and my two favorite people into the same room together—and laugh at the ensuing interaction.

When I've closed my eyes and smell honeysuckle, I linger in the flowers, peeking out at the library, half expecting something to have changed in the time I was away. Nothing is different, the trees as still as ever in the high sunlight, undisturbed leaves about the old building. Aidyn left the little note—which is safely tucked in my pocket and will be in my desk drawer later—so I slept better knowing he was well enough to walk to my barn.

"Aidyn," I call once inside. "How did you know which house was mine?"

The same dry chuckle drifts through the old stacks of books, seeming to disturb the dust motes. Nudging open his door, I peek inside and find him lying along his pillows and blankets by the fire—between the hot summer air and the burning hearth, I'm glad I wore a dress with no sleeves and thin fabric—one leg lounging off, whittling at a rough patch of his cane with a small blade.

"Did you make it?" I ask.

Giving the walking stick a twirl between his fingers, he considers. "No . . . I found it here. It needed a few bits of fixing, but it was quite close to perfect for me. I sometimes wonder who left it."

His head cocks, eyes refocusing on me. Such a sight of him gives me pause. I am unaccustomed to seeing him reclined in such a way, and I cannot tell if he is feeling poorly and needs to relax or better and therefore less embarrassed by lounging.

"I saw you go to the barn," he says lazily. "I was worried of speaking to you on your side of the border, what with all the others making their shrines. I simply wanted to leave a note."

"I received it, yes," I say, setting down my basket containing, among other things, many of the eggshells I collected from the shrines once the others left. "Though if you were going for subtle, you didn't manage it."

He spreads his lips in a too-wide wolfish smile. I shake

my head, but after the other night, I'm ridiculously happy to see him.

He is alive.

He is well.

He is smiling at me.

Ignoring the butterflies in my chest, I plop myself down onto the side of his bed, close enough I imagine I feel his warmth. Tucking my arms around my knees, I gaze down at him.

"Not subtle at all," I prompt. "How did you know you weren't going to hit me with all that debris?"

He appears nearly offended. "I was not going to make it so strong if you did not sit down. I am better with my magic than that. It was not difficult. I would not have wounded you."

He appears so purely and greatly injured by the insinuation that I can't help a smile. Holding out my hand, I show him the tiniest of nicks a branch of oak leaf gave me. Gasping, he grasps my wrist in both hands, pulling me forward to kiss off the unoffensive little mark. It's so fully unexpected that I don't have time to appreciate it before he's throwing one arm dramatically over his eyes, still not releasing my wrist.

"I have been shamed," he mumbles, his lips fighting to keep their fake sadness as I double over in laughter. Apparently, sarcasm isn't much of a lie—unless he believes it enough.

"You're ridiculous," I tell him, though I do not attempt to extract my arm. Despite his dramatics, his thumb is drifting soft circles over the scratch, which didn't even sting past the second I received it.

"You shouldn't have done that, you know," I tell him, unable to put conviction into the words. "I've no idea how the other villagers would react. We love the fae, but we fear them in equal measure. One solitary faerie wandering around and causing strange things with the wind might make them less friendly toward you."

"Oh?" he asks, not sounding surprised at all.

"We are taught to fear the more solitary fae, unless they are the friendly ones we know." I suppose we fear the Unblessed, by Aidyn's explanation.

"No fae are friendly," he says, his arm still over his eyes. "Some are simply uninterested in harm."

"How comfortingly morbid. So, you're not friendly?"

Finally, he lets his arm drop from his face, but still he does not release my wrist. If I wriggled my hand a bit, I could probably move it into his. More likely, he would pull away. I don't wish to take the chance, not with my heart beating out of my chest at the prolonged contact.

"Are you frightened of me?" he whispers. His eyes are burning sharp, his hair slightly disheveled, as if he walked back through the woods he caused a storm in. He smells of honeysuckle and something else I cannot articulate—clean skin and magic.

"I should be," I tell him.

In the dim warmth of the library, on the side of Faerie I should not be in, does it not feel forbidden? Perhaps, but only in the strangest sweet way.

"But are you?"

I take a long breath, considering, feeling the warm air fill my lungs and empty. "No, I don't believe so."

His lips quirk at the corners. "So, a little bit, then?"

I can't help another giggle, nervous and strangely happy. "Most likely."

The smile stretches. "How was your time away from Faerie?"

"Very nice," I say, a little bit of a lie. *He did not answer my question.* "Everyone is preparing for midsummer, it's so hot I'm constantly sweating, and it's not as if I run out of people to cook for. But it smells like rain is coming. I love the rain."

He continues to gaze at me, unblinking.

"Please blink," I tell him, and he does so several times more than necessary, chuckling. "Thank you."

"Humans are funny things," he muses, blinking thrice more. "I see you had an unwelcome visitor."

I wrinkle my nose. There was no use hoping he wouldn't speak of it, but I'm about as ready to avoid the details as he is to avoid the details of his other *kin* should I ask.

Could he name those who came to our lands? The memory of the woman and her wild voice sticks in my mind, and I open my mouth to ask after her instead but steady myself. We are unweaving the threads about each other bit by bit—no use in tugging them apart too violently.

"He lives the village over. We are not friends. I do not know why he keeps bothering me. He is not harmful, just vastly irritating."

There is a narrowness to his eyes. "He keeps visiting though you do not wish him?"

There is something dangerous in that expression, but I answer, "Yes. Why?"

He turns my hand over in both of his absently, as if he does not realize he is doing so. His fingers run through and among mine, and I force myself not to grasp at them in return, worried of stopping his little exploration. His skin is much paler than mine—we are a tiny village and rather light in appearance in general, tending to be born with straw hair and light eyes that squint at the sun. But we spend our days working outside, and my hands are tan against his; they're oddly soft in appearance atop it all. Still, I feel the rough patches from that pretty blade he has somewhere near him though I cannot see its presence.

" 'Tis a great dishonor to force oneself upon another who does not wish them in their presence." His voice has become so low and soft I barely catch it over the dim crackle of the fire. It's such an unfamiliar tone in him that I wish I knew better how to respond.

"Yes," I say, adjusting my skirts as if his hands are not around mine. "Well, we humans aren't too great at sticking to *honor* at all times. I think it doesn't really enter our thoughts unless it's brought to our attention."

Carefully, I dare to close my thumb over his. He glances down. As I feared, he carefully folds his hands away but gazes at me with no less enjoyment in his wild eyes.

"Who is bringing it to your attention?"

I blink. "What?"

"You have much honor. Is someone bringing it to your attention?"

From him, with the strange weight behind his words, I feel as if he has given me a great compliment. "Thank you. No, I don't think anyone is bringing it to my attention, not right now. You seem quite honorable yourself."

The amusement falls from his eyes. He glances away, at the fire. "It is kind you think that."

The sudden change hurts. I know very little of how to comfort him, not enough about him to offer any soothing words, and not enough friendship or bravery to reach for his hand again. "Why shouldn't I?"

"You? No reason, no reason," he murmurs, rolling a bit more onto his side, decidedly *closer* to me. Retrieving the poker, he nudges a few of the coals.

"Were you all right?" I ask softly. "The other night. It was . . . frightening."

"Yes, I heard," he mumbles. "I was not harmed."

Not exactly an answer to the question. Leaning over, I get directly into his line of sight. "Are you all right?"

Some of the humor finally returns. "Are all humans so pushy?"

"Yes."

Rolling his eyes, he finally sits, and I'm back to tilting my head to look at him. My face is right beneath his chin. I scoot back so I can see him better, and he leans his arms against his legs, evening the height.

"Shall we go to the kitchen?" he asks, and I raise my eyebrows at the avoidance.

Getting to my feet and checking in on the sleeping kittens, I say, "Yes, but shall you answer my question?"

"I will be all right," he tells me, which is the same response as last time.

It is coming upon a few weeks, and I do not appreciate how he still appears to ail, but I feel as unequal to the task of bringing it up as ever.

"You did not go outside at night, did you now?"

I open my mouth to say, *No, I did not,* but he is sitting *right there*, staring directly into my eyes. He may be forced by the creation of his soul not to lie, but I am forced by the intensity of his gaze. Besides, I would not like it much if *he* lied to me should he be human.

Sighing, I admit, "I climbed onto the roof."

"Oh?"

He is following me down the steps, so I no longer see his expression, disappointed or otherwise.

"I couldn't quite convince myself not to," I say. "I could hear them and see their shapes in the trees, and I felt as if I must look. I did not go outside though. I climbed through the attic door. The hounds did not see me."

That last part I am less certain of, but the woman dispatched of the one I thought for a moment might have been meeting my gaze.

"I should have supposed," he says, handing me firewood as I nurture the stove to life. "They were in your lands—it is difficult for your kind to not be drawn to their presence."

I send him a dry glance at the irony of me being here so often, to stay in his presence; he shrugs a shoulder, unbothered. He leans too heavily against his cane, worse than last time. It has been days since we had our little stroll in the human side of the woods, and the weight he puts on the walking stick has me desperately concerned in a way I do not know how to voice. He is already avoiding my questions.

Would he be angry should I press the topic?

Setting out my basket, I take a few mushrooms and watch him seat himself carefully along the same chair as before. It seems a proper place for the two of us, carefully aware of each other's presence and spending easy time together, even in the strangeness of this old place.

"There is a brownie here," he says suddenly, as if aware I am watching his every move.

I blink.

"Yes," he says, stealing one of the mushrooms, still covered in flecks of dark earth, and nibbling on the ends of the cap. "They do not settle alone, so it must have realized I am here. It is in the rafters near the trees. I shall show it to you."

I glance out at the edge of the tree roots I can see from this angle. "I miss getting them in my house."

"Put cold water on your sill at night; they will come in the summer."

I stare at him, open-mouthed, for a moment before laughing and shaking my head.

"What?" he asks, returning the mushroom. After he stuffed his face with my raw ingredients the last few times, I frown at his lack of appetite.

"You are such marvelous creatures, capable of amazing magics, and you live so much longer than us . . . and you're so drawn in by little things. It's . . . sweet."

He raises an eyebrow, resting his chin in his hand and gazing at me in a way that makes my cheeks hot once more. "I found a cellar as well."

Changing the topic? "Anything down there?"

"Wine," he says bluntly.

I snort. "Where is it?"

He points to the left of the little kitchen, down the hall I haven't properly explored, at a slightly different angle from the path we took to the strange basement door.

"Are you drunk?"

"*No* . . . I tried some last night. It was rather awful."

Washing the dirt from the mushrooms in the sink, still marveling that the water pump works with enough force put into it, I tell him, "I have some raspberry wine in my house from last year. Would that be sweet enough for you?"

"Only if you wish it. I do not need it."

Perhaps it's better I don't. I've no idea what a drunk faerie man would be like . . . even Aidyn. Instead, I say, "Tell me something about Faerie."

When I turn back to the counter, starting on dough for bread while the mushrooms simmer, he's gazing at me oddly. Truly, I cannot tell if he is unwell or simply in a strange mood from the events of the other night. Perhaps the more I encourage him to speak in any way possible, the more I'll learn about him. Enough to piece together something I can do to help, even in the smallest way.

"What about it?" he asks, drawing a circle in the flour I've spread on the old table.

"I don't know. We know very little about your lands. Tell me something you love about it."

This brings a slightly more genuine tug of a smile to his lips.

"My magic can do a great many things, as you've seen. They are not all particularly useful."

I glower.

He ignores me. "If I try with enough effort, I can lift myself off the ground. There are many fae with wings, but this is the closest I will certainly get to flying. There are hundreds of mountains here, if you go far enough and deep enough into this realm. I am not even sure about the others. I'm certain there are all sorts of creatures even we do not know about. Maybe one day I can take myself there, if my magic ever grows strong enough."

His eyes are not on me, not on anything here in this library. When he eventually takes up a new topic, about some of the meals he is familiar with that he once claimed a human will have never heard of, his gaze remains faraway as ever.

Late that night, Una is helping with some of my baking—or rather I'm testing a few different pies for midsummer and she's hovering about licking the ingredients off her fingers, but it's nice to have her. I did not miss the relief in her features when I returned from Faerie in one piece and within a reasonable time before dusk.

Olivia and Andrew are smoking their pipes on the front porch. Everyone is jumpy of being outside after the other night, and they have seated themselves right before the door. Night air drifts in the windows, as well as puffs of sweet herby smoke in swirling fingers past the moon. Rain clouds are finally gathering, and the spare droplets hit the window.

I've told Una all of what happened today in bits and pieces and whispers when we think her parents won't overhear. Niall is sitting at the kitchen table—given that he hasn't yet left for the night, he'll probably end up sleeping on the carpets before the fire instead of walking home at midnight. His facial expressions change with my pieces of information, so I know he's listening.

Truth be told, there isn't much to tell. I cooked for a while, and Aidyn spoke of little random things about his own lands, and neither of us truly had any revelations. We did not have to. I know little of whether he thinks of me as I think of him, but he seemed to enjoy my company.

Any little interaction with him feels as if I've had the strangest, most worthy-of-speaking-of experience. Perhaps I am wrong, but Una seems vastly interested. Niall can pretend he isn't invested in the gossip as he likes, but he's still chuckling quietly to himself at what Aidyn said about *dishonor*.

"Truly, I can't believe neither of you has asked me to bring him to meet you," I say casually, and both look equally appalled and interested. Niall settles on a grimace, and Una shakes her head.

"We're not even sure if we should be encouraging *you* to speak to him," she whispers. "Are you *certain* you have never mentioned our names?"

"Yes, very. Nor my own."

"That does not anger him?"

The question feels odd. "He doesn't anger easily. At all, really. The only time I saw a temper was when I startled him and when he was worried I'd get myself killed wandering deeper into Faerie."

Una gives me a skeptical look.

"I'm not stupid," I tease, then wince. "I was frightened out of being stupid."

Una leans against me, cheek on my shoulder. From behind us, Niall says, "If Blain ever comes near your house again, I'm going to beat him until he can't have children."

From outside, there's a sharp laugh from Olivia as I glower at Niall's perfectly innocent expression. He spoke *that* particular sentence loud enough I'm surprised the nearest cottage didn't hear. I set the pies on the sill to cool in the cold night air while Una tries picking apart the newest one without burning her fingers. Wiping my hands on my skirt, I plop myself into the chair beside Niall.

"You're not bigger than him, you know," I say. "And he's had swordsmanship lessons."

He gives me a look accurately portraying how I've stung his ego. "Yes, but I'm *quite* scary with an axe, remember?"

Smacking his leg and then ruffling his hair, I make a face back at him when he sticks his tongue out. Cara is in bed, but her attitude seems to have taken over Niall for the moment.

"Well, we've heard no more hounds, nor have we seen any evidence there are more," Una says, joining us with a slice of the blueberry pie. I'll take a bit of each to Aidyn tomorrow. "Though after the other night, if they ever showed up again, I'd be shocked."

"Thrice is the charm," Niall grumbles, eyeballing the pie and trying to steal her piece.

"I don't think he's well," I murmur, finally voicing what's been nagging at me all day and long after I bid him goodbye for the night.

Both glance at me.

I take a long breath. "For one thing, he seems to be staying the same at best. He is evidently still in some sort of pain or ill—I'm unsure. Today, I don't think he felt well at all, though he said nothing of it. He didn't eat much. It's an unusual thing for him."

Una's expression turns sympathetic, Niall's considering.

"He hasn't told you what's wrong?" he asks.

I shake my head. "I believe if he *could* lie, he'd simply tell me nothing's wrong. He's quite proud."

"How would you even help a creature like him?"

"I don't know," I mumble. "I do not believe he trusts me—not enough, at least."

Una snorts a tad, and I glance her way.

"Do you trust *him*?" she asks, and I realize the point she is making.

"Probably not enough," I admit. I don't know what else to do for him—it seems he will never tell me how I might help, or there is no way I can possibly help. It seems incorrect. He may be of the fae, but they are creatures of flesh and blood as any human.

Perhaps tomorrow I will edge a little closer to gaining enough trust.

In the morning, I watch the men across the field as they ensure the grasses are trampled down enough for the dancing. A few familiars from the neighboring villages are filtering in. It is less than a week now—a few days really, if I bother to count them—and I am little enthralled with the idea and more forgetful of my baking aspirations, instead stumbling about with my thoughts full of Aidyn.

That I might help him somehow.

The only *somehow* I know is to return and speak to him, perhaps cook him another meal that is comforting and wholesome for healing and hope he provides me with something I can do.

"Here," Una whispers, dropping a jar of salve into my hand as I stand in the garden, watching the sun get high enough I feel safe to return to Faerie, helping Olivia with her gardening. "I know you brought him medicines already, but this is elm bark for infections, in case he decides to confide in you at some point. Doesn't hurt to be prepared."

I hug her about the shoulders. "I'm going to tell him my friends are concerned."

"You'd better not," she hisses. "Just imagining him frightens me. Besides, most of it was your idea to begin with."

When I finally slip away, I glance again toward the preparations and wonder if Blain will dare show his face again. I believe I see Mister Haskel's wagon, but that doesn't mean his son had the guts to follow. I hope not. Each time he appears, my nerves fray further and further. All my little excursions to Faerie cannot be helping. Strangely enough, perhaps Aidyn himself may be. I know those lands are full of magic, as is the man himself, but his presence is calming, comforting. The more and more time I spend near him, the more I feel as if I have known him forever.

For a few moments, I simply stand inside the border of Faerie, breathing in the honeysuckle and considering the trees. They are calm as ever.

I shall ask Aidyn about the strange faerie woman I saw. Perhaps he will know her. It is time we have a few honest conversations with each other. Besides, he can ask me most anything. I feel as if I may *not* ask him most anything. We should even the grounds of the conversations, just a bit. Even if we don't get anywhere today, it will be good to start.

Pleased with the determination I've scraped together, I shove open the old door and weave through the maze of books I've come to know well. The other halves of the pies I baked are in my basket—it will be good to get Aidyn's vote on his favorite, or pick berries on this side of the border if his eyes don't light up at any of them.

I should simply pick berries on this side of the border anyway. A guaranteed win.

"Aidyn?" I call, trotting toward his room. "I brought pies. I need another taste tester—"

Pausing in the door, I watch the shape of him under the blankets near the hearth. His sides rise and fall slowly, but he appears more asleep than lounging. I press my lips together. Lying there still and comfortable, he looks entirely human and unthreatening.

"Are you still asleep?" I whisper, creeping along the old creaking floorboards to his side, worry beginning to nag at me. "Aidyn?"

As carefully as possible, aware it may not be a wise idea, I brush my fingers across his shoulder. His hair has partially fallen across his face, and my fingers twist to brush that aside instead. I'm not sure he'd appreciate such a thing.

"Aidyn?" I whisper again, partially unwilling to wake him but even more unwilling to let him sleep without knowing if he is all right.

I give his shoulder a slight squeeze through the blankets.

His eyes flicker open.

20

Plum Tree

Relief takes hold at the gentle silver gazing up at me, and I smile, hoping it doesn't look too worried. "Hello—"

He starts, jerking as if a monster stands just over my shoulder, nearly pushing me off the side of the pillows. My heart leaps. Falling still, I see the moment he realizes it is only the little human he's made friends with, not something far worse. We gaze at each other for a long moment as I wonder what monsters he must be remembering.

Are they the same as mine?

"Hi," I whisper again, thinking of doing something to comfort him but still shy of simply wrapping my arms about him. I settle for, "I brought more pie. I need your expertise."

He lets out a long strange sound I take for a sigh, glancing about the room. I sit as quiet as I can, waiting for him to wake fully, not wishing to frighten him. The idea I *could* is unsettling, but he looks so purely flustered by my presence that I don't wish to speak, not yet.

Finally, he rolls back onto his side, expression tense, and puts his hand across his eyes, rubbing his temples.

Manners be damned, I ask, "Are you hurting worse?"

He doesn't answer.

"Aidyn," I warn in my best motherly tone. "Please stop avoiding the topic. I am not a danger to you."

He blinks, moving his fingers aside enough to gaze at me oddly. Still, he doesn't speak.

Ignoring the heat in my face, I tell him, "I am worried."

His expression is unreadable, but I guess a sort of exasperation. Pointing to above the pillows, he faintly says, "Will you feed the kittens please?"

Glancing at the little jar of honey, I tell him, "It's empty."

Frowning, he makes a jerking motion with his chin, glancing at the shelf where he keeps all his little trinkets. " 'Twas not last night—" He returns his hand to over his face. "Brownie."

"Oh," I say, forcing myself not to chuckle. The library has taken up a resident brownie—of course it would get into the food while Aidyn slept. I wonder if it's eaten the mushroom soup in the kitchen. Hopefully it only prefers sweet things. We'll need to guard the pie.

Glancing down at Aidyn, I realize he may not be well enough to stand. It would be cruel to wait on food for the little creatures until he feels well again.

Remembering his warnings about their bees and their

sting, I say, "How about I . . . go back into Nevyan and find some of the places I've marked in Faerie that have berries. They'll eat berries, won't they?"

He peeks at me through the crack in his fingers. I cock my head at him, wishing he would smile or make any sort of human expression.

"Aidyn, I do not like you in such a state. Will you—"

"You think I like *myself* in such a state?" he snaps, and a few of the fallen leaves along the floorboards skitter past. I jump, flinching despite myself. His expression falls, and we gaze at each other for a long moment. He simply returns to covering his eyes with his hand. Frustration wars with sympathy in my chest. I know little of what he has endured, so I cannot rightfully judge, but surely by now he must realize I am only concerned.

Huffing, I set my basket with its pies down above the pillows. "Very well. I shall go look for berries. But no human berries, since they are picky little things."

"There is a plum tree," he says, and I blink, surprised. He extends a finger to the other side of the library. "I believe I saw it by the brambles the last time we stepped out near the falls. I meant to go back. Should not be out of sight of the library, if you return through the passageway door."

My mind collects a vague memory of seeing a fruit tree of sorts when I was by the brambles, but I was quite preoccupied by the strange creature hiding in the bushes themselves until Aidyn came to chase it away. After that, I was much too nervous of following him into the woods to consider a tree.

"I remember . . . I think."

Again, he peeks out at me from between his fingers. I still cannot read his expression but have a difficult time not putting a negative emotion to the hard press of his lips. I tell myself again that if he is lying down in such a way, not bothering to accompany me out the back, he must truly feel poorly. It likely has nothing to do with me that his gaze is unfriendly. More so, the fae are strange folk. I should not be reading his expression in this situation as I would another mortal's.

"Do not go into the trees," he says, and that intensity has returned. "The door should put you out right beside the plum tree. Do not go out if it doesn't. Do not go farther past the tree. You remember what I told you—"

"Yes, yes, never venture into the trees without you," I say lightly. It worries me less all of a sudden, the idea of walking into the back of the library and out into the woods. I will be all by myself. Without anyone there, I will be fine. I can worry about myself and myself alone.

" 'Tis right near the brambles—"

"Yes, so you said," I say, trying to offer a teasing smile. I do not like the way his eyes follow me with such sharp inspection. "I will not go into the trees. I have been quite scared off."

Glancing at the window, I think of the hunt hound Aidyn dispatched of and the fact that I haven't stepped foot there since. "Would you like me to go elsewhere and find berries?"

" 'Tis more dangerous."

"Is it?" I've been doing so since I was a child.

"You are incredibly lucky you never found yourself lost to begin with."

"Oh."

"If you can keep the library in your sight, it is difficult to lose your way. The door should put you right beside it; just think of it as strongly as you can. And do not venture away from the entrance it makes for you."

I know this, but the way he says it has me pausing. I glance at the basket where the kittens are still sleeping and consider if this cannot wait until tomorrow, until he is recovered. Yesterday he was not himself, no matter how I spoke to him or made him comforting food. Today he is worse.

The longer I stare, the colder his gaze feels. I came with a great deal of determination to find more truths about him, but it withers under his chill. I hate how laid vulnerable he is. I do not believe I would hate it so if he allowed me to offer help in some way. Then I would only be worried.

I am helping by doing this.

After taking the things out of my basket, I loop it back over my arm for something to carry the plums in, considering a pie if I can gather enough, and put a log onto the fire, not knowing what else to do.

"Here."

When I turn, he is working the tiniest ring off his finger, offering it. Automatically, I hold out my palm.

"Do *not* go anywhere else. If for any reason you cannot find your way back, picture this place, and this will point your steps in the correct direction."

Anxiety twines in my chest at the suggestion I may need such a thing, but I slip the ring onto my thumb, where it fits nicely. It is light as air, but the pressure of it seems to weigh upon my finger. It feels strange to be wearing something from these lands.

Shifting on the pillows, Aidyn makes a movement as if he is going to sit, then goes still, something flickering across his expression. He keeps his eyes closed and does not speak to me again. I glance at the little jars of salves along the window, which he has not touched, and think perhaps it was a foolish thing for a human to assume she could offer aid to a creature of Faerie with a few jars of human herbs.

Gathering my nerves, I touch the back of his hand. His eyes don't open, and he curls his arm away from my touch, under the blanket.

I do not push him—not everyone wishes for company when they are feeling poorly.

Pausing on my way out, I return to the kittens and place them in the circle he has created out of his arms. They mewl and crawl under his chin to settle.

"Flower," he says with much exasperation, but he does not try to push them back to their basket. If he will not accept comfort from me, perhaps he can from the little creatures he loves.

Satisfied, I tell him, "I'll be back in a few minutes."

He says nothing more, and I trot out of the warm little room and down the hallway, weaving through the maze of books, finding it strangely easy to follow the disturbed dust along the floor where we last ventured through. Aidyn's footsteps are decidedly less messy, as if he barely walked by at all.

Laying my hand against the ancient handle, I feel the strange cool of it, the otherworldly assurance that there is magic swirling about this place as it does about Aidyn. I picture the edges of the plum tree I saw, just past the brambles.

For good measure, I whisper, "I need to go to the plum tree just outside the library please. It is important."

Turning the handle, I step carefully down into the tunnel, finding the same sprites hanging from the roots of the ceiling, unfurling their little limbs to gaze at me and scatter aside as I pass.

"Sorry," I whisper, wondering how long they sleep when not disturbed.

When I press out through the opening, I half expect to find the same brambles as last time, beside the waterfall. Instead, I am looking up at a thick twisted trunk of a plum tree heavy with fruit. A grin tugs at my lips, a small laugh along with it.

"Library, you are a marvel," I say.

Pushing myself out into the open and glancing back, I brace myself to find the rotting corpse of some hound spread among the leaves. It has been quite a time, and I'm not sure what else would have happened to it. Perhaps animals here scavenge as they do on my side of the trees. Perhaps the other fae took away any remnants of the hounds they let come too close to the border.

Where did Aidyn hide from them? Would they simply not check the library?

As ever, the trees are calm and open and empty. A few birds flicker through the branches this time, and the leaves rustle in the calm air. Carefully, I take a few steps past the small tree the library sent me through, standing on the crinkly carpet of leaves. Nothing presents itself. The library chimney puffs smoke a short distance away.

"You're being suspicious," I tell myself, then remember

Aidyn telling me my words will be heard among the trees of Faerie and click my jaw shut.

The beehive sits just in my line of sight. Even if the little creatures were not too dangerous for me to approach, Aidyn has been worried of stealing too much honey. I will collect as many plums as I can within a few minutes, then run back through the burrow still safely open by my feet. Even alone, I am nervous. The open, bright nature of the trees both helps and intensifies my turning stomach.

I gaze up into the heavy branches of the plum tree. A few maples crowd against it, but it sits comfortably in the dim soupy sunlight of Faerie, a bird taking flight from its branches.

I relax further.

This is nothing to fear.

I have gone almost this far into Faerie on my own many a time. This time, there is the library to keep in my sight and the burrow by my feet, so it shall be even easier. Turning the ring on my finger, I take a few experimental steps around the tree. Bees buzz faintly, far off, but come no closer to me than last time.

In the quiet between the trees, I very much expect the strange little creature that drinks off emotions to come peeking its odd face at me through the brambles. No such thing presents itself, though I grip the handle of my basket and think about giving it a good smack if it does. I'm not sure I've ever taken up violence against another living creature, but I'm prepared to try.

Sugary fragrant fruit fills my senses. The taste of the air settles along the back of my tongue, and I'm reminded of *exactly* why, at a little age, I started tripping my way into Faerie. The fruit on the other side was simply irresistible to human eyes and noses. The first time was an accident, but when I finally stumbled back out into the bright daylight of the mortal realm, both parents in an entire tizzy about my whereabouts in a village where disappeared children means being trapped forever in the eternal realm, I'd returned with my pockets full of blackberries, not to mention what was smeared across my face from all the eating. Faint lines existed for a long time on my hands and arms from crawling past the thorns and brambles to the sweet fruit hiding among the moths and fallen leaves. They faded with time, though if I look hard enough, I can find one or two. The much-larger scar on my hand and arm overwhelms any desire to do so.

I rub my fingers against my skirts, casting a glance around, but there is no such thing as hounds here—not right now. It is bright daylight, and I am not wandering in any strange in-between space where time plays tricks. The library is there, the remains of an old giant coated in leaves and time. Sun shines bright and deep through the trunks. I do not smell or hear or sense anything dangerous, just the few passing birds and the nearby hive.

Bees buzz around the dripping nectar, too high and few in number to pay me much mind. The branches hang heavy and low. I push one aside, gazing into the cool dark about the trunk created by all the low branches, but let the leaves fall back into place. I am wary of venturing into shadows now, even ones cast by a fruit-laden tree.

A bee buzzes close by my head, and I shy from its wings,

but it is only drifting by, fat on the few flowers remaining on the tree and the dripping nectar itself. Picking the closest plum so ripe it falls into my palm with a brush of my fingers, I settle it into my basket. Another and another go in, my head whipping about every time I crack even the smallest twig or drop the plum with too much of a squish into the basket. Nothing presents itself. Smoke curls from Aidyn's hearth in the library, and I do not allow myself to become distracted with the idea of him—he is unwell, and I know little of how to aid him.

No. Right now is not the time to let my mind wander to such things. I can worry when I am safely back in his gaze, sour as it may be today.

Mumbling to myself about strange faerie men and bees and kittens, I fill the large basket halfway to its brim. I am in no fear of taking too many. I have barely managed to take the tips of a few bundles of fruit of just three clusters of small branches. The tree, massive as it is, has so many I could make a dozen pies and feed the kittens for a month and likely never run out. They will fall to the ground and rot before I can gather them all.

I'm grateful Aidyn noticed the tree during our last venture. Hearing the bees buzzing about, I would not want to brave trying to take from their hive. They are much larger than our little mortal honeybees.

Licking my fingers, I glance again into the woods. The sugar and tartness make my cheeks hurt. I pick another from the tree and slurp most of it down without chewing, juice dribbling.

All things considered, it's rather a shock no one else likes to go traipsing into Faerie.

Blain.

I pause, a second plum halfway to my mouth, and consider. Many men think themselves brave enough to go into Faerie, daring one another to run in and back unharmed, though the idea itself is mostly harmless. I've done so hundreds of times, thousands. It is nothing.

Putting the fruit into my mouth, I chew and collect more, glowering at the leaves, considering and considering.

Does he want something from Faerie? I could not believe he would wish anything else from *me*, specifically. He once wished me to show him these lands, those years ago, but I thought nothing of it. It was a common thing, after all, and I was a strange girl—the wild and moon-born oddity who skips into Faerie to return unharmed.

Perhaps it is not him. Mister Haskel approached me first, after all. Business with my father, perhaps? But no, Da would have him thrown into the dirt—

"Back again, are we?"

I jump, annoyed at having let my thoughts wander, and scowl at the creature perched between a cluster of the plums. I weigh the basket full of plums in my hands and consider that I could perhaps take out a grown man with it.

It cocks its head at me, still drooling, and I see that it does, in fact, have no teeth. Knowing it can't do me any true harm, just dig at any old wounds I cling to in my heart, it's almost pathetic. Picking a plum out of my basket, I toss it at the creature. It fumbles, snatching it with one overly long limb before it can be struck in the face.

"Eat a plum," I tell it, then turn on my heel for the burrow in the roots of the nearest tree.

"Step on a mushroom, eat your eyes . . ." it hisses in a strangely familiar feminine voice. Whatever it's trying for, I ignore it and its morbid little poem, giving the bees a watchful eye as three buzz near the tree I'm approaching.

"Pluck your teeth, one by one . . ."

I nearly roll my eyes, but chills are crawling across my skin, so I keep walking, ignoring it as I ignored Blain. Evidently, I am annoying it, since it is trying so hard to get me to come back.

"Oh, look how the little one cries . . ."

Una. It's making itself sound like Una.

Aidyn didn't mention *that* particular talent—he must not have known.

How does it know what she sounds like?

Irritation flutters up my chest. Picking another plum out of my basket, I turn to give it a good throw at the stupid thing. I have quite a decent throwing arm, most likely from spending too many years hurling various harmless objects at both Niall and Una and getting them thrown back in return. Might as well knock the creature right out of its roost, and maybe next time it won't try—

A flurry of limbs, and I smack the creature away with a yelp as it jumps from the nearest branch right for my face. Its skin is cold and dry as paper. I stumble, and my shoe catches on a root of the brambles. I smack down too hard onto the forest floor, irritated with myself at being so startled and clumsy at the same time.

"Stupid thing," I grumble, coughing and glaring at the tree canopy before sitting upright. "I'm going to send Aidyn after you—"

My voice dies in my throat, and I stare at the dark thick trunks of trees.

"You're not right," I mumble, just to hear my own voice.

The plum tree is gone, as are the brambles and the goblin creature—though it could be hidden behind the nearest trunk and I'd know no better—and it takes me a moment to gather my nerves and glance over my shoulder.

Clusters of dark trees. A dim haze of fading light as sudden twilight turns to falling night. A few stars blink between the branches of the canopy, strangely close.

No burrow. No library.

21

Dark Woods, Bright Eyes

Rolling onto my knees, my ankle throbbing where I twisted it tripping like a fool, I stare at the place both the plum tree and burrow should be. No matter how I squint, no library appears amid the dim of the trees. After a moment of hearing nothing but my own heartbeat, it dawns on me what must've happened.

I fell, and I closed my eyes.

If I stumbled back at all, with my eyes closed, would Faerie consider that lost as when I run a dozen steps in? I have never tried simply closing my eyes and taking two or three steps.

I didn't realize I'd done it this time.

I stumbled backward and must have closed my eyes as I fell. A natural instinct. Even Aidyn would have done such a thing.

But Aidyn cannot lose himself in Faerie—at least not here.

A few bees still buzz in the air, but I do not trust their existence. Their presence does not mean I am anywhere close to the library and its open, bright woods.

Maple trees and a bright sky thick with the scent of honeysuckle have been replaced by old oaks twisted and warped with age, bent over themselves in a strange dance. Rotting leaves and something overly sweet, like too many of the plums or overripe autumn apples, fill the air.

Carefully, I collect the scattered fruits back into their basket, abandoning the ones that have tumbled out of reach, unwilling to move from my spot until my heart stops pounding and my mind clears. The straps along the top I never use work to tie the top closed. If I fall again, I don't want to lose the kittens' food.

Keeping the basket looped over my elbow, I force myself to let out a breath, ignoring the all-enveloping nature of the air, and twist Aidyn's ring gently about my finger. It was touching of him to give it to me, but I didn't believe I would need it.

If for any reason you cannot find your way back, picture this place, and this will point your steps in the correct direction.

Simple enough. Something cracks in the woods, and I jump, chest aching. Something resembling a deer gazes at me, too many eyes too large and bright in the shadowy woods. Flowers cling to its back, lilies or something else I've only ever seen in faded ink illustrations in the pages of old books. Its antlers are black wood—even from here I can see the grains. Its legs stand perfectly straight.

It turns and moves on without a sound. I watch the place it

disappears without breathing.

Isn't Faerie supposed to be enchanting?

Perhaps that is only the borders. Perhaps the rest of these lands are dangerous and like the fae themselves: unpredictable. Besides, who knows where I've been deposited. I think of Aidyn's stories and his warnings of the fae they call *Unblessed.* I don't know if they are truly any more dangerous, but I hope the frightening nature of the trees is no indication of the folk dwelling within them.

Standing, I grimace, but I twisted my ankle worse when I was a child. I can walk on it.

Since I must.

Basket still over my arm, I turn the ring carefully, trying to sense whatever magic it was forged in, not knowing if I would recognize it if I could. I take three steps in the direction the library *should* be, holding the picture of it in my mind as best I can. It is a tad like picturing Aidyn when I am not with him—strangely fuzzy, like a dream from years ago called forth.

"A big old library," I mumble to myself, then think better of it with how the woods may be listening in and think the words instead.

It is two stories, with a strange basement door and a hole in the roof where leaves float in. Two big maple trees are growing inside the floor. Vines are growing over the door, but there is another door and a back door with a metal staircase and a winding staircase going up to the roof. Several chimneys, and a small kitchen, and lots and lots of books—

Again, as if the ring will hear me, I whisper, "A big old library—"

"Well, that won't help you—"

The moment I catch sight of the creature from the corner of my eye, I leap upon it, grabbing it by the neck like I'm wresting a snake, hauling it from the bark of the tree it clings to. Its little fingers peel off bits of bark with a hundred cracks, and it squeaks. It is considerably heavier than I expected, and I end up pinning it to the ground rather than attempting to hold it up.

"You followed me here?" I ask, giving it a little shake, the snarl in my voice easier with the panic. "So you know the way back. *Show me.*"

Snarling and squeaking, it flails its arms and legs, achieving nothing as they smack against my body like the finest branches, not even tearing my thin dress. Sneaky and tricky it may be, but Aidyn's right: it *certainly* is no physical threat. I keep my hands locked about its collarbones, ignoring the plums it's scattering, waiting for it to flail itself into exhaustion.

That strange sharp pain starts in my chest. Feeding on my distress, very likely.

Giving it another harsh shake, I snap, "Don't even consider it! I'm not letting you go until you take me back to the library!"

"Humans are evil, ugly things!" it wails, spitting drool thick like fat.

I grimace and let it continue for a moment before considering there are certainly *other things* watching from the eyes of the Faerie woods. I clamp my hand over its toothless mouth. If possible, it looks more pathetic.

"I'm much bigger than you," I warn. "And it isn't as if I have *anywhere else to be.*"

It continues struggling, albeit weaker, the pain in my chest remaining but not growing, until it finally flops still, glowering in return.

Releasing its mouth, I ask, "Do you know how to take me back?"

"You got yourself lost, silly human—"

"Do you want my hand over your face again?"

Spitting, it flails a bit more before falling still.

"Show me the way back."

"Why woulds I?"

Scrambling for something and biting the insides of my cheeks so I don't cry in frustration, I say, "Well, I'll have to take you with me, and you can bask in me being miserable the whole time, now can't you?"

Spreading its lips in a horrifying approximation of a smile, it says, "I donst need you for that. You can't be rid of me. I can follow you wherever you be—"

It bends one of its strangely jointed legs in my direction, and I realize what it's doing in time to turn my head so its little toe doesn't jab right into my eye.

Aidyn's ring digs into my hand.

I don't need it either.

Sitting on its chest while it screeches like a banshee, I tear the hem of my dress into one large strip. After tying the creature up in an intricate bundle of limbs and stained cloth, I snatch up my basket and *run.* Turning through my mind all the little details of the library I can and trying not to so much as blink against the hot sticky air, I'm slowed fairly quickly by my ankle.

A twisted ankle isn't permanent. Faerie is. Ignore it and get home.

When I've run out of all the details I can recall, I think them again in a different panicked order, and then I list everything I can call to mind about Aidyn: the obvious features he maintains, then how his voice sounds in the gentle light of the evening, the way his eyes crinkle at the corners when he smiles, the fact that he is ill and I should be returning to him, hoping that the ring perhaps knows its last owner.

The sun sets, and I slow to a walk. I am going to lose my footing more in the utter dark—

And should it be taking so long?

Aidyn never said. It feels as if hours have passed, though perhaps that is my mind playing tricks.

"Aidyn?" I whisper, to be careful.

More bees buzz past in no distinct direction, and I consider if they are perhaps constant companions of Faerie.

At night? Bees fly at night?

Instead of utter darkness, I am greeted more and more by strange shimmering flowers. Pollen floats in the air, and I would be drawn to the beauty were I not fearful that breathing it in would enchant me forever.

How long can a human go unnoticed in Faerie?

Voices drift through the trees, and I lock my legs into place, leaning against the nearest tree for support.

It is not Aidyn's voice.

It may very well be the creature having struggled out of its bonds and tracked me down, but there are more than one, and they are not familiar.

Letting my breath out in a long huff, I consider my next steps. If I move forward, toward the voices, who knows what I'll be greeted with. But I cannot turn *away*. This is the direction I've been heading, and even if Aidyn's gift is guiding me, I do not know if changing directions is wise.

Momentarily, I consider closing my eyes and simply losing myself *elsewhere* of the strange voices, but I very well may deposit myself somewhere much worse. Swaying, I creep forward as quietly as I can, breathing too loud behind my ears, fingers trembling.

I step around the nearest tree, and the song fades. Nothing but a small clearing greets me, and in the dark of the night, I see a handful of shapes. They could be nothing more than the undergrowth of the woods. I am *not* stepping into the open, not in the dark. Picking my way around the clearing, I watch the shadows from the corner of my eye, hoping none will do me the disservice of moving, intent on keeping to my path as best I can.

Another note of music, long and lyrical and strange, and I shove my fingers into my ears, tripping over roots and stars know what else as I finally pass the clearing and try to run. I still hear it, whatever it may be, a lingering whisper inside my ears, disregarding my fingers. It is very strange here. Warm and comforting. If I sit down, my ankle won't hurt so much. If I merely—

Stop.

Hands remove mine, a circle of fingers strung daintily

about my wrists. Breath like sweet flowers wilted in the sun brushes my cheeks. I blink more than once, gazing up at the face.

She is beautiful and strange and inhuman. Something akin to a face and eyes and jaw filter blearily before my eyes, but I don't much mind. Sleep tugs at my limbs, my tongue still heavy with the taste of plums and sugar. Vaguely, I recall something about a library, but I cannot bring it to mind.

A dream, perhaps.

A hum ripples through the air, rolling over my bones, tugging at my chest. They are not human words, but I believe I understand them. No wonder we disappear into Faerie, never to return. *Who would wish to?*

The hands tug gently, and I follow along, the basket still weighing down my shoulder, straps tangled around my arm. Bees buzz nearby, closer and closer. Rough dry skin brushes the sore pinkie on my weaker hand—

Who is touching my hand?

I blink, stumbling to a stop.

Who is with me in the woods?

The grip around my wrists tightens, the song continuing.

I look up.

Four pure-white eyes gaze down at me from one face, a long length of hair black as the surrounding night, too-long limbs in every fashion. A gentle song flows from its lips, and she cocks her head daintily, all teeth and skin and eyes.

"Let go of me," I say numbly, my lips not yet catching the building panic in my chest.

It twitches.

"*Let go of me!*" I scream, putting all my weight into my heels and yanking *hard.*

The gentle loop of her spider leg fingers turns into an unbreakable grasp, muscles like snake bellies ripping around the bones in my wrists, which suddenly feel too fragile. She pulls back with much less effort, and I smack into a sharp rib cage, my vision flickering where my temple cracks against bone.

No, no, no, I'm not letting this happen again.

The woman—if I can call her such—hisses at my blood smeared across her neck. The moon has broken the canopy, and I realize she's led me back to her clearing. What she plans on doing with me, I've no intention of finding out. Shrieking and not caring whatever else hears, I struggle away as best I can, stomping at her clawed feet and kicking at the double bends where her knees should be. On and on she drags me toward the center. More bees buzz. Something smacks into my cheek, the humming of wings just against my ear. Fire erupts against my neck, a weakened sensation flooding my left side, fire dripping down the inside of my skin. I scream hard enough my throat feels as if it may tear.

The woman yanks me nearer, her face bending close. I have never fought off another creature, not unless I count wrestling with Niall when we were barely grown or holding down sheep to get them sheared for the first time. Neither applies. I know nothing of fighting, and something tells me I'd have no use for a weapon even if I'd brought one.

Her breath brushes my face. Her nose is quite prominent, a long needle of a thing to match her many teeth. She has far, *far* too many eyes. I cannot poke them with my hands captured.

Launching forward, I sink my teeth into the bridge of her nose. Foul, sour blood fills my mouth, and a scream like a tear in the sky stabs my ears. I'm on the ground a second later. Another sharp sting catches right on the back of my sore hand, and I smack it into the ground before I can think better. Rolling over, knocking into the stupid basket of plumbs, I scramble for my feet. Its hand snatches my hair, pulling me back and wailing.

Something in the woods starts up a hard shriek of calls—dozens, hundreds.

Another beesting.

I'm off-balance but swing the ridiculous heavy basket of fruit right around as it drags me back, a satisfying jar in my shoulders as the heavy burden strikes true. It doesn't do as much as I'd hoped, but the creature stumbles, her hand still in my hair. My locks have long been cut short, and she has so much of it gripped that her hand slips right off when I yank.

Another beesting, and I find myself on my back, dizzy, numb fingers slithering through my bones, my muscles.

Aidyn did warn me about the bees, I think vaguely as I catch the woman flailing at them as well. *So many bees.*

A hand grabs my ankle, and I hear my own scream like something far off as I'm dragged into the bushes, fern fronds and winter brambles tearing at my dress. I'm not letting it eat me or sing to me, and I can't find my ears to put my fingers in, so I smack at the creature, striking something hard with my better hand.

"Stop it," the voice hisses, a strange deep burble like water over stones. "Stop, quiet, *quiet*!"

Another scream hurts my throat, and a long warm hand clamps over my mouth. A heavy body covers mine, pinning me completely. Rings dig into my skin.

"Bluebell, quiet, quiet," the voice hisses, and I flinch, finding a familiar set of eyes, pure silver and terribly bright in the dark of the night, gazing down at me.

Aidyn, I want to say, but his hand is still covering the entire bottom half of my face.

"Hush, Flower," he whispers, keeping me pinned in the bush, glancing out at the creature shrieking and spitting in the clearing.

Aidyn. Tears burn the backs of my eyes. I grip his shoulder, and he nods to me, expression twisted. One hand remains over my mouth, the other under the back of my head. He is heavier than I ever imagined, utterly pinning me down, strangely warm and grounding.

"Quiet and still," he murmurs, keeping his hand looser, gentler, thumb rubbing small circles into the tear tracks along my cheek.

His eyes flicker out and over the creature. Whispering, he tells me, "It must have been following you; otherwise, the ring would've worked. If it sang to you, I can imagine you would not have made your way back."

Somewhere within the back of my mind, I have the wherewithal to realize this is a good thing—he was not misleading me about the ring, and I was doing nothing incorrectly. At the forefront of my thoughts is the shrieking creature, and the stinging pain in my neck and hand and shoulder spreading throughout my body, and the uncomfortable way my ankle is lying, and the comforting weight of Aidyn pressing me into the fragrant grass.

Finally, the woman stops screaming. I catch glimpses of her through the dark leaves. She grips her face where I bit her, blood trickling in droplets against the moonlight. Aidyn's breath slows to nothing. His sword is strapped around his hips, his walking cane lying in the grass right alongside us.

Slowly, its face turns toward us. My heartbeat thumps so loud I'm certain she hears. Aidyn makes a soft noise, like a hum of a line of song. The creature flinches.

And dives for our hidden spot in the bushes.

Aidyn's weight leaves me. Before I can think of rolling away, he's shoved the end of his walking cane up and through something with a wet crunch. My throat makes a strange startled noise. Something hot and wet splashes my cheek, leaves falling about us, disturbed by the creature's presence. Bees hum, and I do scramble back as much as I can, just a few steps' worth on my hands and bottom, caught on the skirts of my dress.

Aidyn twists the cane, hissing a bone-chilling noise like steel on steel, blood and wolves howling at the moon, the silhouette of the woman bending low over him, and he gazing into her face in return. Her hand is twisted in his shirt, and he yanks the cane out with a sickening crack.

Flailing away all at once with a sharp keen, one eye broken and bleeding, she fails back into the grass, more howls in the night joining her cries, growing closer and closer.

"Get up," Aidyn hisses, grabbing my hand and hauling me up. My feet stumble under me, and the world pitches sideways. I wish to grab him, to cling to his support, but I can't reach in the right direction. Besides, I still see well enough to realize he's caught himself on the nearest trunk, in no better condition. His hand touches his middle where the woman grabbed his shirt. Hair pools over his shoulders like familiar ink.

"Aidyn," I say, intent on asking . . . *something.*

I should help him, shouldn't I?

I can't even help myself.

"Picture the library," he says. "A dozen steps. Count them."

He tugs me along, and we stumble as fast as we both can manage through the dark woods, counting up and up and up, the woman's screams ringing terror into my ears, Aidyn's hand clasped about mine.

22

Matching Wounds

For a terrible moment, I fear we shall never find the library again in the dark, but only a few steps later we are plowing right into the edge of a familiar plum tree. Aidyn trips but manages to keep his footing, dragging me along while my head spins.

"Where is the burrow?" he asks as my mind struggles to grasp at his words. "The way you came through, where is it?"

I blink, pointing to the little maple tree where I first crawled out and finding . . . nothing. Aidyn puts his hand to the trunk of the tree, more as if he's seeking support than searching for the path I took to the plums.

"It was here," I say, my voice faraway. "This is where I came. I'm certain . . ."

Glancing at the nearest trees and back over his shoulder,

Aidyn shakes his head and drags me along, abandoning the search for the little tunnel. I take a final glimpse for it, but my eyes find nothing before the brambles cover any chance of finding it again. Clinging to Aidyn's hand, I let him lead me away.

It is pitch-dark. Even the library is less a comforting presence and more a looming giant in the shadows and strange bird calls. Bees still buzz but don't pay us much mind as we trip and stumble in our return to the back door. I nearly trip up the back steps, catching myself on the railing before the stillness of the old structure envelops us.

Aidyn shuts the door behind us and pauses, leaning against it like we both did when the hunt hound first came around the side door.

My head spins, and I sit down hard all at once the moment we are no longer running for our lives. Aidyn slides down beside me. There is no light in the old place, just a faint glow down the hallway from Aidyn's hearth flicking warmth into his room.

"Look at me," Aidyn says, then takes my jaw in his hand, turning my face toward him. "Do you still know who you are?"

I fumble with his words, attempting to make sense of them. "What?"

"Your name, do you know it? Don't tell it to me, just think it to yourself."

Niamh, I think immediately, and it clears some of the blur from my thoughts. "Yes."

"And my name?"

"*Aidyn*," I breathe.

"And where you are?"

"At the old library on the edge of Faerie," I tell him, understanding more and more why he is asking me these things: because I was sung to by a strange creature of these lands. I may very well be cursed, entranced, destined to wander back into the eternal woods with nothing but these lands in the forefront of my thoughts. "Am I cursed? Did that thing . . . ?"

"No, you're well," he says, sitting back. "I must tend to those stings, but you're well enough."

Well enough. Tears burn my eyes. Embarrassed, I bury my face in my hands and cry. Stupid, stupid girl. I could've died.

Why didn't I run past that clearing faster? Why didn't I ignore that stupid creature when it was sending me those stupid little poems?

"Flower," Aidyn says, and his breath tickles my hair against my ear. His fingers pull some of the locks aside so he can gaze at what there is to see of my face through my fingers. " 'Tis all well now."

I shake my head, though he cannot be lying. We may be safe enough, but *nothing* is well. "Where did the passageway go?"

"I am uncertain," he admits. "We can search for it later. Anything that wanders in cannot get through the door. There is nothing to worry over."

I sniffle. He is right, after all; the door was heavy to open and the lock sturdy. Safer than the small side door. *We are safe.*

"How did you become lost?" he asks, and I shake my head again. I feel foolish enough already and do not need to be admitting it to him. He should still be in bed. Still be resting.

Still be a bit sulky—

"You should be in bed," I tell him.

I receive a gentle scoff, and I finally glare, ignoring my puffy eyes and wet cheeks.

"I should be many things," he mumbles, then pushes himself to his feet with great effort, grimacing, offering his hands. I think of not taking them, but then I'm unsure I would ever be getting off the floor. The warmth of his fingers is oddly stabilizing, comforting.

Wobbling, he nearly catches himself against me, and I frown, more determined to put him to bed. Night has fallen, and I do not know if I should be returning across the border this late—no matter how I wish to. Besides, I'm unsure I could make it down the stairs.

"You're stung," he says, running his thumb across the burning spot on my hand.

I flinch without meaning to, then simply pull him along toward the bedroom. "Tell me what is wrong with you."

"Hmm," he says as we shut the door to his room, a strange safety washing over me.

The kittens are mewling in their basket, and I remember the heavy burden of plums still looped over my shoulder, weighing me down as I walk.

Since he won't answer, I ask, "How long will I be dizzy?"

As I fumble with their blankets, I dump some of the fruit onto the floor beside them. They crawl over it with little paws, ripping open the purple flesh and licking at the juice. Satisfied, I slump onto the pillows, shivering in the warmth, finally understanding why Aidyn keeps his room so heated if this is how he feels.

"Show me," he says, seated beside me, silver eyes on the side of my face.

I stare up at him, thinking of the creature and her face bent over his, his harsh glare in return. There is something dark on the bottom of his cane—I know precisely what it is and don't wish to think too hard on it.

"What?" I ask again, feeling dull. I have never passed out before, though I may simply do so now.

Sighing, he pulls me around. Startled by the contact but finding it nothing like that strange creature and her song, I attempt to move my body in the direction he wishes while he mumbles something about monsters and silly humans.

I feel silly, I think about telling him, but I find no determination.

His hands turn over my own, touching again at the beesting and then at some of the small scrapes from my struggle before tugging at the shoulder of my torn dress where another sting is. His shoulders are slumped. He wavers slightly, wobbling even as he is sitting. I want to lay him in bed and put blankets over him, smooth his hair from his forehead.

Scowling, he returns to my wrist and puts it up to his lips.

"What are you doing?" I ask, giving a weak tug at the idea of him putting my ruined finger against his pretty face.

Rolling his eyes, he ignores my weak protests and presses his lips around the sting. A sharp pain follows, but the strange numbness retreats. I'm not entirely certain what he's doing . . . Sucking the venom out as one would a snakebite? It feels almost as if his teeth broke skin but does not hurt enough.

Some of the haze clears from my thoughts. It must be the

venom of the stings, not the words of the creature still echoing in my mind.

"You are all so susceptible to Faerie," he mumbles, spitting
into the ashes of the fire. I think of putting another log on but
can't quite move my body correctly. "These could drive you
mad if you let them fester. But I suppose you're susceptible to
our magics in good ways as well. This will work better than
any of your little tonics you're sneaking in."

Somewhere in the back of my thoughts, I have the wherewithal to be annoyed by the statement, to roll my eyes in
return at the fact he has known about the medicines and not
mentioned it.

"Well," I mumble, "you did not tell me anything, so I had
to try *something*."

I say it with a fair bit of attitude, but he gives me such a
strangely sad expression that all hints of annoyance flee.

"I appreciate your trying," he whispers. His face is very close
to mine. I look down, at his two hands wrapped around my
smaller one, ruined fingers resting between his. The pain there
is mostly gone. Gently, he removes his gifted ring, returning
it to his own finger.

"Do that for the others," I tell him. "Then tell me what is
ailing you. Even if I cannot help, I wish to know."

"Of course you do, tiny Bluebell," he murmurs, making an
expression somewhere close to a smile. He presses his lips to
my finger again for a moment before spitting the venom out
into the hearth. This time, I do move to place another log onto
the fire. He gives an appreciative hum.

"I'm tall for a woman," I repeat grumpily.

Brushing my hair aside, he glances at me with a strangely shy expression, then does the same to the burning wound along my neck, his hand cupping the other side of my face. Embarrassment pecks at me, though the pain is winning out. There is a third along my shoulder, and I do not have time to consider the implications of such before he simply moves aside the torn fabric to repeat his little healing session.

"What else hurts?" he asks, paying special attention to my hand, though the pain has mostly cleared. It was the worst sting by far. His thumb touches near the cut along my brow, but it no longer bleeds and does not bother me much in comparison.

"My ankle," I say, "but I don't think you have any special faerie spit for a rolled ankle."

He gives another approximation of a half smile and glances at my feet, which are now beside him as one of my legs is resting over his. "No. Which one? You should take your shoes off."

He's quite correct. Fumbling with the few laces—I should've worn my boots to begin with and not rolled my silly ankle—I pull both off as carefully as possible. The right one is swollen, but not as terribly as I anticipated. Aidyn must see, as he touches it immediately, careful enough not to hurt.

"Anything else?"

"Yes," I say in exhaustion. "*Everything.*"

He chuckles tiredly, leaning against the closest desk where the pillows create a little wall.

"Tell me," I say again. His eyes are closed—he doesn't appear to be listening. "*Aidyn.*"

"Hmm?"

"Show me what's wrong with you. I'm only a human, I know, but you're going to tell me." Carefully, limping more than before, I gather all the silly little human herbs and jars off the window and deposit them onto the bed, sorting for whatever I can attempt to use to soothe the remains of the stings and all the many cuts and scrapes. His bright eyes follow my movements, low lidded and strange in the dying firelight.

"You should not go back tonight," he murmurs, glancing at the window. " 'Tis too dark. I cannot walk you back."

Nodding, I frown at the salve I'm smearing across my shoulder, ignoring the sting. "I'd rather not walk again for a little while, certainly. This is going to ruin midsummer."

"Midsummer . . ." he mumbles, half a question, half a breath of a thought.

"Yes, the festival," I remind him. "When the faerie world is closest to ours. We dance all night, and the fae come out to dance with us. Well, not fae much like *you*, but the little ones. Sometimes bigger ones, but they're only shadows in the trees, you see? It is a lovely time. I will bake a pie and win the contest this year. If I bake you a plum pie, will you taste test it for me?"

I'm aware I'm rambling, but my mind is still spinning, and I feel like crying.

"A pie contest?" he asks, amused by the concept.

"Yes. And we wear masks. Some we make ourselves, some we all make, but that's usually for the children. There's much eating and drinking and dancing. If you are in love, you put flowers in the hair of your love, and they dance with you. My friends shall put flowers in each other's hair."

I think for a long moment of telling him more about Niall and Una, but I have not even told him my name, not yet, so I put the thought from my mind.

"Who will you dance with?" he asks. His eyes are oddly intense, as if this worries him greatly.

Who are you dancing with, Niamh? I wrinkle my nose.

"Well, I'm not certain with anyone *now*." I gesture to my ankle. "But no one in particular to begin with. Just my friends. If my parents were here, I'd dance with them. They may return home in time, but it is a long journey on those roads, and they are often delayed. Next year, perhaps."

"Hmm," he hums again.

I stare at him in the dim light, the soft red orange of the dying embers painting the side of his face and catching in the wrinkles of his clothing where he lies against the pillows. He is draped like a soaked cloth across the side of his bed, gazing at me in equal measure, and I am suddenly having none of it. I survived being lost in Faerie, and a great deal of it is owed to him. He came searching for me when I did not return, and in his condition. He may be grumpy with me all he likes for my pushy nature—he does not mean it.

Scooting closer and grimacing at how each movement annoys my ankle, at how fragile my skin feels, I tell him, "Take your shirt off."

He blinks. "Pardon?"

"That woman did not hurt *your* ears—you heard me just fine. Come here."

I take hold of the front of his shirt and tug him up until

he is sitting in front of me, albeit slumped. His expression is somewhere between amused and uncomfortable. I do not mind. As if *I* were not uncomfortable with his little administrations for my injuries. I do not know who he is or why his pride prevents him so deeply from allowing help, but I'm having none of it—not after tonight.

Working at the few laces at the front of his tunic, I ignore his glaring eyes. My fingers are not moving so well, but they are warming from the fire, and I will not be dissuaded.

" 'Tis a little presumptuous for so early in our friendship, is it not?" he asks, teasing in his voice.

My cheeks turn red-hot, but I raise my chin, undeterred. "Your mouth was on my neck."

He laughs but tugs his shirt tight when I attempt to remove it. Glowering up at him, I find his face quite close to my own, eyes fixed on mine.

"I want to help you," I say gently, carefully, a strange and sudden quiet across the room. "Are you truly going to tell me I cannot?"

This appears to flummox him considerably, his eyes flickering away to the fire, a distinct downturn to his lips. He mumbles something that sounds suspiciously like "not proper."

I snort and give his shirt a gentle tug. "*Aidyn.*"

"Are you going to tell me what happened tonight?" he asks.

A weak distraction. Still, I scowl. "I might. If you let me help."

His mouth pops open, brow furrowing, offended. I raise my brows, attempting not to laugh at his expression.

"I think . . ." he says, casting his gaze back at the fire. I hold my breath, not wanting to interrupt any sort of truth I might be pulling from his chest. "I think . . . an infection has possibly settled. Some of the pain . . . is only staying, worsening sometimes."

My stomach twists. Infections are tough to fight, tougher still when he declares his kind are not susceptible to our medicines.

"Yes?" I encourage.

" 'Tis on my back," he says, still avoiding my eyes. "I cannot reach it well. I am quite capable of caring for my own injuries."

I nod. I wouldn't doubt such a thing even if he *could* lie. "Yes. Show me."

His lips turn down further at the corners. My own are tugging at a smile. I grasp the hem of his shirt and carefully, *carefully*, ease it over his head. He does not resist this time, though there is a definite tightness to his shoulders.

A few of the kittens wobble over to sit against our pressed-together legs, having finished their meal. With the log on the fire, it is warming again, my arm closest to the flames growing hot under the thin fabric of my dress. Carefully, I drop his shirt aside and brush the hair away from his shoulder. He has bandaged himself quite neatly about his torso and his shoulder where I accidentally tore at his clothing.

"Your . . . leg?" I ask, not suspecting he will have me unbuckling his belt.

"It's healing," he murmurs. "Slowly, but 'tis not the worst of it."

I nod, glancing at his leg but leaving it be, my eyes drifting back up. He is as much a man on the rest of him as he is in the face and arms, and I ignore the heat in my face.

Remembering what I am doing, I tell him, "Stay," then get up unsteadily and limp down to the kitchen. I scrub my hands as best I can with nothing else to cleanse them, then take a pot with a little water back to set on the fire. Aidyn gazes at me morosely as I do so, back to leaning against the pillows, one hand tugging absently at the edge of a bandage. Holding my fingers back to the fire to rid them of the ice cold of the water, I mumble about not having proper *anything* to help him. But I cannot take him to the village, and he has been doing well enough here on his own.

Well, he is not resisting me, so I may as well speak.

Sitting, I scoot carefully beside him, feeling his eyes on me while I find where he has tied off the strips of fabric and work the knots loose. Nothing seeps through the cloth, but I have not yet looked at his back.

"That . . . strange little creature that eats emotions?" I start, wondering exactly how silly I will sound telling this tale.

"Hmm," he says with much less lightness, as if someone has tracked mud upon his bed.

"It was hanging in the trees trying to upset me, I suppose. It was saying this weird little poem, and it made its voice sound like Un—like my friend's voice. It made me angry, so I turned around to throw a plum at it, and it jumped at my face. I tripped on one of the brambles. I suppose I must've closed my eyes when I fell, because when I sat up, I was in those dark woods and it was nearly night."

He nods slowly, thoughtfully, helping me unwind the

cloth from about his chest. "I did not know they could do such things. It must have been watching you to pick up your friend's voice. There are no other humans in Faerie anywhere near here. I do not precisely know how its magic works."

"It went with me when I got lost. I don't know how. But it showed up a few moments later."

"The same way I found you, most likely. It knows your smell now. Besides, those trees are not terribly far from these. I heard you scream."

I nod as well, wishing to ask him more about how he came to the clearing. I can ask after I finish my story. I made a deal, after all. Most of it is told, anyway.

"I tried to find my way back like you told me. What . . . What was that creature?"

He moves a shoulder. "An Unblessed. I did not get a close look. I know more about the creatures of Faerie than the species of the Keepers. Unblessed, though, certainly. There are enough of them in this realm."

I shiver, glancing again at Aidyn's cane. It sits along the floorboards, beside his sword in its scabbard, with the dried blood on its end. He follows my gaze and wrinkles his nose.

"You're lucky," he says softly, like a breath he doesn't want to let be heard.

"Lucky I have you," I say. "But yes, I know. I didn't mean for it to happen."

He shakes his head slowly. "It was not your fault. I should not have let you walk out there."

"*You* shouldn't have had to follow me out," I counter.

"Hmm."

"You say *hmm* every time I say something you either don't like or don't want to answer."

"Hmm."

I'd put my face in my hands if I weren't trying to keep them clean. Unwrapping the bandages as best I can, I tug them gently away from the dried wounds while Aidyn gives a weak flinch.

"Sorry," I mumble. I've taken care of minor things before, but never this. "Oh."

Something has raked its claws across him. All down his middle, from collarbone to hips—and I'm assuming farther given the state of his cane—is a large mess of deep wounds. A smaller one marks his shoulder where I pulled the bandage off weeks back. The tips of those along his shoulders and down his back are visible from this angle. For the most part, they appear to be healing, puckered and red and certainly painful, but none of them remain open. Gazing at them for a long moment, I consider why they appear quite so familiar, with the jagged way the wounds healed at the edges and the space between them.

I hold up my damaged hand with its withered pinkie, look-ing at the awful matching decorations, which shouldn't seem as if they can harm both human and faerie.

"Yes," he agrees sadly. "*Oh.*"

23

Old Stories

"Will you tell me how?" I whisper, pressing my finger ever so gently beside one of the angry half-healed wounds. One has reopened slightly, where the woman grabbed him, though the bleeding has already slowed to nothing.

He lets out a long whisper of a sigh, and a few leaves skitter across the floorboards, disturbing the kittens. "Must I?"

"You must do nothing in particular," I tell him. "Are these healing?"

He nods tiredly, hair slipping over his shoulder to cover the things on his chest that will certainly turn to scars.

Didn't he tell me my own injury did not heal well? And yet he is here, hiding.

Carefully, I make a motion for him to put his back to me,

my hands drifting against his sides, aware in a small part of my mind that I have my hands on a very strange faerie man with little of his clothing to cover him. He is very much human in appearance. Every so often, when he shifts, I nearly believe I see something beneath the surface of his skin, like vines or veins of rock, as if he is not made from the same things underneath as I am. Tenderly, he turns, leaning against the pillows, hands bracing against the old mattress. Moving aside the remnants of the bandages, I see what has him in pain.

Claw marks continue along his back and down his spine in a way I'm shocked lets him stand so straight. One is a much angrier shade of crimson than the others, a large blister of pale skin as if something is caught beneath. Given the extent of the injuries and how difficult it would be for him to keep such a wound clean at his middle back, I wouldn't be surprised.

"My family is a violent one," he murmurs, voice so soft that the crackle of the fire mostly overwhelms it. "Not to one another or to the helpless, but we are a warring kin. We, specifically, among other families, are those you think of who keep the edge of Faerie safe. The hounds are becoming worse and worse these centuries. We often have many scuffles with them. 'Tis our nature to clash. We have been doing so since long before your village existed and will do so long after they are no longer angry at you."

Such explains the injuries, or at least hints at an explanation, but not the rest. Not why he is here. Alone.

"I am not much of a fighter," he whispers. Pain seeps into his voice. I wish to tell him that even if such a thing were true—he seems rather dangerous to me—it would be nothing to be ashamed of. But I know little of their ways, of his family or much of the Gentry to begin with, so I don't speak. "I realize I am an embarrassment to my kin. My sister is quite competent. She is fierce. My father is proud. As am I."

I hear it in his tone, a strange hint to his voice I've never before grasped. Love, I suppose. He speaks of her warmly as the hearth and does not sound jealous atop it.

"Is she frightening?" I ask softly, careful not to break the spell of his words.

He gives a weak chuckle. "To you, I am certain. Not to me."

I nod, my thumb absently rubbing a soothing pattern on a part of his uninjured spine. His skin feels paper-thin, though I believe it tough as iron, and much warmer than expected— though I should have guessed from the comforting nature of his hands.

"My father is a strong creature," he says, voice softer, drifting away, back to the place he once lived where bluebells grew around the walls. "As is my sister. I am not. Do you know how much pride it takes for a house of the Gentry to grow? Weak, shriveled little things must be snipped like withered buds."

He picks at one of the jars of salves I've dumped nearby. A horrifying picture of the situation begins taking place in my mind. "They—"

"No," he says before I can get the words out. "They did not discard me."

He is quiet for so long I'm forced to ask, "Then what happened?"

A long sigh follows, and I believe the only reason he is telling me is because I sit with his back to me, my hands resting ever so carefully against his lower ribs. We do not have to look face to face, not right now.

"I have lost to . . . monsters on many an occasion. I have no mind for such strategy, and my sister has often endangered herself in attempts to aid me. My father will not set me aside. Such a thing would be a disgrace. So I took the opportunity—I set myself aside."

He gives a weak flip of his hand toward his wounds, and I believe I understand.

He clarifies, "It would be easy enough to believe those hounds carried off a body. I stumbled across this library, and it was a good-enough place to heal. Evidently, I am not doing such a fair job of it."

"You can't be expected to," I tell him, spinning the new information around in my thoughts. "So, your father and sister think you're . . . dead?"

I cannot imagine a situation in which a parent or sibling would prefer such a thing. I do not know his relationship with the two, but he seems to love them both. I cannot wrap my thoughts about it all.

"I should hope," he murmurs finally. "I am finished being a burden to them. Abandoning them under other circumstances would be a shame to them. There is no shame in kin who die in defense of their lands."

I do not wish to argue, to make him any more upset than the soft tone of his voice tells me he is, but I cannot help but say, "I think if I had a child, I'd rather know they're alive over anything."

"Perhaps," he agrees. "But such things will fade in time.

For me . . . Well, many fae live solitary lives. 'Tis not so bad a thing."

It is for you. If I try, I can bring myself to understand that perhaps injured and alone, he thought this was the correct decision. That, obviously unwell still, he does not wish to return home if his family are greatly concerned with their pride and strength.

But I cannot abide such a thing, and if his father is as good a man as he claims, Aidyn should not either.

Under these circumstances, I don't believe I can convince him. Touching near the angry red wound along his spine, I tell him, "It looks as if something is caught beneath the skin. You may be correct about the infection."

His head twitches. "That will kill me."

My heart jumps into my throat. "What?"

"If it is a bit of their claws or teeth—I cannot rightly remember exactly what happened—it will poison me slowly. They are deadly creatures, even slaughtered."

"I can take it out," I say immediately, without consideration. "I do not have a weak stomach."

He is quiet, face turned slightly toward the fire. I force myself not to interrupt whatever he is factoring.

Finally, I mumble, "You cannot tell me this will kill you and then expect me to do nothing about it."

He doesn't wish to die, does he?

Letting out a long sigh, he simply rests his head between his knees. Glancing at the little jars of salves and herbs, I consider what best I can use to ensure any infection doesn't worsen. I am not a healer, though I have tended to minor things, as has anyone who lives in a small village.

"Did you drink all of that wine you found?"

He makes a noncommittal noise.

He may be miserable, but he's going to answer my questions. "Aidyn."

"No, it was awful."

I huff a small laugh, glancing about the room. "Where is it? Do I have to walk down to the cellar?"

After a moment, he points to the windowsill, where his other items are collected. I squint at it, head hurting, and spy a tiny decorative bottle behind a few old candlestick holders. Walking on my knees to spare my ankle, I use one of the clean cloths as a cover to pick up the dusty glass. Intricate designs of grapes and vines swirl across the glass; I've never seen the like. I can admire it later.

Again, I glance at the dusty old box on his shelf. "What do you have in your little box here?"

He peeks briefly over his shoulder. "Many of the books downstairs had dropped leaflets. They were rotting on the floor. I . . . collected a few I like—information on creatures I've not heard of, different plants, notes on weather changes in Faerie. Such things as that."

For a moment, I'm disappointed it holds no cure for his wounds, no special magic only available to the fair folk, but I cannot help the affectionate way my heart squeezes. I crawl back to him, old bottle of wine wrapped in the cloth.

"I'm going to use this so nothing else gets into the wound," I tell him, sniffing the contents and being greeted with the bitter bite of fermented grapes. "Do you have a little knife?

The kitchen ones are all dull—"

He begins pulling his shirt back over his shoulders.

"Oh, no," I tell him, tugging it back down and pointing to the pillows. "Here, lie down. I can get it out. I can see it—it's a little black piece just under your skin. I know it'll hurt, but it's going to hurt less than dying. Here, you can drink the rest of this after I use some—"

He's giving me such a suspicious, low-lidded gaze that I'm forced to pause. With the way he's looking back over his shoulder, he's every bit a strange creature cowering in the shadows created by the fire. To me, he barely looks frightening—not after tonight. Scooting around until I'm facing him, my leg pressed close against his so I don't tip off the edge of the old mattress, I give my best glare in return.

"You think I'm going to let you suffer?" I ask.

This has him glancing away, gaze skittering over the leaf-strewn floor.

Feeling brave, I ask, "You went out there looking for me in the dark, and you think I'm not going to help you? Don't be dense. Lie down."

His focus remains on the floor, but I can see the warring thoughts behind those bright eyes. If he believed he must hide here, away from everyone he loves, because he is not enough for them, I realize I'm struggling uphill.

For him, I will struggle uphill gladly.

Softly, he says, "You are a lovely creature."

I blink.

"Must you see me so?"

My throat burns, but I nod. "I must."

His eyes flicker to mine, a displeased turn to his lips. I inspect them before leaning forward and pressing a gentle kiss to his cheek. How very forward it is hardly matters—not on this side of Faerie, not after all that has happened. He lets out a long soft breath that tickles the hair hanging about my face, and I gaze up at him, trying without success to read past the sadness in his gaze.

"Thank you for saving me tonight," I whisper.

He cracks a weak smile. " 'Twas nothing."

" 'Twas to me."

Another sigh. He's more soft breaths than words tonight. I cannot blame him—not in such a state.

"Aidyn," I say gently, with the tone Una uses on me when I'm being unreasonable. "Lie down. It's either that or find one of your own kin to help."

He wrinkles his nose. "I cannot."

"I know. So I must."

His shoulders slump. Rather miserably, he turns, and I keep my hand on his side as he lies down on the pillows, mumbling something in that strange singsong language I cannot keep in my mind for more than a few seconds. His fingers pull a tiny, slim knife like a needle with its sheath from his pocket. I did not realize it was there. It is silver as his sword blade. Setting it into the fire, I let it grow hot before placing it aside to cool.

Busying myself with the cloths, the little jars of herbs, and the hot water, I take another sniff at the bitter wine. My head still hurts, and my muscles are complaining. I'm ready for quite a long sleep, but my mind is clear enough. Having nothing better, I use a bit of the wine on both my hands and a cloth dabbed carefully against the wound. Muscles in his back ripple, but he makes no complaint.

"Strong stuff," I mumble, handing him the bottle. "Want the rest?"

He regards the bottle as if it may bite him, but he takes it and tips the contents into his mouth, rolling back onto his stomach with a noise of displeasure at the taste. I'd laugh if I weren't looking at the terrible thing that has been causing him pain.

"I'll try to be quick about it," I tell him.

He gives no indication he heard me, eyes closed, a tiny furrow between his eyebrows. One arm is curled under his head, partially hiding his expression, the other lying under him where I cannot see. He is not lying fully upon his stomach, but his back is to the fire, so I can see quite well. The kittens have all returned to their blankets beside the basket, so they're in no danger of disturbing us.

"I didn't know any better," I tell him, for he confided in me, and I very much and all of a sudden wish to tell him everything. He has not beguiled me, has never given me any reason not to trust him. It should be the beginnings of a distraction against the pain. "I'd never been in love before. Well, I don't truly believe it was love. I was younger, and I'd never had a crush, so that was very likely all that it was. We were basically children. I still do not precisely know why, but he asked me to show him into Faerie. It wasn't such an odd thing to ask. Some of the boys in the village would dare one another across the border, which was silly, and most of them didn't end up doing it, or they went a ways into the woods, never made it to Faerie, but went in far enough the trees began to look strange and they could claim they did so. So, I thought very little of it."

The skin is fragile around the piece of claw or tooth buried beneath.

"I was probably a little proud of myself, actually. He was charming and handsome, and he thought I was special, evidently. So, we snuck out one night, and I meant to take him into Faerie. Just the edge, just for a moment."

The knife is uncanny and sharp, and I think suddenly of diamonds, though I've never seen the stones in person.

"We never actually made it in. We were talking and getting distracted the whole way. I don't remember all the details. It was such an odd, quick thing. I remember leaning against a tree, and he was leaning on me, and we were saying silly things to each other like people do. I think he probably kissed me, but I don't remember fully. It could have been a dream, later that night, while I was hurt."

Aidyn makes another soft noise, this one of more pain, but the wound drains. I keep one of the soft cloths against his skin so it doesn't ruin his blankets.

"Then something growled in the woods, and I heard three barks. I remember that part very specifically. We'd all heard the tales, of course. But hearing stories doesn't mean you recognize when it happens right before your eyes. So we just stood there, looking around. Maybe if we'd run, it wouldn't have made a difference, but sometimes I still feel silly for that: just standing there."

Aidyn's breath is less labored than it was, though the pinch remains between his brows.

"And then they came out of the woods. I remember very little of that part, just that he was afraid, yelling and screaming. And so was I. I fell. Sometimes I think I remember his hands on me, like perhaps he shoved me out of the way in his fear. I don't know if that's real either. For a while after, I wondered if he ever looked back and regretted it, but I don't think so. I don't know which would make me feel better."

Dabbing at the wound, I use the tip of the blade to—carefully as possible, as if I'm touching a filament of sugar—pick out the tiny black shape from his skin, knocking it into my hand. It sits there, a definite tip of what I'd imagine to be a claw, against the scar covering my palm made by the same. Gently, I hold it over to Aidyn. His eyes flicker open long enough to gaze at it with a curl of his lip.

"Toss it out the window," he rasps. "Not into the fire. Such things should not be burned."

The window is closed, and I'm still tending to his wound, so I toss it onto the nearest shelf, in the open where it won't be lost and high enough the kittens can't wander to it. I'll dispose of it shortly.

Using another clean cloth and the cooled water, I wash the raw skin as best I can. He still twitches at each administration but doesn't complain.

"I don't know why they didn't kill me," I mumble. "I'm not even sure they injured me on purpose. I think one of their claws tangled in my hair—quite a bit of it was broken until my mam had to trim it even. Maybe they realized I wasn't whatever they were looking for. I just remember their eyes and teeth and the way their paws hit the earth. How their eyes were more intelligent than any person's. And I remember waking up at home, my parents and friends quite upset, as you might imagine. My friends fussed over me for ages, my best friend in particular. She is like a sister to me."

Selecting the little jar Una gave me, I make a small poultice for the wound, arranging a little pad out of cloth around the edges so it won't have so much pressure on it. I will take it out in the morning and rebandage it. Mam did it for me with blisters and the one time I burned myself rather badly on our big stove, so I hope it's of some aid.

"Can you sit?" I ask softly. "I'll get a bandage back about you."

Pressing his hand to the mattress, he moves himself ever so slowly. Sympathy squeezes my chest, and I loop my arm about him as carefully as I can manage, easing him up, still holding the pad of clean cloths in place. He's larger than me, but I seem to be of some help.

"I hope you know," I tell him, since my cheeks feel hot and he is not meeting my eyes, "that I despise entering the woods with anyone, as you might imagine, and you have tricked me into it on several occasions."

His lips nearly quirk, and under the circumstances, that is enough.

Despite how he claimed our human remedies are of little help, I dab more onto the few places where the skin has not quite healed over, including where that creature grabbed at his chest and caused him to bleed. As I replace the bandages, I'm grateful I had the forethought to sneak so many in.

"Why was he visiting you?" he asks. I wasn't sure he'd truly comprehended my words.

I let out a sigh. "I don't know. I think his father wants something from mine. They're both businessmen. They're probably just trying to sidle up to me because if I'm not angry, my da won't be. But I don't rightfully know."

"His manhood should be disposed of."

I stare at him, open-mouthed, before a half-hysterical laugh bubbles out of my chest. One of the kittens starts at the outburst.

His frown doubles. " 'Twas not a joke."

"I know," I nearly cry, face buried in my hands. I collapse back onto the mattress and giggle. Aidyn gazes at me severely. Rubbing his middle, he snatches at a fresh shirt folded neatly beside his bed with a finger, taking slow moments to put it back on. I manage to sit myself up and help him, though his expression only grows more sour.

"Oh, don't glare at me! That's *funny*."

If possible, his mouth turns down more. Giggling as I bundle up the old bandages and his ruined shirt and drop them aside where I can wash them later—after *sleep*—I scramble to think of anything that he might find amusing enough to even out his expression.

"Well, as I said, that stupid little creature that drinks off emotions followed me into those other woods," I tell him. "And you're right, they're not very harmful, are they?"

His scowling frown turns into a confused one.

"I held it down and tried to get it to tell me how to get back to the library. It wouldn't and threatened to follow me, so

I sat on it and used a piece of my dress to tie it up."

"*Pardon?*"

I shrug. "I'm sure it'll get out eventually."

He stares at me so long I can't figure out how to read his expression.

Then his lips press together.

I cackle, not caring how ridiculous I sound, while he stares at the wall and tries very hard to maintain his rage. His shoulders tremble a little. Leaning his face against his palm, he shakes his head, forehead thumping against my chest bone. Giggling, I loop my arms around his neck while the two of us continue having fits for quite a good while.

"I wish very much I could have seen such a thing," he mumbles.

Now that the laughter has faded, I'm very aware of him leaning against me and the way my cheek has been resting against his hair for a time now. Exhaustion tugs at me, and I think about moving, but we've managed to balance out leaning against each other.

"Next time it comes around, I'll chase it down," I mumble in return.

"Hmm."

When he raises his head, I tip forward a little before righting myself, feeling slightly drunk even though *I'm* not the one who drank a few mouthfuls of bad faerie wine.

His face hovers before mine, both of us slumped. "You cannot return tonight. 'Tis too dark."

I nod. "I'll sleep here. I just . . . have to go back as soon as the sun comes up. My friends are probably having a fright about me. They won't come into Faerie though."

His eyes flicker down, coming to rest on my neck, or perhaps my lips. "Do you feel well?"

"Tired."

"Sleep. It will fix much of it."

"Yes."

He lowers his face, nose resting between my own and my eye, his skin warm and soft. Even with his coat off, he smells of honeysuckle.

A brush of his lips against mine, like the softest whisper of silk against skin.

Once more, a little longer.

"Thank you, Flower," he whispers, such a low breath of a few words.

I tell him the same in return.

He lets out another long soft sigh. My hands manage to find his. We sit in such a way for a long while before I realize he's struggling not to lean his weight too greatly against me. Guiding him back carefully, I ensure he's lying down before pulling all his blankets over him. Watching him lie there, tucked up ungracefully in blankets, I push aside the quilts and unbuckle his boots while he makes a noise of protest but cannot sit up to take over the job. Setting them aside, I tuck his feet back in and smile under the weight of his bright tired glare over the edge of the quilt.

After tossing the little piece of claw out the window and returning the kittens to their basket, I wash my hands and face in what remains of the water, feeling his heavy-lidded eyes on my back. My head and muscles are too heavy for my body. The rest I can deal with in the morning.

Glancing at him, I lie down along the open space on the bed between him and the fire. Moonlight filters in a few slim fingers past the window glass. The hearth crackles, but the world is otherwise silent. The weight of his blankets falls over me, his close warmth seeping through my clothes. His fingers brush against the back of my neck and remain there.

24

Midsummer Eve

The fire has died, and only coals shimmer among the bricks, but the room remains warm. Now that I've woken with my head clearer but my body upset with me, I notice the utter and complete quiet of this place. The kittens are asleep, one of them purring. Aidyn seems to be as well, as he made no remark when I yawned, and his breath tickles my ear without sound.

I've no intention of moving, not only because my body feels twice the weight it should, but because somehow, in some way, at some time in the night, I ended up tucked back into the mattress, and Aidyn's arm is draped heavily over me. His chest is pressed to my back. I'm not yet awake enough to be embarrassed.

I am, however, aware than Una and Niall are going to murder me. Banshees would be less a threat.

Heaving a sigh, I nearly start when Aidyn mumbles, "Are you well?"

"My friends shall be quite cross with me," I tell him, finally shy now I know he's also awake.

"Ah." He doesn't move his arm.

Smug creature.

But I am not ready to simply run—or limp, unfortunately—into the mortal trees, not after glancing about at the mess we made last night and not knowing the state of him now that he's gotten some sleep.

There were no dreams last night. I suppose utter and complete exhaustion will do such a thing.

An image of the Unblessed woman's face merely passed through my mind the moment I woke. The gray light filtering through the window chased it away soon enough.

Sitting myself up as if his arm does not drop to my lap in the process, I sit on the mattress and stare at the wall, considering if I *truly* want to get my feet under me.

" 'Tis not morning there yet," he slurs, still sleepy.

"What do you mean?"

"The sun rises earlier here. Then sometimes later. Or time works different." He makes a noncommittal motion with his hand before letting it flop back onto the covers. "Whichever. The sun might not be up yet."

"You did not tell me that."

He cracks an eye. "I thought to. Then I thought that you might be showing up earlier and getting yourself eaten. Seemed safe enough letting you keep up with your normal times and come later."

I fold my arms at him.

"The fact you're giving me that little scowl means I was quite correct."

I roll my eyes and manage not to smile. He's correct, but I don't have to tell him so. I should've known, given the strangeness of the setting sun. Taking Aidyn's cane, I poke at the discarded bandages and shirt, thinking of the best way to get them washed and drying without walking very much.

"No," he says.

I send him a look.

"You do not need to do that. I will. Eat something before you return to your friends. I will have too much time to do little things like that."

I continue to give him my best, most level stare possible.

"I am feeling much better," he says, his expression not as even, instead quite amused.

He can't be lying. Squinting, I try to figure how he might be dancing around the truth with such a blunt statement. When nothing comes into my heavy, sleepy head, I ignore him and stoke the fire to life. My cheeks are still warm, as if I have not moved out from the weight of his arm. I feel the ghost of his touch over my shoulders and on my lips and go about straightening the mess the kittens made of the plums they ate, sorting through the many remaining for the best ones to attempt a pie. I am going home, but I will be returning. I must see to his wounds again. And as long as I am here, I may as well bake, given that midsummer is only days away.

Someone is going to think I was accosted in the woods, I think, glancing at my torn dress, speckled with dirt and red splatters from the plums but which looks considerably worse.

Rubbing my shoulders, I ask, "Did you eat the rest of the mushroom soup I made you?"

"No. I did not feel well the other day, I fear."

Grunting, I finally get to my feet and make for the kitchen, suddenly starving.

"Would you like my cane?" he calls after.

It doesn't sound like a joke, but I call back a laugh as I hobble down the steps, cursing that stupid creature and the fact I did not wear my boots. It is quite early, and the wood is silent beneath my bare feet. Dust hangs in the sunlight. Something jumps between the branches, but I catch the flash of pale blue fur I remember from every brownie I've ever seen, and eyes peek out as it chitters at me only to disappear into the rafters.

I must remember to leave some food out for it—perhaps it is too shy to come down otherwise.

When I've returned with the soup, Aidyn is sitting and has some of yesterday's pie halfway into his mouth.

Good, he's eating. He looks minorly guilty for no reason, watching me set the pot on the fire to boil. Though I was considering reasons why he could be lying, he does appear stronger today, not sitting straight but not sagging quite so much.

All of a sudden, I don't know what to do with myself. He appears equally flummoxed and focuses on his pie. By the way he's quite pleased with the apple slices, I imagine I could recreate that if the plum pie doesn't turn out the way I wish. I know I should still go home early so I can take a slow walk around the trees to my own cottage, but I don't wish to.

I can eat first, at least.

Taking a long breath, I ask the question that came to my mind beside the plum tree. "Do humans want anything from the fae?"

Pausing with a scrap of piecrust near his lips, Aidyn cocks his head. "Protection, I suppose. Though as far as I know, that has mostly fallen into prayer. How do you mean?"

"I'm not sure," I admit. "I just had the thought that Bl— er, um, the uh, *coward*"—Aidyn makes a face—"might want something from me because I'm constantly going into Faerie, but for the life of me, I don't know what it would be."

Chewing slowly, he leans his shoulder against the warm bricks surrounding the hearth, inspecting me with those sharp eyes. Casually, he says, "I'm not certain. If you told me his name, I could find him in a heartbeat, no matter where he is. I could make him tell me."

My mouth pops open, and I can't help the chill that settles over my skin. He only raises an eyebrow at my expression, unbothered. I'm not sure which unsettles me more: the reminder of how acute his magic is when given the proper tools and that I am in as much danger if he were to decide he does not like me . . .

Or that I nearly opened my mouth to tell him.

As if sensing this, he says, "You can think it over."

Shaking my head—at which part I'm uncertain—I ask, "But you cannot think of anything?"

Disappointment flickers across his face, but he tells me, "It is not as if we trade with humans. We have such a specific relationship with your folk, and it is not as equals. I'm sure your kin find anything within our lands more valuable than our own, but other than dipping into the edges to gather food"—he gives me a smirk—"I don't know what any of you would desire."

Besides, so much as crushing an incorrect mushroom can bring down the wrath of the Keepers. Most humans don't want to step foot in here, let alone attempt to take anything.

"I don't suppose he's interested in a basketful of berries here or there," I mutter. "Maybe it has nothing to do with me. I'm being paranoid."

Aidyn still regards me with those overly intelligent, low-lidded eyes.

I let the topic fade, chilled by the reminder of his magic.

"I do not wish you to think badly of my kin," he says quite suddenly, voice low. Maneuvering closer alongside me, hand on his shoulder, he stares at the soup I'm stirring with a long-handled spoon. "I am very proud to be my father's. As I said, I am through being a weight upon them."

Though the statement grates on me, it's an oddly sweet thing—he is so concerned I may think badly of his family. Not a surprise. Though there have been a few bouts of anger and frightening expressions, he seems an oddly sweet thing for a creature born of Faerie. It isn't as if humans do not have little outbursts when stressed or injured. His are simply a touch more terrifying. For the most part, he seems kinder than many humans I've met.

Whoever they are, they do not deserve him.

"Why are you not answering?" he asks.

I snort. "I don't know how to answer. As I said, I don't

think I'd like it very much at all if my child decided to remove himself by pretending monsters took him. If your father is half as good as you say he is, he must agree."

He's quiet until I've pulled the pot off the stove—I forgot to bring up bowls, so I pass my spoon to him after blowing away the steam and drinking a salty bite.

Finally, he whispers, "We are not the same creatures as you. Love means not the same thing."

He may be correct, but I don't see why I have to believe so. "So, you'd think it was good if your son did such a thing?"

He does not answer, simply keeps passing the spoon back and forth, and that, in and of itself, is answer enough.

When I eventually stumble back across the border, cursing to myself at the uneven ground, I find the sun not yet cresting the trees. Some of the village will be awake, but not all. I take a long slow path around to our cottage, listening to Primrose lowing at my approach.

"Hi, girl," I say, leaning against her warm broad head. "I'll be down in a little bit."

It's still early, so I make my way back inside, finding a change of clothes and lighting a fire under the bath. It will be hot later, but I'm in no mood for cold water. Gazing into the mirror, I tug off my pretty torn dress, regarding it unhappily. It isn't past saving, at least once I wash it. Staring at the faded bumps of beestings, I let out a long slow breath.

His lips were on my skin.

Shaking myself, I get into the water while it's still only a little warm, curling into a ball before gathering the soaps off the wall and washing my hair until the whole room smells of herbs and sweet pea and honeysuckle. Dipping under the surface, I hold my breath until my lungs are close to bursting before sitting and shoving my hair out of my face.

Una is most certainly going to kill me.

I can't bring myself to mind. If it were Niall in that library, she'd bonk me over the head with my own milk pail if I tried to hinder her return.

Is that what Aidyn and I are to each other?

It was nothing like the one other kiss I've had, with that man I don't wish to think about. Truth be told, it was not much of a kiss at all, just a chaste brush of the lips, almost mistakable for nothing. I touch my fingers to my lips, considering with a long sigh. If I were a little braver, I might have tried for another this morning. Apparently, I am not so brave as I sometimes feel.

As far as I know, that little bit of strong wine muddled his thoughts. Perhaps he does not remember he did it and will not do it again.

I sigh.

When the sun is finally peeking over the trees, sending light through the washroom window, I force myself out of the cooling bath, then dunk my hair into a pail of fresh water until it is clean of soap before plastering it back into two short braids while it's wet and manageable. It's already warming, and I find the thinnest dress I have. Peering out the front door, I ensure no one is wandering up the path, then head to the barn. Down in the village, I see a particular head of golden hair pause as Una catches sight of me. I hurry into the barn, head down. If she's going to come shriek at me, at least she'll do it away from the eyes of the village.

The village may *hear* her, but I can't do much about that other than run back into the woods, which wouldn't improve the situation.

I'm halfway through filling the milk pail when I feel myself being watched. Glancing sideways, I find Una standing in the doorway, hands on hips, and suddenly wonder if I *shouldn't* have come into the barn, where there are plenty of objects to be flung at my head.

"Before you leave my body in the woods," I say, "I'll have you know I did *not* stay overnight by choice, and I had a very frightening time."

The glare remains, as do the angry shoulders.

"I'm almost entirely certain something nearly ate me," I tell her conversationally, though the memory has me shivering in the hot morning. "But in case you need further reason to like Aidyn, I'm also certain he killed it, or close. It was too dark to find my way back, so I slept there."

Her eyebrow goes up.

"Don't worry," I mutter a little bitterly. "He didn't ravish me in my sleep."

Despite the evident curiosity, I see her eyeball the nearby stack of hay. She can't lift one of the bales on her own, but I imagine she might very well try.

Finishing the milking, I scoot around on the stool, careful of my ankle. "It really was an accident."

Finally, she says, "*What'd* I say I would do if you didn't come back by sundown?"

"Cry at me?"

"That is correct."

"Does it help that I cried when I was there?"

"*No!*"

I stare at her for a long moment. "Can you just cry at me now so I expect it?"

She throws her hands into the air. "Niamh!"

A distant part of me remembers that Aidyn was once by this barn and that he could be eavesdropping and hear my name being spoken. A larger part of me doesn't care.

"Does it help that I cried in front of Aidyn?"

She glowers and chews on her lips. "Was it embarrassing?"

"A little."

"Then yes, a little."

I don't mention that I'll be visiting him again. She doesn't need to hear it right now, and it'll do me good to stay here for a few hours.

"You look terrible," she tells me, still eyeing that hay bale.

"I feel terrible. If anyone else asks, I slipped and fell down a hill, all right?"

"No one will believe that."

I shrug. "Whatever alternative they come up with, it still won't be what happened."

"And you're going back, aren't you?"

Or I'll tell her now. "Yes. I know what's wrong with him now."

This has her attention. She squints at me, glances over her

shoulder, and then kicks some of the hay beneath her shoes. "I'm going to get gray hair. You're going to give me gray hair."

"I really am sorry."

"Well, don't be so genuine. *I'm trying to be angry!*"

I put my face in my hands so she won't see me smirk. "Una, I can't even believe it was all real."

Footsteps announce themselves, and I have a moment of panic before Niall slides into view, skidding to a halt on the straw.

He opens his mouth before Una's hand flies up. "I already yelled at her! She's going to say something incredible, I can tell—don't interrupt!"

His mouth clicks shut, but he evens a stare at the back of her head. They most certainly were planning an ambush.

Finally, he says, "If you ever make me come into Faerie to get you, whatever is in there won't be nearly as scary as I'll be."

"Don't *ever* come into Faerie looking for me."

"Don't ever *make me*."

I clamp down on the childish desire to stick my tongue out at him. He scowls but looks more relieved than anything, hugging me before glaring out the barn door as if he's too angry to speak. It isn't convincing.

"You—" Una points at me. "I'm going to get my dress, because I was *worried* about you yesterday and didn't finish it, and you're going to tell me everything."

Niall clears his throat.

"Tell *us* everything—are you limping?"

"I twisted my ankle. I fell."

Glowering, Niall stomps over and picks up the milk, muttering something I can't make out while he stalks to the house. Una and I exchange glances before she remembers she's angry for the same reason. "Get in the house!"

"The chickens—"

"I'll feed the chickens!" Niall hollers from the other side of the barn.

I manage not to smile. It's such a vastly different world on this side of the trees. It doesn't call to me nearly as much, but the people certainly do.

"Does it help at all that Aidyn threatened to, er . . . remove Blain's . . . manhood?"

Una's mouth pops open, and then she turns on her heel and trots off to get her sewing. It doesn't hide her giggling as she hurries down the path. Niall is giving me such an odd look when I round the door of the barn that I know he's trying to keep a hard expression.

Finally, he says, "Introduce me to him. I'll help."

Rolling my eyes, I limp inside after him, trying to piece together everything that happened the day before so that I can properly tell them the story.

It is not long before I return, pausing once where the trees meet the village clearing to glance at the meadow valley where the dancing will take place. Another storm is gathering heavy in the air. I'm relieved not to find any familiar wagons or horses or pale heads of hair I don't wish to see.

Closing my eyes, I find the now-familiar woods about the

library and the gentle tendril of smoke from the correct chimney.

"Aidyn!" I call, trotting ungracefully through the walls of books mostly on one foot, the ingredients I need for the pie-crust set over my arm in a smaller basket. There's extra bread, cheese, honey Una pilfered from her own pantry, and what I took from my own to make him more soup, but it isn't a heavy burden. It's not as if I have more medicines I can unsuccessfully pester him to utilize.

Before I can call out again, a soft breeze swirls down from the upper level. Relief lodges in my chest. He is evidently well enough to be sending a bit of magic my way.

"Are you cooking?" comes his voice from above. "I shall come down."

"Yes!" I call, feeling strangely shy to return after the events of last night.

Spreading my things out on the kitchen table, I find a pot of something already warm on the stove. Aidyn appears momentarily, walking slowly but with straight, comfortable shoulders. He pauses in the doorway, and we regard each other in the late-afternoon light sent through the dusty window.

His lips quirk.

"Why so concerned?" he asks, as if I were not forced to take a knife to his skin less than a full day ago. As he says it, his eyes flicker to my neck where the bee stung me, then to my ankle I'm leaning off.

Why so concerned, indeed.

I peer up at him, trying to pretend my thoughts are not swirling on whether or not he meant to kiss me. "How do you feel?"

He wrinkles his nose, gazes at the ceiling, and says, "Lazy."

I tamp down the sudden desire to smack him with one of his own pillows. "Don't test me, faerie."

My fake annoyance only has him pressing his lips together, mouth crinkling at the corners. I suppose if he's well enough for this amount of amusement, he can't be suffering. Hopefully he got more sleep.

Watching him pull the loaf of bread from my basket and press it to his nose, I tell him, "I'm going to make a plum pie."

"Mmm," he says, nose still in the bread as he takes a deep breath.

Una thinks him much more frightening than he is.

"What did you make on the stove? Were you walking much?"

"I told you I am perfectly able to cook for myself," he tells me, unbothered.

While he takes a knife to the bread, I open the pot to find some sort of dish of a variety of mushrooms he must've taken from the nearby trees. I decide not to give him grief about walking . . . yet.

"What are these?" I ask mildly. "Have you found something else poisonous to eat?"

Handing me a slice of bread, he deposits a tied-up cloth into my hand. I find a bundle of leftover wood hedgehog mushrooms, perfectly edible.

"These usually grow in the fall," I tell him, and he shrugs.

"Faerie," he says. At my even stare, he supplies, "They were sprouting under the edge of the library. A few dozen paces."

I consider making him swear it, but I suppose he already

has, given their ways. Picking at the food, I find something light in texture and a little spongy, not as flavorful as it could possibly be, but he has so few ingredients out here—

"Is the chef impressed?" He's a tad too pleased with himself, lips pressed together. I can't help but look at them.

"She is."

The sparkle in his eyes erases my annoyance at his outside venture. Nibbling on the bread, I scramble my thoughts together and set to work on my pie.

It isn't long before I realize the brownie has taken up full residence as she slinks from her tree in an attempt to steal my ingredients. Half my time is spent keeping an eye on the flashes of pale fur as the long-limbed creature appears from all the nooks and crannies of the kitchen. Eventually, Aidyn catches her, mumbling in his singsong language before setting her on the counter, where she folds up and scowls at him. She is vaguely human in shape, if no larger than a house cat, with some sort of fabric like fall leaves draped about her, and she chatters back at him in an approximation of the same words, though much less elegant and charming. I've never heard one speak before. I give her a cup of cold water and two of the plums, and she quiets down, glowering at the kittens Aidyn has let loose along the floor to explore.

She keeps on chattering at him while he tries not to laugh. "She has little ones."

"What?"

"In her tree nest. She has little ones." Before I can open my mouth to ask where, he tells me, "No, you may not look. They are very protective. It will give her too much stress if you try."

Disappointed, I consider if I can somehow bribe the creature with enough sugary treats for her to want to introduce me. Aidyn smirks, and I wonder if my thoughts are obvious on my face. He has already seated himself along the closest table, leaning against the wall in such a way it doesn't press against his back, and nudges the stool toward me with the toe of his boot. I sit, glad I needn't worry about my ankle, and scheme about dancing at midsummer without hurting myself.

His eyes are still on my face.

I manage not to look at him too often as I test out every possible option for the pie filling. A comfortable silence descends across the kitchen, interrupted only by the brownie muttering to herself, the kittens getting into the cupboards, and the soft whisper of Aidyn humming. With no words, it feels entirely unthreatening.

When the stove has been fed enough wood and both pies are inside—two slightly different recipes, to see which Aidyn and Una and Niall like the best—I gaze at him pointedly.

He pauses with the four kittens he's managed to balance in his hands, eyebrows going up, and asks, "Yes?"

"I want to see your back."

His nose wrinkles, a hilariously human expression. "I—"

"Just out of curiosity, do you think you'll win this argument?" Taking the pot of water I've been boiling over the stove this time and unbundling some of the other clean bandages left over from my previous sneaking in of supplies, I wait for an argument.

I receive none.

"You know, you'd think a terrifying faerie would be able to

outwit a little human like me."

When I glance up, I'm receiving the same even stare of mild annoyance and exhaustion. Blandly, he says, "The tales never tell of humans so pushy as you."

"Thank you," I say brightly. "Am I going to waddle over to you, or you to me?"

His lips press into a thin line as he fights to stay severe. Well, there's only the one stool I'm taking up, so I maneuver onto the counter beside him. Boosting myself alongside his hip, I feel *nearly* as tall as him. Much of his height must be in those legs. He is only wearing one of his light but finely made tunics. Taking the hem of the pale cloth, I lift it carefully until I can hook it over his shoulder and inspect the bandages. His back is to me, and though a rainstorm is gathering here as well as in the mortal lands, daylight drifts through the glass behind and above us, so I have a clearer view than last night. My cheeks heat, and I'm quite glad he's staring forward and at the floor, where the kittens are stumbling against one another.

I am no doctor, but with the poultice removed, the painful wound beside his spine appears improved. He winces but does not object to my cleaning it with the cooled water. Carefully replacing the bandages, I assure myself he is unlikely to get himself killed somehow while I'm home for a few days for midsummer.

"Are you like this with all your friends?"

"Excuse me?"

"Are you this pushy with all your friends?" He only sounds a little exhausted.

"Do you mean am I loving and caring to all my friends?

Yes, I am. Thank you for noticing."

He snorts, turning a bit, and suddenly his face is right there, so very close to mine as he gazes over his shoulder. His hand readjusts on the edge of the counter, fingers sliding under my knee. My skirts are thin, but it's likely my imagination I can feel his skin against mine.

His eyes flicker all down me, drifting over my lips and back up to my eyes. "Have you satisfactorily doctored me?"

I clear my throat. "I think so?"

Lips tugging at the corners, he slides off the edge of the counter and disappears out the door. I scowl after him, considering if he was waiting for me to kiss *him* and wondering all the more if there is any great difference in how fae and humans approach such things.

Am I supposed to be doing something?

Faerie only knows why I don't simply ask him.

"Where are you—" I clear my throat. "Where are you going?"

Moments later, he returns with a book I vaguely recognize from the first time I was here. Scooting himself back onto the edge of the counter, he flips through with great care for the old pages.

"Would you like me to show you the constellations of our world? I saw you left it out."

"I didn't recognize any of them," I mumble. "I was distracted. There was a strange faerie in the library I was not expecting."

His smirk widens.

I am aware he is attempting to distract me, either from

what we went through the other day or from my comfort around him leading to questions he doesn't wish to answer. Right now, with the Gentry gone and the hounds with them, Aidyn on the mend as far as I can tell, and midsummer less than two days away, I don't feel quite so desperate to rush our conversations. Let him keep his secrets for a few days or a few weeks—he seems to have no intention of leaving, and there is nothing I am desperate to know past curiosity.

"Yes, show me," I say, scooting closer to his arm.

Midsummer morning falls upon us with a wash of hot summer rain. The clouds are not thick, and I remember many dances through the years where the morning was damp and drizzling and the night hot and humid. Today will be no different.

It only chases the preparations inside or under the shelter of the festival tents for the early hours of the morning. Niall doesn't seem particularly worried about getting wet. Neither does Cara. Una glowers at the clouds and eyes both our dresses, finally finished.

"It'll pass," I console her. "There will be plenty of flowers for Niall to put in your hair."

She bites her lip, pleased with this reminder. Her parents and Niall's are going to have a night with this little development—unless they, like Emma, have realized yet said nothing.

I wonder how quickly Aidyn would catch on.

Immediately, if the rest of him is any indication.

My ankle is resting as I sit on the counter and bake an

extra pie with the recipe we settled on, letting a few dozen more bowls of pastry dough rise. I find myself lost in the last conversation: the careful turn of the book pages too old for a creature like me to comprehend, his fingers along the inked stars and linked constellations, the lull of his voice as he spoke for an hour with little pause until the words came together as their own song I was awash under the spell of.

After, he showed me the loose pages he'd collected into his box, dozens of drawings and lines upon lines of beautiful writings he explained in human words.

Glancing out the open window letting in the damp scent of hot dirt meeting the rain, I squint through the mist to where the trees rise over the horizon and wonder if he is looking this direction in return.

The storm does indeed pass, and the rain turns to a damp freshness in the hot air as morning fades to afternoon. Both Una and Niall help me with the baking for this evening in between making masks for the children, who are gathered outside. The shrines built on the edges of the trees are being set with offerings—sugary things and eggs and little pots of milk for whatever creatures leave their world for ours tonight. Eventually, Emma joins us, depositing her grandchildren with the other little ones and their strips of paper and rolling up her sleeves, eyeing the finished baskets of steaming breads and pastries with an eyebrow raise that's close enough to impressed.

When she pulls up the cloth over the plum pies cooling in the window, I point my dough-covered wooden spoon at her and say, "Don't touch."

She snorts. "What's in it?"

"Plums."

"I didn't know there were plum trees on the border of Faerie."

I can feel Una staring at the back of my head. "A little ways in. Not far."

"Hmm." She says nothing more on the matter.

For a while, as the festival comes together little pieces at a time, I stay in Una's house with the others, sending Niall and some of the other men off with batches of pastries.

Music has started. Many of the children have gone scampering off with their carts of paper masks. The sun is heading toward the horizon, reds and oranges on the clouds with a colorful early sunset. When I step into Una's garden, I find lines of wagons that have gathered, the field of villagers from all around spilling into the streets of our village.

In the distance, a low call like a horn over the hills drifts across the trees.

Just inside the open window, Emma looks out and says mildly, "They've arrived."

Part 3
Salt & Wildflowers

25

A Fae Dancing

"Arrived" seems a tad dramatic on Emma's part, particularly when most fae who will slip out the borders tonight, here and all along the other places of our kingdom where the faerie realm meets mortal, are nothing like Aidyn. Perhaps in other villages, other border cities, other places wild enough, the Gentry themselves come dancing with the people who dwell along their borders.

For the most part, there will be little brownies and goblins and all sorts of nameless small things that will climb into our hair or onto our roofs and into the food we've prepared.

Still, the low shrill of the unknown horn over the treetops has a twist of excitement worming its way up my chest. It is the closest our two worlds come to becoming one, and even Aidyn's presence these past few weeks does not blind me to the wonder. I never have discovered what causes the noise, and neither has anyone I've ever spoken to.

Birds flock over the hazy horizon, landing in trees and watching us with low lids and large eyes. Other than a few rustles in the trees and grasses, there is not much else to announce them. Nothing else, at least, but the shift in the air I can only now describe as magic.

"Ahh, they're *here*!" Una sings, prancing out the door to hug me from behind, almost tipping both of us over. Conspiratorial, she stands on her toes to whisper into my ear, "What if he arrives?"

My cheeks turn hot. Imagining Aidyn among the villagers, even on midsummer, has a laugh bubbling up my chest. "I would never hear the end of it, that's what."

"Mmm, it would be amazing . . . and hilarious for me. Let's put our dresses on!"

"I have the last batch to put in. I'll help with yours."

After I slide Una's dress over her shoulders, we take a look at her in the little mirror against the side of her wall. Finally finished, it is a fall of cream lace and pale green that sets off her eyes and hair perfectly.

I wasn't particularly worried about how I would look at midsummer, not without anyone to dance with—now I'm slightly more concerned about my lack of interest.

At least my dress is blue like the end of a summer sky.

As I help Una into her ribbons and lace, I try my very best to picture Aidyn here, in the village, but can't wrap my head about it. Just because I saw him in this side of the human woods while we were searching for mushrooms does not mean he would melt into a gathering of humans. Even hidden by all the bodies of those brought together to dance in torchlight through the night, I can't imagine he would not stand out. Given I stand tall enough as most men, I'm not sure there's anyone in this village or the next few joining us who would be taller than our resident library faerie.

With the last of the pastries in the oven and the rest on their way to the festivities courtesy of Niall, his friends, and some of the neighbor kids—who are certainly going to be eating them as they go—I let Una haul me into her room and take me out of the apron and old dress I've been wearing for all the cooking. She rambles on about how handsome Niall looks in something other than the clothes he wears for smithing and ignores when I grin at her. My dress is a simple thing—less likely to be caught on any undergrowth if I end up escaping into the woods at some point—but swoops a tad lower than my others and better hugs my waist and shows off my shoulders.

"Let me do something with your hair!" Una practically cries as I slip on some of the softer, daintier shoes I don't usually have cause to wear. They're comfortable enough for dancing, particularly since my ankle isn't hurting nearly as much.

"I like it down! There's not much of it."

"Yes, and I like it just a *little* pulled back in the front. Come over here."

After fifteen minutes of wrangling a few front locks of my hair into the perfect twists, Una deems I am beautiful and ready to dance before all the men from the next village over. From the other room, Emma snorts as if she knows I have a particular man in mind I now wish would appear on the day when the faerie world opens to the human.

"Are you coming?" I ask, checking the ribbons on the back of my dress absently as I find Emma on the front porch.

"In a bit. I like to watch the dancing. Right now everyone is getting drunk and playing games."

I snort. Everyone will be happily into the wine all afternoon and night until we fall into sleep sometime early next morning. There're usually one or two scuffles, but nothing serious. It is midsummer, and the magic of the realm beside ours hangs thick in the air. We are drunk on it as much as any human wine we've mulled, and that is a different type of intoxication entirely.

"Don't anger any fae!" Emma calls after us as Una and I go trotting down the path, hand in hand. I wave back over my head.

"Yes, Niamh, don't anger any fae," Una hisses, half joking, half glaring.

"I don't know why you're telling me. Obviously, they find me delightful."

She scoffs, then laughs properly.

The festival has exploded across the valley with a colorful tapestry of open-walled tents with ribbons drifting from the tops, the maypole's scraps of pure-white fabric being wound about and about by children, and the impossible mess of dancers who have already begun bouncing about the flattened grasses. In the shadows of the trees casting longer and longer fingers of shade across the land, and with the fiddles that have taken up harmonizing, it seems almost as if there must be fae dancing within them. More music seems to join in, though I cannot pinpoint the source or the sweet sound of the instrument.

Despite all our little jokes and warnings about Faerie, Una pauses with me and inhales shakily, eyes catching mine. I grin. We only receive the smallest bit of faerie magic at midsummer, and still, we're nearly drunk on it before the sun has set. It is only by the help of the fears and stories sunk into our minds since childhood that folk are not lulled into the woods at night.

Even so, every few years, there is always a man or woman who wanders off into the gloaming woods to stumble back at dawn, left over from being drunk, remembering nothing but whispering of lovely things. They are themselves again after a few days, and I've always wondered what kind of peace we have strung with the fae that they only come out for a few fun hours on a warm midsummer night before retreating forever and eternally into their woods.

Until one in particular holed himself up in a little library on the edge of the mortal trees.

I smile.

"Masks," Una whispers, dragging me sideways to one of the carts of paper masks the children have made. I pull one off the top, not entirely seeing it, rubbing the layers of pulpy paper between my fingers. When I glance down, it somewhat resembles a fox, though the faces are nothing in particular. Smirking, I tie it over my face, my mouth left exposed, and laugh at Una with her somewhat-rabbit-resembling mask, complete with flowers, hopping after the toddlers, who are shrieking and laughing.

Bonfires are being lit on the edges of the dancing, where no one is likely to get too close, along with smaller ones for roasting meat and vegetables. Even the children are already gathering the wildflowers growing along the edges of the trees. Niall will need to hurry if he's going to gather any for Una.

"Niall's somewhere," Una says, prancing back to me and grasping both hands. "Let's dance!"

I trot after her, avoiding running children, until we're swallowed up by the bodies of our families and friends from the next villages dancing and singing.

As evening settles into night, all three villages have finally arrived in full, and Una has dragged me into dancing more times than my ankle appreciates. I find a seat on the edge of the field, closer to the village than the trees, and eat a slice of roasted ham. A little creature flies by on papery wings, tries to grab the slice, and immediately flutters off with a series of angry noises before I can even pull away a smaller piece. Leaning over to watch it leave, I chuckle and wonder what name Aidyn would know for it.

I glance into the trees and force myself not to sigh.

My plum pie was successfully delivered to the judges, two of the older women from our village and another half dozen from the two villages over, and now all I have to do is wait. Pushing my silly paper mask onto my forehead, I try to find Una and Niall in the mix of bodies and bouncing dancers but can't quite pick out her lacy dress or the pale flowery mask she chose.

I do, however, spot the man attempting to make eye contact with me across all the dancing and ribbons.

I should've kept my mask on.

I don't suppose it would've made much of a difference—there aren't many women with reddish hair in all the three villages.

Finishing my ham and licking the salt from my fingers, I drag my mask back into place and slide to my feet, determined to disappear into the swirl of bodies. Perhaps Emma has decided to join the festivities. Hiding next to her and her walking stick seems like a fine idea—

Blain drops off the wheel of one of the wagons encircling the field and heads in my direction.

"Fantastic," I mutter. I've had a small glass of wine and am not feeling terribly polite. Not even the faerie magic hanging in the air is going to help.

I imagine I'd become rather unpleasant if Blain were to be in my vicinity after I'd drunk that strange strong wine Aidyn had.

Perhaps if I put Blain and Aidyn *in the same room with Aidyn a little drunk . . .*

I snort, then clear my throat.

The current dance is more of a group festivity than a partnered one, so I'm happily drawn into the mix by one of the village boys I don't know. By the time I've passed through a dozen sets of hands and have received plenty of smiles from familiar and unfamiliar faces, I can no longer see Blain from my place near the center of the dancing and consider myself quite smart for my escape. Finally catching sight of Una and Niall, I notice a handful of lupine flowers peeking out from his back pocket. He pulls one out and tucks it into her hair as they move. In the distance, I spot Olivia and Andrew watching, Niall's father joining in similar surprise. Soon, all such flowers will be woven into Una's braids, noticeable to everyone. I manage not to laugh too loudly, my heart squeezing.

The music changes tempo, and everyone begins partnering off, mostly with whoever they happened to be standing with at the time. I've found myself with a cute little boy no older than twelve who's giving another girl across the field a sad look.

"Go ask her to dance," I say, then send him trotting off across the flattened grass while I grin after. Somewhere, Cara is probably asking the boy she has a crush on to dance as well. Midsummer is not necessarily love in the air, but it might as well be.

In the past, would the Gentry truly slip from the trees and dance with us humans until we collapsed?

If there was ever a time when it happened, it seems quite far off.

A hand curls under my elbow, and suspicion lodges in my chest even before I glance back and see Blain's pale hair in the moonlight. In no mood, I grab his wrist and remove his hand, shaking my palm as if he's dirtied my fingers.

He chuckles, which only serves to heighten my annoyance. "I wanted to see if you'll dance with me?"

"I will not—" I start, then pause, turning to face him fully. "*Why?*"

"Pardon?"

We're barely avoiding getting bumped into by dozens of dancers swirling around us. I don't particularly care to move or try to maneuver out of the field with Blain scampering after me.

"Why do you keep trying to speak to me? Any man with a pinch of dignity under these circumstances would not be asking me to dance."

The pleasant smile turns a little harsh, then twists back into place with some effort. "Perhaps a man with a *pinch of dignity* wishes to be friendly."

I cannot tell if that is supposed to impress or soften me. It does neither.

"I'd prefer if you didn't."

I mean to turn and walk away with some amount of calm, but he catches me again by the hem of my sleeve, making to put his hand on my waist. "One dance, that won't—"

"Would you like me to scream?"

Across the field, Niall has noticed the situation, and both he and Una have paused to stare. If I show any signs of distress, the fight that breaks out this midsummer will be right in front of me.

I'm very tempted to show a sign of distress.

"Lots of girls scream on midsummer," he says with a chuckle, but it doesn't sound the same as if such a joke came from any other man. "There are too many fae about not to. And you've been into Faerie too many times to be worried about me. Come along, one dance won't be so bad. You'll—"

My back bumps into someone else's chest. Someone

rather tall. Honeysuckle overwhelms the scents of pastries and cooked meats and women's perfumes. My cheeks burn without needing to see the shadow cast across me, even as my heart leaps. Blain's expression drains of all emotion as he stares over my head. I'm assuming he'd run if he were slightly less startled.

Aidyn's nose brushes ever so slightly against my ear, sending a chill down my neck and into my shoulder. "Flower, would you like to dance?"

"Very much so," I whisper, stepping back farther against him as Blain's hand slides off my sleeve with no resistance.

"I'm not used to such dances; you may have to lead," Aidyn says, and nevertheless steps gracefully into the other dancers with his arm around my waist, the two of us spinning away from the human left flummoxed in the middle of the field.

"Lovely mask," I tell him, staring up into the paper mask he must have snatched from one of the carts—it seems ridiculous on him, a little like a wolf, particularly when no one else seems to have noticed a sudden and true faerie among their dancing. It only covers the top half of his face, so I see his grin perfectly well.

"Aren't you supposed to be resting?"

Carefully, he withdraws his hand from mine to adjust my mask which fell crooked with Blain's handling, still leading the dance despite his claims.

"But 'tis midsummer," he objects with that teasing little tone that crops up every time he is attempting to distract me from fussing over him.

I purse my lips, trying with all my strength not to smile too much at his sudden appearance, but to no avail. I am unreasonably pleased. He still has his cane—I feel it against my back where his arm is woven around me, keeping my body pressed to his. We're dancing a little slower, and he seems to be treading carefully on his sore leg as far as I can tell—or as far as he is putting on a good show. I don't have enough conviction to tell him to stop spinning me about under the stars on midsummer and realize I sound like quite the silly lovestruck child.

I don't care much about that either.

"One dance," I tell him, holding up a finger from where our hands are folded together. "Then we go find a place we can get off our feet."

"Yes, yes, my dear pushy little human."

It sounds like a compliment coming from him. "I'm not the one *dancing* when he should be healing."

"No, but I do believe you would if given half a chance." He drops his head back to gaze at the stars, and I'm impressed he doesn't spin us into one of the other couples. "How fares your ankle?"

He has me there . . . a little. "Doing quite well, thank you."

He grins and returns his face to just over mine. "Why the masks, hmm? This is not a tradition I am familiar with."

"So you may dance with the fae all night and all morning until sunrise, and they know neither your name nor your face to find you again."

"Oh? What if I wish to find you again?"

I lean closer. "I think *you'll* have an easy time of it. Besides, no true faerie has come out to dance in decades, as far as I've heard."

"No? What a pity. I should've come dancing sooner."

I laugh. "I would've been like everyone else here: not seeing you unless you wanted."

"Hmm," he agrees, glancing at our fellow dancers. "They will not see me unless I am drawn to their attention. I doubt they will remember me much. I didn't interrupt anything, did I?"

I've almost forgotten I was extracting myself from Blain's newfound interest. "You were a few minutes late, I think."

He quirks an eyebrow through the gaps in the papery-thin mask, and I get the impression that he would've liked to do something much more *faerie* in nature to Blain if I and so many villagers hadn't been swarming him. Or perhaps if I hadn't been watching. After the story I told, I cannot blame him much. If Una told me such a story, I'd become a sudden and intense acquaintance to violence.

"Nonsense, my timing is impeccable. *He'll* remember me." He says the last part wickedly.

I cannot imagine what Aidyn would look like to me were I not swept up in his arms. As I attempt to call to mind how frightening he appeared when first I laid eyes upon him, all I see are those same eyes when they peered down at me in the dark of Faerie, pressing me safely into the grass, and how they watch me now.

" 'Tis a shame you didn't bring flowers," I mumble too softly over the music and all the laughter.

From inside the neck of his shirt, he draws out a little blue-bell much like the one he left on my barn fence.

I laugh so much it makes it difficult to keep up the dance

steps. "Where do you keep *finding* those?"

" 'Tis a secret," he declares, quite pleased with himself, twirling the flower between two fingers, the rest still woven between mine. "I believe you told me it is for your hair?"

My cheeks turn warmer—between the moonlight and the mask, I wonder if his eyes see it. "Well, it is quite a tradition to do so before you wish to kiss a girl."

"Oh?" he asks again, still twirling the flower. "I missed the tradition that first time, then, didn't I?"

Well, he certainly remembers. "Yes, but it hardly counts. We were almost asleep."

"Very true," he says, then tucks the flower into my hair. I am suddenly quite happy Una insisted on weaving back a few of my locks where his fingers are tucking in the stem.

"Much better," I tell him, though my heart is tapping away at the inside of my ribs.

"Hmm," he agrees, stepping into a small gap in the dancers to slow to a standstill. His face tips to mine, hand cupping my cheek and around the back of my neck, and he presses our lips ever so softly together. I lean up onto my toes to let him better hold me, one arm still around his neck, other hand on his chin. Our masks brush with a gentle rustle of paper. I want to run my fingers across every bit of him, more so when his lips part and he leans back enough to breathe and kiss me again.

A couple bumps into us, startling me much more than Aidyn. Someone calls out an apology as they're spun away across the field of dancers.

Aidyn chuckles, and the music changes tempo again.

I suck in a long breath and find my voice enough to tell

him, "That was your one dance."

"Oh—" He gets no chance to argue his case as I grasp his hand and lead him away, weaving through all the dancing and brushes of hands to the edge of the field where the wagons and carts have circled us in. I don't know the time and am not sure when I should check back on my pie, but if I've won, the ribbon will be there when I return.

"Into the woods at night, hmm?" There is laughter in Aidyn's voice.

"This is hardly the woods," I tell him, pausing only a dozen steps into the trees and the long grass, among a patch of lupine the children haven't harvested. Turning, I release his hand to pull his mask carefully over his head. The mischief in his eyes matches that in his voice. "I made plenty of pastries. There should still be some left. Shall I steal some?"

This almost appears to distract him, and then he seats him-self in the grass, toppling me down alongside him and half lying over me. "Perhaps shortly."

"Something else on your mind?" I ask as he leans over, not quite trapping me beneath him but keeping me warm in the grasses, which are cooling in the summer night. The air still smells of rain, but the ground is not damp enough to notice.

Maneuvering until his cheek is propped against his hand, eyes just over mine, he unwinds my mask ribbons carefully, as if it's my dress instead, running his fingers along my cheeks and around the corners of my eyes. The cool of his rings against his otherwise warm skin startles me. His brow furrows slightly, as if he can't decide, as if my lips are not still warm from kissing him moments ago. I would decide for him if I could remind myself how to break this silence, the intense gaze of his eyes locked onto mine. Gently, he tips his head until the side of his nose skims mine.

"Are you afraid?" he whispers, voice rough.

I shake my head, and it brushes my bottom lip against his.

"Not at all?" It is not a tease or a flirt or a little toss of banter. His tone is soft, concerned, genuine. If I were far enough back to look into his eyes again, I imagine they'd match.

My breath unlocks enough for me to whisper, "Not at all."

Another long hum of a breath follows, that soft sound I've come to associate with amusement or contentment . . . or a little bit of avoidance when I'm asking uncomfortable questions. His breath drifts against my cheek, and his lips press tenderly to mine. Weaving my fingers carefully around the back of his neck, I lean against him where we're curled together in the grasses. Everything about him smells sweet, the sugary taste of the plums on his lips.

When he leans back, forehead resting against mine, his thumb drifts over my bottom lip. Running my fingers through his hair, I think offhandedly about how soft it is, about how I've been thinking of doing this since I met him. His lips drag down the side of my cheek, nose pressed to the curve of my neck, before he straightens enough to kiss me again. I don't know whether to close my eyes or keep watching the perfect planes of his face so close to mine.

"Can I tell you my name?" I whisper.

"If you wish." His voice matches mine, tickling my skin. "I do not need it. You may save it as long as you wish."

"I know, that is why I—"

Aidyn's exploration of my neck stills, and I along with him. His head rises, silver eyes flickering into the dark of the woods. When I follow, I see nothing of note. His sudden stillness urges me to stay quiet. Instead, I squeeze his wrist.

His hand slips into mine, tightening in return. Soundlessly, he presses a finger to his lips and eases back onto his knees, pulling me along. The grass whispers under my movement, loud in comparison to all the sound he *doesn't* make. My heart is pounding for reasons having nothing to do with his closeness. Standing, he helps me to my feet and points to the dancing. I want to say his name, but I am afraid of running through the grasses, let alone speaking. His eyes flicker to mine, and I try to impart my questions without sound. He opens his mouth, then glares back at the festival, then at the forest and at me.

Something rustles in the deep dark of the woods, and a set of giant paws steps out.

26

A Certain Conviction

In the dark, I do not know if it is a hound or a wildcat or something else entirely. No sound comes from its throat to signal if we may meet our death.

All I know is our wolves are not so large.

My hand tightens painfully around Aidyn's, and he squeezes in return. I'm certain that with his sharp eyes, he knows exactly what stands only a few yards away, but he is not speaking, and I dare not. My skin is hot, heart pounding, urging me to run.

Can it hear my heartbeat? My quickening breath? I feel as if Aidyn is standing much stiller than I am, if only because I am trembling out of my skin.

Ever so slowly, Aidyn's hand releases mine, weaving around my waist, locking me against his chest. His heartbeat hammers against my shoulder.

"Close your eyes," he says in such a soft breath I barely hear it over the rush behind my ears.

Everything inside me screams *no, no, no*, but I remember him doing such before, when we found the body of the wildcat, and he returned us to the library in a few steps.

A sharp yip, and a blur of movement.

I clap my hand over my eyes. The world falls out from beneath my feet, something loud and snapping has me flinching, and grass smacks into my cheeks as we're deposited elsewhere in much less quiet and dignified a fashion than last time. I can't help the yelp that's yanked from my throat even as Aidyn's arm stays solid. My other hand is grasping his, palm still clamped over my eyes. His breath tickles my ear as he stays utterly still. For a moment, I do not know if I should dare to move. Then the tremble in those calm breaths of his makes itself known, as well as something warm and damp against my shoulder.

"Aidyn?" I choke, still unable to uncover my eyes.

"It isn't here," he says, and his voice holds the same tremble as he begins to sit, unsteady and nearly tipping back atop me.

Rolling over, I attempt to sit him up under the realization he's much too heavy for me. My hands are sticky. He says something in that breathy language with the tone of a swear, and I say the same in my own.

"That one . . . was fast," he tells me.

In the moonlight, I cannot see much of his expression or exactly where he is injured. It moved toward us, before I closed my eyes. I put my hands on his shoulder and back and along his chest until I feel the tear in the skin in the soft divot beneath his collarbone beside his shoulder. He seems to be working on pulling off his coat, but I tear a strip off the clean underskirt of my dress and use it as a rough stuffing for the wound as best I can. I can still hear the festivities—we are not in Faerie, and I am glad for it, because there are at least three people on this side of the border who will help.

It also means the beast must still be close by.

And that there are so many villagers dancing nearby.

"Will it attack the others?" I whisper, glancing about for any sign of it, ignoring the tears burning the backs of my eyes.

"Unlikely. They are so clustered together."

"Lots of people sneak off to make love during midsummer," I tell him, but he does not appear to entirely be listening, instead staring off into the deep woods with that intense inhuman head-cocked stare he's unsettled me with before. I glance into the dark but cannot see anything.

"Is it here?"

Slowly, he shakes his head, murmuring, "Does not make sense . . ."

"What does not?"

"They are not mindless. They are monsters, but not mindless." Finally, he turns his chin, and I catch his bright eyes looking at me in confusion for answers I cannot give. "What has angered them? Something in this little village?"

Shaking my head, I tell him, "I don't know. Can you stand? I have a friend—"

"It smells strange here."

Momentarily, I wonder if he's lost grip on a little of his

sanity, if any faerie has sanity to begin with. "It . . . smells like grass? And food?"

It smells like him.

He shakes his head, back to staring into the woods. Patting the grass, he comes up with his cane and pushes himself to his feet. I stumble upright, wrapping my arms around his waist when he wobbles, keeping his unoccupied hand on the cloth I've used on the new scar that shall litter his poor body. He barely seems to be affected by it, but I know he is much more disturbed by the presence of those wounds than he lets on; he cannot be accepting of another one.

"Aidyn," I say more firmly, because if his nose says there is something wrong in this section of the woods, I've no desire to walk toward it.

After giving my hand a squeeze, he wanders deeper into the trees.

Momentarily, I consider either swearing at him or not following, but then I scurry after, wrapping my arm through his, lending what little support I can.

"Must we investigate your nose?" I hiss. "What if it finds us?"

"I smell it too," he says. "It's still across the field, pacing. I wasn't paying attention . . . before."

My mind swirls around that monster anywhere near the festival.

What if Una and Niall wander off to kiss in the trees the same as well did? What if Cara goes to pick flowers inside the trees? What if—

I smell it.

Something different, at least. An oddly musky scent, incorrect and strange, unlike anything I've quite come across before.

When I stop, it forces Aidyn to pause as well.

"What is that?" I ask.

"I . . ." He does not finish the thought, continuing forward, arm slipping out of mine. I follow again, glancing at the lights of the lanterns and bonfires around the dancing.

Aidyn pushes aside a branch, and a soft light touches his face. Softly, he says, "Oh."

His tone has me pausing. Perhaps I do not wish to see.

Perhaps it is nothing to do with me or any other human.

Perhaps we can turn away and never know.

My feet carry me forward until I am pressed against the warmth of his arm, and I see what exactly he has found in the dark.

Someone has maneuvered a wagon into the space between the thickest of the trees, squashing bushes in the process. Wildflowers are crushed beneath the heavy wheels. A single small lantern hangs from the buggy seat, nearly dead. Piles of animal skins are rolled into the corner of the wooden planks, which is not particularly unusual in and of itself. Hunters, trappers, and traders wander up to the edges of Faerie when they are feeling bold, as animals tend to flourish here, and this side of the woods is not too dangerous. Not too unusual at all—

If it weren't for the covered cage.

There is something else under the foul scent of whatever animals have been hunted and skinned, a more familiar otherworldly smell hanging over the space.

Aidyn's breaths are quickening in his chest.

In a haunting whisper of a breath, he says, "We must *leave*."

"Aidyn?" I ask. "Aidyn, what is in the cage—"

Three sharp yips, a tremor in the wooden planks of the wagon, and Aidyn has snatched me around the waist, covered my eyes, and whisked us somewhere else. This time feels particularly *wrong*, my stomach twisting, as if his magic is failing him on this side of the trees or he is too wounded to be continuing. A scent like wind over rotting leaves washes over us. As if to confirm, he nearly topples us both over as his body slumps against mine. More muttered oaths from him as well as a few ridiculous apologies, but we are in another border section of the woods, not very close to the library but close enough I see the house I want.

Wrapping my arms back around him, I point to the cottage. "Flower—"

"It is midsummer, there are many fae."

Warningly, he says, "*Flower*—"

"Aidyn, you cannot *die in my arms*, do you understand?"

"I'm not *dying*—" he begins to mumble.

"Are you saying that because it's true or just because you've managed to convince yourself no matter the truth?"

This appears to considerably flummox him but makes it easier to help him in the direction I wish.

Barely anyone walks the paths of the village when there is so much dancing and wine to be had, and anyone in their homes is likely to have succumbed to too much liquor early. Aidyn is trying his hardest not to make me help him, but he's in no position. I'm not sure he should've been here dancing to begin with, let alone *this*.

Don't cry, Niamh. It's not going to help.

I pound on the wooden door and momentarily consider what I will do if no one answers—

And then I am staring into Emma's eyes.

She blinks slowly, once, looking at my stricken expression, then at Aidyn right above me. Whatever magic that has the few people in the streets unable to truly see him either appears to have no effect on her or Aidyn is allowing it. She can see him, if the barrage of emotions crashing over her expression is any indication.

"Oh, Blessed help us," she mumbles.

I've no time to consider the oddity of the phrase before she's grabbing me by the arm and dragging us inside with a great deal of strength. Aidyn, less graceful than usual, nearly smacks his head on the doorframe.

"Who are you?" Emma asks, taking Aidyn by the arms and seating him on her padded couch by the cold hearth. Her boldness unsettles me. "Are you Gentry or—"

"I am Gentry, yes," Aidyn says, unsurprised by the sudden intensity. He is gazing up at Emma's face with a passing of that curiosity I've seen from him so often, even as he leans back, weak. "I shall not harm you, elder one. I am too gentle for my kind."

This seems to pacify her, if slightly. Instead, Emma turns her sharp gaze in my direction. "I figured you'd met some faerie. This is more than I was bargaining for, Ni—girl."

Aidyn doesn't so much as quirk an eyebrow at the first sound of my name.

"He's been staying in the library," I tell her, in no position not to spill every fact I have. I do not know what I am supposed to do about the hound stalking our woods. I am just one woman, one *human* woman, and not a fighter at that. I've never had to be brave enough to attempt such a thing. "He's been hurt before, and I kept going back to visit him. Em—um, we saw more hounds on the edge of the trees."

She stands, her back straight as a needle, no longer irritated with me and glancing at the nearest window.

"Someone has caught one. I think they are skinning fae they find near the edge of the border."

Her eyes darken.

" 'Tis why they are here," Aidyn mumbles, and Emma starts as if remembering he is slumped right before her. She looks at my hand, and I realize I've been curling my fingers into his hair, tucking it back soothingly without meaning to.

"I don't know what to do," I admit.

Emma draws in a long breath. "Neither do I. Let me think." She begins to pace, lighting a second small lantern and setting it on the flat wooden arm of the couch. "Girl, take cloth from my washroom and tend to his wounds."

Nodding, I momentarily forget where her washroom is as I scurry to the back of her little cottage, head spinning and hands jittery. Digging through her drawers, I find the rolls of clean cloths most everyone has saved up. It's always good to have plenty of bandages when you do not live near any city and cloth takes time to make. A few jars of salves sit alongside them, and I grab what I can, even if Aidyn says it doesn't have much effect on his kind. Taking a washbasin, I fill it with water and return.

Aidyn appears quite fascinated with Emma, watching her every move as she shuffles about, glancing out the windows and probably considering, like I am, that standing on a wagon and shouting to everyone from three villages clustered together that there is a monster in the woods is a good way to cause so much panic it may just spook the creature.

If anyone would believe me.

The wild woman who runs into Faerie shouting about monsters during midsummer isn't likely to convince anyone save for those who know me the best.

I'll merely be laughed at and ignored, if not mocked.

Could Aidyn do it?

One look at him slumped along Emma's cushions says *no*, not unless we think of no other options.

Are Una and Niall safe?

Are they safe? Are they safe? Are they safe?

Aidyn makes a disconcerted noise when I pull away the cloth I've been using on his shoulder but otherwise does not object. Somehow, sitting here, in Emma's house, with her reaction to him moments ago, I am much more aware of how dangerous a creature I have come to befriend, how much trust he is offering me to help him. He could certainly fling me out the window with a toss of his hand. In this normal little cottage, he appears ever more out of place, and it has my heartbeat picking up even as I find it easy to touch him.

"I've never met an elder human before," Aidyn murmurs, his voice far off, as if he doesn't know he's speaking. "Your faces age differently than ours. You have lovely paths across your skin."

Emma regards him for a moment before scoffing gently. "Well, you've managed to befriend the gentlest faerie I've ever heard tales of."

"There are no tales of me." Aidyn rolls his eyes, head resting back against the cushions. "I am much too young."

Another eyebrow quirk, but Emma nods softly and does not speak. I press my lips together, feeling both as if I should laugh but also weep. My heart is tapping an uneven pattern against my ribs, even now.

"Should we tell B—I mean, our tax collector?" I ask. He is closest to the head of our village along with my parents, though he may be just as drunk as many of the other villagers by now.

"I . . . do not know," Emma admits. "Where are your other two?"

"Dancing, last I saw. I should—"

There's a brief knock on the door, and Una scrambles in before I can finish the thought. "Emma, have you—"

She halts, face flushed from dancing and hair disheveled with wildflowers but looking otherwise excited until she sees me and Aidyn, and her jaw falls open.

Emma stares at her, the overly loud sound of her name spoken seeming to hang in the air.

Aidyn, cocking his head at the next human he's meeting up close, glances at Emma. " 'Tis a beautiful name. I've no desire to use it."

Emma heaves out a long frustrated breath while Una blinks more times than she should, eyes finally sliding up to mine. "*What*—"

Niall joins her, starts, and recovers quicker, pulling them both inside and shutting the door. He sets his axe against the wall.

"There are more hounds," I say before either of them can begin yelling, then repeat everything I said to Emma.

Niall, to his credit, seems to be keeping up and nodding. Una still hasn't closed her mouth.

"Are these the friends who were worried I'd enchant you?" Aidyn asks dryly, words more slurred than before.

Una closes her mouth.

"Yes," I say awkwardly, then apologize when he starts at the herbs I'm applying.

Una's eyebrows finally crinkle with concern, and she edges closer. I've told her dozens of gentle stories about the creature, but that does not quite comfort her in the face of meeting one of the fae we've only heard stories of—the kind who come in the night, sing strange songs, and chase away the worst monsters of their lands. Her eyes are wide when they stare into Aidyn's soft curious gaze.

A short silence falls. Emma has taken back up her pacing. Niall sucks in a long determined breath. I can see him winding up to deciding he's going to fix everything.

Still, he merely asks, "What do we do?"

"That's what we were trying to figure out," I say, then look to Una. "Someone should get your sister and both your parents, at the very least. They'll listen. We can't go anywhere near the woods—"

"I'll get them," Niall says. "They were all near the pies only a few minutes ago."

The pie contest, I think blandly, nearly amused at how unimportant it has become. I do not like the idea of him returning to the dancing, not when there are dangerous things creeping along the edges of the trees, but I like the idea of everyone else I love out there even less.

"Careful," I whisper, and Una frowns at him as well, kissing him before he grabs his ax and trots back out the door. I do not need to tell him not to speak of Aidyn—we all know.

Finally, Una whispers, "What is happening?"

"I don't know," I say all over again.

"Who would be enough a fool?" Aidyn whispers. There is a distinct furrow between his brows, and not of confusion. He should be seeing a true healer. I smooth the bandages down, thinking of pulling off his shirt and looking at his back but wondering if he will fight against it with other eyes watching.

No, he should be helped by one of his own.

He lets his head roll against the cushions until he is looking at me. "Do not all your people know not to anger Faerie?"

"Yes, we know." This is not an accident. This is no careless step on a mushroom. "Anyone who lives anywhere near this area of the woods is much too frightened to—"

Aidyn blinks when I do not continue. Glancing at Una, I see understanding in her expression. I read the same thoughts in her eyes, and when Emma glances our way, I wonder if she can see the sudden realization or if she's just come to it herself.

"You know who," Aidyn says, a little clearer, and I hear the hint of that unearthly noble faerie voice that is too often hidden beneath teasing and gentleness. "Do you know, Flower?"

"I—" Unsure how to continue, I glance at the door.

Something hot kindles behind my chest bone, a sudden and certain conviction, along with the knowledge I was being used. At least, I was *trying* to be used and would've been had I not been so convicted in my anger all these years later.

And what has *begun* from those actions—what could become of all of *us* should those hounds decide a large crowd is not something they want to avoid.

Even that wildcat Aidyn and I found near the path, with the smaller wounds along its fur—

Unsteadily, I rise, and Aidyn's hand slides off my leg. I step out the front door.

"Ni—um, *don't*—" Una squeaks after me.

Stalking down the path, I weave through the dancers and people wandering with food and drink from the edges of the village spreading out into the field. A few shoulders bump into mine, and some familiar voice calls out to ask if I'm well. My heart thumps, and I barely hear the words atop the rush behind my ears.

He isn't difficult to find, not standing beside his father and one of his overly bright stitched suits. Someone has left their shoes on the ground. Numbly, I pick up one of the heavier boots—they're not going to find them again until morning, anyway—and keep walking. Una's voice trails after me, but she doesn't go quite far enough to grab me.

"You," I say, ducking under someone's arm as Blain hears me and glances in my direction, expression unbothered. "Cowardly, spineless *worm!*"

The sole of the boot I've stolen collides solidly into his cheek. I may be smaller than him, but not by much, and he's in the middle of turning to me. A moment later and he's on his behind in the dirt, blinking. A few people yelp. Someone in the crowd, probably someone who *knows me*, laughs so loudly it actually has me turning to search the sea of faces. So many people are chuckling that I can't pick them out. Whatever they think is happening, that I am in my cups or this is some sort of lover's quarrel, I don't much care. Everyone is going to think I'm the wild woman during midsummer anyway, so it doesn't matter.

"Niamh—" Mister Haskel says, as if he has any right to be offended.

Briefly, I consider going after him, but I am not quite violent enough to hit someone not as young and physically well as I am.

"What did you think was going to happen?" I hiss at Blain as he climbs to his feet, a certain glint in his eyes that has changed quite nicely and suddenly from the version of him trying to charm me. "Someone stepped on a cursed mushroom and we both nearly died. What did you *think would happen*! Or did it not matter since you're perfectly well when you do not live as close to the trees as we do?"

"Your pretty fae took care of it, did they not? Everyone says they all came from the woods and handled it." He shrugs. "They must. It is their duty. No humans would be hurt. I would not do such a thing."

I open my mouth, not having expected him to actually give a half-sensible reply.

He's no concept of how the fae do not have *to do anything.* They owe us nothing. Somehow, they are kinder than the humans on our own side of the border, simply because they choose to protect us from their own.

Numbly, I say, "Why don't you take another walk with me into the woods, and we can see if they did?"

His mouth turns down.

"Come along," I say, holding out my hand with the ruined finger, as if he would ever take it. "Why don't you walk into the woods with me again since you are so eager to take my hand and court me? Come along, Blain. Let us go into the trees like lovers do, and we'll find out if our pretty fae have protected us completely."

His jaw feathers, and he glances at the few sets of eyes now watching with much less amusement. I feel Una just behind me and can imagine her expression with my hand held out as it is. From the corner of my eye, I catch Niall's familiar set of shoulders edging past the crowd, observing. His hand is held loosely around the hilt of his wood-chopping axe.

"No," I agree, dropping my hand. "I suspected not."

"It is *different*," he says, and his voice cracks against the music. "You and I know it is different. It was not my fault the first time, and it is not my fault now."

So, he does think on that night. It gives me none of the comfort I thought it would. "It is not different at all, and you are the same as you were then. You're half right: it wasn't your fault, not that night."

His jaw tips up, just a little, eyes glossy in the torchlight.

"It is tonight. You can take yourself and your father and your wagon full of death and your crumbling excuse for a spine and head back to the city—"

His hand grabs my arm, yanking me forward. I have barely a moment to consider if it would be worth striking him again before Niall has taken care of that decision. A fumble of movement and I'm knocked to the ground as Niall tackles Blain into the dirt, grass flying and a scuffle ensuing as the watching crowd dissolves into more fits of laughter interspersed with egging on the fight. Olivia and Andrew have paused on the edge of the crowd, expressions tight, the only others who've any idea that this isn't some silly little lover's quarrel. Una is dragging at my arm to pull me up with little success.

Apparently, Niall is getting that opportunity he was looking for. They're not drastically different in size, and I'm mildly worried that Blain, with his fighting lessons, might do some damage. He knocks Niall off him once, getting a good crack in on his cheek before Niall is atop him again. Blain may have the practiced skill, but Niall is all shoulders and hardworking strength—

A sharp bark breaks the night sky.

The music doesn't stop, but a good half of the people around us fall still, glancing into the sky and about the field toward the wooded edge. The men scuffling most likely didn't hear. Una and I exchange a glance, her eyes wide and pale in the dark. One bark could be anything. It is midsummer, after all, and there are all sorts of unknown creatures ready to dance through the dark hours of the night—

A second bark.

"Niall, we have to go!" I yell, grabbing his belt with both hands and yanking him back with all the force I have.

"I'm not *finished*—" he snaps as he lands, off-balance, on

his behind before his expression drops. His hand finds the hilt of his axe in the grass. Blain, struggling up with his clothes all off-kilter, wiping at his bleeding lip with a handkerchief, freezes. His eyes slide to his father, then meet mine. There's nothing else to be said. Whatever happens to all of us, he is here as well. A strange sense of justice sparks in my chest for only a moment before there are more barks, and I regret leaving Emma's house.

There is also another horn across the sky and some low wail of a noise.

The faerie woman.

"That's the same—" Una says before someone screams and the mild discomfort of those sober enough to dance turns into shouts of panic and scrambling feet. It isn't chaos yet, but it may be eventually.

I grab Una's hand and drag Niall up by the shirt, and the three of us bolt back through the crowd. Una shouts to her parents that we'll be at Emma's and they should go home with Cara, and I hope with all my heart that they don't follow us to where Aidyn is hiding. Pausing at Emma's doorstep, I catch sight of the old woman glancing out the window, down the path closer to the side of Faerie where I normally get myself lost. As Niall herds Una inside and tugs on my sleeve, I squint at the moonlit path down toward the trees.

Other figures ripple along the edges of the trees, different in their forms than the hounds the shapes of which I know so well.

The singing cut off moments ago, but I search for her shape in the dark, wondering if Aidyn knows her. I hear him saying my nickname just inside and remember that the last time he was hiding out in the library. Why he hid, I still cannot wrap my head about, though I know the reason.

"What are you doing? Come inside!" Una hisses, leaning out to tug on my sleeve. I back into the doorframe, pausing to catch a last glance at the man I see instead of the woman, perhaps the one who cut the hound down last time, perhaps different. This time, I see his face more clearly in the dark.

Sharp silver eyes slide to mine.

27

Beautiful Name

Heart hammering, I back inside the safety of the cottage, tripping over my sore ankle before shutting the door with both hands. My breath stutters, and I keep my hands where they are, taking strength from leaning against the stable wood, staring absently at the handle.

From the corner of my eye, I see Una watching with a mixture of questioning and concern.

I stare at Aidyn over my shoulder. He's where I left him, draped along one side of Emma's couch, a little too long for the pillows, one leg folded up beneath him, long hands curled together as if he must cling to something or flee from the human world entirely. His eyes drag over me, then to the door, then out the window overlooking the kitchen . . . toward where the Gentry have arrived. Something knowing sits in the lines around his eyes and the set of his mouth.

Does he know his kin have arrived? Does he know the creature whose eyes found mine?

"Emma?" I ask, and my voice rasps more than I wish it would.

"I heard screams," she says, voice grim. "Have they come out of the woods?"

Her eyes are out the other window, that which points vaguely in the direction of the festival.

"I saw your grandchildren go inside with their parents," I tell her, and her shoulders visibly relax. "The Gentry are here."

"The what?" Niall asks.

"The ones who protect our borders. Emma?" I ask again. "Do you have a way onto the roof?"

"No," Aidyn says before she can answer, and I start at the sound of his voice, as if I were not intoxicated by it less than an hour ago. "Stay inside. You can do nothing but endanger yourself."

I open my mouth to argue, for what reason I'm unsure. Because I must see what is happening to those in the village. Because I must see what the Gentry do to the hounds that haunt my nightmares.

Because I wish to call out to the man who shares Aidyn's eyes the moment he may walk past?

Foolish woman. Weeks ago I was terrified to even glimpse a hair on Aidyn's head, and now I wish to call out to strange fae?

Still, I glance at Emma's bedroom—her cottage is laid out a little like Una's, and there is likely a set of stairs to the attic as well.

"*No,*" Aidyn says again, his tone reminding me very well what complete and utter control he could have over anyone whose name he holds.

Una and Niall flinch, shoulders hunching, Niall edging in front of Una as if there is a threat to be had. He glances at me as if for confirmation this is the creature I've been speaking of so kindly the last few weeks, even if his tone is meant to keep us all safe. Only Emma is not cowed, her eyes sliding to mine with a strange understanding.

Wobbly, I walk to the back of the couch and lean against the wooden supports, both hands finding Aidyn's uninjured shoulder and tidying his hair back from his face. He gazes up at me with such intensity I wonder if he will simply use magic to pull me back if I try to venture outside, even as his hand rises to mine.

"Do we simply wait?" I whisper.

It is what we did last time. It didn't seem so very long a time until both the Gentry and the hounds were gone.

This time, something is different.

This time, perhaps I know what is happening.

Someone should tell him.

"What is his name?" I ask, and Aidyn looks up at me with a mixture of knowing and likely false confusion. I never did learn if fae can lie with their eyes. "Your father. His name?"

The cottage is so quiet with the weight of the other three humans' unasked questions crushing us and the faint sounds of music and calling out and a few barking hounds. Something else howls, and it sounds afraid.

Do all creatures of Faerie fear the hounds as we do? It seems a strange thing we should all fear creatures of their lands.

Aidyn whispers something so soft that I frown so he will repeat.

"Tynan. My father's name is Tynan."

I mouth the name to myself, committing it to memory. I'm surprised he told me, what with his fear I'll step outside.

"Beautiful name," I say offhandedly, as if names are not precious to fae and he has not imparted something of utmost importance. I cannot do anything with it, not the way Aidyn could with mine, but it feels important anyhow.

"You do not understand," he says, a long whisper of breathy words I barely hear, as if reminding me that what I think he should do is not the same as his own convictions.

That their love is not the same as ours.

"I know," I tell him, then wince when another howl echoes outside. There is the softest comfort that they are not, this time, angry with *me*. No one stepped on a mushroom. I did not enter their territory. Someone else and his greed enraged them, and if they are likely to hunt anyone down, it is more likely Blain and his father.

Perhaps this should make me sick, and my stomach turns, but I cannot convince myself to be grieved in this moment. There are hounds on our side of the trees, and it is their fault; whatever fate they reach has nothing to do with me.

"It was probably that day that he realized," I say without meaning to.

"What?" Niall asks. Una leans out from behind his protection to peer at Aidyn.

I clear my throat, and Emma stops her pacing to frown.

"That night when the hounds attacked the first time. It obviously scared him, but he probably realized how to lure monsters out of Faerie. We don't take anything here, all those little trinkets they sell in the city . . . We didn't even think anyone really would."

The ruined half of my hand hurts, though I know it isn't real. Aidyn's fingers tighten between mine with the utmost softness, as if he knows, his thumb ghosting over my littlest finger. The cool of his many rings is becoming a strangely familiar comfort.

To my surprise, Niall comes close enough to sit on the other side of the couch. "He was sniffing around you because you go into Faerie so much."

"Possibly," I agree.

"It was the Haskel boy, was it?" Emma says blandly, and all three of us stare at her in shock. Aidyn raises an eyebrow, and I see his lips make the sound of the family name without speaking it.

"What?" the old woman asks in the same tone, then goes to the kitchen to peer out the window.

I finally mutter, "We think so," as if she were actually asking the question.

Aidyn makes the same gesture of whispering to himself.

"Stop it," I tell him, and he shuts his mouth, not looking remotely chastised. With a long breath, I say, "They have a lot of family—not all of them can be to blame."

He presses his lips together but does not argue. I am correct—there are more innocents with the name Haskel than guilty—and he realizes.

Joining Emma at the window, I lean over the counter and squint as far out the glass as I can. Nothing unusual is to be seen, save for wisps of *something* on the dark horizon. They are flying, so it cannot be the hounds. My heart picks up either way. Hounds are not the only dangerous things in Faerie, especially during midsummer.

"How did they know?" I ask Aidyn. "The Gentry came tonight. Why?"

He shakes his head. "Perhaps they have been keeping watch. I am not precisely certain."

I wonder if he's managed to work a lie into that. He isn't *precisely* certain but has a theory he isn't telling me. We make strong eye contact over the back of the couch until I give it up.

"How did they know the first time?"

He opens his mouth, then closes it. At the time, he told me quite dismissively that he had his own ways, but we did not know each other then, had not lain in the grasses together with our arms tangled around one another.

Finally, he gives a little twirl of his hand, a gentle breeze picking up even within the stuffy air of the cottage. Niall backs off the edge of the couch but doesn't make for the door.

I let off a long sigh but nod. Somehow, his magic told them. I do not need to know the details. Perhaps it made them suspicious enough to return, if they know the magic of their kin who should be dead.

That same long haunting wail of a sound begins once more. We all jump, the image of the woman from that night, with her long shadow of hair and familiar countenance, still fresh behind my eyes. I can picture her perfectly now that I hear her strange voice echoing across the trees and meadows. Aidyn's expression droops, his eyes flickering out the window with a faraway gaze, eyebrows pulling together. Something about him sitting there, a long pale shape near the lantern Emma set beside him, his hair fallen over his shoulders as if he can disappear into the dark shadows of the room, makes me see it.

Did Aidyn not mention a sister?

Aidyn is resting his temple against the pillows. Slowly, I step around Una and Niall clinging to each other and watch him. His eyes have fallen closed, his chest taking short labored breaths. The wound wasn't too deep on its own, but it is another weight upon a body already too heavy. Perhaps whatever poison that shred of claw contained had already taken root before I could remove it.

"Aidyn," I whisper, not certain what I am asking for, watching his eyes flicker open only briefly. Sitting on the pillows beside his curled-up legs, I murmur again, "Aidyn."

His hands are uncomfortably cold, and I drag one of Emma's quilts over him, though it's much too hot even in the whitewashed walls of the cottage.

Offhandedly, my finger rubs against his rings. I glance down, looking at the pretty little band he let me wear when I went hunting for plums. It did not work well because I had been immediately found by that strange creature.

He gave it to me. A gift.

And never actually asked for it back.

His eyes do not open when I work it gently over his knuckle and onto my thumb. I am not planning on needing it but feel safer with its pressure around my finger. I slide the quilt higher up around him and kiss him gently on the corner of his mouth. Una makes a funny noise.

When I turn, Emma is still staring out the window, but both Una and Niall are watching me.

"I don't think we can help him," I say softly. Una's eyebrows pinch, and she comes to gaze at him, head cocked.

"The healer?" Niall asks in a tone suggesting he already knows such a thing is too dangerous.

"I don't know."

Bustling over, Emma says, "I'll have a look at his shoulder."

"It's not merely that," I say, then briefly describe his other injuries. I know he has well and fully fallen asleep when this does not rouse any sort of reaction. Still, I stay as vague as possible, trying to give him what dignity I can.

"I am not good for such things," Emma says. "Still, I will look at his shoulder."

I stand out of the way so she can fuss over the poor creature. Niall squeezes my arm. There is the beginning of a bruise on his cheek where Blain struck him. I lean onto my toes to give it a kiss. He is looking at me as if he wishes to be given instructions on what to do. I understand the sentiment.

Tell me the right course of action so I may carry it out. The path feels as unclear as one through Faerie itself.

"I'm not going outside," I tell him, because I don't want Una following me, then slip into Emma's bedroom.

I've never been in here, but it's much as the rest of the cottage, littered with remnants of her knitting and neatly arranged with dried flowers on the writing desk and bed carefully made. More flowers hang in the windows, foxgloves and grass seedlings. A small bowl of clear water joins them. For some reason, my throat tightens.

There are indeed steps to an attic, and I find my way out onto the thatching of her roof shortly enough, noting that next summer it will likely be in need of replacing. Drizzling rain catches on my cheeks, but it has not yet returned to the hot summer downpour of this morning. The scent of wet earth hangs in the air. Moonlight still glances through in places, enough I see fully well the outline of the trees. Torchlight from the dancing and festival still stands, as many people have not scattered, though the music has stopped. Either not everyone knows the loud yips of the hunt hounds or they did not hear over the music. It occurs to me, with a sudden discomfort, that perhaps just as Aidyn is not seen unless he wishes to be, perhaps the hounds are only heard by the ones they intend to hunt.

If such a thing is true, hopefully it means none of the villagers are in danger.

I push stray strands of hair out of my face, now plastered to my skin with the heavy mist of the night. No longer singing, the woman is nowhere to be seen. More so, I do not know what I would've done had I seen her.

Tried to catch her eyes again? Called across the meadow and trees that her brother is here?

I do not know if she is the sister he spoke of—also, I do not know if they are on good terms. Aidyn may be withholding much more than he lets on.

A shadow of a long shape slithers down the paths between the houses, pursued by others. All through the air, strange little fae I've never seen flap overhead, most leaving, others hovering. I hope the brownie in Aidyn's library is safe.

And the kittens.

Are they hunting them?

No. It doesn't seem correct. They fought with the wildcats on the border, but they are here for a different reason entirely. My eyes find the spot far across the meadows where there must be a wagon hiding faerie skins and one of the beasts themselves.

What must Blain have done to trap something so dangerous and otherworldly as to frighten the Gentry?

Apparently, any faerie must be swayed by sweet things.

Someone must tell the Gentry who arrived. Aidyn will not. At least, I don't believe he will. If that tampering done to the faerie world is left unresolved, the hounds are likely to come back and back and back again.

I open my mouth, as if saying *Tynan* aloud from the rooftop will bring the fae directly to us. I know not if that will work and don't think it wise I try.

Someone must tell them.

"A few weeks ago you were terrified of Aidyn. This is not a good idea," I tell myself. "Not a good idea. A very, very foolish idea."

Someone must tell them.

As of now, I don't know where *they* are. Among all the shadows slipping in and about the houses and across the meadows, I can scarcely differentiate hounds from Gentry from villagers returning to their homes. Though there were some shouts, they have mostly died down, and if someone had been attacked, panic would've erupted. Down the line of cottages, I see Andrew peek his head out the glass window, then push himself and Cara back inside.

"What do you see?" Una hisses at me where she pokes her head out from under the thatching.

"Not much," I admit.

A wolf howl sounds across the night, a blanket of normalcy and comfort among the strangeness. A part of me wonders if wolves go dancing with hounds during midsummer. Or perhaps they do so with wildcats and are missing them during these hot summer nights.

Across the meadow, nearest to the trees, a shape slithers into solidity, as if he grew from the shadows themselves. Even across all the distance, the silver in his eyes is visible. The woman dances up to him, an ethereal shape in the moonlight, and I can't help but wonder if this is how Aidyn moves when not weighed by injury. My breath comes out in trembling, unsteady movements.

"Is Emma keeping the blanket on him?" I find myself asking. "He gets cold so quickly."

"I think so. Come *down* before one of them sees you."

Tynan's shoulder turns to me, and he steps back in the direction of the woods.

The edge of the roof is not far from the ground, not with all the thatching easily reached just above Emma's patch of carrots. Careful of my ankle, I go sliding down and off the side while Una hisses after me, too frightened to actually scream. I land none too gracefully in the vegetables, knocking aside a cabbage, but succeed in neither twisting my good ankle nor worsening my sore one. A few people stop in the path, looking concerned and then curious about my actions.

"Go inside!" I call, then bolt down the path before Una can scramble back downstairs and attempt to drag me in the front door.

Thanking the heavens and the fae my ankle has healed up quicker than expected, I pull up the silly pretty fabric of my dancing dress and bolt to the end of the path and into the thick grasses. Dew drenches me, and my legs burn, and I'd think of calling out to the retreating figures if I weren't so frightened of the hounds hearing.

The female disappears into the trees toward the dancing as more howls pierce the sky, followed swiftly by the three barking yips of the hounds, hopefully far enough away it is not me they have found in their hunting eyes.

"Wait, wait, wait," I whisper against my burning lungs, and then do call out, "*Wait!*"

If he hears me, he gives no indication, striding toward the edge of the trees. A long bright silver blade is balanced in his hand, point held back toward me. His clothing is barely discernible in the night, just the pale of his skin where his hair does not cover him.

"Follow him, follow him," I whisper, gripping the ring in case him stepping into the trees takes him immediately into Faerie. I cannot run back on my own. I cannot turn back to whatever hounds might be chasing.

And someone must tell him there are more hunting us.

I am afraid your son is going to die. I know you love him, and he is going to die.

I come to the edge of the trees, a barely familiar section I do not know, grasses smacking into my legs and a spare branch whistling past my cheek.

"Wait!" I call. "Tynan!"

My fingertips brush the back of his tunic, and the moonlit dark disappears.

28

Into the Night

I realize I'm falling in time to roll on the forest floor. Head spinning, I shake leaves out of my hair, getting onto my elbows before understanding what must have happened. My breath catches, the oppressive weight of the very air of Faerie blanketing me, the reddish leaves between my fingers strangely wisped, as if I'm gazing at a smudged painting. I blink, and the illusion does not fade. My hands are clear enough.

Raising my head, I gaze up at the faerie creature whose attention I've snared. Pushing onto my knees and leaning away does not help the sensation that he is much too tall, and I remember offhandedly that Aidyn mentioned himself a shorter faerie among his kin.

The little circle of leaves among the trees paints the same

image, the trunks faintly out of focus, as if I should not be seeing them at all. This is not what Faerie should look like.

It is not even what Faerie looked like when I lost myself in the wrong trees.

My mouth opens, but I cannot speak.

"Who are you?" Tynan asks, cocking his head.

The air is soaked with magic, and my lips part again to answer him; I barely stop myself from saying *Niamh.* I cannot imagine what he could do with my name if his mere suggestion makes me wish to answer.

I also remember Aidyn saying he is not too terribly frightening for one of his own.

"Just a girl from the village," I whisper. "I-I think I know—"

His head cocks the other way, as if I am a strange thing he has nearly stepped upon. He has many different features than Aidyn, his face holding none of the gentle slopes or kind countenance, though his ears bear the same little slits. He is all sharp edges and strangeness, an immortal ageless face that should be dust for the number of years he's lived—though his eyes, they are identical in every way to his son's, enough so it is terrifying how little a change in intention can make them appear as frozen and unkind as winter ice.

"Know?" he coaxes, and I get the distinct impression he will not be as fascinated with me as long as Aidyn was at first meeting.

Swallowing, I say, "I think I know . . . why those hounds have been attacking us. Someone . . . from a different village, I think . . . I think he's been hunting creatures on the edges of Faerie. I saw a hound in a cage."

Despite their battle with the creatures, I see a distinct flash of rage pass across the perfect angles of his face. His head straightens, and he gazes down at me sharply.

"Your name?"

Again, I almost speak it. I *want* to speak, want this creature to look at me kindly, want him to be pleased. Pulled by the power behind his words, I realize Aidyn could've had me giving my name at any moment had he wished it. He could've done anything to me, and he did not.

I manage to shake my head. "Please do not make me."

"You spoke mine."

"Your son told it to me."

All expression falls out of his face. I do not dare get my feet under me. A part of me thinks I should've stayed on my stomach, prostrate on the leaves in the face of something so much more powerful and simply *other.* Now I dare not even bend lower or look away.

I am aware that if I survive this, Una may simply dispose of me herself. I bite the inside off my lip so I do not cry.

Finally, his mouth opens. "How dare—"

Shaking the leaves off my hand, I show him the ring on my finger, staring at the ground so I can collect my thoughts enough to speak past the fear. "I am not lying. He showed me all his rings. He gave this one to me so I would not get lost in Faerie. He showed me the one you gave him. It is braided silver. He is in a cottage in the village. I am afraid he is going to die."

The silence is so long and sharp I bite my lip harder, wondering if he can hear my hands shaking against the crisp, brittle leaves. Finally, I hear a harsh let out of breath, as if in relief or a withheld sob. Not another sound passes. Then a long pale hand encircles my wrist, set with rings of his own, and I start at the warm dry feel of his palm. He turns my hand over, thumb pushing at the ring as if to assure himself it is real.

"My son is dead," he tells me, his breath ghosting over my hair, making me flinch.

"Aidyn," I say softly, and his breath catches again, "is still alive. But I am afraid he will die. We do not know how to care for faerie wounds. I do not think he has told me everything. And he . . . I do not think the rest of my village should know he is there. He—" I swallow, some sort of bravery twining up my chest, because he obviously loves his son, and I do as well. "He said many kind things about you. He says you are wonderful. And his sister as well. He says no such kind things about himself."

Finally, I manage to glance up. Perhaps I should not have said those last few sentences. But a small part of me still angry at Aidyn's words wishes to know and know *now* if his own father agrees with such a sentiment.

His eyes are barely inches from mine when I raise my head, the precise same eyes as his son, too wide and owlish and not correct compared to a night of dancing with other humans.

They have much more emotion now, and *now*, now they look like Aidyn's. And they distinctively say, *No, no he does not agree with such a sentiment.*

A soft breeze whispers through the trees, and he glances up and about, into the nearest trunks as if they are speaking to him. He sniffs, eyes wandering over my hair. Another huff of a breath pushes out his chest.

"Take me," he says, and he winds his hand under my arm, pulling me up as if I weigh nothing, barely remembering to set me on my feet.

"Where are we?" I ask, torn between grabbing his sleeve for reassurance and recoiling from something I should be leaving offerings to, not touching. His hand remaining under my elbow decides it for me.

"In between," he says. "How did you find your way into Faerie?"

"I . . . close my eyes and get lost—"

He lets out a soft noise much like Aidyn's little huffs, and his other hand briefly shadows my eyes before we're in the mortal trees once more, moonlight shimmering down. I take a long gulp of fresher human air, feeling the stormy chill of it hit the tears on my cheeks.

A long shadow of a hound stands in the grasses between us and the village.

Tynan tenses, turning so he is positioned in front of me, an unsettling sound like a hiss coming from the back of his throat. A whimper of a squeak comes from mine, my other hand finally grabbing his sleeve, the soft fabric strangely grounding. There was no scent to that strange in-between place of Faerie—I notice it now that all I smell is grass and an odd sweetness from the faerie I'm clinging to. No honeysuckle, but there is a strange familiarity to it. I wonder if all fae smell the same, just a little, or if it is so benign as the little clan of fae sharing the same soap.

I do not know why, but I expected no fear from him. He is

so much older, and Aidyn implied there are much more dangerous magics than his.

Shouldn't one of the Gentry not be frightened of these monsters? Perhaps there is no such thing as a Gentry who does not fear an Unblessed.

The hound is not so bold as it was with Aidyn. Its shoulders hunch, a shadow of smoky fur along its back rising, ears pinned. It stalks to the side a few paces before stopping and growling a long low sound. Three sharp barks follow, but it does not pounce. Another three. Tynan does not flinch, his back straight as a needle, head low. There is still that long blade in his other hand, and I notice offhandedly that the carvings match Aidyn's.

Another three barks.

I can't help but flinch, astonished at the same time that it is *not attacking*. It is as afraid of Tynan as he is of it, perhaps more.

I dare not ask what it is waiting for.

A voice rises over the grasses, the familiar terror of it a strange comfort all of a sudden, as the hound jumps, attacked from both sides, and a whistle of a sword's blade sends it dissolving into the grasses. This time, I hear the thump of its body hitting the earth and flinch. It's only now I see the woman accompanying her voice as it shimmers to nothing in the drizzling night air. Her eyes are darker, but there is something more openly familiar about them, an obvious interest and mild concern that brings her closer to human.

"Dauna," Tynan says, "come."

Wordlessly, she drifts after, a gentle wave of movements, as if she dances upon her toes after us. We are out of the grasses and into the houses in merely a few moments, and I blink, clinging tighter to Tynan's arm lest I topple over.

"Where?" he asks, though there is a set to his eyes focused on Emma's house, and he is already pointing us in that direction. Those scampering inside or simply wandering into the safety of the village don't appear to notice us, and those who do only squint as if in a strange dream. Everything seems a tad too fuzzy at the edges, as if he dragged the strangeness of Faerie along with him and this is what hides us from the others.

Does he feel the presence of his child now he knows enough to believe him alive?

Still, he's slowed his steps, and I wonder if he's seen many more humans than his son. Pointing, I force my feet to work of their own accord and tug him toward Emma's cottage before stopping.

"Wait," I say. "Please let me go in first, just for a moment? You'll frighten them half to death."

A tad ironic, considering the pounding in my chest and my shaking hands.

"I will not harm them," he says, releasing me beside the door.

More howls and barks pierce the sky. Tynan glances upward, then back to me. Evidently, he is more concerned with Aidyn than finding the wagon, and I cannot be unhappy with that priority.

Blessedly, Emma did not lock the door, and I find myself face-to-face with Una. She opens her mouth, looks as if she might strike me, then backs immediately into the room, hand over her mouth. Niall is sitting near a still-sleeping Aidyn, frowning in the dark. Emma is in the kitchen and likely has seen the entire interaction.

Before I can even attempt an explanation, Emma is saying, "Let them in."

Feeling oddly bold, I reach back to snag the cuff of Tynan's long tunic and tug him inside. Like his son, he must duck his head to enter, much more of a sweeping movement than poor Aidyn's stumble while he leaned against me. Dauna has paused outside, not near the door, and is frowning at the field of dancers.

Niall scrambles away from the couch, looking to me for reassurance before relaxing, still bowing his head. I take Una's hand, and she squeezes me tight.

Before I can speak, Tynan drifts around me, stepping toward his son. I mean to say something, to explain more of what has happened, but cannot bring forth the words. One faerie was an odd thing in Emma's little homey cottage—this feels something other entirely. I suddenly do not know if I have done the right thing, not when Aidyn has decided to hide himself away. But if it saves him, I cannot be sorry.

Momentarily, Tynan does nothing but stand over him, gazing down. Aidyn looks remarkably small in comparison, curled against the pillows and under a few more quilts, and I force myself not to go and stand beside him as some sort of defense.

Tynan's hand drifts out, the tips of his fingers brushing Aidyn's hair. Bending, he cradles his son's face between his hands so softly it does not rouse him, brushing his thumbs over his closed eyelids and temples.

"Aidyn," he whispers, then kisses his forehead as Aidyn shifts, called by whatever magic is settled in his name. "Aidyn . . ."

Una cocks her head at the two, and my throat grows tight. Glancing at Emma, I find a matching expression of concern and softness touched with mild confusion.

I am not sure how to react, or what to do, before Tynan's soft voice interrupts my worrying. "What has happened to him?"

Giving Una's hand a squeeze, I shuffle closer. "We were attacked by a hound tonight . . . He had an injury from before . . . I tried to help. I think maybe we helped a little, but I'm not sure what I'm doing."

"Tonight?" he murmurs, moving aside the quilts and touching the new bandage on Aidyn's shoulder but not disturbing it. Instead, his palm presses to Aidyn's chest as if he can fix his painful breaths with merely a touch.

"We were . . . just inside the trees near the dancing," I provide, not wishing to say that we were distracted because our hands were tangled in each other's hair. "It was too fast for us to get away . . . I think Aidyn got in front of me before he made us disappear."

Guilt nudges me into saying that last part, because if I had not been there, certainly he would've been faster to escape. Tynan glances my way but only nods as if he understands perfectly why his son would do such a thing. Once more, Aidyn stirs but does not wake, even when I place my hand on his shoulder.

"Can you help?" I ask, trying not to consider the implication of him taking Aidyn away where he will not return.

Blinking as if remembering I am here, he nods ever so slightly. "This is not a fine place for him to remain."

I knew already but chew the inside of my cheek so hard I taste iron. Feet brush the doorway, and I find Dauna stepping inside, likewise ducking her head.

"Who are you?" she asks, dark eyes on me. Her voice is much the same as that low wail she enchanted the hounds with, a whispering song of words that both makes me wish to shrink away and stand and watch her singing. "Why have you called us—"

Her eyes fall on Aidyn hidden behind Tynan and me, and she turns silent. With a soft cry, she flies across the room to drape herself around him, nearly toppling him off his pillows. He stirs slightly more, his hand brushing against her arm, still not waking in full.

Three more barks, and Una, Niall and I start, turning toward the door Emma shuts.

"How many of them are there?" Una whispers, then shrinks when Tynan merely glances in her direction. I give her hand another squeeze. If he did not harm me after I chased him into the Faerie woods, I doubt he will fly into a rage simply for her asking a question.

In fact, he answers, "A few dozen."

My stomach drops. "*Dozen?*"

"Most likely," he says, as if someone has inquired about the weather.

I saw him frightened of that hound that confronted us, saw the way he tensed and heard the strange, uncanny hiss of warning that came from his throat, and Aidyn himself said they are consistently fighting with these creatures—I know he cannot be unafraid.

Perhaps this is where Aidyn learned to put on a fine show of being unbothered.

"They're not attacking anyone," I say. "Why aren't they attacking anyone?"

He is not so ancient and otherworldly that I cannot see the thoughts swirling behind his eyes, the ever so slight furrow of his brow. Leaning his chin against Aidyn's temple, he stares at the wall, thoughtful. At his silence, I glance at Emma, but though she's moved closer, arms folded, she looks likewise confused.

"Where has he been sleeping?" Tynan asks, fingers absently unwinding a knot in Aidyn's hair.

"There's a library right on the inside of Faerie," I tell him. "It's ancient, but it's safe."

Tynan cocks his head, his lips parting in slight confusion.

"It seems to find people," Emma supplies, and we all turn to her. She shrugs, something in her expression I cannot read, her eyes soft and faraway as she gazes at the creatures who've taken over her cottage. "I was lost once as well. It tends to find those who seem to need it."

She glances at me, and I wonder if she is correct—Aidyn believed so as well. I wonder what I needed there so desperately that Faerie would rearrange its landscape for me. My eyes drift to Aidyn.

"I know precisely where to find it," I murmur. "He'll be safe."

Tynan nods, accepting Emma's explanation, extracting Aidyn from his sister's grasp with the utmost care and taking notice where he holds him as he eases him up into his arms.

Una grasps my hand once more. "I'm going with you."

Despite everything, I raise my eyebrows.

Before I can remind her of her fear of those Faerie woods, her mouth sets stubbornly. "I'm *going*."

"As am I," Niall says lowly, retrieving his axe and looking particularly unhappy, if determined.

"Careful," Emma murmurs, and I am both glad she is staying here where it is safe and longing for her to accompany us. Her eyes catch mine, and she nods gently. Perhaps she cannot step into Faerie again, cannot bring herself to travel back into those lands where unknown and untold things happened. She has only ever spoken with a strange fondness, if not warning, of those other lands. Perhaps that is what makes it too much. I try to smile, try to give her all the understanding I can, and she gives my chin a gentle squeeze.

Tynan's mouth pinches, but he does not object to my friends. "Where do we need to go?"

"There is a hawthorn tree just there." I point in the correct direction. "Will the hounds—"

"Dauna," he says. "They must close their eyes. Take them."

Una and Niall are both already gripping my hand and arm, so when Dauna rises in a long fluid movement, approaching us, both flinch but do not step away. I look up into her dark eyes, which are upset and glassy with tears, but not unkind. Perhaps a little grateful.

"Close your eyes," she whispers, and her hand takes mine,

the other covering my eyes. With a sudden step forward, the comforting smell of Emma's cottage turns to the trees and night air. Both Una and Niall make shocked noises, but I'm accustomed to it enough I merely suck in a sharp breath. I did not know such magic was possible inside the walls of a cottage. Perhaps hers is that much stronger than her brother's at the moment.

"Where is your path in?" she asks, gazing about the trees.

Over her shoulder, I catch the lantern and bonfire lights of the village, many still dancing and eating. It is almost impossible to believe they have not heard the hounds, or perhaps their minds are too drunk on midsummer air. Even past my pounding heart, I'm drawn to the light and magic drifting through the air, and I shake myself, trying to throw the enchantment from my shoulders.

"Here," I say, dragging Una behind me as Niall walks on his own, watching Dauna with some mixture of alarm and fascination. It's difficult not to. I want to stop and stare at such an otherworldly creature about as much as I wish to run back to Aidyn.

As if called by the thought, I turn and find Tynan stepping out from behind the nearest tree, his son bundled in his arms. He gazes at the hawthorn where I first lost myself into finding the library.

"Ah," he says, as if it all makes sense with the sighting of this one tree, then steps around it, disappearing.

"It's all right," I tell my humans as Dauna offers her hand to take us across. "Close your eyes, I've done it hundreds of times."

Niall grits his jaw and nods, gazing up at the dark trees and back at the welcoming lights of midsummer, his hand finding Una's as she's already clinging to me. Her eyes have never left my face. I wish I could tell her how much I love them for coming with me, even if they are no protection against creatures of Faerie.

Instead, I kiss her on the cheek and say, "Close your eyes."

On the other side of the mortal trees, honeysuckle and the heavy storm-laden scent of the fae I have come to know settles across us. Tynan has already found his way inside the one accessible door, and Una and Niall do not have much chance to gaze about the dark trees of this other world before I am hauling them across the short space and inside the sanctuary of the ancient walls, faint yipping barks of hounds following after. Dauna pulls the door shut tight and sniffs about the dusty books as she follows.

"Upstairs!" I call to Tynan. "The first room there, he has a fire in the hearth."

Una makes a breathy noise, gazing up at the maple trees sprouting through the ancient roof, but I hurry them along after Dauna, anxious to have them in the safety of Aidyn's room, even if we're already sealed within the library.

Tynan has laid Aidyn partially out upon the pillows and blankets, his hand beneath his head as if he cannot quite release him. Even still, he glances about the tiny room full of odds and ends Aidyn has collected, touching the side of the basket where the kittens have begun mewling at the sound of footsteps. Una, despite her fear, shuffles to them and pulls back the blanket.

"The hounds?" I ask softly, still hearing their barks across the night.

"When did they arrive?" Tynan asks, voice matching his faraway gaze.

"Um," I say, glancing at the moonlight out the window. "I'm not sure. Not long. Less than an hour?"

"Hmm," he hums in the same tone as his son, then settles Aidyn's sleeping form into Dauna's arms before drifting to the window and glancing out. "Your human who has been skinning fae—"

"He is *not* my human."

His eyes flick to me in annoyance, and I remember I shouldn't be interrupting such a creature.

"Either way," he continues. " 'Tis not an easy feat. Do you know how he is accomplishing it?"

I shake my head. "No. But we left fairly quickly. It . . . scared me."

Having seen Aidyn's reaction, I'm certain it scared him as well, but he would hate if I gave his father such an impression.

"Can you remember that place as well?"

"Yes."

Una elbows me.

"What?" I whisper, though Tynan looks at us as if he hears quite clearly.

"You're not going back out there with those things. You can't fight them."

"Well, Aidyn is in no position to show him, is he?" I whisper back, though I'm convinced it does no good to the two sets of faerie ears still awake enough to listen. "They need to get rid of them."

Una sets her jaw, sending a glance toward Tynan only to shrink as she realizes he is staring directly at her. I'm surprised he doesn't intervene.

"I could go with you," Niall begins to offer.

"I don't think having two humans to watch over is going to help," I point out, my stomach turning. "We can take the passageway through the library. It will put me right where I want to go; we don't have to go back out through Faerie. It's all right."

Tynan's eyes flicker to Niall. "I have no need of you."

Niall sets his jaw, looking as if he wishes to say more. As much as I appreciate the offer and wish him there, an extra layer of familiar comfort and protection, it would bring more danger. Niall is of no use against hounds, just as I am not. Tynan would have to protect both of us as well as deal with the caged monster.

"There are more of us in the trees," Tynan says, rising off the windowsill. "We are not alone."

Passing by Aidyn's makeshift bed, he touches his son's temple once more. "Dauna, stay with him. We shall only be a moment. Little human, come with me."

Una's nails dig into my hand. Whispering, she says, "Please do not take my sister away. She already bears scars from you folk."

I grab her in my arms and hug her. She is smaller than me, and I end up crushing her to my chest. In her ear, I say, "This is all I can do to protect us. You'd do it in my place. Let me go with him. He already protected me from one—I do not believe he will let anything happen to me."

My words are much braver than my heart currently breaking free against my ribs. Through blurred eyes, I see Aidyn still limp and wounded in his sister's arms, her matching hair falling partially over his face, her whole body, nearly as tall as his, seeming to form a gentle nest about him. Her darker eyes have found mine. For all Aidyn's claims that he bears his mother's countenance, his eyes match his father's, where his sister has those of a faerie I've never met.

"It'll be all right," I tell Una again.

Tynan takes me under the arm, but it does not require much strength to move me. I can go with him and help. Unlatching the door, he lets the cool of the library air wash over us. Glancing back, I find Aidyn's eyes flickering open. He gazes up at Dauna's face, a finger touching her chin as she leans down to brush her nose against his.

He does not speak, and Tynan does not turn to see as I lead him down the steps, past the books, and through the strange door with its heavy handle, out into the night.

29

Salt and Wildflowers

Hounds are barking, and though the dancing music has mostly faded, picking up in uncertain intervals, most of the festivalgoers have not realized they are in danger. We've stepped right out into the trees, wildflowers poking at my ankles, secluded from the eyes of villagers. I glance back at the root-bound crack in the tree we've climbed from. Hopefully we will not lose the burrow once we step away from it. Tynan peers back at it, mumbling something to himself, a distinct fascination passing across his expression before his eyes dart across the trees.

"Does no one hear them?" I whisper.

"Do they all live here, in those cottages?"

"No, many are from the neighboring villages."

"They are not accustomed. They do not hear the same."

"Oh," I say meekly, and consider I should be much more afraid than I am, though my heart is pounding, my eyes are burning, and my limbs feel weak. Somehow, being in the woods with this strange faerie is not the most terrifying part of this venture. I have the feeling that Tynan, with his hand still under my elbow, will simply drag me out of danger should it arise. Of all the impressions Aidyn gave me of his father, there were never any that he was a coward. Quite the opposite.

"What scars?" Tynan murmurs suddenly. We are stepping through the trees, not quite going deeper but skirting the edges, and I wonder if he shall do the strange movement again that brings the world together quickly, and if it is something every faerie can do.

Numbly, I ask, "What?"

"Your tiny sister, she said you already bear scars from our kin."

We're nearly the same age, and hearing Una called my *tiny sister* has a giggle bubbling up my chest. She isn't *that* much smaller than I am, though I suppose we all look small to Tynan. I swallow back the laugh before he can think I'm mad.

Instead, I hold up my hand.

"Ah," he says, spying the twisted finger even in the dark, his bright eyes narrowing. There is a decided downturn to his mouth, just as there was with Aidyn. "That should never have happened."

I must tell Aidyn that he looks quite a bit like his father indeed. "It was a long time ago now . . . long enough, I think."

He grunts. "Can you point us in the direction?"

We've left the greatest cluster of trees, the trampled-down

grassy fields greeting us. It seems so strange and incorrect that there should still be dancing and singing and lantern lights floating among the smaller fae frolicking through the grasses. One little dandelion puff of a creature trundles up to us on strange wings, and Tynan redirects it with a careful hand. If it were not for the hounds, the festivities would go well into the first light of the next morning.

They may still despite the danger. No one appears to notice the chorus of faint barking along the tree line. Taking a long breath, I squint at the trees, trying to find a landmark, and spot a familiar cluster of bushes Aidyn and I pushed through. "There, I think. It's difficult to tell. Aidyn was using his magic to take us."

Nodding, Tynan ducks under the nearest branch and returns to the shadows of the trunks, my arm remaining in his grasp. If he releases me, I may very well succumb to panic.

The scent of the trees is cool and damp in the warm air, droplets of misting rain condensing and dripping onto our shoulders and off the regal bridge of Tynan's nose. He does not flinch.

"Where are they?" I whisper, no longer hearing the sharp barks of the hounds.

"It may not be so much about the human as you think," he says in a matching tone, still not stepping forward. "They may have troubled *you* for this reason, but we are constantly at odds."

It takes me a moment to catch up to his reasoning. "You think they're luring you out?"

"Not me, per se. As many of us as possible. They are incredibly intelligent and will protect one another—that does not mean they have the concept of compassion. We are locked in battle and always shall be."

"Then what—"

"We should not be locked in battle on *your* side of the trees."

I understand a bit more. What is an uncommon and frightening incident to us is a common war on the other side of the trees between the Keepers of Faerie. Tynan and his kin are only trying to end the danger *here*, not permanently.

"Are you going to kill it?" I ask. "The one in the cage?"

A muscle feathers in his jaw, but he does not answer. Taking in a long, deep breath, he finally steps forward, leading me through the damp grasses. I cannot precisely remember the trees around where the wagon was hidden, but that thick unnatural scent is in the air, if weaker.

Blain wouldn't be able to leave without those beasts catching him alone in the woods, would he?

Momentarily, I consider what would happen if we were to come across the threads of his corpse in the woods, torn apart by hunt hounds. Despite everything, I swallow so I am not sick.

The small clearing in the trees opens, but it is empty.

He'll think I've lied to him . . .

I open my mouth, unsure of what to say, before Tynan is releasing me and stepping carefully around the small space. Now I see the wagon tracks in the damp ground, disturbing the grass, and the faint hoofprints of whatever donkey or horse pulled it. Momentarily, I wish I hadn't confronted

Blain, hadn't tipped him off that I know what he's done, but I also hadn't realized the *Gentry* themselves would arrive, that I would be speaking to Aidyn's father.

I begin, "How far could they have gone—"

Tynan's head is tipped sideways, and he is gazing at something I cannot see in the trees. It appears this is quite the faerie habit, and I find my stomach twisting, my words dying on my lips. He is fairly close to me still, but whatever he sees in the dark feels much more dangerous when I am not standing behind his shoulder. I rub my hands into the fabric of my skirts, too frightened to move toward him, vulnerable in the night air.

Straightening but not taking his eyes from what he's found, he merely reaches over and takes me back under the arm until I'm stumbling after him.

"Do not let your sight leave me," he mumbles, then releases me again.

I keep on his heels as he steps lightly over tree roots, my hand near his back, ready to grab him as if I'm a child wandering after my own father—who I am suddenly quite glad is not here to put himself in danger—and finally see in the dark what he has discovered among the grass.

Found out by us and alerted to the hounds nearby, it seems Blain took it upon himself to rid his wagon of the cage and the beast within it before departing. He'll be much lighter without the weight, and it's much less likely the hounds will track him down.

They will merely stay here, in our village, as they always have when provoked, since our pretty fae will evidently take care of it.

Rage bubbles up in my chest, but there is nowhere for it

to go, so I merely stare at the cage toppled onto its side, still half covered with the thin old blanket. My fingers find Aidyn's ring and twist it round and round. Tynan wrinkles his nose, snorting as if he's smelled something terrible, though I only catch the reek of the hound and its heavy breathing past the cloth. The ancient faerie nudges at something with the toe of his boot, and I spy pale flecks of something in the grass.

"Salt?" I ask. It's thrown around the edges of gardens and on the windowsills of those frightened of malevolent fae, but I never knew it could be of any use. It certainly didn't dissuade any of the brownies who break into the kitchen and steal food. It didn't dissuade Aidyn from eating my soups.

"It troubles our sense of smell," Tynan supplies, still eyeing the cage. He reaches down to touch the grains before withdrawing his finger without touching. "It does not hurt us—we may eat it, even—but I have heard in your human cities, it is often mixed with flecks of iron so that we are caused pain if we step upon it."

I blink. In the moonlight, it only looks to be a handful of scattered salt, but I had no idea such a thing could be done.

"Bring some up out of the grass," he says, waving a hand in its direction.

Confused, I dig up a handful, mixed with damp earth, and run my fingers through the grains. I cannot tell the difference, but Tynan turns my wrist toward him, inspecting it without touching, and hums.

"Most likely," he says. "I am not going to test the hypothesis."

"That's how he was doing it?" I ask. "Salt so they can't smell anything and iron in case they get too close?"

"Most likely," he says again, nodding to the handful. "Keep that in your pocket."

For protection, I realize, glad I still sewed pockets into my dancing dress as I scoop a few handfuls of the mixture in where they can fit. It is mostly dirt, anyhow. A bag or bowl of it was likely spilled on accident. There are several other things that seem to have been dropped: a glove; an old paper bag, perhaps for food; and splinters of wood, likely from the cage being dropped to the ground and abandoned.

From under a piece of board, I tug out the handkerchief Blain used to wipe at his split lip. The corner is embroidered with the *H* from his family name. Tynan is not looking at me, and I put it into my pocket as well, though I'm not sure why. It seems strange to leave it.

With the edge of his sword, Tynan lifts the hem of the tattered cloth covering the cage. I see nothing but a shifting shape but hear the responding growl. As before, Tynan visibly flinches, shoulders tightening, upper lip peeling back in a slight grimace.

We may fear them, but he despises the beasts.

He thought they took his son from him.

The bars on the cage glisten in the faint moonlight—iron, most likely. It is a relatively difficult substance to come by, if I recall correctly, but it appears Blain and his father have amassed quite the wealth in their little scheme, enough to afford something so heavy that can trap even a faerie hound. The inside bars, at least, are covered with planks of wood. Only a shadow exists inside, but I see a bright eye gazing out at me for a moment.

"Are you going to kill it?" I whisper again. Despite the rage currently burning behind my ribs, I am not much of a violent person, and the idea of slaughtering something not actively attacking fills my throat with bile.

Again, Tynan does not answer. I suspect he does not know and does not wish to admit such a thing.

"What happens if we let it go?" I ask.

This earns me a glance from the corner of his eye, narrowed and unkind.

"All I mean is that we are helpless," I tell him. "We cannot fight them if they have any more rage aimed our direction, and you are not always here. If you let it go, will they all return to Faerie?"

I know how it sounds—*can you not deal with it in your own lands?* But the longer these other hounds remain—dozens, according to Tynan—the more danger we all face.

When he does not answer, I ask, "If you kill it, will the others stay?"

I know they have already killed more than one—I saw with my own eyes as he did it right before me—but I wonder if disposing of this caged beast will mean the difference, if it will be the end of us.

If he tells me no, I will have to believe.

He sucks in a long, deep breath and admits, "I do not know."

I nod, strangely relieved he is not as put together as he seems, that I am not the only one frightened and confused. But I also wish he knew how to fix this.

"These have killed others of our kind."

I think of the wildcat and her kittens asleep in the library and all the other fae in Aidyn's position who weren't lucky enough to come away from the hunt hounds' claws with their lives. My throat burns. Aidyn's wounds come to mind. "I know. I am not asking you not to fight them. But can't you send them all back to Faerie?"

He releases another long breath, jerking his chin ever so slightly, and I know he understands my pleas.

"Do not scream," he warns me.

Maneuvering me aside, he dips the tip of his blade around the lock where it will break from the bars should he give it a harsh tug. Despite my questions, my stomach flips, my breath catching. He speaks something in a long string of breath, those strange words I hear Aidyn murmur so often that I have no prayer of remembering. They make my eyes burn and my throat tight, and I wonder if my soul knows the warning behind them even if my ears do not understand.

He snaps the lock aside, and there is a splintering of wood.

The creature slinks out and away like a living shadow, something dark emerald and unseeable in the nightly woods. It circles Tynan in the fingernail light of the moon dappling the grass through the branches, then turns its eye on me. The faerie's broad back is to me, his long sword held comfortably and willingly between us, so I do not believe the creature is likely to pounce. They have more logic than I imagined in all the nightmares I've had through the years.

The growl that comes from its throat almost sounds to be their own version of the Gentry's gentle language, and then it is a shape disappearing into the trees, a shadow of a branch rustling in the night air. What few raindrops hit the ground cover its steps.

I realize how much my breath has been picking up when Tynan glances at me, and the slight movement of his own chest is so calm. I swallow with difficulty.

"Good," he says, and only now do I remember he told me not to cry out.

Nodding numbly, I say, "Can we go back to Aidyn?"

"Yes," he says without hesitation, though his eyes dart about with distrust. "They have not left. Let us take you back, then."

"Will you have to chase them off?"

"Most likely. They will still be angry. We must find that human, but not this night."

All the stories of fae and their curses, of falling-out teeth and dancing until limbs fall off, come to mind. Despite it all, pity chokes up my throat. "Will you enchant him into Faerie?"

Tynan quirks an eyebrow, taking my arm and leading me through the woods though I was already following. "We only wish for beautiful things in Faerie. He will die."

The chill in his tone settles across my skin, but I do not know what else I expected. No, I did not expect anything else, not truly. I expected something worse than a fast death.

Truly, I do not know what else *Blain* expected.

"Foolish man," I mutter, and Tynan glances at me curiously, though he does not ask. I am grateful, for I do not wish to tell him I was once kissing that man on the edge of the woods.

With another growl and a splinter of branches, I am knocked to the ground, my breath forced out of me. Light as a feather, Tynan still huffs as he hits the earth beside me, hissing and sitting up, brushing aside the burning salt on his exposed wrist. He did not lose his grip on his sword but goes utterly still, gazing at the hound that bore down upon us. It is a different one, I can tell by the slope of its shoulders, massive in comparison. Its long teeth and green-black fur flash in the moonlight, snapping so close to my face I forget to let out any sort of scream.

A soft hum ripples off Tynan's blade, the fingers of his left hand pinching together in a purposeful gesture, and the air around us cracks. I blink, watching moonlight shimmer, a web of cracks forming around us at once, then shattering as glass, startling the creature back. I flinch, but they do not touch me. Red blood trails the monster's snout and legs. I never expected its blood to be the same color.

There are much more frightening magics, Aidyn had implied.

I glance at Tynan, on his knees in the long grass but seeming to tower nonetheless, the sword hilt clasped in his hands, his eyes sharp and focused. Aidyn's gentle summer breezes seem comforting in comparison.

The hound circles us, growl reverberating off the trees. The dancing is so close by, I'm sure someone must hear, but all I catch is laughter floating to us, the comforting upbeat tune of a fiddle. I wonder if all the little folk have begun to run and if we humans simply haven't yet noticed.

More barking.

Tynan's eyes flicker about, not quite afraid but growing in concern. Another shape appears from the trees and is immediately cut down, falling into ribbons in the grass beside my leg. This time I do give off the slightest whimper, scooting aside until I bump against Tynan's arm.

He opens his mouth, some sort of song beginning on his lips, but the wind picks up.

Momentarily, it is nothing but a gentle gust, until it slams hard and all at once into the trees and the nearest hound, knocking me over and setting Tynan off-balance but crashing the monster beside us into the trees. Several more hounds run past, scattering. Honeysuckle drifts along with it. Tynan makes a frustrated noise, shoving himself up out of the grasses, long unbound hair askew, stuck to the corner of his mouth.

From the corner of the burrow, Aidyn's eyes glare sharp and harsh as his father's, his breath coming labored and full of otherworldly rage as he climbs out and toward us.

My relief turns at once to concern—he cannot be out here, cannot be exerting his magic. Still, I scramble to my feet, away from the hound and directly into his grasp, throwing my arms about his chest. He looks angrier than I've ever seen, if off-balance, leaning against the nearest tree, his arm coming up to lock around me with surprising strength. I see the moment his eyes fall upon his father half kneeling in the wildflowers, still between us and the disheveled hound, and his expression crumples.

"Da?" he whispers.

30

Teeth and Claws

Tynan opens his mouth. A sharp yip bounces off the trees. Glancing back, he springs at once to his feet, looping his arms about the two of us and nearly yanking me off the ground. I yelp, but we're deposited by the nook in the tree where we appeared.

"Go in," Tynan says, unwinding me from Aidyn in order to help his son stay upon his feet.

His hand remains a ghost along my back as I pick up my skirts and stumble through the root-coated little burrow. When it widens enough we can straighten, I hear Aidyn murmuring something to his father in that whispering language, and I glance back to see the older faerie duck and scoop his son into his arms. A weak protest follows, but I'm surprised Aidyn managed his way down here at all. Tynan is not remotely flummoxed by his child's strained annoyance.

"*Aidyn!*" comes Dauna's voice as she flies through the book-shelves, pulling me through the basement door and hissing at her brother in a string of words I do not understand but is clear enough in tone.

She and Una will get along.

"I looked into another room for a *moment*," she protests, flailing a hand in Aidyn's direction. He isn't looking at her, one arm looped loosely around Tynan's neck as he gazes at me. I grab his other hand, feeling the dig of his rings into my palm. I will return mine to him soon, but not before all this is over.

Tynan glances at the basement door. "They are on this side of the border. They did not come into the tunnel."

"How do you know?" I squeak, to which statement I'm uncertain.

"I hear them," he says in that cool unassuming tone, then heads up the stairs. "Come."

"Come, come," Dauna says as if I did not hear, taking me under the arm and dragging me up.

Stumbling after and feeling incredibly human in compari-son to her steps, I ask, "Is there something else in the library?"

"A brownie," she says, which feels less than noteworthy. "And some strange little bug creature; I'm sure Aidyn knows its origin."

My lip curls. "The thing with no teeth that makes your chest hurt?"

She glances back. "Yes?"

"Aidyn says it drinks your emotions. It's mostly just

annoying."

She wrinkles her nose as well. "It ran away from me, at least."

At the top of the stairs, Niall's head of hair is the first thing I see, followed quickly by Una bouncing on her toes and clinging to the railing until she gets sight of me.

"I tried to tell him he shouldn't get up," Niall says when Dauna deposits me near them, leaning over the railing and squinting her sharp eyes into all the corners of the library. "Thought he might kill me for suggesting it."

Remembering how Aidyn's predator-bird gaze once frightened me, a strained giggle bubbles up my throat. I clap a hand over my mouth, grabbing Una and hauling her back to Aidyn's room. I should not be laughing, and Dauna sends me a look from the side of her eyes confirming I sound like a crazy little human her brother has collected.

"Look who's brought more humans to the pretty fae . . ." whispers the familiar little goblin voice. Squinting into the dim shadows of the nighttime library, I spot the long limbs folded atop one of the nearest bookshelves, its two huge eyes blinking at me in the dark.

"What in Faerie—" Niall whispers.

"Ignore it," I say, giving them a shove into Aidyn's room while it crawls down to face height on the shelves. "It can't actually hurt you."

In a perfect imitation of Niall's voice, it says, "How many—"

Grabbing the nearest book off a shelf, I brandish it in the creature's direction. "Do you want to get tied up again?"

It hisses, more drool dribbling down its chin. From the

tree, the brownie shrieks at it. Apparently, the two don't get along. Una pokes me in the back while I continue to glare at the creature, scowling and slowly backing away until we're all safely in Aidyn's room. Dauna steps inside, muttering to herself. Poor Niall's brow is furrowed, lips pursed. If he wants to ask about that creature and his voice, he keeps it to himself, rubbing his throat.

"It's harmless," I tell him lest his thoughts run away with the idea of faerie curses.

He looks at me as if I've lost my mind but nods.

Tynan is settling Aidyn back onto his bed, saying something I have no hope of understanding, smoothing his hair back. Hopefully he's telling his son what an idiotic thing it was to leave in such a way. Aidyn's eyes are mostly unfocused, but he gazes up at him as if clinging to the words.

To Dauna, I whisper, "What now?"

She gives a tilt of her chin, as if considering, her eyes on the two men. "There are more of us here. We shall drive them off. We will find who has committed crimes against our folk. After, you need not fear the woods."

I swallow thickly, keeping my arms limply around Una's shoulders, feeling her quick breaths. I'm not certain Dauna is quite right about that and wonder suddenly if I am the first human she has truly met, as I was to Aidyn.

We will always fear the woods, even if the hounds are gone forever.

Glancing at the kittens, I count each to ensure they are all there, then cover them once more with a quilt before easing the basket into one of the nearest cabinets. If anything dangerous, hound or otherwise, makes it in here, I do not want any chance that it might kill the helpless things when the two creatures are at such odds. They are all asleep and in no danger of wandering out.

If some monster finds its way in here, I'm not sure what will happen to the kittens if we are all gone. I swallow painfully.

Tynan's head lifts, and he gazes back at us, eyes drifting over the three humans in these lands he likely considers his own. My mouth clicks shut as if I've been caught saying something terrible. Dauna only cocks her head farther.

"It's terribly quiet," he muses.

I glance about. It is always quiet in Faerie, though perhaps not for creatures with such sharp ears. Aidyn lets out a soft breath, winding his hand under his father's arm, but his eyes remain mostly closed. His stubborn ability to make himself fight even near death makes me want to scream . . . and probably his father as well, given the state of things.

Out in the library, I can hear the creature still muttering to itself. Frowning, I release Una to step just outside the door, gazing out at the quiet vastness of the library. A few chitters from the brownie float down, but nothing more. When the little goblin hisses at me, I pick the book back up. I squint out the hole in the roof where the tree grows through as it casts leaves ever so gently onto the floor. The outside world is dead quiet.

"How did you get in here?" I ask, turning back to the leggy creature.

It cocks its head at me. I feel rather than hear Dauna step out behind me.

"The brownie didn't let you in," I say, pointing back at the tree and feeling my heart thump against my ribs. "Which way did you come in?"

"Through the door under the plum trees, funny little human," it spits. "Mean human. I was stung by a bee!"

I put the book down.

"The back door?" I ask.

It shakes its head. "Too heavy. Tall blessed with pretty knife kept it closed."

I glance back at Aidyn. Of course he kept all the doors closed—this strange little faerie is not even the worst thing that could make it into this sanctuary. Dauna's expression is pinched, hand on her chest, and I wonder if it is not causing me discomfort because it is drinking off her soul. A moment later, she whisper-sings something back to her father and trots off down the stacks of books, disappearing into the overgrown branches of the maple tree. A gentle rustle of leaves is the only indication she's likely made it onto the roof. The brownie pays her no mind but hisses again at the goblin drooling along the bookshelves.

Silence descends across the library. My breathing picks up as I squint at the wall in the direction the plum tree should rest.

The door near the plum tree.

Could its little hands open the handle on that door?

"Tynan," I whisper, creeping back to the door. He spares me a glance away from his son, over his shoulder. "There was one time when I took the door out into Faerie to collect food for the kittens. I got lost, and Aidyn had to bring me back . . . We could never find the passageway back again, as if it had grown over. Aidyn could not find it again either. If that creature somehow found it and opened the door to get in here, what if one of the hounds followed?"

Tynan turns farther toward me, his hand still around Aidyn's, and frowns. "Perhaps they could dig it up if it grew over itself. I do not know how the goblin came in. I believe I can find the passageway and close it. It is not a terribly difficult magic when you are my age—"

He pauses, cocking his head and sitting up straighter, glancing about the room.

How much more of this place does he see than I ever will?

Aidyn murmurs something too low to catch, and Tynan's nose wrinkles. Slowly, he stands, a long easy movement that sends Niall and Una shuffling back. He pauses beside me in the doorway, breathing in a long, deep breath. The goblin hisses at him, then shuffles away shrieking when Tynan's lip curls.

Slowly, he shakes his head. "I'll go now. It is still late, and there are many hounds. I do not wish one to come in—"

Aidyn murmurs something else that has Tynan's shoulders tightening. Looking back, I find he's pushed himself up onto his elbows.

Catching my eye, he says, "I smell them. They must be here."

Tynan glances back.

"I know their smell. Better than I can describe."

Tynan's jaw feathers. I watch something pass between them I cannot name. Carefully, Tynan maneuvers me back inside the room before shutting the door between us. Aidyn makes an uncomfortable noise, trying to sit up farther, but Niall catches him by the arm. The look that passes across the faerie's face has me hurrying to his side so poor Niall isn't the only one telling him not to stand.

"Stop it," I say, holding a finger before his face. "You're not getting yourself killed or so help me I will go right behind you and you'll put me in danger too."

Aidyn's lips part in offense. If I didn't know him so well, the look in his sharp eyes would have me withering. Niall, bless him, *does* release Aidyn's arm and back away, though only by a step this time. Una maneuvers behind him, the four of us crouched on the pillows against the wall, listening, while Aidyn and I keep frighteningly intense eye contact.

Finally, his eyes flicker to the door. His fingertips brush against his middle, against his still-healing wounds. Whispering, he says, "Not him too."

My throat burns, and I do not know what to say to such a thing, for I would not want my da going out to look for a monster. My father is not a terrifying ancient faerie who has already slain many of such creatures, but I suspect it would be no less horrifying.

"Your father is insanely terrifying," I murmur. "I think he'll be all right."

As I say it, I'm not sure it's true. Against one or two of the hounds, perhaps it would be simple, though Tynan was certainly unsettled each time we were confronted with one of the creatures.

If there are more, will he put himself back into safety? How far did Dauna go in her search? I know there are more Keepers skirting the borders of Faerie and the human world, but they are busy rounding up dozens of other monsters. I wonder if there are many more Unblessed than there are Gentry.

The roof above us creaks as if something is skittering across, and Una gives a restrained squeak, putting her hand on my arm.

"Is there a level above us?" I whisper. I've never seen stairs going up from here.

Aidyn gives a little shake of the head, glancing up. I cannot read his expression, though the way his arm winds around my waist says he is more concerned than he lets on. No barking can be heard—surely, if they were hunting us, we would hear. Perhaps it's only the goblin finding its way onto the roof despite the brownie. Or it's Dauna, though a part of me insists she wouldn't make so much noise, not with how silently and softly Aidyn walks even when injured.

The room is dark save for the fire still crackling low in the hearth, sending soft moving silhouettes into the corners of the walls. Still, my eyes tell me I see shadows of feet from the other side of the door. Aidyn pushes himself up, leaning his chest against my back as he readjusts his sword into his palm, a soft breeze rustling my skirts. Una's breath catches. I reach back and grab her hand where she's hidden behind Niall.

Aidyn's breath tickles my ear. Another set of heavy pants ghosts from the other side of the door. From the way his arm weaves about my waist, I think he's trying to ease me behind him. It doesn't move me much. I'm afraid to breathe, let alone crawl around him and risk making a sound. Instead, I grasp his arm woven about me.

There's another pant of hot breath and a soft creak against the wood, as if a weight is pressing against it. Aidyn is whispering something that has my head fuzzy and my ears dull to noise as if full of water. My heart flutters faster, but I know better by now than to think he is enchanting *me*. Still, I give Una's hand another squeeze in case she is beginning to panic. Niall's breath is picking up, but he isn't trying to get away.

The old brass lock snaps, and I flinch. Aidyn's voice falls still, his blade brushing against the grains of the wooden floor. A familiar dark shadow slides within the crack of the doorway, bright eyes gazing at us in utter stillness. With Aidyn's spell gone, my eyes burn and my throat tightens, but I'm holding myself too tight to cry.

Its shoulders push in, filling the doorframe, but still, it merely looks at us. I've never seen one so close and so lacking in violence. Shadows seem to drip off its shoulders onto the floor, and I cannot discern if it's the firelight or my eyes playing tricks. A second one slides up behind it, smaller and no less terrifying, hunkered lower to the ground as it looks between its pack mate's legs.

Aidyn whispers something in his own tongue, and the bigger hound cocks its head. I can only image what he's trying to impart—that we are not the ones they're looking for, that we mean it no harm, that we only wish to be left alone . . .

Do the Unblessed understand such things?

My lungs burn, and my breath shakes when I let it out. It sets another paw into the room, easing inward in a slippery strange movement, lips rippling over its teeth in a silent growl. Hopefully nothing has happened to Tynan. I wonder if

Aidyn would know, would feel it in his soul. The softest breeze still flutters across the floor, but I do not know if Aidyn has the strength to throw this beast through the wall as he did only a short time before. Certainly he hasn't the strength to fight with his blade, and Niall with his little axe will be no protection.

The smell of a storm fills the air again. The smaller hound yips and scatters as the air around it crackles and snaps, and through the larger's legs I spot Tynan frozen on the steps, hair tangled and a trickle of blood on his cheek. His lips part, one hand held up from the last burst of magic. In the dark, those eyes matching his son's look terribly bright. And afraid.

Would his magic kill us if used so close?

He leans forward as if meaning to step closer, though the remaining hound does not turn to check the threat behind it. Aidyn's head shakes ever so slightly, a soft word falling from his lips I know no meaning of but must mean *no*.

Tynan falls utterly still.

The beast's eye rolls across the room, and I get the distinct feeling it has settled on me, my partially ruined hand held tight to Aidyn's arm across my chest.

Does it know me? It cannot know me, cannot be one of the same ones from all those years ago, can it?

The hound steps forward once, pulling its paw back as I notice the salt and iron spilled from my pockets onto the wooden planks. I do not believe such a little thing will give it pause for long.

Without meaning to, I slide my hand over to squeeze Aidyn's. His thumb locks over the back of my knuckles.

Throat burning, I release him to slide my fingers down into my pocket, brushing over the piece of fabric I picked up. When I drag it out, the hound's eyes flicker to the scrap of white speckled with blood from what Niall's fists accomplished. I cannot quite bring myself to hold it out entirely but move my hand in front of me where its face won't come too close to ours. Aidyn's fingers clamp around my forearm anyhow, preventing anything worse. The handkerchief doesn't quite cover my ruined finger.

"We didn't do it," I say, voice cracking so terribly I wonder if it understands, if it understands human language at all. "Only him. Just the one. We are not all like that."

Its head cocks, a bright angry intelligence in the large sliver of an eye pointed in my direction. The handkerchief flutters between my fingers, shaking as they are. I open my mouth several times and close it just as many. How simple it would be to send it away from us and to another human on the other side of the trees. Even when he brought it upon himself and threw us all into danger before him, it seems a terrible thing to let fall from my lips.

Finally, I say, "I'll make a bargain with you."

Aidyn whispers something that sounds like a warning, but I cannot catch the words.

I swallow thickly. "Leave him be as long as he stays out of your woods. As long as he stays on the paths and returns to the city, let him. If he ever steps foot back in these trees or lays a hand on your kind again, do whatever you will. None of the rest of us here mean you any harm. Let him take his fate into his own hands."

Its breath lets out in a huff, sending back the leaves Aidyn's magic scattered its direction.

"If you do, I will give you his name," I whisper. "You may hunt him anywhere."

Its breath comes out in another long snort, surprisingly warm along my skin. Aidyn's hand tightens nearly painfully around my arm. Its paws stand a little closer together, avoiding the salt, shoulder blades sharper and straighter, as if it's drawing itself up. A dark red tongue licks over a tooth.

A voice shivers out so deep it wraps about my chest and clings to my soul. I cower back into Aidyn's arms, letting him pull me farther away as Una gives off the tiniest squeak and Niall breathes out an oath. The handkerchief drops from my hand, fluttering to the floor in a lick of white against the shadowy room.

In my ear, Aidyn whispers, "It agrees to your bargain."

I swallow again, my voice lost to a tight throat, and manage to whisper, "Blain. His name is Blain Haskel."

Its head cocks, the one closest bright eye caught on mine. It slides to Aidyn next, and I can't help but wonder if this one looks familiar to him after gaining all these wounds. Another soft groan rolls over the floor, leaves brushing over its feet, as Aidyn's magic has not quite left the room. Una's hand tightens painfully about mine.

With a jump that has Aidyn snatching me back, the hound twitches to the handkerchief, breathing in a deep snuffle of noise before blowing it aside with a snort. With a sweep of its tail, it flees the room, ghosting past Tynan on the steps, where he flattens himself against the wall. His hand rises with that bright long blade, but he does not strike, some unreadable expression on his face. As soon as it passes, he crawls up the last few steps and gets to his feet, bounding to our sides and putting a hand against Aidyn's shoulder.

A few quiet moments pass.

Softly, Aidyn says, "They have left."

The pressure around my chest unwinds, and I glance up at Tynan, who wipes the fleck of blood from his cheek and nods, sliding his sword back into its sheath. Una's breath catches, and I hear her dissolve into soft crying. Numbly, I scoot back over Aidyn's leg to hug her while Niall continues staring up at Tynan with confusion and relief. With my other arm, I drag Niall over—he starts, then wraps us in his big arms. Gently, Tynan nudges us onto the side of the pillows and puts his son back properly on the bed, laying him down while Aidyn scowls.

"All will be well," Tynan says a little shakily, though it strikes me that it cannot be a lie. "I could not entirely find the passageway. I will barricade the blue door and wait for Dauna to return."

I squeeze Una's shoulders, picturing exactly what will happen in the dark to the man likely still guiding his wagon back to the city if he steps off the path. My stomach turns, but no regret has sunk in. We know better than to wound Faerie. He knew as well, from the time he fled the woods those years ago. I gave him a chance to save himself, and if he returns, I will tell him so myself. Midsummer is not quite over until the sun rises once again.

"All will be well," Tynan murmurs again, and places a hand on Aidyn's hair.

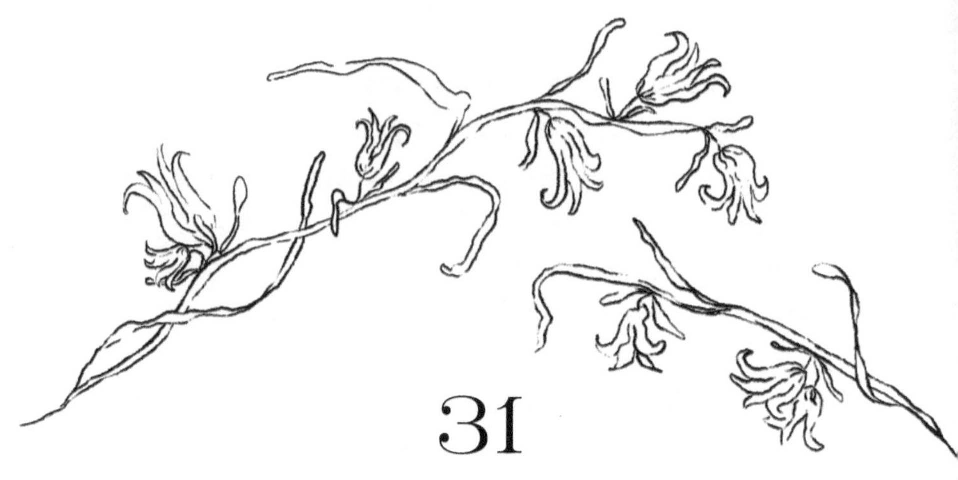

31

Coming Home

By the time Dauna returns and keeps a watchful eye on us as Tynan assures the old blue door is closed, it is nearing early morning. Aidyn has spoken little, leaning against the pillows near the fire I'm keeping and watching his sister and father with sleepy low-lidded eyes. Terror is exhausting, and Una and Niall slept for several hours on the pillows beside me. Now I hear them wandering just outside the door, curious of all the books in this strange place. Dauna's steady eyes move back and forth, never leaving them as she perches against the wall, her leg over Aidyn's knee as if frightened to lose his touch.

The kittens are fed and wandering about on their unsteady legs. One sits and yawns, tiny eyes on me. I cannot help but wonder what would've happened had I never stumbled across them or if *someone else* had.

I scratch its tiny chin.

"Will they grow as large as the one we found?" I murmur.

Aidyn blinks slowly, as if remembering I am here, though I've felt the weight of his eyes along my back for quite a time now.

"Yes," he murmurs. "They will be no less wild for being creatures of the Gentry. They fall somewhere a little more in between, if I am correct."

Dauna raises a thin eyebrow as if such a concept is uncertain to her.

"They will always remember you," he continues, softer. "I think they shall always come to you in the woods, if you choose to come into Faerie after this."

I'll be safer in Faerie now than I have ever been. Now does not seem the time to mention such things, especially with Una and Niall listening. I am in no hurry to think about it. Exhaustion drags at me, and I am ready to sleep for ages and be done with this midsummer until next year and hope the next is not quite so eventful.

I lay my hand near his where it rests limply along the covers. His fingers fold through mine, but with his sister watching us with tired amusement, I feel too sheepish to simply crawl over and kiss him.

Tynan brushes through the doorway with careful movements, startling me with his sudden and quiet appearance. He is considerably ruffled compared to hours ago when I chased after him, but the tangled hair and a tear in his loose shirt do not cut upon the imposing figure, let alone make me forget that I am looking at a creature who might've known humans when they were still new to these lands. With less danger draped over us, I find myself dipping my head and lowering my eyes.

He regards the three of us equally, carefully moving one of the stray kittens off his boot. I cannot fathom what he thinks of such things.

Finally, he gazes at me. "I owe you several favors, little human. Are there any you wish to ask of me now?"

My mouth pops open, eyes coming back up, thoughts swirling around the unexpected gesture. "I . . . no? Oh, *wait.* Um . . . my parents. They're likely returning from the city by now. If they come across the hounds on the road back—"

He gives a small nod and the barest hint of something that might be an amused smile. "We can watch over them, though I do not believe those creatures will cross along the human roads. 'Tis not in their nature, as you have seen."

I swallow thickly, nodding.

My expression must be doubtful, for he says, "We will ensure they arrive safely."

"Thank you," I whisper.

Dauna's gaze flickers between her father and brother, and she rises in a fluid motion. "I shall find them. I will not frighten them; they will not see me."

She offers a quick smile with those last words. I open my mouth to ask if she is all right after the night, if she shouldn't sleep, but the thought of her watching over my da and mam is more comforting than I realized.

"Thank you," I say again.

She points to her brother. "If he moves too much, remind him I shall knot his hair and throw him into a lake."

Aidyn's lips press together in annoyed amusement despite the haziness in his eyes, but I giggle nervously.

After kissing Aidyn and then her father on the cheek, Dauna slips out the door. I hear her soft voice saying something to Una and Niall.

When I look up, Tynan is still gazing at me. "If you'll pardon, I must tend to and speak with my son."

All of Aidyn's words about his father flood back, and I find myself nodding before I can truly wrap my head around the fact he's asking me to leave the room. Glancing at Aidyn, I find no alarm or discomfort in his expression, just glossy tears hanging in his eyes. Despite Tynan's watchful eyes, I lean over and hug Aidyn about his shoulders. His arms weave about me with overwhelming strength, his face pressed into my neck, breathing in deeply.

"It is well," he says softly, and I wish I knew what passed between them when they were speaking in their own tongue. When I lean back, he wrinkles his nose. "Do *not* cross back on your own so early."

I shake my head, getting unsteadily to my feet and stepping over a kitten. "I have no such ideas, believe me."

His mouth twists in doubt, but I've no intention of leaving the safety of the library until the sun is quite high. Tynan nods to me as I ease my way out the door, closing it as quietly as I can. Una is alone near the railing, leaning over the branch of the tree and handing one of the plums into the leaves. A moment later, the brownie comes down, chatters at her, and snatches it. From deep inside the branches, I believe I see a few tiny hands reaching out to their mother.

Una glances at me with a bit of tired amusement. "Dauna offered to take us back. N—uh, he went. Our parents are probably having fits."

I grimace. I can only imagine how my own mam and da are going to react when I retell this tale.

Her eyes flicker to the door. "Are they all right in there?"

"I don't know," I admit, glancing at the keyhole. They must be able to hear our words, but I stay still and silent before crouching and pressing my eye to the crack.

If Tynan knows I'm near the door, he gives no indication. I cannot hear what they are saying to each other and doubt I would understand if I could. Tynan has seated himself along the pillows against Aidyn's side, his head lowered. Crouched together, they appear much less the terrifying creatures we are warned of, as if we should not be leaving them shrines but going into the woods to befriend them.

I know better, but only hardly.

Aidyn's lips are moving ever so slightly, and Tynan is undoing the bandages and pulling aside the collar of his shirt with utmost care. I see his shoulders move as if sighing, and even in another language, the soft frustration in his tone cannot be mistaken. Aidyn says something else, jaw clenched and a wobble in his chin. Tynan's hand drifts up to touch his cheek before he bends to kiss him and pull him into his lap as if he is a child.

My throat burns, and I ease away from the door, embarrassed I intruded. Creeping across the old wooden floor, I join

Una near the other side of the wall where I first picked up the book of constellations. She's seated on the edge with her legs through the slats of wood, dangling in the air. I sit beside her, resting my chin against the railing, which is still shockingly stable after so long.

"Yes, I think they are going to be all right," I murmur, and she nods. "Will you be?"

She heaves a quiet sigh. "Well, I didn't have that monster breathing right into my face, so yes."

I wrinkle my nose and shiver. "Perhaps don't tell my folks about that detail. It's not as if I'm keen on repeating it."

She glowers but rolls her eyes. After a moment, she asks, "Do you ever think about what caused it the first time?"

It takes my tired thoughts a moment to catch up to what she must be asking. "You mean with me and Blain?"

She glances back.

I wrinkle my nose again. "I gave that creature his name."

"He turned over his own grave." She matches my grimace. "I cannot imagine angering fae and bringing them into the homes of people I've been laughing and joking with."

I shake my head, leaning my temple against the railing. "I thought I could brush off everything he did. It was far outside of me, I suppose."

"You bargained for him."

"I did. It didn't seem right not to. At least he has his own fate in his own hands now."

She hums. "What do you think they'll do to him if he steps near Faerie again?"

"I don't wish to think about it much."

She makes a soft noise of agreement, and we fall into silence before she asks again, "Do you? Think about it?"

I shrug. "Not often. We all figured *someone* probably stepped on a mushroom. It doesn't seem as if it matters much. Something caused it, and it was a long time ago, and they evidently are not interested in us once they realize we have not overstepped. They could've killed me that night. They didn't."

Una is quiet.

"Why do you ask?"

She shrugs one shoulder, arms draped over the railing, her finger nudging my ruined one offhandedly. "I just think about it sometimes. It could've been any of us kicking over a mushroom or stepping on something else we shouldn't have trod upon. It could've been hours or days before you and Blain went into the woods." Her eyes flicker briefly to mine. "Niall and I went into the woods once at night, maybe a week before. Did you know?"

I snort. "Hmm, you and Niall kissing in the moonlight . . . My goodness, you've been hiding it for ages. I wouldn't have the self-control. I came and told you about Aidyn immediately."

She rocks into me. A wilting flower falls out of her hair. I touch my askew braid for Aidyn's bluebell and find it clinging.

"I think about it sometimes," she murmurs. I don't know what she means until she whispers, "It could've been us. We could've knocked over a mushroom, stepped into a faerie circle without ever realizing in the dark. It could've been me who did it."

I open my mouth, then close it. Such a thing has never occurred to me, and I don't suppose it ever would have. From

Una's tone, I suppose I should feel more strongly about it, but it seems a silly sentiment after a night proving the unpredictable and wild nature of Faerie.

Eventually, a tired little giggle bubbles up. Una glances at me, and her upset expression doesn't help. "It could've been any of us. If we're working on likelihood, there's much more chance it was *me* accidentally stepping on one in any of the previous days and weeks and *years* I spent digging around for berries over here. We'll never truly know, and that doesn't bother me. It barely did then, it truly doesn't now. What else do we expect, living right on the edge of the Faerie trees?"

She stares at me over the edge of her arms, eyes glossy.

I let out a long breath. "Don't think about it anymore. Even if it happened to be you, you're still the best sister I could ever ask for."

She claps her hands over her face. "You're impossible."

"I'm very right. I was born under moonlight—I know things."

She makes an unhappy noise. Scooting over, I lock my arms around her shoulders and pull her over, rolling us onto the floor. She turns, hugging up against my side, quiet.

"I love you," I tell her, staring at the leaves and the lightening sky through the broken roof. The brownie looks down and chatters at us softly.

"I know," she mumbles, as if I have offended her. "I love you too."

When the sky is lighter, I limp downstairs on my sore ankle, Una following with one of the kittens, and nurture the stove back to life. My stomach is angry with me, and I cannot remember the last time I ate . . . perhaps at Midsummer.

Aidyn should eat something anyhow if he isn't sleeping. I've heard no other sounds from his room, and neither has his father left, but I'm restraining myself from knocking.

As if hearing our movement, Tynan appears seconds later, observing the makeshift kitchen I've set up, and takes a pot from over the stove before disappearing around the corner. Una gives me a mildly concerned look, and I shrug. I was introduced to the Gentry much slower than she was, so it's likely much more unsettling.

I still have plenty of ingredients stashed here from the last time I cooked Aidyn a meal—luckily, the brownie has only stolen some leftover pie—and I start with bread I can knead quickly and cook in a skillet. Most everything is dry ingredients, and I riffle through for something that will make a more suitable meal without leaving the library—

Reappearing in the doorway, Tynan sets half a dozen eggs of all sizes and colors on the table, along with the pot, now full of mushrooms and blackberries.

Softly, he says, "Aidyn has informed me you're cooking. Would you like anything else from me?"

For no reason, embarrassment floods me. "No, no, this is perfect. Yes . . . I like to cook. Thank you."

He nods and appears to glide back up the stairs despite tiredness tugging at his shoulders. Una and I exchange another look before I sigh and look into the pot, finding suitably edible mushrooms. I place another pot over the now-hot stove and crack the eggs into them, then set the shells aside, contentedly putting something together where everyone can have at least a little.

When I open the dusty window over the table, the world is quiet, soft birdsong floating in.

"I never thought I'd go into Faerie," Una murmurs, nibbling one of the berries as if it may spring alive. "It's not *so* different, but it is."

I nod. "Want to come back?"

Her nose wrinkles up. "I don't think so."

I laugh, and several sore muscles protest. "Even to see the kittens?"

If anything, she looks more perturbed. "Maybe."

By the time the sun is high and everyone has been fed, I leave a sleeping Aidyn under the watchful eye of his father—who appears as if he may doze himself, once he's not distracted by the kittens—take Una's hand, and lead her across the border with no troubles, both of us tripping over the roots of the hawthorn tree.

Glancing into the now-mortal trees, she shivers, though the chill of yesterday's storm has blown out, leaving a blistering summer sun with a tad too much damp to the air. Under the canopy of trees, the grasses are still coated in dew, and our legs and shoes are wet by the time we finally step out onto the sunny hillside. A soft breeze has picked up, the air no less hot for it.

Despite how many have crowded into our village for midsummer, few are wandering around. Those who didn't drink or dance too much are cleaning the mess made the night before, but most everyone is sitting on their porches or inside their houses, likely a great deal still in bed or taken up in the barns they've slept in after so much dancing. A few days will pass before everyone makes it home to their own village.

Emma is sitting in her own front yard when we make it down the grassy slope, Una's hand still in mine. Tiredness hangs in her eyes, and I have a feeling she was waiting up worrying over us after we left. I step over her carrots until I can reach over and hug her, then see Una to her parents' cottage.

Niall wanders down the path, his father yawning and watching him blearily from their porch. I can't imagine what he told him. Niall's hair is askew, and he looks as tired as us as we pause before Una's yard. He sighs, and none of us speak. He takes each of us under one arm and crushes us to his chest. I close my eyes and lean against him, trapped between and around the two of them. Sometime later, he releases us and gives my hand a squeeze before taking Una up to her cottage. Momentarily, I see Andrew and Olivia duck out of the window as if they weren't watching.

Smiling, I return home.

Primrose is lowing at me after not being milked, and I tell her, "I know, I know," as I find the pail.

By sometime nearing afternoon, I take Aidyn's bluebell from my hair and press it between the pages of a few heavy books before crawling into bed for sleep.

When I wake, darkness has fallen. Patting the desk for my

pocket watch, I find early morning. Rolling onto my back and feeling my ankle and most of my joints protesting, I stare at the wooden grains in the ceiling barely visible in the early light and let out a long breath. It's quiet enough that it could be Faerie, though the shapes of the familiar trees through the gossamer curtains assure me it is not.

Momentarily, I put my hand over my face and feel tears burning down my cheeks, more from relief and leftover emotion, because I am not frightened, not anymore. Eventually, I push aside the covers and draw a long bath. My fingers twist Aidyn's ring around my thumb. Wrinkling my nose at the bedding I slept in so dirty, I strip it and haul it downstairs to the washing barrel and set to work. It is just early enough it is only warm, and I've found a dress I haven't managed to soil or tear that's thin enough to be comfortable in the summer and roll the sleeves all the way up until they're beneath my armpits. My shoes are inside, and the damp cold of the ground sticks between my toes.

By the time I've hung the sheets and wrangled the thicker blanket into the water, the sun is over the trees. Three wagons bounce down the path, two I recognize. From this distance, I can't tell if Mister Haskel or Blain has decided to return— either way, they must not have stepped off the path—but they're not the ones who make my heart leap.

Carefully, I pick my way down the path, avoiding pebbles, before breaking into a quicker trot when my parents' wagon turns off the main road and ambles up the path to our cottage. Blackberry snorts and comes to a halt as if my presence means she's reached her barn and food. I rub her velvet nose while Mam shuffles down off the wagon with a series of happy noises and lets me choke her in a hug. Da, chuckling, clicks and flicks the reins at Blackberry until he gets the horse to haul the wagon all the way into the barn.

"Oh, love, you look tired. Midsummer couldn't have been so mad." Mam laughs and runs my unbrushed hair through her fingers. I caught a look at myself in the mirror after the bath this morning, and I know I appear a little too much like a wild woman lost in Faerie.

I gnaw at the inside of my lip. "You have no idea."

"We meant to be here a few days back and not miss the dancing, then the storm rolled over the city, and we didn't want to find ourselves stuck in the mud."

I shrug, merely happy that Dauna watched over them and that they weren't here the other night lest the hounds have found them after knowing my smell.

"The dancing was nice," I say, remembering Aidyn's arm around my waist and the silly mask he stole.

Over Mam's shoulder, I spot both men in the other wagon and grab her hand, pulling her toward our cottage. "Let's go, hurry."

Glancing back, her pretty face wrinkles up. "Yes," she says dully. "We saw him. That—"

Laughing over whatever insult was on the tip of her tongue, I haul her back home. "They might just come over here. I'll tell you in a bit."

"Have they been here while we were gone?" Her voice rises in offense. "Did he try to talk to you?"

"Mam—"

"He didn't come to the dancing, did he? I'll—"

"*Mam*. Please hurry."

Huffing and picking up her heavier traveling skirts, she follows me up the path, muttering the whole time while I try to keep a schooled expression. Da is unhooking Blackberry from the cart, stopping to scoop me up once we reach the shade of the barn. I groan dramatically as he swings me side to side, hiding my face in his shoulder. It feels as if they've been gone much longer than a few hot summer weeks.

"What is he doing?" Da mutters, and I know Blain and his father have indeed decided it's wise to make their way to our cottage. I glance at the wood-chopping axe in the corner and hope Da doesn't remember its presence.

"Long story," I say when he sets me down. "I think at least Blain is coming to talk to me. I think—"

Da glances at me as if daring me to offer a good reason for their visit. Considering the hound last night, I manage not to smile at the rage in his expression. If Faerie does not take its revenge, my father is not restricted to the woods.

"They were luring out and killing faerie animals. The hounds came back. Just . . . trust me."

His mouth pops open, but before either can ask further questions, Mister Haskel is shouting a hello from outside the garden. When I turn, Blain's expression is unreadable, his eyes on mine. There is something haunted in his cheeks. I am not surprised after the other night and must wonder if he already stepped within the trees. My hand goes into my pocket where I stashed his handkerchief this morning.

Midsummer should've been warning enough.

"You two missed the dancing," Mister Haskel says, his face stretching into a smile I'm unsure is real. "I've been hoping to catch you. I have some business to discuss."

Down the path behind them, I see Una hustling up, Niall trotting ahead, something shimmering in his hand I'm assuming is his own axe once again. I bite the insides of my cheeks.

My da's eyes are stony cold, something warring in his expression, anger against the temptation to be polite out of curiosity. Instead, he glances at me. I put my hand in his, and his rough finger rubs against my littlest one. His touch presses Aidyn's ring firmer against my skin.

"You should go back down the path," I say, turning to Blain. His eyes haven't left mine. "And don't leave it. Go back to the city and stay there. Don't go looking for your crate."

His eyes narrow, and he doesn't glance back when Niall—looking considerably more rested, the bruise on his face fading—comes to a stop a dozen paces behind, gaze flickering over us, trying to decide if it's his place to intervene.

"Niamh—" Mister Haskel begins, and I shoot him a look that has his lips pressing into a thin line.

Barely above a whisper, Blain says, "You think because you go in and out of their lands so often and one of them comes to dance with you that you know best?"

"No," I say with enough honesty it surprises me. Stepping over, I pull his handkerchief out and push it into his chest. His hand jerks up to catch it. "But I never meant them harm. You did."

His jaw clenches, eyes widening ever so slightly. Mister Haskel has gone silent, the hand that was waving in my direction in a feeble attempt to get my attention falling still.

"They are not like us," Blain whispers.

"You're right. They would've killed you outright. I made a bargain on your behalf you didn't deserve," I tell him. "Do not step into the woods again. They'll know."

"They know you better than me."

"They do," I agree, releasing the fabric into his grip. "But they don't have my name. They have yours."

His lips part, and despite it all, I believe he knows precisely what I am saying and what I am trying to impart, one human to another on the edge of Faerie. A long sharp whistle of a breath tugs in between his teeth, a mixture of anger and horror flickering across his face before settling on something intense but unknowable.

His mouth opens again, and then his fist drops the handkerchief to grasp at my arms. His expression does not look dangerous—he is too much a desperate child to look dangerous to me now.

Da seizes him by the front of his fine wrinkled shirt, dragging him up onto his toes, precisely how tall and broad he is in the shoulders becoming obvious. Blain releases me to scowl up into the face of a man he has no hope or dream of fighting.

"I don't know what you've done this time, but your hands will stay off my daughter. And you." He glares at Mister Haskel, who has begun to give a weak protest. "We have no business. Keep your child away from mine."

From halfway behind a smirking and glowering Niall, Una has her hand over her mouth, trying not to laugh. My chest warms. I rub my father's arm until he decides to drop Blain into the hay.

"Get out," he says, annoyance dripping from his tone as he brushes a hand in the older man's direction. "Or I'll let Niall over there do what he's itching to do."

Niall taps the flat head of the axe against his thigh, smile muscled into a serious expression even if the glint doesn't leave his eyes. Da's always liked Niall—I don't doubt for a minute he'd send him Blain's way, even if I asked him not to.

Slowly, Blain rises with his father's hand under his elbow, eyes flickering toward the broad barn door behind us, at the trees rustling in the breeze. They are not Faerie trees, but I'm sure they look it to him. Mister Haskel gives him a tug, and Blain follows him out. Niall smiles pleasantly as they pass.

I rest my hands on my hips and hang my chin against my chest, letting out a long sigh, aware of my parents exchanging glances. Una trots over to hug them both while Niall strolls alongside, spinning the handle of his axe and looking pleased.

"I didn't follow half of that," Mam admits.

I say, "Una and Niall kissed at midsummer."

"*Niamh!*" Una smacks me on the arm as if she were not the one kissing Niall in the middle of all the dancing. I giggle while confusion, amusement, and mild disappointment flicker over my parents' faces before settling on something close to affection. As much as they've been nudging me into considering taking Niall as a husband, they can't be unhappy that my two best friends have fallen in love with each other—not when they watched them grow up almost as children of their own.

"How long have you known about that?" Da asks while

Niall avoids eye contact, turns beet red, and smirks.

"A while," I admit.

"Niamh," he says with more warning in his tone.

"Yes?"

"What was that he said about you dancing with a faerie?" He pauses. "Where are those kittens?"

I rub my face, feeling Aidyn's ring against my skin, then run my hands through my knotted hair until a few untangle. "It's going to take a bit of explaining. I'll make breakfast. We can talk about it." At Una's stare, I add, "Maybe he'd like to meet you."

32

Whisper-Song

That night, early in the morning, a whisper wakes me. It ceases the moment I raise my head, and a soft tap knocks on the window glass. Heart jumping, I lean forward and brush aside the curtain to find Dauna's dark eyes gazing back at me. Disappointment knocks against my chest, but I know it's better that Aidyn is staying off his feet. Getting fully out from under the covers, I shove the curtains aside properly, dried foxgloves and bee balm rustling, and edge open the glass.

"You'll fall," I hiss, though as I say it, it strikes me as ridiculous. She looks perfectly comfortable on the slim branch nearest this side of the cottage, fingers resting against the windowpane.

Indeed, her eyes roll. "Aidyn wished me to tell you that you are safe to come if you would like, but keep it to the daytime. He is much more awake now."

My heart jumps, but the moon is still out and the morning dim. I have several hours to wait.

"Thank you. I'm sorry he sent you here to give messages," I say, laughing quietly.

She shrugs, and her mouth quirks at the corner. "I do not mind. His eyes light up when he talks about you."

My face heats. "And thank you for watching over my parents. They're here safe."

"I saw. They have warm countenances."

I smile. "Yes, they do." I glance back into my room, feeling strange. "Would you . . . like to come in?"

She chuckles, and I hear the trace of magic in her voice, just the barest thread compared to the long haunting wail that enraptures anything within its grasp. I shiver. Shaking her head, she says, "I am happy out in the dark. I will see you again."

She slips off the trees with barely a brush of sound, and by the time she reaches the grasses below, I've lost all sight and sound of her. I lean out over the edge of the window, into the cool morning air, my hair hanging about my face.

"Aidyn," I murmur, as if he is not safe in his warm bed as he should be. "I've missed you."

After a few more hours of light sleep and waking a half dozen times to check the sunrise, I'm out the door with one of the baskets I haven't ruined or left in the library, a note to my mam and da on the kitchen table. Despite the long and rather intense conversation that ensued from breakfast into dinner, they have both returned from a long and tiring trip and likely won't be awake for a few more hours.

Emma is out early again, and I bring her a few of the muffins I baked yesterday in preparation for something sweet to bring to Aidyn. She raises her eyebrows over her tea, her pipe smoking in her hand on the table.

"How are you, girl? Saw that scoundrel and his father looking rather upset as they left yesterday."

Grinning sheepishly, I tell her as simply as I can what has transpired. Her eyebrows go up, which is likely as much as I can surprise her, other than showing up with an injured faerie right on her doorstep.

Finally, after a long silence, I tell her, "And I'm sorry. For bringing Aidyn here so suddenly. I was frightened."

She lets out a snort, then a sigh. "All things considered, you did rather well."

My face heats once more.

"Besides, it's the most fun I've had in ages. I can't tell you how many years have passed since I've seen a proper faerie. Are you going to him now?"

I nod, looking at my shoes.

"Will he heal?"

"Tynan says so. He seems to care a great deal."

"Good, tell him I'm glad. And tell him to keep my name to himself; I'm too old for any fae to have any interest in it, anyway."

I nod and give her a kiss before picking my way out of the garden. Pausing, I turn back. "Emma?"

"Hmm?"

"A faerie had your name at one time, didn't they?"

She taps her pipe against the arm of her rocking chair. "He never had my name. He had my love though."

For no good reason, my throat burns, and I nod. I know precisely how she feels, though even as I'm taking my time to hike up the hill, waiting for the sun to rise higher, my name is on my lips, as if even speaking it into the trees will carry it back to Aidyn.

Perhaps it will. They are listening in on everything, after all.

I wait beneath the branches of the hawthorn, brushing my fingers against it respectfully, until the sunlight touches its roots, then close my eyes and step into the Faerie woods.

Trotting through the silent trees, I let myself in through the side door and bounce lightly up the steps, wincing at my ankle. No one is in the kitchen, and I knock softly on the mostly closed door to Aidyn's room.

"Are you asleep?"

When I peek my head in, I'm greeted with a soft, "Hello, Flower."

He's still on his bed but half out of the covers, lying on his side, feet bare and clothes ruffled, a leaf in his fingers one of the kittens is batting at and hissing. Grinning in a most ridiculous manner, I step inside, setting my basket near the hearth and taking off my shoes. The wood is cool, warmer where the low fire has been burning.

"Where is everyone?" I ask, not believing for a moment

Tynan would have left.

Aidyn's lips quirk. "Father has many duties at home. He was rather upset about it. I had to chase him away. Blew him off his feet a tad. He will return tomorrow."

I raise my eyebrows, picturing the terrifying creature upset over leaving the son he just discovered still lives . . . and getting his hair blown into knots again. "Your poor da."

He chuckles, and it's good to hear the sound. "Dauna is still here; 'tis the only reason he did not drag me along with him." He waves a hand gently. "She left only minutes ago. They are keeping a watch on the woods around your village. I believe she is giving us privacy."

I relax knowing neither of Aidyn's terrifying relatives will appear from between the walls, sitting on the pillows and taking his hands.

"She is wandering out that way," he murmurs, waving a hand again, this time with mine trapped inside his. "I can feel where she is in the trees now that she is close."

I smile. "That's sweet. I like her, even if she scares me."

"Hmm." He picks one of the kittens up, setting it alongside the bed. "She likes you."

Again, I feel quite pleased with myself. Leaning over, I wrap my arms about his shoulders once more, burying my face into the warm bend of his neck. Humming, he drags his hands across my spine, holding me tight to him, breath tickling my shoulders. The kitten mewls from somewhere close by, and one of Aidyn's hands drops to pet it. His lips press softly against my skin where the dress has slipped aside. We stay this way so long I'm certain I could fall asleep against his chest were my heart not pattering against my ribs.

All of a sudden, he murmurs, "You were very brave."

I take his face in my hands and kiss him. No longer distracted by exhaustion or the strong panicky excitement wrapped about me during midsummer, I can properly appreciate his lips between my own, the drift of his breath when we part, and his nose brushing the bridge of mine. His finger curls into a lock of my hair, then another, and he sets the kitten into its basket with the others before looping his arms around me.

"How is your shoulder?" I whisper, parting the collar of his loose shirt and looking at the neat bandages Tynan has been tending to.

"I am quite sure I shall survive," he murmurs, amusement in his voice.

"And the rest of you?"

"Much better."

I squint, reminding myself that he must be telling the truth in some form. His lips curl back up. He *does* look much improved, even if he's still lounging across the pillows. Hopefully it is only because he has grown comfortable around me.

"Oh, I have something of yours," I say, holding up my hand and working off the ring. "I figured you'd want it back, even if you did, technically, give it to me."

He cocks his head, taking it with care. "I wondered where it went. When did you take it?"

"When you were asleep at Emma's—she says don't you dare use her name, also—so I could chase after your father." I snort at my own foolish decision, even if it was the correct one. "How are you two? You seem all right, and he was talking to you the other day, wasn't he?"

I chew my lip, not wishing to reveal how I was peeking in on them.

Rolling the ring between his fingers, he gazes at me with an expression somewhere between contentment and an emotion I cannot name. "He was quite upset with me. It helped, I think."

I nod. It's an understandable thing to say. I wouldn't imagine anything less than Tynan being worried and fussing over him would've helped.

"He understands it," he murmurs. Before I can feel angry, he continues, "Don't misunderstand, he hated it, but he realized why I had my thoughts. And he understands creatures do strange things when they are in pain. I do not believe he is angry in that fashion. He was upset by the idea he'd given me that impression . . ."

Swallowing, he glances to the side, but I only give his hands a squeeze, encouraging and happy he has decided to confide in me these private things.

"He did not," he clarifies, turning back to me. "I did not give you that impression, did I?"

I shake my head. "You didn't. Just that your world gave you that impression."

He takes in a long breath and rolls his eyes up to the ceiling and across to the kittens. "He has asked me to return with him and has declared he shall curse and swear out anyone who dares say anything in my direction."

Another laugh bubbles out, and I clap a hand over my

mouth, picturing perfectly and horrifyingly how such a creature would go about such things.

Aidyn rolls his eyes again, rather aggressively, even if something about his face says he is pleased with this. "I believe him. I do not know if I shall." He finally drops his gaze back to mine. "Not for a while yet."

I cock my head, looking into the little silver flecks in his eyes. They appear so incredibly gentle now that I cannot remember how I ever imagined him as anything other.

"I must redecorate the library, after all," he supplies.

I grin. "Of course."

"And care for the kittens."

"Ah, yes, only the kittens."

"Yes. What else?"

"I wouldn't know. Would you like to meet my parents?"

His eyes widen for a moment even as he's holding back a laugh. "Would I now? How do they feel about the fair folk?"

"Do you remember how I screamed and ran away the first time?"

"Vividly."

"I can say it certainly won't be that dramatic. They've had warning."

He gnaws on the inside of his lip with a low chuckle. "Perhaps I shall, then. When I have a moment away. From the kittens, of course."

"And the redecorating."

"Yes."

Grinning, I lean over again, utterly happy that he is so much improved and his eyes are lighter again. Taking my face in his hand, he pulls me the rest of the way down to offer another kiss.

"Are you rested?" he murmurs. "Are you well?"

"Very well, thank you. I've slept quite a bit. I think U—my friend was rather worried I'd end up enchanted by Faerie anyhow. She's been checking in on me. Really, I think it scared her more than it did me. Somehow."

He chuckles, and I'm sure he caught how I nearly spoke her name once more. "Your little friend with the long hair?"

I nod, our noses brushing.

"The two seem delightful. I am glad you have them. We shall have to find something I can call them."

"I'll ask," I say, then return to drifting my lips along his jaw and up to his ear.

He makes a long contented sigh of a noise, whispering, "I dreamt of you each time I slept. You walked just out of my reach until I chased you and woke. Can I tell you something?"

"Yes, yes, tell me."

He slides the ring back onto his finger. "I'd already taken the ring back. It didn't count as my gift to you. Not anymore."

Propping myself up a little more, eyebrows pulling together, I ask, "Oh?"

"Hmm. I must've given you something else."

It seems as if he is hinting at something quite important. "What else could you have given me without me knowing?"

He peers up at me with the little curl to his lips before twining his hand into my hair and guiding me back. "Something," he murmurs between kisses, tucking me down into his arms until I am pressed up against him and am forced to wriggle the blankets away to get closer. "Something very important."

His heartbeat thumps a gentle quick rhythm under my hand, and I think less of what he is saying, the specifics of it not mattering more than the strangest understanding enveloping me. My thumb runs over the dual point of his ear as I brush his soft silken hair over his shoulder and touch his back with the slightest pressure, careful of his healing.

"You're not frightened now, are you, Flower?" he murmurs again, genuine concern in his voice as last time.

"Niamh," I tell him.

His lips fall still on my neck until he murmurs, "What?"

"My name is Niamh."

A moment more he is quiet. Then he murmurs, "Niamh."

Though I do not believe he is putting any magic into the word, it is certainly there. A warmth settles across my shoulders and in between my ribs, a wash of cool water followed by sunlight. I murmur, "Aidyn."

"Niamh," he whispers again, then rises back up to kiss me properly.

A furry little paw digs into my cheek, and Aidyn huffs as one of the kittens tumbles between our faces. I clap my hand over my mouth, trying to stifle my laughter with little success.

"We are going to crush one," he mumbles, wincing as he attempts to move the little thing off the side of the bed.

Rolling over, I pick up the two who've woken and tumbled out, putting them back into their basket with the few plums they're much more interested in.

"I keep getting interrupted," he mutters, dragging me back

over to his chest. "All of Faerie is against me."

"How is your shoulder—"

"I'm not planning on using my *shoulder* very much."

I keep on giggling despite how much I tell myself it's too much, wrapping my arms around his neck. His hand makes a little brush of movement, and leaves scatter across the floor as the door clicks almost closed on the broken lock. I give another huff of a laugh. My hands drift to his shoulder, and despite his proclamations, I still encounter the bandages under the thick fabric of his shirt.

Sitting up, I nudge him off his side and onto his back, half propped up on the pillows, while his eyebrows pucker together in mild distress.

"Hush," I tell him. "You have a tendency for hurting yourself all over again, you know?"

"It isn't on *purpose*—"

Grinning, I kiss him, then on his nose, and then the corners of each of his eyes. He narrows those eyes at me, hands still clasped against my ribs, their warmth seeping through the thin dress and underclothing. Carefully, I unwind the ties of his shirt, taking the hem and sliding it upward while he eases his shoulders up with a wince, helping me slip it over his head. I smooth my hands over the bandages with the utmost care, trying to assure myself he is feeling as better as he claims, even if he cannot be lying about it.

"You need not be quite so concerned," he says so softly the barest crackle of the hearth almost overwhelms it.

"Shh," I murmur, running my fingers over and around the divots of his ribs and under his chest bone, wondering if he is indeed made of something different than I am under his skin, where the strange ripples almost like vines or something else of equal magic sit. Still, he is incredibly soft, an entirely warm and living being. He shivers when I take a long slow path of touches down his chest and to his sides.

His hands slide around to the buttons between my shoulder blades, carefully plucking them one at a time and sliding the fabric from my shoulders. It is quite warm in this little room even in the gray morning, and I push the fabric the rest of the way off until the thinner underdress is left, the sleeves slipping off my shoulders and soon mostly maneuvered out of the way as well.

He mumbles something in his own tongue, gaze wandering lower than usual.

"You do realize," I say against his cheek, "that I cannot understand you. I would like to hear what you are thinking."

"I named you correctly," he mumbles into my hair. "Your skin feels like flower petals. You smell sweet."

"Oh?"

"Warm grass in the sun," he says, sounding as if this is the greatest compliment he can give me. Silly as it sounds, it still sits just as warmly in my heart.

"Keep your arms about me," I tell him. "Do not ever release me."

"Do you know what else?" he asks, and I make a questioning noise, wanting him both to be quieter and keep speaking forever and forever. "You did not wait for the sun to come up."

"It was light on my side," I tell him. "And I had not finished kissing you either."

He lets off a soft hum as I touch my lips to the base of his throat and against his collarbone before returning to his mouth, where he has taken up murmuring my name when his lips are not otherwise occupied. Twining his fingers into my hair, some of the rings catching in an uncombed lock, he pulls me harder to him, mouth sweet and hungry. I cling to his unbruised arms, nervous and overly warm and happy.

Shuffling the thin cotton the rest of the way from me, he bundles it somewhere off to the side, pulling me over him where I won't hurt anything still healing. My hands find what little remains of his clothing and make quick fumbling work of getting them out of the way.

"Aidyn," I say gently, happily terrified of all the things I wish him to do, wondering if I can say his name the same way he says my own; perhaps being on this side of Faerie will lend me that power to bewitch him as thoroughly as he has bewitched me.

By the noise that rises from his chest, stopping short as if it has caught in his throat, I feel enough as if I have succeeded.

"Aidyn," I say again, and he mumbles my name back to me in a way that feels as if I finally understand his whisper-song language.

His mouth touches every place I've been imagining, and he bundles me down into the blankets alongside him and in between his arms until we're both trembling and his face is tucked into my neck.

I mumble, "Oh," against his shoulder and feel his agreeing, "Hmm," more as a hum in his chest than a word.

A short time later, he is tucked over me, my back against

his chest where I feel the bandages and wince at the thought, though he seems quite pleased, his leg bent through the two of mine, his hand drawing lazy circles in the air, tugging gently at locks of my hair. I turn the ring around and around on his finger, the one he gifted me then did not, and feel tears prickling at my eyes. My throat bobs a little too much when I swallow, and I try to consider everything that brought us here and cannot wrap my thoughts about it. My breath is a tad unsteady. Moments later, his hand falls still.

"What is wrong? Did I—"

"I'm *happy*, stop fussing," I mumble.

He is momentarily quiet before pushing up onto his elbow to look over into my face. I see very little but his large silver eyes squinting at me in the low light. After a thorough study, he falls back with a contented huff. I'd roll my eyes if it weren't terribly endearing. His arm tightens, tucking me flush back against his chest once more.

"Will you take me somewhere in Faerie that you love?" I ask, reaching over to tap against the wooden floor to get the attention of the nearest kitten wobbling about. It hisses and wanders its head into my palm.

Blowing out a long breath over my ear, he says, "All that happened at your midsummer, and you want me dragging you about the wild woods?"

"As long as we don't find any waterfalls where time moves strangely," I say, grinning. "And remember to close the passageway upon our return."

He mumbles something in his own tongue that sounds vaguely exasperated and a little fascinated.

"Why did it overgrow?"

"I do not know. Neither does my da, though he thinks perhaps we went too far from it. We shall not get lost this time."

Not with him, I certainly will not. "So, can you think of no places?"

After a pause, he admits, "I can."

"Would you like to, then?"

Another pause. "Very much so."

I grin again, pressing my lips into his arm and rolling over enough to see his face. He gazes down at me with a strange mixture of exasperation and smug contentment—perhaps a bit of excitement, even if his eyelids look as if they're drooping. He nudges his nose into the side of my cheek.

"When you are well, then," I murmur, and kiss him against the corner of his eye.

Epilogue

 usk has settled across the valley, and I've left Una
and Niall to their dancing.

Two weeks have passed since midsummer, but
the air remains hot and hangs heavily about us. A few storms
have trundled in and passed, and everyone who happened to
hear the hounds has recovered from their fright and decided
more dancing and drinking is in order, even with no fae to
join and no occasion to mark.

I have done considerably less baking for this evening, as
only a few dozen of us are gathered about a bonfire roasting
pork and newly harvested corn. I danced with both Una and
Niall a dozen times, my skin hot against the fire and the night
air, my hair tumbled about. I wonder if Aidyn will be up and
about as to do any such thing. If he tried, Tynan or Dauna
would take to yelling at him.

The two other Gentry have been a constant presence about

the library, felt nearby even when I do not see them. With the danger passed, Tynan is a much quieter creature than his son, usually watching me in an unblinking silence when he decides to remain in the room and speaking little to either of us.

The glances exchanged between father and son seem much more meaningful than any sentences on which I could eavesdrop. Though he is often returned to his home, wherever that may be and whatever bluebells may be growing around its gates, Aidyn appears no less happy for it. Something is smoothing out between them even if I cannot put words to it.

I wonder often if Tynan feels his age in his mind though he does not in body.

Dauna is livelier, even if she is more often in the trees than the library. Sometimes, at night, I think I see the ghost of her passing by the window and feel strangely watched over. Often, under the moonlight, I hear a long song of a sound I am certain is her, even if I cannot discern the direction or reason.

We've seen no sign of the hounds. Likewise, neither have we of Blain or his father, though one of the girls from the next village was heard lamenting the fact he has taken to living in the city permanently.

"I will be back soon. Watch for me in the trees," I say, then kiss my mam and da on the cheek.

Aidyn is waiting inside the woods, sitting against the broad front door coated in vines, legs stretched out, the basket of kittens beside him, though they're beginning to outgrow the little space. Picking my way across the leaves, shoes forgotten in the long grasses, I still search for signs of things that should not be here in the near dark. Aidyn asked me to come as the sun set, and I do not believe he would have so little fear if we were not well and truly safe.

"What is it you're showing me?" I ask, bending over to touch his face and kiss his lips. His eyes fall warmly upon the bluebell he offered me last night, which I looped into my braid. He finally showed me where he's been picking them, from a little patch sprouting from under the back porch of the library, a little bundle of springtime in the fallen leaves.

I have been considering how they grow here, by themselves, he told me. *I wonder if perhaps they must have grown because I needed them, as I needed this place. And you.*

I squeeze his hands as he peers up at me happily.

Climbing to his feet, cane in one hand, basket in the other, he says, "Come, hold on to me."

Eyebrows raised, I take the basket of squeaking kittens and loop my arm around his. He leads me around the side of the library and across the deteriorated wall of honeysuckle, stepping into the woods where I would normally return to the human lands. Without closing my eyes, I am only traveling farther into an unknown part of Faerie. My hand slides down into his, and his fingers weave between mine.

"I've been hearing her for a few nights now," he says, then seats himself tenderly on the carpet of leaves. Folding myself beside him, I watch three of the kittens fumble out and into my lap. They're nearly twice the size they were the day I found them and have begun to learn not to gnaw so hard on my fingers. "I think she's waiting for us to come out."

"Who?"

He presses a finger to his lips and murmurs a gentle, soft

song. I shiver, breathing in the spell he is setting, thick with sweet autumn leaves, fresh wind along grass, and something strangely animalistic in a way I cannot name. I press my nose into the kittens and catch something similar. Before I can think of gathering my words, a rustle begins along the fallen leaves, and Aidyn's song fades.

A wildcat's heavy paws touch the earth. My shoulders clench, my legs ready to flee even as Aidyn's comforting arm slides about my shoulders.

"They are wild and dangerous but take no pleasure in malice. You rescued many of its own. You need not be afraid." He breathes out gently. "I wondered if she would come out. I never knew if I would see one like this."

My mouth falls open as the creature—much like the one we found among the grasses, though living and breathing—darts its keen eyes back and forth along us. Its teeth are long and sharp in a different way from the hounds', its bruise-blue fur rippling across its body as it moves. From my place on the forest floor, seeing it living and moving, I realize simply how large a creature it is, likely as tall as my head were I standing. It paces a dozen steps away, regarding us with a strange intelligence I do not understand. It does not speak, not like the hound or in any other way I can fathom.

"Can she understand me?" I whisper.

"I am not certain," he admits. "I would believe so." Louder, he says, "We have little ones of your own kind. We are caring for them until they are old enough."

I'm ready to ask if he needs to speak in his own tongue, in that beautiful language I do not comprehend, when the wildcat cocks her head, stepping forward, eyes still on me. Despite Aidyn's words, a soft breeze washes across the leaves. Paying him no heed, the cat drops its face low, a gentle noise rumbling from its chest, a grown sound compared to the kittens' purring. My hand half reaches up, but the wildcat snorts and tucks its head, instead nuzzling the kittens sniffing at its paws.

A similar sensation to Aidyn's spell takes hold—quick legs breezing through the woods, a thousand sweet and subtle smells of places too far into Faerie for me to ever know, the woodland air heavy and sugared. I lean my head against Aidyn's shoulder and tear my eyes away from the creature just long enough to see the calm gentle awe settled across his features. His silver eyes catch mine for a spare moment, and his lips quirk at the corners.

The wildcat snuffles and nudges the kittens for only a few moments before trotting into the trees without a final glance. The next moment, it has disappeared into them with a shimmer like summer heat over grass, and I realize I only saw it because it made itself known to me, as Aidyn does.

We sit for a time, my head tucked under Aidyn's chin, letting the kittens run and tug one another's tiny tails, before silently rising and counting them up into their basket. It is a short slow walk returning to the shadow of the library, Aidyn's hand and mine drifting to and fro together.

Once the little creatures are returned to his room, already sleeping after their tumbling about, I squeeze his fingers and say, "Come with me."

In the mortal trees, the scent of honeysuckle drifting along behind, I lead him around the hawthorn tree and to the edge of the human woods where the dancing and faint singing can be heard. Night has fallen in full, moonlight lying across the valley, and Aidyn cocks his head at the firelight.

"It's very soft here," he says, and I wonder which of a thousand things he could mean. Before I can ask, he bends and kisses me.

"Everyone is a little drunk," I admit, "but they did not get enough dancing at midsummer before they had a fright. I made more pie."

"I am not going to dance. I will frighten them." He looks down at me from the corner of his eye in an unsettling expression I know to be shyness. A grin tugs at the corners of my mouth.

"One little dance, something slow, and smile at them as you smile at the kittens. I will not tell your father or sister, I swear it."

His lips press together in a mixture of amusement and decided exasperation.

"They are feeling quite grateful for the fae, as you'll understand," I remind him. "And Emma will be delighted. They may not even realize you are of Faerie if you dance and smile a little and do not attempt to enchant them. It is too late in the evening to expect anything else. They may not even see you or remember you, as last time. They will think you a lovely dream."

"Hmm," he says, poking at the bluebell in my hair. "One dance, then."

"One dance."

Down the dark shadows of the valley lit with summer

bonfires, my parents are gazing up at the tree line as I asked, searching. "And my mam and da are eager to meet you."

His lip quirks in less amusement, more nervous mischief. "Might I enchant them?"

"Hmm. Only a little."

"Only a little," he agrees with a broad grin. I kiss him under the chin.

Sighing out a breeze that rustles the grasses, he lets me weave my fingers between his and lead him down through the drifting wildflowers and into the firelight.

The End
~ of Niamh & Aidyn's story ~

Niamh's Honey Cake

3/4 cup honey*
1 cup butter, melted
1/2 cup brown sugar
4 eggs
2 and 1/2 cups flour
1 tsp vanilla

Pinch or two of salt
1/2 tsp cinnamon
1 tsp baking powder
2 tsp baking soda
1 cup strong coffee

Mix all wet ingredients, then mix all dry.

Bake at 350° for 30-40 minutes, or until golden brown
and a toothpick comes out clean from the center.

Dust with powdered sugar or drizzle with honey if desired.

*preferably from Faerie bees

Niamh's Plum Crumble Pie

Filling
4 cups chopped plums*
1/2 cup sugar
1 tbsp lemon juice
1/4 cup flour
1/4 tsp cinnamon
1/4 tsp nutmeg
Pinch or two of salt

Crust
1/2 cup butter, melted
1 and 1/2 cup flour
3/4 cup brown sugar

For filling, mix sugar and lemon juice into chopped plums. Mix all dry ingredients and mix into plum filling until thoroughly coated.

For crust, mix sugar and flour into melted butter with a fork until crumbly. Sprinkle atop the filling. If desired, sprinkle some of the crumble on the bottom before the filling goes in.

Bake at 375° for 30 minutes or until crust is golden brown and filling is bubbly.

*preferably picked from a Faerie tree

Thank You For Reading

Thank you so much for reading *The Wind and the Wild*! Leaving a review on Amazon, Goodreads, or the platform of your choice helps support this book and reach new readers!

To follow along with Emily McCosh's works, including the next books in the *Keepers of Faerie* series, you can sign up for her author newsletter at *oceansinthesky.com* to be the first to learn about new releases, artwork, unreleased content, and any other bookish news.

Playlist

Enjoy some of the amazing songs I listened to while writing *The Wind and the Wild*. A big thank you to these amazing artists for their hours of inspiration.

Mark Kozelek & Jimmy Lavalle - Ceiling Gazing
The Irrepressibles - In This Shirt
Ludovico Einaudi - Experience
Message To Bears - You Are A Memory
Phoebe Bridgers - I Know the End
M83 - Outro

About the Author

Emily McCosh is a graphic designer and writer of strange things. She currently lives in California with her two parents, one tree swing, and innumerable characters who need to learn some manners. Her short fiction has appeared in *Beneath Ceasless Skies, Shimmer, Galaxy's Edge, Flash Fiction Online, Nature: Futures*, and elsewhere.

She is the author of *All the Woods She Watches Over: Stories & Poetry; Under the Earth, Over the Sky; In Dying Starlight;* and *The Sea at the End of Everything*.

Find her online and keep up with her upcoming novels and illustration projects at:

Youtube: Emily McCosh

Instagram: emily_mccosh

TikTok: emilymccosh

Newsletter: oceansinthesky.com

Acknowledgments

First off, I'd like to thank the past version of Emily that gleefully began writing this book as a "short little novella." She was optimistic and innocent and had no idea the story that would bloom from there.

Secondly, I'd like to thank my best friend and writing buddy, Saf, for listening to every theory I had in the outlining stage, and for reading the rough draft one chapter at a time and leaving thousands of encouraging comments.

A big thanks to my beta readers Freya and Megan for all their comments and advice, and as always to my lovely editor Natalia Leigh for fixing my commas and pointing out all my sentence fragments. I'm so sorry, but I kept many of them.

Of course, to my mom, for reading the rough draft, making cute comments about the characters, and for asking when she gets to read the next sections.

To my dad, for first encouraging me to write, and for continuing to be so supportive through the entire process.

And finally to my puppy dogs Alice and Rosie, who often sat with me as I was drafting this book, and interrupted for attention and play. You are missed.

Acknowledgments

Thank you to everyone on Kickstarter who have supported this project and given it so much love. Over seven hundred lovely people made this an amazing book launch—I couldn't have imagined a more amazing campaign, my gratitude to each and every one of you.

Flower

Aleesa B	Anthony Haevermaet	Dakota
Morgan Nichols	LN Emmert	June Crispell
David DeHaan	Gretel Schroeder	Nick M.
Sofiya Kritsula	E. A. Hendryx	June Crispell
Riccardo Sartori	Claire J	Alessandra
Dakota Turnbough	Brittany aka Royalty/	Sofiya Kritsula
Jessica Cline	Ruei	Mackenzie Clawson
Kit Kat	Elizabeth Troolines	

Solene

Poluc

Ju Transcendancing

Susan Wilson

@lovelylandingsreads

Stephanie Owen

Elizabeth Graham

Lucy Dembski

Korvus F. M.

Nava Starling

Regina Rouse

Wyngarde

Ashley Binder

Kate Donlon

Austin M.

Carla Marleny

Paredes

Crysella

Natalie

Caitlin Jacobsen

E.R. Paskey

Shannara M Stanchly

Laura Whitaker

Midnightmare

Austin M.

Susan Laspe

Jenni Strand

Honey

Kris Marchu

Sarah Kuna

Suzanne

Gwyn E

Brianna W.

Mandy Puffenbarger

Bekah

Sydney Umaña

JullesT

Tiffani Sahara

Emily Rennison

Gee Rothvoss

Amy Cokenour

Rory

Morgan Reilly

Ahmee

Abigail Spears

Lexi Rose

Shreya Srivatsan

Devin Jane

Corley

Rachael Welch

Franchesca Caram

Andi

Victor Arellano

Amy McLaughlin

Mackenzie Goldman

Sonja Moorhoff

Meaghan McDermott

spot_the_jay

Ayla Genesky

Caitlin Roberson

Madelynn Beus

Morwenna

Dalila Enriquez

Natalie Jolin

Bumblingbriars

C. H. Knyght

Nathalie DeFelice

Madisyn

Jessica Watkins

Dimari

Carla L.

Erica Blankenship

Kathryn Brisson

Emily Eikost

R Hunt

Malayka

Maegan S

Caitlyn

K. "Cyanide" Stauffer

Buntany

Teeka

Freya Stone

Liz Kommer

Connie Webster

AuntieErrica

Miriam E. Monical

EL

Ceri Smith

Morgana Follmann

Summer Fazzone

Nate & Britt Brown

Shelby Hamden

Iio

Brianna C.

Cyndi Taylor

Anna Adler

Samantha Newberry

Mo Vitche

Charbi the Tea Witch

starpainter

Natalie Jolin

Gee Rothvoss

Carla L.

Brittany Hannan

Abigail Spears

Plum

Shylia

Rebecca Thiel

Katie Holmes

Breeana Groves

Oroniel

Sarah Ogden

Sam Games

Lynn Kaeding

Wall Twins

Rachel Boyes

Grae

Natasha L

Lynnsie Diamond

Destinee Roach

Linda J. Wakefield

Maire O'Brien

Chelsea Rogers

Fatima Silva Mendez

Ryan M. Williams

Lychnobia

Verity

Amanda Kennedy

Lark Cunningham

Hailey Christine

Chappell

Christy Clark

Brooks Moses

Willow G

Ashley Koch

Alyssa Line

Whitney McGruder

G Terkuile-Green

Isabella Miles

Elena Kigel

Abigail Lanier

Michelle Favorite

Ileana

Apolline

Anne Higinbotham

Lennea Ashley

Lisa Packard

Coiluna Petrichor

Kerry

Mojo Samurai

Karey

Victoria Van Wamel

Liz Carlberg

Mojo Samurai

Aurora Shea

Honeysuckle

A.R. Lett

Melissa Graham

Annarose Willhite

Kayti Egolf

Mary Livingston

@prettylittleshelfie

Ronja Haugen

Kayla Power

Megan Dunn

Anais

Ashley M. Orndorff

Katherine Fox

stormi

Boo Culliton

Djamila Kurbanova

Amanda Gylling

KleinesMue

Jessica Beatty

Brenna Greenfield

Suzanne van der Heide

Katie Miller

Amanda Feness

Heather P.

Charlotte Zang

AJ Giblin

Taylor Trudeau

Sam Hutteman

Karissa Fortney

alaa.

Roberta Miller

NanashiNova

Deimako

Marlene Renteria

Elvina Patino

Haru Jang

Krista Westermayer

Ashlee Murphy

Reese Dube

Fira Richardson

Amanda Balter

Loren Wilson

Samantha Landström

Carol MacLennan-Gonzales

Titania D.

Tanya-Lee Williams

Cassie Theobald

Emerson Fratzke

Jennifer Norton

K Hendrick

Billye Herndon

Sophie Allen

Roberta.O

Chumyshka

Fiona De La Huerga

Servat

Karan Singh

Susan Terry

Katie Grimes

Krys Galvez

Taylor O'Donnell

Rachel Brown

Cassidy Logan

Lynzy B.

Mary Mikadze

Stephanie Barnett

Sabrina Raimondo

Rebecca Baubé

Sarah Jean Maura

Kelsey Stenberg

Susannah Mansky

Alicia Petroff

Cassius Oliver

Kiarah Keppers

Jessica Hoyal

Kai Yee

Nora Storet

Sofi St. John

Pinky

Catherine McP

Angelina K.

Ky Town

Elodie

Nic Jeffreys

Emma F

Caitlin Millsaps

Annie Lilac

jon marshall

Faith E. Nickel

Rosa Thill

Meghan Dzurichko

Lore

Rue

lulu

A. Alex Thomas

Liana

Samantha Kuxhaus

Kathryn McKil-
lop-Knibbe

K. L. Duran

Kristin L

Andrea Martin kidder

Kirsten Diamond

Kayti Egolf

Elizabeth Davies

ShadowKlutz

Brogan Reid

Katelyn Gray

Caitlin Pollastro

Adelle Williams

Caitlin Meechan

Britain Rogers

Iona

Yoliany Baez

Chanel H.

Sweet Pepper Books

Katherine Malloy

Loretta Fryer

SJK

Haelee Mitchell

Matthea W. Ross

Maggie Carmichael

Billye Herndon

Mandi Kane

C.Wilson

Grant C

Melanie J. Vasquez

Lauren Wayman

Sarah S.

tarian jackson

Nelda Iznaga

Christine Detrick

Michaela Seaton

Kathleen Pham

Merissa Mayhew

Nikole C.

Sarah Phillips

Alyssa from Nerdy

Nurse Reads

Rebecca Kokorda

Sofia Cerdas

Ari Miller

Valentina Volpi

Stormi Flowers

Heather Gearhart

Deya Soto

C Gay

Crystal Middleton

Trent Langston II

Alexa Cortes

Kassie Ziegler

A.R. Lett

Stacy Ward

Nicole Haarstad

Joanna Lane

Sarah Forssander

Andrea Grabowski

Vicki Hsu

Alice Bretzius

Leanna Thornsberry

Courtney Rummell

Maria Francis

Karen M

Casey Loehrke

Jane Q. T. Nguyen

Rachael Knieser

Davin Greenwood

Sophie Wyatt

Anna Liang

Annie Lilac

Kristen Schleif

Morgan G.

Meagan Chalifoux

Yumemi

Corinne Brucks

Kierstyn V Bristow

Jessica Lucille

Geena

Annie Greenman

Fallon Woodbury

Ariel Doherty

Jenny

Xiomara M. Gonzalez

Melanie Rutledge

Katherine Shipman

Michelle Badillo

Lindsay Stringer

Adriana Loughridge

Lizzee Bee

Anaïs-Sophie

Elvira Contreras

Vanessa Perry

Johnna Anthony

Lisa Fane

Nic Jeffreys

Alice Ticha

Kimberly Florendo

Katoro

Merriel Ashley

Shanna Loughridge

Rosalinda Vargas

Raychel Kill

Courtney Brolly

Hannah Levin

Jessica Beatty

Trent Langston II

Emily Sims

Anna Thiel

Mandi Kane

Stephanie Barnett

Sarah Pennington

Amanda Gylling

Casey Loehrke

Nicollette Winiewicz

Kayla Willman

Valentina Volpi

Rachel S

Holly A.

Summer S.

Haru Jang

Tiffany Lay

Loretta Fryer

Lauren Wayman

Tara Kat

Annie Lilac

Megan Borrego

Sarah Abraham

Briana Rae

Corinne Brucks

Susan Terry

A. R. Lett

Annarose Willhite

Mary Livingston

Thomas Siodlak

Xiomara M. Gonzalez

Sam Hutteman

Maria Francis

Elena Kigel

Jessica Beatty

Tarian Jackson

Krys Galvez

tarian jackson

Miranda Heather

Valentina Volpi

Ari Miller

Marissa I.

Nic Jeffreys

tarian jackson

Sarah Phillips

Grant Cothren

Meghan Dzurichko

Bluebells

Cat Parker

Courtney R. Delgado

Lauren K.

Madeleine Couvillion

Sherry Mock

Emerald Bruce

Cyann Ava

Mickey Spencer

Kordi Steck

J.S. Baehr

Tatum

M.A. Zanz

Kristina Seyfarth

Tayler S

Kimberly L

Shell Boyd

Lynnette Pritchett

Kimberly L

Samantha Cicio

Kristina Seyfarth

Christina Averett

Katherine Carney

Veronica Franklin

J. S. Baehr

Emerald Bruce

Niki Kuhlman

Eileen Charette

Kordi Steck

MonPtitChou

Jessica Oster

Courtney R Delgado

Kyle Butler

9 781960 433312